UNMASKED HEART

Challenge of the Soul: Book 1

Vanessa Riley

Books by Vanessa Riley

The Bewildered Bride

The Butterfly Bride

The Bargain, A Port Elizabeth Tale, Book I

Look for A Duke, The Lady, And A Baby - Summer 2020

Sign up at VanessaRiley.com for contests, early releases, and more.

Published by BM Books
A Division of Gallium Books
Suite 236B, Atlanta, GA 30308

* * *

ISBN-13: 978-0-9907437-6-7

Shy, nearsighted caregiver, Gaia Telfair always wondered why her father treated her a little differently than her siblings, but she never guessed she couldn't claim his love because of a family secret, her illicit birth. With everything she knows to be true evaporating before her spectacles, can the mulatto passing for white survive being exposed and shunned by the powerful duke who has taken an interest in her?

Ex-warrior, William St. Landon, the Duke of Cheshire, will do anything to protect his mute daughter from his late wife's scandals. With a blackmailer at large, hiding in a small village near the cliffs of Devonshire seems the best option, particularly since he can gain help from the talented Miss Telfair, who has the ability to help children learn to speak. If only he could do a better job at shielding his heart from the young lady, whose honest hazel eyes see through his jests as her tender lips challenge his desire to remain a single man.

Unmasked Heart is the first Challenge of the Soul Regency novel.

Dedication

I dedicate this book to my copy editor supreme, my mother, Louise, my loving hubby, Frank, and my daughter, Ellen. Their patience and support have meant the world to me.

I also dedicate this labor of love to critique partners extraordinaire: June, Mildred, Lori, Connie, Gail.

Love to my mentor, Laurie Alice, for answering all my endless questions.

And I am grateful for my team of encouragers: Sandra, Michela, Kim, and Rhonda.

Cast of Primary Characters

Gaia Telfair: the second daughter of Henry and Delilah Telfair.

William St. Landon: the Duke of Cheshire and the son of the late Rev. St. Landon.

Serendip Hallow: Gaia's best friend. She is also called Seren.

Sarah Telfair: the second wife of Henry Telfair, stepmother to Julia and Gaia, mother to Helena, Lydia, and Timothy.

Henry Telfair: the man who has raised Gaia Telfair, father of Julia, Helena, Lydia, Timothy, and three deceased sons.

Elliot Whimple: a neighbor to the Telfairs. He is a botanist.

Julia Telfair: Gaia's older sister.

Millicent Rance: a cousin to the Telfair's who was once engaged to Mr. Whimple.

Deborah Smithen: the duke's cousin and long time admirer.

Benjamin Stelford: the duke's best friend.

Mrs. Wingate: the housekeeper at Ontredale.

Albert: a loyal servant to the duke

Miss Oliver: a woman disgraced in public for her out of wedlock pregnancy.

CHAPTER ONE

March, 1819, Devonshire, England

Mud seeped into Gaia Telfair's slippers as she slogged to the old church. Out of breath, she clutched the rough-hewn rail of the cemetery's fence. A heavy shake of her foot didn't keep the wetness from leaching through the kid leather or the peeling satin lining. If there had been more time, she'd have grabbed her sister's sturdy boots or begged for the cook's stilt-like pattens.

Yet there wasn't time. Her heart beat hard as she tried to imagine her brother's sweet smile. Two miles of fruitless searching between here and home had worn her to a thread. How could he vanish?

Something must've upset him and made him run. Unlike her younger sisters, the incorrigible twins, Timothy wouldn't grieve her like this.

A heavy sigh fell from her lips. If Gaia hadn't been glorying over Elliot's broken engagement, she'd have paid more attention to the six-year-old.

Balling her fist, she rapped the top of the fence, stinging her knuckles. This wasn't Elliot Whimple's fault. It was hers. If Elliot knew of this trouble, the gallant scholar would lead a search party. Such a dear man.

She cleaned her fogged spectacles against the edge of her short spencer, her best jacket, and then shoved the lenses onto the bridge of her nose. Straining, she scanned the graveyard. Everywhere were puddles and soggy earth, thick like cold porridge. Anyone lost in these woods would be soaked to the bone. Poor Timothy.

She swiped at her eyes and leaned her full weight against the crossed timbers. The tang of rainwater perfumed the air. Lil' Timothy loved spring showers.

Something small and dark fluttered the bushes edging the corner. Was it her imagination, or did a blur knock against the lone elm? Timothy?

Fingering the oak rail for a splinter-free patch, she swung her legs over the fence. *Lord, let him be well.*

Pulse pounding, she cupped a hand to her mouth. "Timothy!"

Her voice echoed then disappeared in the breeze. No response, no crowds or foolish talk or repetition of the silly teases from her *friends*. The tweaks of how the afternoon sun would further darken her skin stung something deep in her chest. The sunshine could do no more damage to her olive-like complexion; well, no more than the blood in her veins or the luck of her birth. Her father called it a pagan inheritance. Why did she have to be the one to show their Spanish heritage and none of her sisters?

Gaia uncurled her tight fingers. She'd accepted she'd never be as pretty as any of the other fair Telfair girls, but it didn't lessen the pain arising from unthinking words, even those made in jests. With a breath, she swallowed the ache and moved forward.

Toes clenching, she trudged past her older brother's marker. The memory of mopping his brow as he succumbed to his war injuries piled more sadness upon her heart. The pressure increased as she stared at his stone and the one shared one of the stillborn twins of her late mother. Shivering, she glanced away to the flattened grass path. How could she tell Father his last son was missing? Would the man's poor health sustain the news?

Slipping to the elm, Gaia hung her head. No Timothy; just a fleeing rabbit and the lone marker for the old vicar. High blades of grass nearly covered the etched limestone. Set apart from the other graves, the caretaker must've missed it.

The afternoon sun filtered through the high stained-glass window of the chapel, casting a scarlet glow upon her snug sleeves and thinning knit gloves. If only the light could wrap about her and somehow spin time in reverse. Then, she would pay more attention to her dear brother, not her dearest friend's gossip and wild encouragement of chasing Elliot Whimple's love.

Gaia whipped her head to the road and spied the approach of her running confidant, Serendip Hallow.

The lovely girl, inside and out, waved. "Have you found Timothy?"

"Not yet." The words caught in her throat, almost bringing forth a sob. She edged in Seren's direction. "Crowds scare him. He's so easily disoriented."

"I've put a footman and a groom out to search; and to do so quietly. My brother's going to look on the moors. He'll do anything for pin money," Seren shook her head and tilted her bisque bonnet. A raven pin curl fell and skirted her vibrant green eyes. "Timothy might have wandered there, like before when *Elliot* found him."

A stamp of Gaia's foot produced a splash of mud, further saturating her skirt and damp petticoat. Her shoulders sagged as she seized the rail. "No, more talk of that man. If I hadn't been so engaged with my own foolishness, I'd have kept Timothy. Our father will be so disappointed in me."

"He's always so stern with you."

True. Father was hard to please. If she were prettier, more like her beautiful elder sister, he might be easier. Stomach twisting, Gaia nodded. "But this lecture will be so deserved."

"It's not. You have too many responsibilities. You deserve happiness." A bright smile spread across Seren's small oval face as she waggled her trademark charm, a four-leaf clover. "Listen to me; your brother will be found. Fortune is headed your way."

Linking hands, Seren guided Gaia's climb over the railing, but, instead of letting go, she pulled her into a deep embrace, mashing her cheek against a fine rose shawl of rich Mechlin lace. "You matter. Tomorrow, when Timothy's safe, do something for Gaia Telfair. Work up the courage to tell Elliot Whimple your heart."

Straightening, she put a finger to Seren's mouth. "Not now; I must find my little brother."

With a half-step backwards, Seren shrugged. "Of course. Where haven't you looked? Maybe he's back at Chevron Manor."

"He's not home, but..." With a final hug, Gaia pivoted toward the woods. "My oak; I took him to it last week. Pray he's there."

Sprinting, Gaia didn't look back.

One button, two, three. She ripped open the bone fobs of her short jacket to allow her arms to swing with greater speed. Elms and pines all blended into a blur of jade. The smell of peppery heather filled her lungs. Soon she'd be at her spot; the crag overlooking the moors 'neath the largest oak in England.

Hopping across a pebble-infested stretch, Gaia stepped to her special place. Through the last few difficult years, this was where she'd sought comfort. Here, she prayed and cried and danced with the wind.

She parted the bushes and stepped on to the clearing.

Wiping her eyes, pushing at her spectacles, she squinted at the reddish-brown locks, the coloring so close to her own. Timothy? Nestled on a limb, perched high in the tree's canopy, lay her brother, a small lump in a dark blue coat. Not wanting to startle him, she crept closer.

"Thank you, God." With one foot on a gnarled root and clasping a thick branch, she lifted close enough to stroke the boy's hair.

Her slippers gave way, and she dropped onto a patch of wet leaves. Pea-green blades of garlic-smelling ransoms stroked her jaw. Cool air rushed her temples. Her bonnet had come loose and lay a few feet away. The brim bore mud stains. She sighed, more things to explain to Father.

Lifting an arm and then a leg, she tested each limb. Nothing seemed hurt but her pride. "Timothy, you had me so afraid."

"G-A-Ya?" The boy's soft blue eyes were swollen red. He clenched the branch as if he'd fall. "H-elp."

"Stay put." She stood and swatted the stains from her dress. "Oh, how am I going to get to you?" At twenty, she was too old to climb trees. Definitely against the ladylike protocol her stepmother and aunt had tried to ingrain, but how else would she retrieve the scared boy?

Lifting up the hem of her ruined skirt, she set her slippers again on the root and craned her neck, searching for a better place to grip. "This is punishment for listening to gossip and praising the end of Elliott's engagement. God, I shouldn't have rejoiced at his unhappiness, no matter how right it is to spare the world another bad match. Probably shouldn't have prayed for the break, either. Let Elliott Whimple not regret—"

"I've heard young women pray for husbands, but I'd never thought one capable of praying for misery," the deep voice transitioned to laughter.

Twisting to see, she fell again, but this time strong arms

caught her and placed her on solid ground.

"Now, what do we have here?" The tall man with the curious blue-green eyes handed her the reins of his pewter horse and wandered closer to Timothy. "Can I help you down, young man?"

"Wait," her voice warbled, "he fears strangers."

"Nonsense; a stranger's just an unknown friend to a daring lad." He reached near the branch.

Her brother rocked his head and tried to scoot away. His low heel caught on the branch and Timothy teetered.

Before she could blink, the stranger grabbed Timothy. His large hands swallowed the boy's middle as he stalked over to Gaia. "Does this brave adventurer belong to you?"

She opened her arms to receive Timothy, but the man turned and put her brother atop his gelding. "I only let brave young men on Magnus. You must be so, for climbing such a big tree."

A smile set on Timothy's lips as he gripped the leather harness on the well-muscled horse, but Gaia still trembled. She wouldn't calm, not until the boy was in her arms. "Sir, we are grateful, but I need to take my brother home."

"Let him get his bearings back. We don't want him to become fearful of heights. My father once... Well..." He tipped his top hat and led Magnus in a circle around Gaia. "A young man needs to believe in himself."

Timothy's high cheekbones held a dimpled smile. Who wouldn't on such magnificent horseflesh? The huge gelding pranced. The gorgeous creature towered. It was as tall as she. Stroking Magnus's onyx mane, her brother looked very comfortable, so different from the frightened boy from moments earlier.

Yet Gaia's stomach knotted. Her little brother was her responsibility, one she cherished when she wasn't swept away in thoughts of Elliot or trying to appear unruffled by polite ridicule. She bit her lip for a second, wondering who this stranger was and when he would leave them. From the cut of his fine grey coat and the shine of his boots, this was a wealthy stranger, someone who wouldn't ordinarily associate with the Telfairs. The sooner Timothy and she returned home, the better. "Please, sir; we can't trespass upon your favor any longer."

The fellow stopped in front of her. His wide shoulders blocked the sun shining through the leafy canopy. A hint of sea air, fresh and salty, hung about man and steed. "Be at ease. I'm enjoying the moors and the coast; so beautiful this time of year. But grant me one token of goodwill as the boy takes a few trots on old Magnus."

Her tongue felt thick, and she fidgeted with the faded ribbons trimming her bodice. "What... would that be?"

"Explain why you've prayed for misery. Hearing the tale seems a fitting hero's reward."

His tone sounded too merry to be sinister, yet her knees wobbled. Only Serendip knew of her unrequited feelings for Elliot. Now a stranger did.

She took a deep swallow. "I spoke... out of anguish. My brother looked as if he'd fall."

"Yes, but such a curious intercession." He patted the horse and tugged the grinning Timothy from the saddle, putting him into Gaia's embrace. "One wonders what you'll ask for next."

With the man's dark hair and solid build, he could've been an older version of Elliot, but scholarly Elliot had manners. He'd never press, and her natural shyness kept her from offering opinions. Leveling her shoulders to portray an air of confidence, she cleared her throat. "Sir, my prayers are for my Lord's ears."

"Then I'm not worthy to hear. Still, my curiosity is not lessened. Have you prayed for anything else?" His baritone bore thick chuckles and a sense of elevation. "A plague or more hostilities with France won't do."

"Horse. Horse." Timothy squirmed and knocked her spectacles askew.

She squeezed him tightly. Righting her lenses, she caught the man's gaze. He was more handsome in focus. Nonetheless, wouldn't the stranger spread this tale at the local pub or wherever men told their stories? Whispers flew through the small village faster than falling rain.

And when Father heard, he'd think her wanton and be so disappointed in her character. Fear squeezed her chest; with her brother's tiny hand secured in hers, she put him to the ground and pivoted back to the path. The sooner they made it home, away from strangers, the better. "Thank you again, sir."

"My pleasure, but please don't option for another war. No relationship is worth the bloodshed."

His mirth fell upon her, picking at the scab covering her battered pride.

She had half a mind to leave without uttering another word, but she turned. "Laugh, if you must, but more people should pray against ill-suited matches. I believe there would be a lot less unhappiness in the world."

Tucking his fist onto his hip, as if he ferried an invisible hat like a shako the militia wore, he marched out of the shadow of the oak. A frown covered his face, his chiseled jaw set into grim lines. His gaze whipped up and down then seemed to settle on her countenance. "So, lass, what makes you an expert?"

"I have eyes, four of them." She tweaked her lenses. "And I use them." Stabbing a few loose pins back into her chignon, she gaped at his polished boots and traced the expensive silver threading of his greatcoat to his thick cravat. She'd just insulted a very rich man; someone Father would try to placate in public, and then complain about ad nauseam at home. "They must also make me forget myself. Sorry."

She bit her lip and loosened the iron grip she had on Timothy's fingers. "I shouldn't be dismissive of the man to whom I'm indebted."

"Such large hazel eyes." He reached close to her ear and plucked a muddy spear-shaped leaf of lousewort from one of her dangling curls. Examining his gloved fingertips almost as much as her locks, he arched his brow. "Very fine. I suppose you see things others miss. I've heard the eyes are a window unto the soul. I think I know now what that means."

He leaned to the side and retrieved her bonnet, wiping off the mud, further soiling his gloves. "Here, misery prayer warrior."

Stepping away, he returned to his horse and swung his mighty legs over the top. "Young man, be kinder to your sister. The lovely lady is becoming quite tanned in this afternoon sun."

With her mouth dropping open, Gaia tried to inhale. She didn't know what to react to first: that the stranger thought her lovely or that he assumed it was Timothy's fault her complexion wasn't snow-white. Maybe it was the combination, which made her pulse race, dull appearance and all. If she spoke her mind to Elliot, perhaps he, too, could see her this way. Hope burned inside.

With a flip of his brim, the stranger set off. Man and horse soon blended into the tree line. Who was he and would he mention her prayers to others?

She blinked, as if the action would push away her questions. None of it mattered. Timothy was safe. She took him in her arms and twirled him. Her quarter-step fell in rhythm to the sway of the oak's limbs.

Gaia hugged the boy again. "Don't run away ever again."

Timothy dropped his head. "Mean boys. Sl-ow wit."

She kissed his forehead. "You're full of wit, no matter the

speed. You are so dear. Let's go home." Hopefully, the scolding she'd receive for losing Timothy wouldn't tamp Father's strength.

William St. Landon, the Duke of Cheshire, left his dapple grey at the stables and started to the main house; nothing he enjoyed more than a day-long ride in his native Devonshire. Spring with the spice of pine and freshly-turned soil had to be his favorite season.

The topper of his adventure? Finding a saucy tree sprite praying for misery. Ah, to be young and headstrong. At the late age of thirty-six, he was above such games.

Oh, Ontredale Lodge. He scanned the pinkish-grey stones, a country home to his lineage, and marveled at the place. Smaller than his estate in Cheshire, it was still very large and grand. As a boy, he only visited once, that awkward day his father informed him he was heir to all this. The man never liked the money or prestige, but he didn't like much. Shrugging off the bad memories, William pounded up the limestone steps.

With a blackmailer after his family, he had more serious things to fill his mind than bad memories. Resigned, he pounded up the limestone steps.

His breathing hitched as he entered the main hall. Little Mary's cries wrapped tightly about his heart; another nightmare for the poor girl.

How was he to help the child? What could replace the love of a mother, even an awful one?

"Your Grace, you've returned." His housekeeper, Mrs. Wingate, shook her head. "Lady Mary won't sleep. Her new maid has been unable to soothe her."

He removed his coat and hat and dropped them onto the close table. "The surroundings are unfamiliar; that must be upsetting her."

If only it were true. He ripped off his smudged leather gloves and handed them to Mrs. Wingate, the principal guardian of Ontredale. "I trust that the house will be fully staffed soon."

She nodded her head, fluttering the frill of her perfectly-starched mobcap. "Yes; it's been difficult to meet your needs so quickly, but it shall be done. If I'd had more *notice* of your arrival, all would've been in place."

Raising a brow at the inflection in her voice, the light admonishing tone, he swallowed and chose to sympathize with the woman clad in stark ash skirts. It wasn't Mrs. Wingate's fault no one could be alerted to his arrival. When his carriage arrived in the middle of the night, the old girl greeted him with a head full of curl papers in her greying hair.

"Sir, don't doubt my dedication," her tone softened, almost absorbed in the ocean of marble lining the entry. "Though the late duke visited often, I thought you'd be more like your father, and seldom come."

To be like him was a curse William wanted no part of. "Mrs. Wingate, I know you will do as well for my family as you did the late earl."

She nodded, and her gaze rose to the top of the stairs as Mary's cries ceased. "What else may I do, Your Grace?"

Absent the blackmailer's head on a platter, nothing. He sighed, thankful his child had calmed. "You will guide us with grace through the transition."

A smile peeked for a moment then disappeared in the aging crinkles of her heart-shaped face. "Should I get a doctor for Lady Mary, my lord?"

"No, she is healthy; physically healthy." What was the best way to ask? He studied the quizzing brown eyes glaring at him. The woman had to know there was a problem with his daughter. "Is there any in the village familiar with caring for a child... with difficulties?"

She looked down at the show table and picked at a pleat on her apron. "The Telfairs; their youngest can now speak, even talk with his hands. With so many daughters, one might need the position of a companion or governess. The quiet one, the one who minds the boy, she definitely has the makings of a governess."

Communicating with hands? That would be better than nothing. He tapped his chin. "Draft a note to start introductions, but, Mrs. Wingate, I'd like to be the final say on any position instructing Mary. And make it plain that my only desire is a governess, not a sly companion hoping for elevation. I'm not looking for a wife."

She nodded, but a wide frown thinned her lips. "Of course, my lord; the quiet one is the one you want. Her hopes couldn't be for more."

There was something ominous in her words, but he'd let the notion fall away. Mary was the only female he needed to puzzle out. In matters of running the house, the stern housekeeper was knowledgeable, but not with concerns to his baby. He marshaled to the stairs to check upon Mary, but pivoted. "Did any correspondence come today?"

"The usual invitations, Your Grace." Wide eyes framed the woman's portly face. Her chin lowered as if to hide them. Those windows to her soul were the only things showing a measure of compassion or feeling from the stoic woman.

Surely she recognized a devoted father. His fingers tightened on the banister. "Anything from Mr. Stelford?"

"None, sir." She brushed at the mud stain on his glove. "Been a quiet day until now."

No word from his confidant?

Or the blackmailer?

William took a cleansing breath; another day of borrowed peace from the blackguard threatening to expose his late wife's infidelity.

He should fall upon his knees and thank God for this respite, but he and God weren't on the best of terms. Maintaining a truce with the Holy Father must be best.

He smoothed his damask waistcoat, splaying its silver button between his fingers; might as well resign himself. "No, I think it will be another late night for me in the nursery." He walked up to the first landing.

Before he could take a step, a fever-pitched sob descended, bellowing.

Mrs. Wingate didn't flinch, as if immune to the child's misery, but a father's heart could never be so hard; at least not *this* father's heart.

"Will you have anything to eat, sir?"

How could he, with Mary suffering? "No."

"But you can't sit up with her again. You'll wear yourself thin, catch all manner of ailments. You should let her flail and outgrow this." Mrs. Wingate picked up his hat and coat and headed toward the kitchen, her dark skirts flapping behind her.

He rubbed his jaw. He'd forgive the woman's cruel advice. When Mary felt secure, she'd not be so easily upset. Trudging the final stairs to the nursery, he tried to soften his boot heels, but they banged against the treads. The drumbeat further soured his mood. Except for his father's strict rules, Devonshire with its greenery and rugged coast meant escape, a sanctuary created by God. Mary should love it here.

The babe was all he had left of his wife, Elizabeth. He must do everything in his power to keep the little girl safe from the evils of this world. If he'd kept better care of his wife, given her a reason not to stray, things would've been different. He rubbed his temples.

The babe's shrieks vibrated the threshold, warbling the grain. It was almost as bad as the bellows of dying men on the fields of Zadorra. Images of the river of death, the battle of Vitoria he fought, filled his head. Yes, no one should pray for more wars with France.

He shook his head. Those memories woke him up at night, but what would make a child of four scream in terror? Why would a God in Heaven make her mute, except for these cries? Where was His mercy?

The late Reverend St. Landon would preach his son's fate, widowed with a hurting child, was judgment. Why not, after disappointing his father and his wife? William straightened his shoulders and pushed open the door to the darkened room. Reaching at the top of a chest of drawers, he lit a candle.

As her incompetent nurse paced back and forth, screeching shushes at his daughter, Mary stood in the middle of the crib, tears dribbling down her chin, her face cherry-red. She must've caught sight of him, for she held her arms up.

Rushing to her, he shuttled across the thick puce carpet, the noise of his heels absorbed in the padding. "You are dismissed, woman!"

The nurse backed from the room, half-curtsying, half-running. The door slammed on its hinge.

Mary leapt at his embrace and wound her chubby arms about his neck. Her moans subsided when he snuggled her close. What an unthinking nurse to let this precious girl scream.

He stroked her sandy-brown curls and wiped tears from her sea-green eyes. This little bonbon held his heart within her tiny palms, perhaps the only person to love him unconditionally. "Papa's here. You're safe. We're both safe."

With the child clinging to his lapels, he moved to the rocking chair in the corner of the buttercream-colored nursery.

Mary burrowed deeper into his arms and played with the

buttons of his waistcoat. What he wouldn't pay to hear her voice given to words and not terror.

He lifted his legs to the child's chestnut trunk and scanned the carved duck and other small toys on the oak bookcase of the glazed-pear cultured room. "Isn't this a pretty place? I had all your things put in here, just as they were in Cheshire."

The little girl knocked two buttons together, as if they were a gong.

Loosening the metal from her fingers, he held her palm. His wide thumb covered the small soft middle. "Would you like to hear of how I led my forces in the battle of Assaye? My regiment spread across the plains of India."

Wide-eyed, she grinned a toothy sigh.

"Say 'Papa', as you once did."

She smiled again and grabbed his nose.

He hugged her tight to his breast. With everything he had, he'd keep the mother's sins quiet. None of the ugliness would fall on Mary's head. No one would question the child's paternity and ruin her chances.

If someone had prayed for his marital happiness, he'd never have wedded Elizabeth, but then he'd never have this joy. "Rest assured, my girl, I'll keep the nightmares at bay."

A short knock assailed the nursery threshold.

Mrs. Wingate entered. "This just came by post," she waved a letter in her hand.

It wasn't written on paper cream, so it wasn't the blackmailer's handiwork. He released a pent-up breath.

Without another word, Mrs. Wingate set it on the dresser, curtsied, and left the room.

Benjamin Stelford's large garnet seal seemed to glow on the blue tinted stationary. It was unmistakable, even at this shorter distance. If William's friend hadn't discovered the blackmailing blackguard, hiding in Devonshire wouldn't conceal the horrid scandal.

CHAPTER TWO

The Day the World Changed

Cold air pimpled Gaia's skin. The flames had died in the small fireplace at the head of her bedchamber. At a minimum, she should crawl out of her thick nest of peach and cream covers, stalk over to the bricked hearth, and make it blaze again. However, that would mean leaving the comfort of her poster bed, the soft lawn sheets nestling her cheek, the wonderful gift from her aunt. Father didn't allow many luxuries. For a while, he'd been a little looser with pocket money for Julia's dance lessons, toiletries for the twins. Alas, Gaia was last on his list, but that had to be because she didn't make a fuss like the others. If only Father could enjoy better health, then he could be more tolerant to all, not just the complainers.

Gaia moved an aching limb then gave up trying to rise. Yesterday's frantic search, the cold mud, Father's disapproving tone, it was all too much. Didn't it matter that she'd found Timothy and no harm had come to him? Well, thanks to the stranger, no harm had come, but hadn't all the Telfairs, save her older sister, attended church?

Each one of them, Father or her stepmother, could've chaperoned Timothy. Why was it Gaia's responsibility? Did

Father even care about how much she'd suffered, thinking her brother had been hurt? It would take days to get those stains out of her slippers.

Serendip was right. It was time to be selfish, to do something for Gaia's happiness. Toes balling, she wiggled to a new spot on her pillow. She'd found the courage to speak her mind to the handsome man at her oak. Surely, it would be easier with Elliott, her long-time neighbor and family friend.

Gaia closed her eyes again. Every detail of Seren's gossip of how Cousin Millicent threw Elliott away for a baron came to mind. How long would he be sad? A week, a few days? Couldn't have been much sentiment for it to end so quickly. The sunny blue of her bedchamber's walls disappeared once more.

High-pitched screams rattled the floorboards. Must be her youngest sisters, Helena and Lydia, squabbling downstairs. For identical twins, they disagreed over everything.

Another voice joined the girls in the hullabaloo.

Too pitchy for Julia. No, her older sister was still touring London with their aunt. *God, let Julia return with an offer.* Then her sister wouldn't be so desperate.

"Children, please. Gaia had a rough day yesterday. Don't disturb her."

Ah, Sarah, her stepmother, must be trying to separate the little girls. The woman would have better luck extricating wild hogs. Last time, Gaia had to cut a beautiful ribbon in two to settle the twins.

With a yawn, she pulled from the bed and headed to the wardrobe. Flip after flip of the folded gowns, shades of muted blue and grey, she sighed, nothing drawing her attention. All the fabrics seemed the same; pale, lifeless. If her mother had lived, surely she would've instilled confidence in Julia and maybe some in Gaia, too. She didn't make it to Gaia's eighth birthday.

With a shake of her head, she grabbed a checked-grey muslin frock. Once she finished her toiletries, she'd speak with Sarah right away about bright fabric, something to attract Elliot's attention.

Two whole days of tutoring the children, of chores, of pretending her world didn't teeter on a precipice and no answer from Sarah. Gaia threw her stained mint-green slipper to the floor and flung herself upon her mattress.

Was the request of fabric too much for Father's pockets, or was it his silly rule of one girl coming out at a time robbing everything?

No more waiting. Sarah must give an answer today. Gaia slipped her slipper back on, smoothed her sprig muslin skirt, and headed down the staircase to the front parlor.

Murmurs filtered under the gap at the bottom of the frame.

She put an ear to the door.

The tones were hushed but heated. A disagreement brewed within, but who would be disagreeable in Sarah's lair? This was a showplace for entertaining, playing music, or endless hours of the woman's craft-making, not arguments.

Maybe she mumbled to herself, as she did when Timothy was born. By his second birthday, it was obvious something was wrong. Gaia's heart clenched. It wasn't Sarah's fault. Who can understand the workings of God?

Popping up, Gaia determined to no longer be passive, and knocked on the door. With the greatest care, she pressed on the door. Its hinges creaked, then swayed, and seemed to halt all conversation inside.

Her father sat near Sarah. Nodding his clean-shaven face, his long ash-blonde sideburns curling to his ears, he waved her forward. "Come in, Gaia."

She hadn't expected him to be in here. He usually took refuge in his study on the far side of the house; that is, if he made it out of bed. This couldn't be good.

Gaia swallowed and almost clasped the pianoforte, tucked in the curved niche at the threshold. Maybe she could lean against it to regain her composure.

Sarah smiled at her before lowering her gaze, and motioned for Gaia to cross the paisley rug framing the sitting area close to the fireplace. "We need to speak with you."

"Does this mean I can't have the fabric? You can see I'm much grown." She tugged at the snug lines of her bodice.

His lips flattened to a line. "Your mother and I have decided you should be aware of all your responsibilities."

"My responsibilities?" At this, she slipped onto the couch. Why did she have the feeling her cheeks would soon color the same shade of burgundy as the sturdy seat?

Sarah tugged upon her treasured coral necklace then started working embroidery thread from the coiled jute basket near her caned chair. Her gaze seemed to be wandering as her tapping foot lifted her cream-and-rose skirt. "You know your father's estate is entailed to the males of the Telfair."

"Yes, Timothy will inherit everything," Father coughed. His lungs raged as if he were coming down with another cold, the third this year. "You've made much progress with him. If you continue to keep him, I think he'll be prepared to manage Chevron Manor."

She stopped her fingers from twitching and then squinted at her unusually-silent stepmother. Her hands shook as she passed a needle through a snowy handkerchief. Something definitely was amiss. "Sarah, Father, I don't understand."

"We, your mother and I, feel you should be his permanent companion."

"Permanent?" Gaia clutched the arm of the sofa, her nails denting the swell of the cushioning.

Sarah raised her head. Her mouth opened and closed and

opened again as her voice went from non-existent to low. "You... will be mistress of Chevron, making sure that he runs things well. My Timothy will always need supervision."

Gaia bounced to her feet and headed for the fireplace. Clasping the dark poker, she stoked the low flame and allowed the heat to dry the water leaking from her eyes. "But what of my hopes?"

Father wheezed, and he pounded the arm of his chair. "You've never been inclined to anything but books. And this will make sure that your sisters and mother will be taken care of always."

"My mother is dead." Gaia spun around and pointed to her stepmother. "This is *her* work. She's only worried about herself."

"Don't talk to her like that." His feeble fingers gripped the woman's hand. "And she's a good woman, unlike…"

"No, dear," Sarah wiped her leaky eyes. "You see she does not wish it."

Father left his chair and took the poker from Gaia's tight fingers. His clammy palms contrasted the blackness of the implement. "If my cousins press that Timothy is unfit, or they dupe his easy mind, all the family will be in jeopardy. I'm convinced your care will keep things well. You're level-headed. You will be the guardian of this manor. That's a worthy calling for you."

With the back of her hand, Gaia swiped at her cheek. The lenses of her spectacles steamed. "Abandon my dreams? Don't you think I want to marry?"

Father guffawed, placed the poker by the fire's grate, and twisted the fob of his pocket watch. "It's not possible; you've never had any inclination."

Why wasn't it possible? She squinted at his creasing forehead. "I want to. In fact, I want to marry Mr. Elliot Whimple."

"You want your cousin's leavings?" Father chuckled. "I can tell you now, Whimple is not looking for a bluestocking. We're even too poor for your sister's pretty face to catch anything. She'll be home on Friday with no offer."

No marriage for Julia. She must be crushed. Tears for her slipped down Gaia's chin.

"Mr. Telfair, she's in love," Sarah put down her needlework, and approached. Her almond eyes scanned up and down. "I suspect she's loved him for a long time."

Father moved toward the boxy pianoforte, his spindle legs drifting. "I wasn't aware, but it is of no consequence. The man doesn't look at you that way. Though he's good to his brother's household, I see him going to study in London. That's too far to watch over Timothy."

"I need a chance to convince him. If he could like me, I'm sure he will help in my brother's care."

He leaned on the instrument. "I can't be at peace if all my children are tossed to the streets. You owe this to me, to all the Telfairs."

Owe? "What do you mean, Father?"

"Don't, Mr. Telfair. She doesn't need to know. Gaia can be reasoned with without saying anything more."

The warning sent a chill down Gaia's spine, but she had to know. "Tell me why I owe my flesh and blood."

Father took her hand and pulled it to his pale face. "Do you think it's possible that fair Telfair blood could produce this?"

Her heart stopped, slamming against her ribs. "My mother's Spanish roots have browned my skin. That's what you've always said."

He dropped her palm as his head shook. "It was a lie, to cover my first wife's harlotry. You're a Telfair because I claimed you."

Gaia couldn't breathe, and crumbled to the floor. Hot tears drenched her face as she wished for a hole to break open and swallow her. "A mistake; please, say this is a mistake."

The man whom she'd called father, whom she'd worshipped, shook his head again.

She lifted a hand to grasp his shoe but stopped, missing the black leather.

Was this why she'd always felt as if she could never grasp a hold of his love? Is this why he treated her a little differently from the rest? "Then who am I? Whose am I?"

"Some traveling bard, some African poet who captivated *her* whilst I travelled. When you came out so close to white, with so little color, the ruse was borne; no scandal would befall my name. I'm just lucky you weren't a boy. Then, Chevron would fall to a mulatto. How would the Telfair line handle that tragedy?"

She waved her fingers, studying the light pigment coloring her skin. Mulatto. All this time she'd blamed her flesh on fate or heritage, not lust. She tugged at her elbows, feeling dirty. Glancing at him between tears, she silently begged for him to say it didn't matter, that he loved her still. "Father?"

With a grimace painting his silent mouth, he buttoned his waistcoat. "I'm going to lie down. Talk to her, Sarah; make her understand."

Desperate, Gaia's hand rose this time, but his back was to her in a blink and he walked from the room. Her fingers felt cold and numb as they sank onto the thin rug. The breath in her lungs burned. Adultery, not a Telfair by blood – these thoughts smashed against her skull.

Sarah knelt beside her and stroked her back. "I'm so sorry. You should never have known."

Gaia shook her head and pulled away. "No more lies."

"Please, I'm not the enemy."

Rearing up, she caught the woman's beady gaze. "You want me to believe you don't want the almost-bastard to be a servant to Timothy? Would you wish one of your children to be given this sentence, to become a governess to their own flesh and blood? Well, at least they can claim to be flesh and blood to Timothy."

Sarah reached again and wiped tears from Gaia's cheek then opened her arms wide. "You are his sister. You love him so. This is no failing of yours."

At first, Gaia fell into the woman's sturdy embrace, then stiffened and pulled away. She needed to flee, to let her brain make sense of the emotions whipping inside. Her slippers started moving. "I must go."

"Sweetheart, wait!"

Gaia shook her head and backed to the threshold. "Why? Is there something else you have to disclose to steal the rest of my dreams?"

Without a thought for a bonnet or coat, she rushed down the hall and out the front door.

Wham! She slammed into a man in fancy, sky-blue livery. The servant was tall and black; black, like some part inside of her. Her eyes fixed on his bronze skin and wouldn't let go.

"Miss? I've come from Ontredale. Are you well, miss? You look pale enough to faint."

Not pale enough; never would be. "Sorry." She ducked her eyes and side-stepped him.

"Ma'am, I bear a note—"

"You want a Telfair. They are inside." She started running and kept going until not a cobble of Chevron Manor could be seen. Salty drops stung and blurred each step, but she strode forward, deeper into the welcoming woods. A hint of spring blooms stroked her nose, but the streaks lining her wet face obscured them.

A fleeting thought to go to Seren's crossed Gaia's mind, but she couldn't let her friend see her like this, even more pitiful than normal. Would Seren even want to be her friend if the truth of her birth became known? "God, I have no hope."

As if her slippers bore a mind of their own, they led Gaia back to her special place. Heather grasses and lousewort danced about her mighty oak, as if there were something to celebrate. Her dance card was now filled with pity. Her fortunes forever changed. Nothing good ever changed for Gaia. "God, spin back time. Let me be ignorant again; ignorant and meek and unnoticed. I won't complain this time."

Anything was better than what she was, a secret bastard. If not for the covering lies of the Telfairs, she would be a by-blow. She studied her shaking hands. If she'd been dark like the servant she'd collided with, would she have been tossed away?

Making a fist, she beat against her oak. The snickers of her *friends,* did they know, too? How many sly remarks were actually hints at her mother's infidelity? The village was small. Gossip burned like a candle's wick, bright and fast.

Did it matter with white and black, all trapped inside her limbs? Her stomach rolled. Nausea flooded her lungs. She lunged away, dropped to her knees, and let her breakfast flow out. Maybe the ugly truth could drain away, too.

Wiping her mouth, she crawled back to her oak and set her wrist against a thick tree root. Her skin was light like butter, compared to the bark. The skin was almost like the Telfairs', just a little tan, a little darker. Not good enough.

She wasn't good enough.

Now she knew she could never be good enough.

Envy of her sisters' fair, pretty skin, had it not always wrestled in her bosom? The English world said the lighter the complexion, the more genteel and the more one would be held in esteem.

But she should have envied their blood instead. They knew with certitude who their father was. Julia, the twins, each had a future that could include love. What did Gaia have?

She stood and wiped her hands against her skirt. The grass stains and dusting of dirt left her palms, but the off-white color of her skin remained. She brushed her hands again and again against the fabric, but the truth wouldn't disappear.

A light wind whipped the boughs of her tree, as if calling her for an embrace. Tripping over the gnarled root, she fell against the rough bark. Arms stretched wide, she held onto the trunk. Moss cushioned her cheek as the rustle of crunching leaves sounded like a hush, as if the oak knew her pain and tried to stop her tears.

More crackling of leaves made her lift her chin, but the strong sun shining through the jade canopy of leaves blinded her. She clutched the scarred bark with trembling fingers, and hoped whoever was near didn't see her. No one should witness her shame.

A white handkerchief waved near her forehead.

Gaia surrendered to the fact that she'd been discovered. Slowly, she stood, smoothed her wrinkled bodice, and turned. Nothing mattered any more, not even the opinion of a stranger. Shame mingling with tears, she took the fine lawn cloth from the man who'd caught her Sunday, praying aloud about Elliott.

CHAPTER THREE

A Stranger's Comfort

William gazed at the young woman wiping her face. With her having no gloves, bonnet, or even a scarf, something terrible must've occurred. Though a quiet dignity settled onto her shoulders, trouble brewed behind the dark rims of her spectacles. Her luminous hazel eyes seemed vacant. Something horrible had to have happened to take her fire.

"I've wrinkled this." She tried to flatten and stretch the linen.

The poor girl should stop. Only Mrs. Wingate's iron could make it pristine again. "That's what a handkerchief is for."

Turning to give her a moment to collect herself, he tied Magnus to one of the long, octopus-like arms of the oak. He'd sought the moors to relieve his own anxiety, not to chaperone a female. No new news of the blackmailer had come, and Mr. Telfair hadn't responded to his note, probably crushing it as Mrs. Wingate had predicted the proud man would do. Perhaps his latest gesture of sending Albert, his loyal footman, to Chevron Manor would fare better.

Yet Mrs. Wingate warned it was a bad idea to send Albert. Why? And why should William cede to the old woman's wishes? This was his daughter's health at stake. No, Albert would return with good news.

The heat of the sun and his anger beaded moisture upon his neck. He swiped at it with every intention to leave, but he couldn't. Alone on the beautiful moors, the upset young lady could get into trouble. He straightened his waistcoat and fanned his face with his top hat. It was his duty as a gentleman to make sure she came to no harm. He marched back to her.

"Here," she handed him the rumpled square. "You needn't interrupt your day. I'm fine."

"Yes, I find my time is cluttered with females crying their eyes red." That was true. Mary had had another bad night.

The young woman pivoted and faced the tree trunk. Her shoulders shook, and the muffled tears that drew him from his ride now sang a haunting melody. Was it regret? Despair?

He fiddled with his tan gloves, and searched for something comforting to say, but no words came to him. His stomach sickened at the false notions shared by his friends and family at Elizabeth's loss.

She loved you and Mary so.

Such a beautiful, accomplished wife.

Any man would be so happy.

Lies.

He rubbed his brow. Never could he toss those sentiments. Laughter was supposed to be good medicine. Maybe it would help them both, he and the misery-prayer warrior.

He walked in front of her, and again extended his handkerchief. "Pleasant weather for a walk… would you take a turn with me?"

Her head moved from side to side as she hugged her limbs. The modest grey broadcloth of her gown clung tightly to her arms. She wasn't delicate, but very feminine and curvy; very different from Elizabeth's lithe form.

"Sir, I'd rather be alone."

"Though the moors are quite picturesque, this is not the place for a young woman alone. If I were your fa... older brother, I'd be very concerned."

For a moment, a dimple twitched as if a smile fought to emerge, no doubt at his slip into vanity. Her thumb traced the gold threads of his initials on the handkerchief. "Privacy, please. Will anyone respect my wishes? No, I don't get anything I want."

He wasn't ready to leave. The only enjoyment he'd had these past days was the memory of his banter with his misery warrior. And wasn't he bemoaning the same thing, about doing what he wanted without censure?

With a bow, he rounded to the other side of the oak and sat down, pushing his back against the trunk. Maybe his intrusion would lift her spirits, getting her to pray again for something outlandish.

"Sir, I asked for privacy."

Smoothing out the charcoal tails of his jacket, he winked at her then pulled his top hat down closer to his eyes. "You are on my side of the tree, miss."

Squinting, he could see her hands lifting to her round hips. He smothered a chuckle.

"As a gentleman, I think you should leave. I was here first."

"Well, you are not a gentleman, and I hope they don't grow men quite so pretty here."

Her eyes widened, and her lips mouthed the word, *pretty*. Cheeks darkening, she folded her arms and tugged on her slim cuffs.

"When I am done enjoying this place and have had my fill of amusement, I could be made to leave."

The flicker in her eyes had the beginnings of a rebellious spirit. This could be quite entertaining.

"No one can make anyone do anything; certainly not me." She went back to the other side and sat. Her trim-less skirt bunched at the legs, exposing neat ankles. "I refuse to do anything that someone tells me to do today. I should be the equal to any. Oh, never mind."

Witnessing the passion of her expressions, with that kissable mouth pouting, was half as fun as her impolitic notions. He scooted a little closer, fully capturing her eyes. "So whatever I say, you'll do the opposite?"

"Why are men so obtuse? You know what I mean. My father, well, Mr. Te... the man who raised me, should know I have dreams, that I want his approval, his love." She put a hand to her mouth then rocked her head against the oak. Her golden auburn curls glistened against the chocolate bark.

Oh, how William wanted his own father's approval, but some things just can't be accomplished. "Well, fathers can be difficult. I take it he disapproved of your misery prayers?"

She shook her head. A few more pinned tresses rained down. "What do you do when everything you knew to be true was just a convenient lie?"

Like Elizabeth swearing before God to love him and to be faithful? A sigh leeched out as his innards groaned. "It's devastating. Parts of your soul you didn't know existed begin to hurt. Maybe even a little bit of your faith dies."

Not meaning to be so transparent, he covered his mouth. "Excuse me."

She blinked, before her large pupils settled upon him. She wasn't looking through him, but right at his face, as if all his painful memories were etched upon his cheek, possibly mirroring hers.

Counting the flecks of cedar and moss-colored specks in her eyes, he was captive, and dared not move or breathe. Never before had he thought a woman's heart could hold such honest hurt, not after Elizabeth.

She blinked violently and bounced to her feet. "I'm leaving now because I choose to leave."

He chuckled. She looked marvelous with her cheeks flushed. "Good; and be more judicious when you come looking for me."

Shaking her head, she pivoted. "Don't tell anyone you saw me crying?" She ran through a bush of aconite. The yellow lobes of the flowers waved her forward.

Perhaps the headstrong girl would now go home and listen. Yet if the lass's father were anything like his, dictatorial and lacking in forgiveness, William could understand why she ran.

With a good stretch, he stood and dusted his buff breeches. How could he mention this visit to anyone? He didn't know the lady's name.

Marching to his gelding, he caught himself humming. Brushing the leaves from the folds of his greatcoat, he stretched to see whether he could catch a final glance of the miss, but she'd disappeared. With a click of his tongue, he turned Magnus toward Ontredale. It's good he didn't know her name. It could be dangerous to a man wishing to remain a bachelor. "Come on, Magnus; Albert should be back with good news to help Mary."

Gaia climbed the steps of Chevron Manor. She should be cold, but her cheeks still held a flush. The audacity of the man! How dare he try to make her laugh! He didn't know her pain.

Yet something in his sea-blue gaze said he did. The way his eyes trailed to the right, as if latching onto a memory, the lines of his lean face hardening, even as he offered humor. Something brewed beneath the surface of his handsome exterior.

Hopefully, the stranger would never see her again. *Lord, let his lips stay quiet on the matter.*

Her face fevered again. Why was she thinking of his

mouth, or any part of him?

With a light push, she opened the door. The soft whine shouldn't have alerted anyone in the chaotic Telfair house. Her younger sisters would be in dance practice. Fa… Mr. Telfair probably sat in his study, counting his pence, Sarah making a hat with dear Timothy's assistance. If Gaia snuck up the stairs, she could finish crying her eyes out in her bedchamber.

Upon closing the main door, she spun and bumped into her stepmother.

The woman held her fast, pushing Gaia deep within her ample bosom. "I was so worried. Please don't run off like that again; we should be able to converse about anything."

Sarah sniffled. Teardrops fell upon Gaia's temple. The embrace was real, filled with a heart Gaia believed cold.

"Come with me." She grabbed Gaia's wrist and tugged her into the parlor. Kicking the door closed, Sarah didn't release her, maintaining a tight grip. Did she think Gaia would escape?

Well, one look at Gaia's dirt-stained slippers said she might.

"I love all my children; Julia, Lydia, Helena, Timothy, and my Gaia. You made me the villain for marrying your father, but I'm no villain. Yes, our first years had difficulties. I was a new wife, and suddenly a mother to you and Julia. I was only a few years older than your grown-up brother, God rest his soul."

Gaia widened her swollen eyes and stared at this red-haired woman. The years had taken her thin frame and put some meat on it, but maybe Sarah had grown in wisdom, too.

Injustice twisted in Gaia's spirit. No, she couldn't be pacified. "The man you married is not my father, is he? What am I to you? What am I to do?"

"Mr. Telfair claimed you. You were born during his

marriage. You are a Telfair, legitimate to the world."

Illegitimate. A by-blow, if not for the legality of a broken marriage. Lifting her lenses, Gaia cleaned her spectacles and peered down. "A Telfair doomed to be a servant. All my hopes are gone."

"Gaia, what were your hopes?"

"I wanted a future. To be loved. To be a gentleman's wife. Who would have me now? What will Elliot think?"

Sniffling more, Sarah released Gaia then leaned against the piano. "True love sees beyond circumstances, but if Mr. Whimple can't see your worth, is there another you want? I've watched you hover around him like a lost pup. When I tried to dissuade you, and show you the admirable qualities of others, you grew angry and fled… just like today."

It had been easier to dislike this lady than to see the good in her heart. Maybe she'd tried to spare Gaia pain. "Did you try to turn me against Elliot because you knew? How long have you known?"

Sarah stood up and inched closer, almost on tip-toes. "Only a few days; not until the Duke of Cheshire sent a note, asking your father for one his girls to attend his daughter. It was highhanded and sent Mr. Telfair into a tirade. That's when he told me, and of his own plans for you."

She put a hand to Gaia's shoulder. "No one knows. We can go on as before. You are one of the beloved daughters of Henry Telfair."

The desire to be loved, to believe she was as good as everyone else, gripped Gaia's insides, cutting away at the numbness consuming her. But this hope wasn't enough, and she swiped her black fingers against her light bodice. "These hands aren't beloved. They don't possess Telfair blood."

Sarah took her palms within hers. "These hands pass for white. Mr. Telfair claimed you. You are his daughter."

She pulled Gaia into another full embrace. They held each

other until they were both soaked in tears. "The love you show for your sisters and your brother, and your father, the man who raised you, makes you every inch a Telfair. That goes beyond skin."

If Father had said the same, maybe it would sink in and warm Gaia's broken heart. No, she was to become Timothy's companion. Gaia pushed free and stepped back. "How am I to believe this? Maybe he wanted me to be Julie's handmaiden, and if I'd been a boy, I'd be tossed to the streets."

"You can't blame him for being hurt at your mother's dealings, but he didn't give you away. He bore the secret. Be fair."

Was it fair to live a lie? Was it fair to always feel inferior and not know why, to reach for a father's love and be rebuffed? "Well, a Telfair has the chance to be loved. Give me one chance to show Elliot that I am his other half." She rent her gown wide. The faded frock blended into the grey tint of the lime-washed parlor walls. "But I can't do that in rags or with Father, Mr. Telfair, attempting to banish me to the netherworld. Convince him."

"It's Father, keep saying it. I've never disobeyed him, but it would hurt nothing if you had a new dress." Sarah walked to the corner closet and drew out a bolt of rose-print fabric. "Sew your dress, but keep it out of sight."

Sarah pulled the end of the silk and brushed Gaia's cheek. "This color will make your sweet eyes glow."

Gaia fingered the smooth damask material. She'd never seen anything so fine. "Sweet? My eyes are a dull."

"Not to a mother." She handed the bolt to Gaia. "Maybe I should have been more willing to tempt your father's displeasure to make you more secure of my love."

Gaia adjusted her spectacles, again trying to see this woman in a new light. Her heart felt a little lighter. "I don't know what to say."

"Give it your best go. If Mr. Whimple is the one, he'll make sure we are not ruined. You will make sure of that, too."

Clutching the fabric, Gaia headed to her room. Elliott had to be the answer. If she could become Mrs. Elliott Whimple, she'd have a name. She'd know, without a doubt, who she was and the feel of true love. But would Elliott want a black wife?

William paced the length of the drawing room as his tall footman, Albert, marched inside. The grimace on his dark face loomed, as did his jittering fingers.

"Be at ease, my temper is no more; it's buried in Cheshire."

Surely, an easier breath pushed out of Albert as his chest puffed beneath his blue mantle. "I'm sorry my news isn't better. Mr. Telfair seemed quite disturbed." His man bowed and closed the doors as he left.

William counted aloud, thought of a Psalm; all the rituals he went through to keep his fury at bay. No help would come from the Telfairs. Mouse-poor family or not, the man wouldn't lend one his daughters in service. He must think there was still a chance of them marrying. None of them must not be on the shelf, as the housekeeper had implied.

He brushed his ever-creasing brow. With the war over, maybe he could find Mary a tutor on the Continent, but that would take time.

Would humbling himself and going in person make a difference?

The smell of the afternoon pastries had waned as he wore a path in the rug. Mrs. Wingate left a tempting silver tray on the table, clustered close to the grand two-story mantel. Scones were meant to be enjoyed hot, fresh from the oven, but who could eat with his stomach knotted?

Pacing the edge of the gold tapestry, he rubbed the stiff

muscles of his neck then parked in front of the mirror above the sideboard. He fluffed the knot of his cravat and gazed at his pained reflection. Where did the carefree soldier go, the one with a pretty wife and new babe waiting for his return home?

He pivoted from the butter-colored paper treatment slathering the walls closest to the entry then checked his gilded timepiece. There wasn't enough time for a social visit before Stelford's arrival. After digesting his friend's intelligence, he'd sleep on it and seek an audience with Telfair in the morn.

Ripping open the brass buttons of his deep blue tailcoat, he grabbed Stelford's stationery from an inner pocket then stalked across the room, passed the small writing desk, his uncle's writing desk, to the grand piano by the bay window. The harp-like curve of the instrument glistened with wood polish. Citrus and oil scented this section of the grand room. Light filtering through the gauzy curtains illuminated the blue paper.

Before he could stuff the note back into his pocket, Stelford, all one hundred and eighty pounds of him, blasted into the center, crossing the beige tapestries flowing around the perimeter. "I have arrived."

Mrs. Wingate was fast on his coat-tails. Her fingers gripped a pristine white apron as her expression mirrored her austere grey gown. "Your Grace, the new footman didn't catch him. I tried to stop him, to announce him properly."

"Be at ease." William gripped his friend's hand. "He's an old friend. We don't stand on ceremony. But inform the footman to be more careful."

The housekeeper nodded, though her gaze could bore holes through Stelford's back.

"You can leave us, Mrs. Wingate. See to it we are not disturbed."

"Yes, Your Grace." She curtsied, gave a frown, and then backed from the room.

Stelford stalked about the place, fingering the wall treatment, the Roman suit of armor in the corner. "This room suits you."

"Only if it had a few more weapons of war, a flintlock or two." He lifted his arms, as if he held a gun, and fired it Stelford's way.

His friend made an audible swallow then stopped next to the sideboard. Stelford popped his shaking fingers into the looping fretwork trimming the furnishing, then to the barrel of the aged firearm mounted on the wall.

"The flintlock was the last Duke of Cheshire's prize possession. I think he shot a bear with it in Scotland. That is how the tale is told."

"I see his favorite marble-top desk by the window. Nothing of your father's? No Bibles to thump?" Stelford chuckled and picked up the decanter and pried at its top. "Should a weapon be so near the liquor?"

With a shake of his head, William ignored the dig at his father. His friend knew the turbulence of that relationship. "You know he only begrudgingly came to this place, as if he tried to hide its existence from us. But do help yourself. I've given up that vice."

Struggling to open the bottle, Stelford's unsteady hands nearly dropped the glass. The man looked particularly horrid; unshaven face, pallid complexion. Was the news that bad?

"No more drink?" Stelford made a 'tsk' sound with his mouth as the stopper released. "The good Reverend St. Landon would be proud."

His honorable father wouldn't be. He disapproved of nearly everything since his only son did, since William decided against studying divinity to go to war… another check mark on his list of guilt. He stepped closer and steadied the bottle. "Drink makes my temper rage."

With a gulp, Stelford downed the liquor. "Then happy abstinence."

Moving the alcohol away got his friend's attention, eyes widening, following the bottle. "Out with it, then you can drain this."

"I've found out nothing new. No new demands from the blackmailers."

Of their own volition, William's fingers tightened about the dimpled glass. He'd throw it and break it against the wall, if not for the mess and the explanation he'd owe Mrs. Wingate. Not to mention backsliding to his old ways of dealing with anger. He eased the bottle back to its position on the Wedgewood tray and backed away from the breakables.

"I'm sorry. I tried as discreetly as I could to determine who was making the threats. A disgruntled footman, one of the maids let go, the cooking staff the late duchess needled.... Nothing. The blackmailer covered his tracks well." His green eyes darted back and forth like a metronome, waiting to meter out more bad news.

William stalked to the emerald sofa and thrust his back deep into the cushions. The tufted fabric swallowed him whole for a moment, but he fought his way back to a seated position. "Just say what you know. I'm in control of myself."

Plodding from the sideboard all the way to the window, Stelford dragged his short heels across the tapestry. His footsteps seemed mired in as much depression as William held guilt.

"I know I was quite upset the last time we met, but if someone tried to malign your late wife's memory, you'd break a few things as a substitute for necks."

Stelford stopped mid-step and pivoted to face William. "Your temper is legendary. That time Elizabeth had you fuming and you threw... What was it? A trunk?"

William's stomach turned. He'd been a fool, a young husband who couldn't understand his wife's changing emotions. "It was a chair. And the hole in the wall was very small."

Chuckles fell out of Stelford's mouth. "Not for Albert. It took him days to patch and paint it."

"I stopped all that and became quite domestic." It still wasn't enough to return Elizabeth's heart to William. But did she seek comfort from calmer waters? Was she unfaithful, like the blackmail notes claimed?

Stelford walked until he reached the window. "I, too, can understand, my dear duke. Lizzy, I mean, the duchess, was a wonderful woman. No one should defame her."

"I know you and my Elizabeth were childhood friends, Benjamin. This must be hard for you too."

The grimace on Stelford's face was comical. He took a long sip. "'Benjamin' is for my doxies and easy conquests. My friends, the ones I care for, call me *Stelford*. I liked the way your duchess said it."

William punched at a pillow. "You knew her well. Do you think there's any truth? Could she have been unfaith... I can't even say it."

Stelford swiped the sweating glass along his forehead. "I know she was very unhappy. She did not like the separation."

"I was at war." William climbed out of the sofa and stomped to the piano. Plopping onto the bench, he plunked at a few keys. "I thought she understood."

Stelford shrugged, but then his lips parted into his typical grin. "Your cousin is desperate to know your location."

Banging his head against the keys, William grimaced. Nothing but confusion surrounded Deborah Smythen; that and her begging him to marry her. William might be lonely, but he wasn't *that* lonely. "Please tell me you held your peace."

"She knows nothing. Tried to cajole me with a bribe, but I stayed strong."

"That woman is up to no good. Elizabeth was barely six months gone and my cousin began pestering me about marriage; that she'd make things easier for Mary." He popped a key. The high note drowned all his thoughts, much like Deborah's voice.

"Miss Smythen might be able to make social connections for Mary."

"My cousin can't stand noise. She definitely couldn't handle my daughter."

A shudder went up his spine, envisioning his obnoxious cousin flying through the doors. "The longer she doesn't know my location, the better."

"Hiding doesn't become you." Swiveling, Stelford approached the back of the huge instrument and ran his hand over the slick polish of the chestnut wood. "Let's go be free. Why not ride to that quaint little village? The fresh air could do us both good. A tavern would do me quite fine."

William waved a hand in the air to stop his eager friend. "Tomorrow we'll head there, but we'll need to stop at Chevron Manor. I must smooth some ruffled feathers to ply Mr. Telfair for one of his daughters."

"What? Now that's what I'm talking about. Why wait for tomorrow, when we can get into mischief today? Forging ahead—"

"I'm seeking a governess, or just advice. I think my overtures have put a burr in the man's saddle. I need to convince Mr. Telfair to lend his daughter gifted with helping children speak. Mary needs her."

Stelford finished his drink. "Mary's not the only one who needs something."

William fumed, but he'd ignore the foolish talk. "Go upstairs. There's a bed waiting for you."

His friend nodded, but took his glass and the bottle of brandy and pounded out of the room.

This Chevron business was about getting his daughter help, but what if smoothing Telfair's ego proved useless? What could be done for Mary then?

CHAPTER FOUR

A Ride to Chevron Manor

Tugging his hat down again, William pushed Magnus into a quicker trot. They leapt a stream and flew down the worn path, past a bank of pines. The crisp morning air greeted his lungs, leaving a tingle on his face. He felt a liveliness that he hadn't known since the Peninsula. This was Devonshire, the place of his birth, the only respite he'd known. And Mary, she must feel it, too. His babe had a good night last night. "Keep up, Stelford."

Farther down the trail, billowing grey smoke popped from the chimneys of the homes and shops of the village coming into view. The streaks tarnished the perfect sky, soiling a hazel-blue canvas. Since his last encounter with the saucy sprite in the heather, William had come to love the color. In the late hours, his undisciplined mind had recalled the turn of her countenance, the shimmer of sunlight on her crinkled curls, the lilt in her voice as she prayed for wretchedness, the tears staining her light eyes. Should've gotten a name. He might be able to inquire on her well-being.

Though a single man should be careful, this woman was smitten over another. Surely, it was safe to think of her. He filled his lungs with the hint of burnt hickory. "I wonder if the old boulangerie is still in business. We'll stop on our return."

Stelford huffed and puffed as he caught up. "You're in the mood for bread?"

"I'm in the mood to remember the innocence of my youth; the good parts." Cutting through town, they edged down the forked lane to Chevron Manor.

"A great honor you offer the Telfairs, my dear Duke, and for such a celibate, paternal cause."

"For my daughter, I'll do nearly anything." He slowed Magnus and leapt down, trudging the path to the modest house with a wide park backing into the woods. Ivy climbed the mottled beige-and-grey undressed limestone forming the facade.

When no groom came to meet them, Stelford grunted then tied the horses to a fence tie. "Are we still in England?"

William dismounted and gave Magnus a pat. "There are no horse thieves about. We should be safe."

Shaking his head, Stelford stumbled forward, leading until they stood on the steps of the low entry. Without warning, a team of wild little girls barreled past, all giggles and flying ribbons. The one whipping a magnifying glass in her palm stepped on William's boot. The light footfall just scuffed his Hessian, no real damage, but the glint of sunlight concentrated by the glass made him blink like a crazed man.

Stelford looked aghast. "Barbarians. This is what you want to associate with, my dear Duke?"

"Friend, they are little children rushing to play; ill-mannered, but children none the less." Neither of the redheads could be the Telfair daughter he sought, or this trip was a waste of time. Towing a handkerchief, he bent to dust off his boot. Before he could move out of the way, a small boy rammed into his hip, pushing William backward. "Whoa, young man."

Stelford pushed them both forward. "You've gained

weight."

William grabbed the boy and swung him in the air. "Where are you going in such a hurry, little man? I think an apology should be tendered."

The boy's eyes grew wide, but he said nothing. The child, frozen within William's grasp was the lad from the woods.

So was his lovely sister near? Was she the Telfair daughter he sought? He hid an anticipating smirk and pulled the lad deeper into his arms. "What's your name?"

The child tugged on a flap of William's greatcoat, as if he could hide within the wool.

"Timothy!" a panicked feminine voice floated from behind.

"Is that you, little man?" He rotated, holding the child to her. "Here, miss."

With luscious sun-kissed ringlets and thin-rimmed spectacles bouncing, William's prayer warrior stood close, with her arms outstretched. She had to be the one. God did work in mysterious ways.

Heart lunging within her chest, Gaia could barely speak; her voice sounding like rushing wind, "Please, sir, he didn't, didn't mean.... You...."

She put a hand to her lips to stop her babbling. The man must think her an idiot.

"Yes, me. And he's been no trouble; just in too large a hurry, like his sisters." He leaned down and placed Timothy in her arms.

A sigh escaped her lips when she held the lad close. The man who saved her brother last week, then caught her crying her eyes out yesterday, stood at the door. The anxiousness and hurt wrapped around her heart again. Eyes closing, she tightened her arms about Timothy.

The boy squirmed, and she set him to the ground. Borrowing courage from the air, she took a deep breath and faced her brother's hero, her forthcoming source of humiliation. Using a few hand motions she'd taught him, she pointed at the tall man. "Timothy, you must apologize."

The boy hung his head. Tears drizzled down his cheek. "So-rr-y."

The handsome man and his red-eyed friend stared at them.

The owner of the steady blue-green eyes tipped his fine beaver top hat. "Is he well? I hope I didn't frighten the boy."

"Did you come to call upon his, our father, Mr. Telfair?"

Timothy reached out toward the man. "Horse. Horse."

Dressed in buff breeches and a turquoise waistcoat, he stooped beside her, seemingly uncaring of dusting his rich clothes. "You remember Magnus. Does the lad have difficulty with his speech?"

Gaia swallowed hard. They weren't supposed to discuss this in public, and especially not with strangers. She snatched up Timothy's hand and proceeded to walk inside.

The man caught up with her, falling into step. "I didn't mean to offend you. I just—"

"What! Are you curious? Will you make sport of this with your friend?" She bit her lip, but also couldn't help but marvel at the new freedom her tongue held. Her protective nature of this little boy knew no bounds.

He crossed in front of her, blocking her retreat deeper into the hall. This man had to be as tall as Elliot, maybe taller.

"I'm not the enemy, miss. And I want to make sure Master Timothy Telfair is unhurt."

"He is well. Now, follow me to the parlor. You may put your hat and gloves on the show table." She pivoted from the green-blue, maybe sea-blue, eyes beaming at her.

Stripping off his outer garments, he kept staring at her. "What is your name, Miss Telfair?"

Wiggling her worn kid slipper beneath her long faded skirt, she wished for a means of escape. The training of being a lady, a gentleman's daughter, spurred into her mind. She would act as one, until exposed to be less than. "This might be the country, but the rules of propriety are obeyed here. We need a proper introduction. Excuse me, sir. I must help with refreshment."

He caught her arm and kissed her hand, as if they were old friends. "How can we have a *proper* introduction, if we continually accost each other? It's up to three separate occasions."

A chuckle fled his mouth when her lips thinned. "If we don't exchange names now, we will have to keep sneaking about."

Her grimace widened as she opened the parlor door. "In here, gentlemen."

His friend, head swiveling toward both of them, slipped inside. Timothy's rescuer stayed. He lowered his voice to a whisper. "Well, thank you, my dear."

"For what?"

"For not calling down any new plagues; it's been a quiet night. I'm grateful." He winked at her before entering Sarah's lair.

Gaia stared at the door, dumbfounded at his jokes. What was he going to say to her stepmother and her father? Had she brought more shame to the Telfairs?

William wanted to turn back and go through the door. The answer for Mary's mute world stood in the hall of this modest home. So close.

"Your grace, to what do we owe the pleasure? It couldn't be again for your audacious request."

Pivoting toward the harsh scold, William squared his shoulders. The man already knew who he was. Ah, the inequity of being on enemy soil. "I deserve your censure, Mr. Telfair. I came myself, to rectify the situation."

The thin older man with light-colored sideburns squinted at him and pointed him to the burgundy divan. "My mind is unchanged, but a civil meeting is better than your first overture or the sending of your *fancy* black servant."

Things were so different in the country. In London, it would be seen as a sign of high regard to send Albert. Quality servants of his race were quite fashionable; not that William followed such trends.

He sat and relaxed his anxious fingers against his knee. His arrogance could ruin any chance of getting Mary aid. Yes, he was Duke of Cheshire, and had command of more land and money than most, but he'd give it all to save Mary from silence. Humility spilled from his pores, wetting his palms. "I must apologize. I was desperate to find a deserving companion for my daughter. I didn't think how outlandish the request must seem to you."

Mr. Telfair smiled for a moment then sank against the curved wood of his chair back. "Good, we have an understanding. None of my daughters are looking for positions. My eldest, though she will be returning from London this evening, is a rare beauty who might be a good acquaintance for you."

Oh, no; the matchmaking commences. "How many daughters do you have, sir?"

Telfair sat back, his posture slumping, as if counting the number was a burden. "There is Julia, my oldest, and then there are my twins, Lydia and Helena."

"And, Gaia; your second-oldest." A buxom woman with reddish hair came into the room with a large silver tea service. The spectacle-wearing prayer warrior followed with a tray of biscuits and other treats.

The men stood.

"Yes, and Gaia," Mr. Telfair's tone was tight, not brimming with joy.

It reminded him of those rare times he'd visited a young lady when he was poor William St. Landon, a low regiment lieutenant. In an odd way, he enjoyed the suspension. He dipped his chin to the ladies. "All the Telfair daughters I've met seem lovely."

The prayer warrior's tray clanged onto the table. She bit her lip as she passed a saucer to Stelford.

The lass must think he'd tell of their unconventional meetings. No, those were something to be savored; a delicious secret. "The twin girls and Miss Gaia greeted me and Mr. Stelford at the entry. Very fine girls."

Hazel eyes beamed with a smile as she handed him a plate holding a chocolate dipped biscuit. Oh, he'd keep a thousand secrets for such a warm gaze.

"Gaia, you can leave us. You, too, Mrs. Telfair; let us men to finish this conversation."

"Yes, sir," the young lady curtsied, exuding grace from her curvy limbs as she balanced then popped up.

She couldn't be leaving. She was the object of this outing. "I also met your young son. He's quite a spry young man. I hear Miss Gaia has been a great influence in his education."

"Oh, yes, she has." Mrs. Telfair, linked an arm about Gaia. "She's quite accomplished in music and languages."

The cheeks of the prayer warrior darkened, making her redden about her mouth. "Your Grace?"

Stelford plopped back onto the divan, and began to chuckle. "Yes, miss. It was in all the papers, telling of his elevation to become the Duke of Cheshire."

There were times when William still wished to exercise his temper and at least heatedly suggest his best friend jump into an ocean. He nodded at Miss Gaia. "Guilty as charged."

The young lady's face tilted up. Her full lips pressed together in a line. There were questions in her eyes. "The Duke of Cheshire."

Why did it feel as if she'd just crossed out any potential friendship because of his station? Another backward moment for this place. That's not how things typically worked. Sycophants, toadies, Deborahs, and other pushy, marriage-minded women all sought him because of his title. "Very pleased to meet you, Miss—"

"That will be all," her father's voice sounded stern. "These gentlemen have business here at Chevron. This is not a social call."

For a moment, William looked down at his chocolate treat, away from the curious hazel eyes and the severe brown ones of the lady's father. "Isn't there a social aspect to everything?"

Mrs. Telfair stepped to him, her cherub-like face grinning, mobcap fluttering. "We hope that this is the beginning of more social calls." She frowned at Mr. Telfair, took a hold of the slimmer Miss Gaia, and traipsed out of the room.

The door closed. One man stood in William's path, keeping him from getting Mary's help. He had to either make peace and humble himself, or let ego stumble him. His short, ill-fated marriage taught an invaluable lesson about the poison of pride. Mary meant the world to him, and deserved the world for such a horrid start, caught between warring parents. With hands drawn to his back, he leveled his shoulders. "Forgive my errant communication, Mr. Telfair. I meant no disrespect. I had heard your daughters are well-esteemed. I want no one around my child but people of the finest spirit and character. Meeting you and those daughters here, I see their reputation is well-placed."

The heartfelt words seemed to soften the old man. He nodded, and he waved his hand more gently this time. "Thank you, Cheshire. Have a seat."

Releasing a pent-up sigh, William tugged at his breeches and joined Stelford in eating the flaky pastry. "I would like to hope for some friendship between our families. I would love to be able to seek advice from you. It is obvious you have done well with these young ladies."

"You have to have a firm hand. Do you intend to be in these parts for long? I'm sure your seat in Parliament requires your attendance."

"If all can remain quiet, we will be in Devonshire at least through the summer." He munched on a bit of the sweet biscuit. Provided neither the blackmailer nor Deborah found him, he and Mary might stay forever.

"Then, it will be good to see you and Mr. Stelford at church on Sunday and the upcoming Hallows' Ball. Fitting into our society is important."

Attend the village church? An image of the pulpit, gleaming mahogany, flashed in William's mind. It would be so much easier just to hire a governess. As he stood, he forced his mouth to smile. "Well, we've a few more stops this morning. Thank you for your hospitality."

"Yes, I, too, have some things to do, with my beautiful Julia returning from London today. Unless you and Mr. Stelford stay another half an hour, I will have to introduce you to her at the Hallows' Ball."

William couldn't say the hundred excuses piling up in his skull. This was a process. He had to be tactful. "Yes, Mr. Telfair. Come along, Stelford."

With his friend's lazy gait tapping behind him, they left the parlor and proceeded to the show table. Miss Gaia waited there.

Back against the wall, head turned to the yard, the young woman fingered his hat; nervous and charming. "So, all is well?"

"Yes; your father has welcomed us to the neighborhood."

Her countenance whipped toward them. Her crinkled forehead smoothed. "Good; we seldom get new neighbors."

William knelt and readjusted the buckle on his boot. An

afternoon of riding would commence the minute they fled Chevron Manor. That would allay the tension in his bones—a member of this community, possibly going to his father's old church. Oh, maybe this wasn't worth it. His hopeful dream of getting Mary to speak was becoming a nightmare.

A tiny voice squeaked outside, "Why did you do that, Lydia?"

"You did it, Helena!" the answer sounded similar in pitch and equally distressed. "I just helped you examine the horse's hair."

Stelford brushed past him and marched all the way to the threshold. "I assume you'd have more visitors, if you didn't set their horse on fire."

The lass shoved the hat at his friend and hurried to the door. She gasped and started running. "Girls, what have you done!"

By the time William made it outside, he caught the blur of Magnus charging into the woods, smoke coming from his tail, and a little boy hanging from his neck. The lovely Miss Gaia chased them.

Mortified, scared, Gaia panted hard. The distance between her and the horse carrying her brother increased. Why did the girls do this?

She didn't waste time interrogating the finger-pointers. Timothy needed her. Maybe Father… Mr. Telfair… was right about Gaia being her brother's companion. None of the other girls felt the same bond, the same desire to help the boy. "Lord, let no harm come to Timothy!"

The duke's horse disappeared around the bend.

Her chest filled with angst, crushing her heart. He could get so hurt.

Hooves sounded behind her. She tried to move out of the way, but it came up on her too fast.

"Give me your hand, woman," the command was stern, giving no chance to question.

Lungs about to explode, she reached for the arm. A band of iron gripped her and towed her into the air. She slammed into the duke's back. Scrambling, she gripped him about his chest to keep from falling and being trampled.

He clasped her fingers for a second then spurred the horse into a faster gait. "Hang on to me, Miss Telfair. We'll get him."

It wasn't as if she had a choice if she hoped to save Timothy. The tree line blurred as the horse gained speed. Wind hit her face, and she pressed her chin against his coat. He sat very high in his seat, and the animal obeyed his commands. Somehow, knowing the duke was near, chasing after her brother, made a little of her fear ease. In the pit of her stomach, she knew God would again use this man to save Timothy.

"Magnus must be headed back to Ontredale."

"Through town?" What would people think, seeing her riding astride with the Duke of Cheshire? "Please, not that way; this will bring such gossip."

"Worse. Magnus is veering toward the cliffs; his favorite place to romp."

Weakness settled between her shoulders as she imagined her little brother tumbling down to the rocks.

Before tears could leak, the duke's bare hand cupped hers. "Buck up. We'll catch 'em before anything worse happens. Just hang on."

Emerald pines parted. The low lapping of waves sounded. The tang of sea air kissed her lips. "Oh, God, let Timothy be unhurt."

"The little fellow's got a good seat, to hang on to Magnus this long. And there he is now."

She leaned a little closer to peer over his shoulder. The scent of warm spice emanated from his neck. She blinked and refocused. It was true; Timothy and the crazed horse were visible again, just beyond the turn in the path.

Within a blink, they were now side by side.

Timothy grinned. His little arms had a tight grip about Magnus's neck. "Horse. Horse."

He appeared well, but her pulse wouldn't slow until she was on the ground, not moving, cuddling Timothy.

As if this was commonplace, the duke leaned over, grabbed the wild horse's reins, and, with the other, he slowed his mount. Forcing both to a walking pace, the duke jumped down. All motion stopped.

Her heart lifted. He was wonderful and in control. Hopefully, the trouble they'd caused him wouldn't make him shun the Telfairs.

In quick succession, he pulled Timothy off the saddle and put him atop his broad shoulders. "Had a good ride this morning, lad?"

"Yeah. Horse."

The grin on the boy's face shattered the glass holding her emotions. Tears swamped her cheeks. Her spectacles steamed.

The duke pivoted and put the warm leather into her hands, his lips drawn into a line. "No tears now, lass. The boy's not hurt."

Humming, the man turned. He and Timothy moved to the animal's rear. "Doesn't look as if your sisters have injured my horse too much, either." His fingers feathered into the dark char of the animal's tail. He marched in front of Magnus. "Nothing time and my groom can't fix."

The beast nuzzled the duke's arm as if indicating, *all will be fine, Master*.

Master; the word *hung in her brain, followed by an image of the duke's tall, black servant. Would that have been her fate if Mr. Telford hadn't lied? What was it like to have a master?*

Another, heavier snort left Magnus.

Her thoughts cleared, and she petted her own mount. "We should be getting back. Everyone must be worried. And we are not exactly chaperoned. I must bring no shame to the Telfairs."

A smile graced the duke's lips. It wasn't a scandalous smirk, so he clearly hadn't misunderstood her intent. Yet, somehow, the urge to bunch her collar itched at her fingers.

The duke nodded. "As we go back, tell me how you taught this young man to speak. That knowledge would be a good reward."

No, that was worse than a flirtation. He wanted to know more of Timothy and his difficulties. Sweat along her palm made the leather slip, but she caught it. "We aren't to talk of this in public."

He inched toward her, his grip on Timothy slight but secure, showing him to possess a skill with handling children. Perhaps he was just naturally gifted, because what man of his station had such experience?

"This isn't a public place. And I won't break your confidence. You should know this by now."

She should. He hadn't told her family of their twice meeting in the woods, and even now looked at her with a mixture of warmth and understanding.

He placed Timothy beside her. "I'd never do anything to disparage you."

Gaia folded her arms about Timothy and pulled his head to her chin. Memories of the boy's first words pressed upon her heart, mixing with the lingering ounce of dread from seeing him hang on to the fleeing horse. Her voice dropped, almost breaking in the whistling wind. "Blocks; I used blocks and hummed the letters."

"Blocks?"

"Wooden ones with bright colors. That and songs kept his

attention. Soon he tried to imitate me. His mouth would open, and he'd mimic my lips. That's when I knew. I knew he could learn to speak."

He took the reins from her fingers, his strong hand warming hers. "Colors, songs. I think I've got it." He nodded, with eyes drifting to the left as if her little story answered an unspoken question. "I'll lead us back."

With a short tug, he made the horses move behind him. The duke's straight posture appeared as if he led an army. What had this man been battling, and what was he fighting now?

Soon the rooftop of Chevron Manor appeared between the trees. In another ten minutes, they'd be back to her family. Her stomach knotted. If she didn't ask about the only other black she'd ever seen, she'd never have the chance. Leaning forward, she held tightly to Timothy, her only anchor to what was real, to what mattered. "The servant you sent..."

"You mean Albert." The duke pivoted, his sea-blue eyes widening as his posture stiffened. "What about him? He was at Chevron the day you ran off. Did he upset you?"

"No."

"Was it his race that offended you? Your father thought it pretentious to send him, but I think his sensibility has less to do with over-handedness and more to do with the servant."

Yes, the man who she thought was her father had a problem with anything that reminded him of her mother's failings. Well, wasn't she also a daily reminder? Gall, hopelessness, all flooded her lungs. It took at least thirty seconds to learn to swallow again. She peered up and caught the duke's gaze, but couldn't hold it. No one could know the feelings of shame pressing at her. Would she always be helpless to the stains of the past?

"Miss Gaia, you have a question." He wrenched at his neck. "Tell me the reason you ran from Chevron shortly after meeting Albert."

She stopped counting the lacings on his boots, and lifted her countenance. "Are you a slaver? Is the manservant a slave?"

A smile bloomed in his eyes then spread to his curling lips. "An abolitionist's spirit runs in the Telfairs. Good. No, Albert works for me. He is a paid servant like others on my staff."

That wasn't her angst. Mr. Telfair probably wanted to banish all of the blacks to the Caribbean or Africa, or wherever else they came from. She balled the tanned fingers holding Timothy in place. If she'd been as dark as the duke's manservant, or hadn't proved to be as useful to Timothy, the heir of all the Telfair entailed estates, she'd be banished, too. The man she'd always called 'Father' didn't love her.

Her horse started moving again. The duke pulled the pair up the last hill. It was for the best. No need to let him know how distant his station in life was from hers.

As they came within the last hundred feet, she could see a carriage stopping at the house. Out popped a tall, rounded figure. Aunt Tabby? Yes, it was her mother's best friend, and Mr. Telfair's sister. That must mean Julia had returned. "Let's hurry. My aunt and sister have arrived from London."

Julia's thin, blurry outline bore a pretty pink pelisse. Oh, hopefully she made a match, and it was to someone as noble and strong as the duke or as kind as Elliot. Before her thoughts could clear, a tall man leapt out. The gait, the short stride... Whimple? The man donned a small domed hat, so typical of unfussy Elliot. Oh, no. It was he.

Gaia's heart beat wildly. He wasn't supposed to see her yet, not without her new dress, not looking wild from chasing after Timothy.

"What's the matter, Miss Telfair? You've put harsh lines on you pretty forehead again."

She let her shoulders slump and fought the urge to pin her

dangling curls. "I look horrid, and we've more guests. I wish I could run."

Timothy wiggled and gripped the horse's reins, whipping them around as if to make their mount move. "Run. Run. Run. Elliot here. Wh.... Whimple."

Part of her so wished the beast would sprint back to the grove of trees. Her cheeks burned hot enough to fall off.

The duke smiled, but, thankfully, didn't turn or draw Elliot's attention, though the devilish curve of his mouth implied mischief. "Haven't you had enough of running? At least I'm here, so you won't have to go looking for me."

She glared at him. It wasn't funny to be unrequited in love. It hurt, cutting up all her insides.

The duke waved a palm. "Now, don't go sending your misery prayers my way. I've my fill already, and now old Magnus too." He lifted Timothy and plopped him again on his shoulders. "Well, the sooner we get you and your brother inside, the sooner you can attend to your guests and ease your stepmother's frown. Your father seemed at peace, knowing you were chasing after this young man." He paused for a second, his face and tone sobering. "A great many responsibilities befall you. You probably haven't the time for another project, not that your father would spare you."

Something very sad sounded in his voice. After all the trouble she and Timothy had caused, there had to be a way to convince Mr. Telfair to not be so suspicious of such a kind man. "Come to the Hallows' Ball at the week's end. Pillars of the community impress not only my family, but the neighbors, too. That may change minds."

A sparkle returned to his eyes, like moonlight beaming on the waves. "A pillar is a hard thing to aspire to, but I could try. Now, let's get you down."

Before she could protest, his hands were about her waist. His firm index finger and thumb squeezed a rib as he hoisted her in the air. Her breath caught; not from the power of his arms, but from seeing Elliot linking hands with Julia, towing her sister into a kiss.

CHAPTER FIVE

The Hallow's Ball

Friday, the week's end, and Gaia still hadn't finished hemming her new dress. If she went to the Hallows' Ball at all, this gown needed to be finished. Yet what was the point? Elliot had again chosen someone else, not Gaia.

Her pricked fingers stung a little less than the cuts in her heart. How could Julia do this to her?

Though her sister never claimed a beau, she never lacked for attention. And when things went badly, who was there to bolster Julia's confidence? Gaia cried with her when she was jilted. Did sisterly loyalty mean nothing?

Maybe she didn't know the misery growing in Gaia's bosom. Julia wouldn't flirt with Elliot if she did. That must be the case. Julia would never be this cruel. And anyone could be taken in by the blue of Elliot's eyes.

What if it was too late, and Julia and Elliot were in love? Could Gaia stand near the couple at the wedding chapel, and wish them happiness? Her stomach twisted, remembering Cousin Millicent flaunting her engagement to him.

Panting, Gaia flung the gown onto her mattress and started to pace. *God, how do I do this? Have I missed my chance because I don't stand up for myself?*

What if there were no chances? Maybe God's gift was the respectability of the Telfair name, and skin that didn't scream her secret. Her face fevered, and that old heart shriveled within. "I should be grateful."

However, only anger filled her veins; anger at her mother for dying and not being able to explain, anger at the lies and the need for them, anger at the engulfing revelation that this was all someone like her, a mulatto, could attain.

Needing cool air, she opened the window. The evening air wafted coconut scent inside, kissing her nose. Peering down, she saw tiny buds and a couple of blooms on the spiny gorse edging the wall. The plant decided to blossom now, the day of the Hallows' Ball. Maybe it was time for Gaia to flower; a future of her own choosing, the hope for which couldn't be gone. The duke thought she was pretty. Could Elliot think her pretty, too? What would happen if she grew as bold in her speech with him as she was with the duke?

Tonight she'd dance with Elliot and find a way to tell him her heart. She and Elliot enjoyed books and learning and the outdoors. Gaia would make an excellent botanist's wife. Elliot was a man of logic. He'd see this if presented the facts. Surely, reason would triumph over Julia's pretty face.

A few taps on the threshold made Gaia turn. The light pounds had to be Julia's small hands.

With a sigh, Gaia went to the door and opened it.

Julia swished back and forth in her fashionable cream gown, with violet threading upon its square neck. Her long, light blonde hair was coiffed with tiny flowers, and twisted into a thick braid. She looked like a goddess.

Gaia swallowed the small bit of hope stuck in her throat. Julia's beauty would win.

Her sister stroked Gaia's chin. "Sarah said that you would be going to the Hallows' Ball. Your first outing; you must be nervous."

Leaning against the door, coddling the crystal knob in her hand, Gaia nodded, but words couldn't form. It was hard to, with the self-doubt flooding inside.

Julia tapped her slipper and folded her hands together. "I thought you might need some help readying."

Licking her dry lips, Gaia backed into the room. "I still have more sewing to do."

"Sarah says you've been working on a dress. May I see?" her words were soft. Her gentle brown eyes looked as if they concealed tears. "I missed you."

Gaia missed her, too. Other than Seren and Julia, no peers had made Gaia feel loved and valued. "A month gone in London is too much."

Julia came forward and wrapped Gaia in her arms. Sisterly love had to come before anything, even Elliot.

Soon tears and flailing arms cleared as they each stepped away, swiping at cheeks, wiping eyes.

"Well, let's have a look," Julia sauntered to the bed and picked up the rose gown. She arrayed it about Gaia and positioned her in front of the mirror. "This color will make you look so well. You will stand out. With all eyes on you, are you ready for that?"

Laying the gown over her arm, she pivoted to Julia. "What are you talking about?"

"The snickers of our friends; you've heard how they talk about me, about anyone different."

Gaia's feet chilled within her slippers. "What are you saying?"

Julia's eyes grew big. "This rose color will draw attention, with everyone else in white or cream gowns. Just prepare yourself for the scrutiny that comes with it."

Anger churned in Gaia stomach. Forgiving her sister for attracting Elliot was difficult, but to make Gaia self-conscious was horrendous. Maybe the girl's shed tears were a trick.

"You don't want me to stand out. You want me to hide."

"I want to spare you. The talk can be cruel to anyone *different*."

Forcing air into her lungs, Gaia let the dress flutter to the floor and sought her sister's eyes. There wasn't cruelty in them, but something genuine, almost fearful. This wasn't about Elliot. She knew. Of course she knew. Six years older than Gaia, she had to have known.

A thousand questions filled her head. Who was Gaia's father? What was he like? Did mother love him, or was it lust? Gaia licked her lips. "Julia—"

Aunt Tabby pattered inside. "Girls, you must not dawdle." The woman picked up the gown from the floor. "This will not do. It will make your face look red and coarse. No." She marched to the closet and pulled out a tired, light-grey, off-white frock. "This is what you will wear."

One of Gaia's old gowns. She would blend with the whitewashed walls. No one would see her.

"Gaia, now hurry. Delilah's girls, my dearest friend's girls, must look well tonight." Aunt Tabby grabbed Julia's hand, towing her from the room.

When the door thudded closed, Gaia let her shoulders sag. What excuse could she come up with to avoid going, that wouldn't disappoint her stepmother? Only the image of Sarah prostrate, begging Mr. Telfair to give permission to allow his less-than daughter to go, filled Gaia's mind. She couldn't disappoint her. What was another day of being ignored?

A tug on her skirt made her turn.

"He'll see." Timothy, who must've snuck out of his favorite hiding spot underneath Gaia's bed, picked up a piece of the thread and let it float to the floor.

She bent and kissed his forehead. "If only that were true."

* * *

When the carriage stopped at Southborne Hall, the Hallows' home, Aunt Tabby pressed against the window. Then, she sat back as if the sight of the decorated estate were commonplace. Maybe it was to a devoted London-dweller, but not for simple county folks, and definitely not to Gaia.

Her first outing. Her first ball. Her palms moistened beneath her tight white gloves. Aunt had brushed Gaia's frizzing curls into a neat chignon. She couldn't stop her feet from tapping on the floorboards.

Her heart beat hard as she scanned the lanterns hooked to iron posts lighting the cobblestone path of the front drive. Smaller lights stood on every other step, offering a welcoming atmosphere. The sandstone brick looked brighter and richer because of them.

In this light, the bare bit of her arm glowed, just like Julia. If only she could believe she was just as good. Maybe veiled in the moonlight she was.

Julia bit her lip and fretted the lace handle of her fan. Why was she nervous? Her hair was coiffed just so, with pearl pins enwrapping her fair locks. Surely, some man other than Elliot would see the beauty in the girl's chestnut eyes.

Aunt descended first and straightened the lines of her moss- green gown. Her chocolate gloves made her thick arms look like a Sycamore tree, but an elegant one.

A liveried servant in his shining light-blue coat held his hand out for Julia. She gripped it and floated from the carriage. Her cream gown with rose embellishments about the waist made her look like a garden after the first snow.

Casting her gaze upon her old gown, a pass-down from one of aunt's daughters, Gaia's palms became wetter. Staying hidden within the dark interior of their carriage held some appeal.

Sarah squeezed Gaia's hand. "It's not about clothes. Don't look for God's approval from others. He has made you special. And his plans for you are special." She towed Gaia from the safe bench and up the stairs to the gleaming entry of Southborne.

The sweetest music flowed down the long gallery framed with Roman columns. Party-goers, the elders of the community, and every eligible maiden lined the passage. The crush of people felt thick. The humid air dampened Gaia's forehead. Sarah's hand tugged on hers, and they trudged deeper, until arriving in the main ballroom.

The music sounded clear, each note no longer muffled by a multitude of conversations. Near the head of the room, men in dark tailcoats plucked long bowstrings across violins, as flautists whipped their obsidian instruments to a jaunty tune. The fine polish of the wood reflected the diamond light of the high chandelier onto her spectacles and the carved trim spanning the ceiling.

Chalked floors made a star pattern similar to the constellation of a Christmas sky. The multitude of revelers spun and orbited about the tables of refreshment.

A few of her sister's friends stared and pointed in her direction. Frowning behind fans, the young ladies didn't seem to share her enthusiasm. Gaia almost laughed. No longer could any of them make her feel more unworthy. Her mother's secret outdid them all.

Massive fluted columns lined the ends of the room, each decorated with garlands of the blooms. Her nostrils filled with lilac. The sweet smell blended with the musk of candle wax from the collection of torches set in the corners of the room.

Adjusting her spectacles, she lifted her gaze to the mesmerizing crystal chandelier. Before she could stop herself, she twirled around. The hem of her skirt whirled and floated before settling back to her ankles. Despite everything, this was her first formal ball. Surely she could forget her inadequacies and the snide girls to enjoy a little bit of the evening.

The set finished, and couples parted. Seren tilted a fan in Gaia's direction. As if she'd held a wand, a gentleman wand, the girl drew two more men to each side, each taller than the next, and attired in onyx tailcoats and creamy waistcoats and stockings. Grabbing a separate hand, each man tugged her back for the next dance. She withdrew her palms, swept into a curtsy, and kept moving until she stood in front of Gaia.

Seren hugged her, wrinkling the front of her snow white gown. A damask ribbon of a lighter purple hue edged her collar and sleeves. With her hair pulled into a bun, and tiny crystals lining the circumference, she could be a princess. A perfect favorite for Prinny, if he dared socialize in the country. Yes, Seren would dazzle any court.

Her friend nodded. "Welcome, Mrs. Telfair, Mrs. Monlin, Julia, Gaia, welcome. Mr. Telfair? Will he be joining us this evening?"

Sarah stroked the falling feather of her headpiece. "Not tonight, but he sends his regards."

Dimpling, as if the absence of the Telfair patriarch gave a license to foolishness, Seren grabbed Gaia's arm. "May I steal this young lady away?"

"Certainly. Look, Mrs. Monlin, there are free chairs in the corner." Taking Aunt by the hand, Sarah fought through the thick press of neighbors, to the seats. Julia smiled then followed.

Tugging at her sleeves, Gaia lifted her head and hoped her painted smile covered her nerves. Everyone else was so wondrous and appointed. Unlike her, they all fit into this world. "Does my shaking show?"

A wrinkle set on Seren's forehead. "You look very pretty, Gaia, but where's the gown you've been working on?"

"My aunt didn't think it suitable. And I don't want to

embarrass the Telfairs, or you, my dear friend."

"Smile, and the world can't stop you." She linked arms with Gaia and took her to the refreshment table.

The largest silver bowl in the world sat on a linen-covered table. Thin brass cups flanked the sides. Gaia took one and eased the dipper into the Negus. The cinnamon-cultured liquid swished as it filled her goblet. The spicy mixture made her tongue itch, but her dry throat welcomed it. "So who has caught your eye?"

With a shy glance about the room, Seren sighed. "I don't think my true love is here, but, tonight, I'd settle for a few more dances with a handsome gentleman. Some of the most exquisite men stay in Father's parlor or have hidden themselves away. The duke hasn't danced once."

"Cheshire attends?"

"Yes, but I fear he's like all the truly eligible catches. Hiding."

There wasn't a fearful bone in the duke's body. He was noble and good. Gaia put down her goblet. "I think he wants to acclimate to our society before he's actively socializing."

A crease settled on Seren's forehead, followed by a pursing of her lips. "He should be well-acclimated, since he grew up in these parts."

Serendip learning about the duke's background? Could the minx have set her goals to include the duke?

Her friend peered down and smoothed her lacy glove against the pristine white cloth covering the table. "Don't look at me like that, Gaia. I'm just curious about anything new to Devonshire; well, somewhat new like Cheshire."

It didn't feel right, her and the duke, almost as bad as Julia and Elliot. Gaia shrugged. "Now that is a tragedy for you, but who needs a duke when I saw you fighting off two handsome beaus?"

A smile bloomed on Seren's face. She clapped as the set

ended. "Yes, it has been fun. This is the best ever, and my dearest friend is finally eligible to attend." The smile disappeared. "That means we've all grown up and soon we will be heading to marriages and families of our own."

Serendip was beautiful. How could she doubt her future, or even be saddened by it? Gaia reached for her fingers. "We shall always be friends. Nothing will ever change that for me."

"I'd like to think that, but your Mr. Whimple will scurry you away to London, or some hunt for obscure plantings. I'll miss my friend."

With a shake of her head, Gaia folded her arms and tugged at the hem of her gloves. "He's not *my* Mr. Whimple."

"Not yet, and maybe my prince will not be far behind."

Ah, Seren still believed in happily ever after. Well, that was possible for her. She knew both parents, and possessed every right to her name. Yet the twitch of her mouth, the wavering of her eyes, indicated doubts. Were they all trapped by a pile of low expectations?

Seren dabbed at her eyes. "Look at me. I'm ruining your first come-out." She waved her hands and pointed. "This is the Hallows' Ball. Dreams come true. Look about. What about you? What memory will you claim?"

With a quick scan of the room, Gaia looked, but didn't see Elliot. She pivoted to her friend. "I hope to dance with Mr. Whimple."

Seren rolled her eyes, but then paused and tapped her chin. "Tell him. That way you will at least know whether his hearing it will make a difference."

Her friend was right. Not knowing was the worst, even more so than living a lie. Gaia shrugged then set her shoulders level to fix her posture. Elliot had to be here somewhere. "I've been speaking my mind as of late, but I don't know what good it will do."

"Well, we will see whether he'll switch to you. Here he comes. Maybe it's your turn."

With a shy hand resting on the lace of her neckline, and a smile on her lips, Gaia turned.

Elliot Whimple walked in her direction. Clad in formal black dress, his slate tailcoat hung on his squared shoulders. His opal-white cravat brightened the twinkle in his blue eyes. Her breath caught in her throat. The music heightened in her ears.

As soon as he came within speaking distance, he bowed. "Miss Telfair, Miss Hallow. You both look very pretty this evening.

It became hard to breathe, but now was her turn. It had to be. "It is a good evening for dancing, sir."

Her hand rose of its own volition, and Gaia hoped he'd take hold and lead her in a dance.

Elliot smiled as his head lifted. His neck swiveled to the corner where Julia, Aunt, and Sarah sat. "There's Miss Julia. I think I promised her a dance. Excuse me." His back was to Gaia before his slight took hold.

Her outstretched hand floated in the air until the weight of her shame made it descend. "I need air."

Seren gripped her shoulder. "He's not worth it. You deserve better than Elliot."

"What exactly is that? Maybe you should say it's not the right time. Or this wasn't for you. All talk the world saves for the cork-brained, those so addled they believe in fairy tales." She covered her mouth for a moment as regret whirled inside. Her friend didn't deserve such talk. "I'm sorry, Seren."

"Dreams do come true, Gaia."

"They aren't for me, not for someone like me." Tears filling her eyes, she shook free from Seren and fought her way through the crowd to the balcony. Closing the double doors behind her, Gaia let the cool air caress her. A small wall torch emitted a little light. This was the perfect place to sob in private.

Almost tripping over her feet, she gripped her arms and steadied herself. The music faded, absorbed by the massive stone facade and the pain in her skull. She cast her eyes to the small stone bench dwarfed in shadows. Maybe if she rammed her head against it, she'd forget wanting to be loved.

She dropped onto the bench and let everything leak from her eyes.

Mr. Telfair was right. He knew she was meant to be a caregiver, a mere companion or governess to her family. Elliot Whimple would never love a by-blow black. No one would. "I'll always be invisible. God, is this what You wanted to show me?"

The doors behind her rattled, and she fled, hiding in the darkest corner. No one should see her this miserable. Rumors and mocking would abound. *Oh Lord, please don't let anyone have heard my cries.*

CHAPTER SIX

A Confession, A Dance, A Plan

Gaia shrank deeper into the corner as her gloves furiously smeared tears along her jaw. A man, a tall one, followed by another of almost equal height, walked out onto the balcony. The broad outline of the former, broad shoulders, oval face, and wide ears, seemed familiar.

She removed her fogged spectacles and squinted. Her cheeks burned. It could be the duke.

The second man pounded the rail. "Cheshire, it's not my fault."

It was the duke. Her heart beat hard, squeezing to burst free from her chest. He'd again catch her crying.

He sighed and planted his hands on the stone framing the edge of the balcony. "Stelford, the notes have found me. How could that happen? You must have said something when you were snooping up north."

"'Pon my word, I didn't, my dear Duke."

"You must have said something. How else would anyone guess that I would be here? This is the last place for me to be discovered because of the difficult history with my father."

Clouds parted and allowed moonlight to gleam upon his snowy cravat and the white shirt tucked behind a check-patterned waistcoat. His raven hair, though brushed to a shine, bore a renegade curl that waggled on his brow. "You were followed. And the fiend could be here now, waiting for the moment to humiliate me. Or..."

"You're not easily cowed, Cheshire. What is it, man?"

"Something more sinister could be at play. There's a desperation or hunger about the notes. They want me to pay or they will hurt Mary."

The anguish in the duke's voice clawed about her heart. He must care for his daughter so much. If only Gaia could be loved like that, but who knows where the man whose blood she shared lived? Or if he lived? What happened to him?

The other fellow, the friend he'd brought to Chevron Manor, slapped his hands together. "I didn't betray you this time. At least we have wind of it. Let's leave."

A wave of sadness struck Gaia, causing a shiver. How could they leave, and why did the thought make her even unhappier?

"No more running!" Cheshire's voice held thunder. He wrenched the back of his neck and lowered his voice. "Mary's finally settled. Maybe the child is beginning to accept this place as home."

"Maybe it's your singing," Mr. Stelford laughed but took a few steps backward, as if the kind-hearted duke would swing a fist at him. "I heard you last night. At least your admirer hasn't found us."

The duke's shoulders slumped. "Don't even mention her. She made a big pest of herself in Cheshire; no telling what she'd do here." He reared back against the brick wall. His head swiveled Gaia's direction.

Panicked, she siphoned a slow breath and hoped they couldn't detect her heart's traitorous thumping. Overhearing a private conversation was worse than being caught crying.

Rubbing his chin, the duke released a groan. "You heard

my singing. Well, Mary seemed to like it. She's even tried to mimic my actions. If only I knew what exactly to sing."

His friend walked to him and posted a few inches in front. "Always the girl. What about you? Why not find a new wife to take care of your daughter and you?"

With a hand now firmly covering his eyes, the duke grunted again. "I am in no mood to court anyone. My daughter is everything."

Mr. Stelford obviously didn't understand the needs of children, or how wonderful it was for a father to act upon his love for his child.

The duke's bachelor colleague moved to the door. "I shall see whether the curvy Telfair chit is around. She made you smile, and you definitely thought of something other than Lady Mary around her. Well, who wouldn't, riding horseback with all that womanhood pressed against your spine."

The man spun and trudged back into the ballroom, shutting the door just shy of a slam.

The duke bolted up and straightened his posture. "You can come out of the shadows, Miss Telfair."

Taking her first full breath, she slunk into the light. "I did not mean to listen."

He took a handkerchief from his pocket and swiped at the stone bench. "Sit and tell me what's made you run to this balcony first."

She folded her arms, not knowing quite what to do with them as she sat. "Why not tell me who's made you run to this balcony second? The *she* and *the notes* sound menacing."

He plopped beside her and raked a hand through his hair. "A nasty business, listening to conversations." His low tones tickled her ear. "But you are right. I'm hiding, too."

She frowned at him. His evasive words were not an answer. And nothing could be as bad as her dilemma. "Why hide at all? Males have options, unlike women. And everyone wants to know a sensible gentleman."

"Sense is in the eye of the beholder. No. They want my income," he sighed, and a sense of sadness emanated from his sagging shoulders. "They want the Duke of Cheshire, not William St Landon."

St. Landon. The name seemed familiar. Why? She shrugged. "I don't understand."

He thumbed his waistcoat. "See, I am invisible, too."

"Impossible." She tried to chuckle, but the incredulity of his statement made her eyes damp. "Please don't patronize me. You'd never trade places to be a poor invisible nobody."

"I came here to find you, Miss Nobody."

"But you told Mr. Stelford—"

"My friend has his own twisted way of helping, and he'd misconstrue my intentions and your charm."

The man talked in riddles, and her head began to hurt. She rubbed her temples. "Say it plainly."

His eyes went up as if he pictured his word choice. A harsh sigh left his lips. "Stelford doesn't know you are in love with another. So he won't realize that I am safe from compromise, or that you couldn't be tempted into some sort of illicit affair." He covered his mouth for a second. "I didn't mean to be so blunt. I respect you far too much to trifle with your emotions or diminish your reputation."

"Honesty is best. I can't stand any more lies."

"More?"

He didn't mention anything about *the she or the notes,* so Gaia didn't feel compelled to mention her secret. What if he knew? Would he still talk to her? Would he shun her, too?

No one needed to know but the man she married. Surely Elliott would understand. Forcing air into her lungs, she tugged at the edges of her gloves. "So you've come to look for me? Well, as you said, it's not wise to go traipsing into the night to find each other."

One of his brows popped up as he stared at her. "The Hallows' Ball doesn't seem to be going well for either of us."

She didn't mean to focus on herself, but it was far too easy to wallow in misery these days. "Not very good for my first one."

"Well, your Mr. Whimple must not be here."

Tears shouldn't come. Surely enough were shed the night she saw Elliot kiss Julia, but wetness still leaked from Gaia's eyes. "He's here, and I'm still invisible."

Cheshire put his bare hand to her cheek and flicked away a droplet. The roughness of his skin contrasted with the gentleness of the stroke. "No first ball should be spent upset."

Her insides warmed, and a vague desire to feel both his palms holding her face washed over her.

"Whimple's a fool not to notice you."

The heat of his breath sent a shiver down her spine; a good tremble that made her feel more alive and prettier than ever.

She pulled away before she forgot herself and batted her lashes like Seren, or said something trite like her awful cousin Millicent, the flirt. "Tell me about Lady Mary."

"My daughter, a precious girl of four, is mute." There was pain in his eyes, and it matched the heaviness in his voice. "I must help my child."

"I'm so sorry, your grace. I wish I had known. I could've been of more help, and not so argumentative."

He lowered his hand, as if he'd just realized it still hung in the air. "I suspect the same reason you don't wish to discuss Master Timothy, is my reason."

Twiddling her fingers, she lifted her chin to him. Sadness seemed to labor his breathing, and cause the increasing frown of his lips. Had she been so overwhelmed by her own misery, she'd forgotten to look around at those who might also be burdened?

"Your ideas of singing and the blocks have helped." He

leaned closer. "I can't leave now, not with the answer to Mary's silence so near. I must gain your father's confidence. I'm convinced your tutelage is the key."

"Mr. Telfair's not here, but I'm sure neighbors will tell him. My aunt will repeat her sighting of you for weeks, if you greet her, but..." She bit her lip. How could she ask something so personal? What notes? What *she*?

His eyes became very focused and steady, as if words were written on her lips. "Ask. Nothing is more attractive than self-assurance."

Something in his stare, maybe how his gaze felt earnest, encompassing her, not judging, made her think she could. "Sir, there is more trouble than your daughter's muteness, isn't there?"

His countenance blanked. "Yes. Yes, there is. My friend was very careless to talk of it. I would hope that you wouldn't mention it either."

He answered but didn't answer. This was a talent, unless he was given to confusion.

She nodded. "I would never break your confidence. You can trust me."

"Perhaps I can. Let's forget my problems tonight. You can only have a first ball once." He stood and made a low bow.

For a moment, his gallantry and the renewed gleam in his eyes made him the most handsome man she'd ever seen; even more so than Elliot, if that were possible.

"Now, Miss Telfair, my fair lady, I usually avoid such." He tugged gloves from his pocket and slipped them on, "but I'd like the next two sets."

"Two? You don't have to be so charitable." She left the bench, took a few steps, and clutched the balcony's rail. "It's not necessary. I've already agreed to help your daughter."

"What are you afraid of, Miss Telfair?"

People would stare at them, judging the gap of their

stations or the differences in their skin. That had to be worse than being ignored by Elliot. She shook her head and searched for her courage. Maybe it lay in the purple sky.

He chuckled, and she could sense his large form coming closer, shadowing her. "Don't you have a prayer to bolster yourself?"

Her voice lowered to a whisper, "I'm not afraid."

She said the words, but even she didn't believe it. Her gaze fixed on the perimeter, where lanterns exposed the array of sculpted hedges encompassing the garden below. She could not look back at the man whose sultry tones made her want to box his ears, as well as stay near and listen to his laugh. "The Hallows lit the landscape so the trees continued to the edges of the pale moon."

Large hands clasped her shoulders. His fingers tapped her stiff muscles, the ones sore from sewing. "Only half of the celestial orb shows. It surrendered to fast moving clouds."

Surrender to what, a seduction on the balcony by a virtual stranger? If she were her cousin or friend, she'd ask him to massage her limbs, but Gaia wasn't a flirt or anything wanton like her mother, and shook free.

This time he cornered her, one large arm on either side of her, holding the rail. "Is dancing with me something to fear, lovely lady? I assure you, I can keep up. Maybe you're frightened by attention. How would you ever withstand your Mr. Whimple's favor?"

What if Elliot stood beside her, talking so sweetly? Her heart flopped down against her ribs, almost hurting within her corset. But he wasn't, and worse, he'd let her hand drop in the air. Did he see Gaia as his poor neighbor and friend, or did he and all the rest of the old families see the girl passing as white? She swallowed. "This close, he'd say I'm too brown and coarse. I should probably shun the outdoors. Didn't you suggest that too when we first met?"

"Nonsense," the duke's deep voice tickled her ear. "You're lovely, Miss Telfair, and I ask again for the honor to dance with you."

Still looking straight ahead, she witnessed the moon shrink to a third. In another minute, it would be swallowed whole. Would it be wrong to be engulfed by something stronger than she, a something that thought her lovely? "Two dances will make everyone think that you've singled me out. That's not your intention. One is best."

He clasped her elbows, and, with great care, he spun her around. Barely an inch distanced her from falling into his chest. Her tight sleeves sent all his warmth to her skin, as if no fabric separated them. What would it be like to surrender and be kissed under a disappearing moon?

He lifted her chin. "If you don't want to be invisible, take chances; live life with both palms open. No more running."

"Are you speaking just to me? You seem to run as well."

His arms slipped to her side. "I'm speaking to myself, too. Let nothing keep you from what you want."

What did she want? A minute ago it was a dance with Elliot. Now to be held by a man who knew she wasn't invisible.

She quivered. Where did these thoughts come from? The clouds should sprinkle and clear her mind of Elliot and the duke.

"Let me dance with the prettiest girl in spectacles, out in the light." He lifted her limp wrist to his arm, and led her to the door. Music seeped through the frame, but who could concentrate on the tempo with a throbbing pulse?

Stopping, with her hands covering the door pull, she glanced at him. "I think... maybe...."

"Come on, Prayer Warrior. I can't stand up to the chalked line alone."

The duke led her into the ballroom, almost as though he

was leading stubborn Magnus. Then he grimaced. "A waltz."

Heads turned their direction, and he clamped her hand onto his arm, as if to keep her near.

"It's that new dance." He tightened his hold on her palm, threading his fingers betwixt hers. "I'm game. I tried it at a dinner party, my last session of Parliament." His voice lowered. "Too late, spry Prayer Warrior."

He seemed to be teasing her into reacting, trying a little too hard, but in an endearing manner. Well, he didn't know that, once she'd made up her mind to walk through those doors, she'd not turn. Stubbornness was a trait she assumed she'd gotten from Mr. Telfair.

With a sigh, she lifted her chin, and slipped into position at the line. As much as she and her sisters practiced, dancing was nothing to fear.

The crowd seemed to hush, and surrounded them as waves of music covered everything. The duke never let go of her hand, and proceeded to twirl her. Her slippers and his buckled shoes, darkness and light, touched and swayed to the melodies of the quartet.

She forgot the hundreds staring in her direction, the increased twittering of fans, the mouths of her sister's friends drawn into Os. Instead, Gaia focused on the angles and plains of Cheshire's kind face. She met his gaze, smiling into his luscious, sea-blue eyes.

His firm hand sank to her waist and guided her in a turn. She missed the weight of it when they parted for the next movement of the waltz. What was happening to her reason? Could her head be so easily turned by a little attention?

William sampled a breath between spins. The girl had heard his complaints. Stupid Stelford. Stupid friend. At least Miss Telfair was like other young women, easily distracted by romantic things. With a little charm and the miracle of candlelight, maybe she'd forget about his admission of blackmail notes and the hideous *she*, his cousin Deborah.

Yet Miss Telfair wasn't like other women. She didn't want him, and could not care less about his title. Her concern to help Mary seemed genuine, without hope of any reward. She was shy and bold all at the same time. He couldn't quite figure out what response she'd offer, and that made her more fun to engage.

Yes, if he weren't so jaded, so spurned by love and marriage, chasing this young woman, showing her what true courtship looked like, might be fun. Then maybe she wouldn't sell herself so short, settling for fantasy love as he had done.

And she wasn't so brown, but possessed a light tan from the sun. Though milky-white skin was the rage, how could anyone reject someone who glowed when she smiled? Miss Telfair possessed a generous mouth, with a cupid's dimple at the top of her praying lips. How would the lady react to a kiss?

Wanting to kick himself for entertaining any such notion, he looked away from her face, settling upon her braided chignon, the soft-looking curls cupping her ears. She was as exotic as Stelford had exclaimed, and William couldn't help being her champion. Somewhere between the first time he'd spied her, and the romp with Magnus's burning tail, he'd developed a soft spot for her.

Stupid, stupid William.

She peered up at him for a second. Those formerly lonely eyes now held hazel lights. A small smile hung on her sweet lips.

And his chest was full. He'd lifted her spirits. That feeling almost washed away the sting of the blackmail note. How did the blackguard find him hiding in Devonshire? When would his wife's adultery be made known to the world? How deeply would the news affect Mary's future? How could she not be stained by such a wanton mother?

"You're frowning. Is something else wrong? Have you had enough?" Miss Gaia's whisper reached his ear, her soft breath sweeping his jaw.

"Never. I mean, I'm enjoying this. Let's keep our places. That was only a half dance. A full reel is starting."

Perhaps Miss Telfair was the solution, not only for Mary's muteness, but to rid himself of fortune hunters and bombastic cousins. A romantic at heart, he could shower Miss Telfair with attention and allow everyone to know his favor was claimed. That might spur Mr. Whimple into action. Nothing makes a buck move more than competition.

How would the prayer warrior respond if she knew the thoughts in his head? And was William as safe as he thought? Miss Gaia claimed to love Mr. Whimple, but a young woman's heart can be changed. William's late wife was proof of this.

The young lady beamed at him. Her crystal lenses focused her eyes like a prism. William's gaze stayed locked upon her as she pivoted about another man. She was the perfect height, tall enough to lay her head on his shoulder, making it easy to siphon the hint of sweet honeysuckle in her auburn hair. Yet the lass was short enough that he could hover about her and protect her within his embrace.

Stelford was correct. Her holding onto him, pressed tightly against him as they rode to save her brother, was a memory he couldn't forget. Oh, the rhythm needed to pick up so he could be about her again.

A few more partner exchanges occurred then she came to him, claiming his fingertips, sending a jolt with the touch. Hand-in-hand, they sashayed underneath the extended arms of a neighboring couple. Another separation, and his palms chilled. Could they possibly be wet with perspiration? Stupid gloves. He wiped his tailcoat as the dance sent her another way. *Focus, William*. Fancy steps weren't enough to help Mary. Without Mr. Telfair's permission, Miss Gaia wouldn't be able to help.

The music of the violins began to subside. The quadrille was ending. It had to be for the best. Another minute so close to those kissable lips, he'd forget himself. Bachelorhood suited him.

A sigh escaped as her hand left his, but he wasn't sure whether it was singular, or a duet. "Miss Telfair, please introduce me to your friends."

"Come, meet my aunt. She's the key to swaying Mr. Telfair." She slipped her palm along his sleeve, to the crook of his arm.

He patted her silk-clad fingers, glanced into her wide eyes, and allowed her to lead the way.

Winding through the crowds, they made it to the corner. Two older women sat in each other's confidence, chatting. One of elegant dress, the other more simply dressed but with a pretty face partially covered by a drooping egret feather. They hushed as soon as William and his prayer warrior stood within earshot.

"Your Grace, this is my aunt, Mrs. Monlin. You remember my stepmother."

Mrs. Telfair's brown eyes held a smile as she reached for Gaia's hand. “Duke, are you enjoying your time in Devonshire?"

"I am. It's always good to be here in the country."

"I heard you've taken residence at Ontredale; such a fine, luxurious property." Mrs. Monlin's gaze whipped over him.

Why did it feel as if she’d just rifled through his banking notes?

The prayer warrior started to fidget as a young man and young lady came near. "Your... Your Grace, this is my sister,

Miss Julia Telfair, and Mr. Elliot Whimple."

Whimple? With a quick glance, he scanned the fellow; tall and thin with a round face, slightly handsome, if you like that sort. "Good to see you again, Miss Julia. Pleased to make your acquaintance, Mr. Whimple."

The young man puffed up his chest. "My father visited with you at Ontredale. He may have told you I just graduated from Oxford."

Many families had darkened William's door these past weeks. Yet the name did hold some curiosity. One glance at his dance partner's brightening cheeks confirmed it. "Yes, I do remember someone mentioning prayers... for your success."

Miss Gaia glanced at the floor.

William didn't mean to make her uncomfortable, but how could he resist the tweak? "Your father mentioned you would be studying plants close to Ontredale."

Extricating his palm from the lovely Julia Telfair, Mr. Whimple extended his arm.

"Yes, but tonight should be about amusement. Miss Gaia, it's the last dance. Should we share this one?"

William wouldn't call it jealousy stiffening his spine, but it was something. Why did it bother him for the man to whom Miss Gaia was partial to ask her to dance?

The final set of the evening. Gaia's heart beat in her ears.

Elliot's gaze settled on her. "May I claim it?"

With her head still spinning from dancing with the duke, she had to squint to focus on Elliot's square chin. He nodded, as if to beckon her forth.

How was this true? Did the man who held her heart want her? What changed his mind?

Deep inside her, a thrill coursed through her blood. This was her chance to be in his arms. Did his reasons matter?

Stomach flipping, Gaia leaned forward to accept the

invitation. As she slipped her palm from the duke's arm, she glanced at her sister's frown. Pretty Julia looked miserable, her chin lowering. Would she be slighted if Gaia accepted Elliot's offer?

Though her sister was insensitive, she should never experience a tenth of the pain Gaia had just lived. No one should. And more so, Julia didn't have a gracious duke to rescue her.

Heart wrenching, Gaia pivoted and looked into the duke's eyes. His gaze swept over her, studying her as if he, too, awaited her response. "I believe I promised the Duke. You did ask, did you not?"

Aunt picked up her punch cup and clinked it against Sarah's. "That would be a second dance. You highly favor our girl, sir."

The flautist and a harpist began to play.

The duke's large palm gripped hers. "I did. Two full dances. The next set is beginning."

Elliot yanked on his flopping cravat as he stared at the duke. Did her choice in partners matter to him?

Julia's eyes went wide, but then a smile bloomed on her countenance. Something in Gaia's soul stung, but she bit her tongue. Where did their sisterly affection go? Why did it only return when Gaia let Julia win?

With a nod to Sarah and Aunt, the duke drew Gaia to his side and led her back to the floor.

An unreadable expression set in his eyes as he twirled her about the chalked floor, though now very little of the flower pattern remained. He said nothing. The humor, which once painted his face, had disappeared, leaving a tense, thin line on his lips. As the music waned, he dropped his head close to her ear. "Do you think you and your parents will join me at Ontredale next week? I have someone whose acquaintance you should claim, Lady Mary's."

She looked to the ground, half-honored and half-grimacing at the potential implications of an association with a man so rich. "I... I can't accept on their behalf."

"Then, I will have to convince them and you, too."

The tone of his voice was full of challenge and charm. Her skin pimpled. There had to be something more to his asking than helping his daughter. Perhaps, he'd let her help with the mystery of the notes and the *she.*

CHAPTER SEVEN

Courting Maybe?

William tapped his foot on the Hallows' drive, waiting for his footman to bring round his carriage. He hadn't thought he'd be out this long at the ball. Quarter past twelve. Hopefully, Mrs. Wingate and the new nurse got Mary to sleep on time. Maybe this attendant would be more competent in child-rearing than the last.

Nevertheless, he'd been able to put his daughter to bed this past week, and she slept through the night. No nightmares.

Stelford walked from the top of the steps to stand by William. "Did you enjoy your evening?"

The man's cheeky grin loomed large in the glow of the lanterns illuminating the facade.

Stretching to appear too tired to respond to the inquisition Stelford would soon bring, William shifted his stance. "Look, my carriage is here."

They settled in for the ride back to Ontredale. The darkness of the compartment would do little to stop the forthcoming Stelford. The man liked a good joke at others' expense, one of his more irritating traits. Yet that sense of humor had helped William this past dark year.

Stelford chuckled and planted his shoes on the floorboard.

"You looked quite pleased with the studious chit. Upon further inspection, she does have a bit more appeal than her glasses."

Oh, that she did; a fine figure, quick wit, and a golden heart for others. She could've forgotten his offer and danced with the man to whom she was clearly partial. From her sister's relieved countenance, it seems Miss Gaia Telfair spared the girl hurt feelings.

Miss Gaia was faithful to his request. Fidelity was a great attribute in a friend. He blinked away his wayward thoughts and stared at his companion. "When did you have a chance to do this inspection? You didn't dance with her."

More insidious chortles fell. "I happened to look through the library window, and saw two sweethearts under a shining moon. Indiscreet ones."

William dropped his head in his hand. "I had to take her mind from your ramblings. She'd overheard our discussing Deborah and the blackmail notes. It is you who must be more careful."

"Tell me, were you thinking of me when the girl was in your arms waltzing, or when you hovered about that fine figure on the darkened balcony?"

Would it condemn William for all eternity if he beat Stelford bloody?

His *friend* reached out and laid a hand on his shoulder. "It's fine to live. Elizabeth would not begrudge you. Maybe if you indulged, it would balance the scales. Then maybe you could forgive Elizabeth's mistake."

"How would the pursuit of a respectable young woman balance a liar?"

Flinging his hand away, as if he'd touched hot coals, Stelford sputtered a mumble before he cleared his throat. "I thought that, maybe, since she'd found a bit of happiness before she died, your finding happiness now would make things better."

Heat began to flood William's stomach and whipped into his lungs. He swallowed hard to control his voice. "You are my oldest friend, but there are some things that I will not discuss."

"Or forgive. I *am* your oldest friend, and I was her friend, too. I just think if you forget the past, you could find peace."

Of his marriage, all he could claim was a bag filled with horrible memories, and little girl broken by them. Miss Gaia Telfair had to be the source of salvation. She could save Mary. That would ease his guilt.

Flashes of the last argument with Elizabeth burned in his head. If he'd stayed in Cheshire instead of escaping to London, maybe he could've calmed her down, kept her from pitching headlong down the stairs. Perhaps he could've spent her last moments asking and accepting forgiveness for the wrongs of their marriage. That would be better than the pile of regrets living in his soul.

He brushed at his hair and stuffed his top hat down harder upon his skull. If he'd been able to make Elizabeth happy, then maybe Mary wouldn't have been harmed. His girl spoke before that night, he was sure of it. Something else happened, and it surely caused Mary's muteness.

The carriage stopped and William bounded out. The lights of his little girl's room blazed more so than the solitary candle her nurse set for sleeping. He ran up the entry and pressed open the door.

Mary's chilling cry gripped him as he stepped into the grand hall. Panicked, he pounded up the stairs and into her room.

Mrs. Wingate met him at the bedchamber. "She's been screaming for the past hour. We don't know how to soothe her."

"Give her to me." William tossed off his hat and held out

his arms to the nurse.

Mary jumped for him. Her chubby fingers locked about his neck.

"Papa's here. Everything will be well."

Her cries lessened, but her wide eyes seemed to look through him.

"Sir, let me take your coat." Mrs. Wingate bent and scooped up his beaver domed hat.

How unusual this must all seem. With one hand pressing Mary to his chest, he used the other to whip off his outer garments. Surely, he'd become a juggler, able to cradle and rock Mary as he stripped off his jacket and gloves.

Mrs. Wingate took the items and nodded to the nurse. They both shot from the room. Good. This was something only a father could do.

Another five minutes of rocking and traipsing back and forth, and Mary finally settled. She reached up and grabbed his ear.

"Ouch, my sweet; let go. I know these big lobes are a target. Everything is all right. Tell Papa what has upset you."

Her sea-green eyes held his gaze.

Carrying Mary to the window, he pointed to the moon and the edges of the crags illuminated by the stars, and hummed.

His girl touched his lips and pinched at her mouth, as if she tried to mimic.

"Music helps, just as Miss Telfair said. 'Til I can get her to you, tell me how to help."

Nothing but Mary's short breaths answered him.

His heart sank as his throat thickened. If Miss Gaia were here, would she cry out to God? Would He answer? Looking down into Mary's reddened face, William almost had the heart to try.

Gaia climbed the stairs and ambled into her bedchamber. It

was well past one in the morning by the time they reached Chevron. Aunt seemed to want to make sure that the duke and Elliot had gone before asking for the carriage. Neither gentleman favored any other lady, so Aunt Tabby's high-handed tactics were for naught.

It would take some time for the cook to attend the others gowns and stays before the woman made it to hers. Swirling in front of the long mirror, she remembered twirling with the duke, his strong arms guiding her. He gave no care for her old clothes and thought her pretty. Pretty Gaia Telfair. Dark Gaia Telfair pretty?

What would the duke think if he learned her skin wasn't tanned by the sun, but by black blood? How he couldn't think well of her, when she didn't know what to think? Why was she borne of lust? What could explain the sin of breaking marital bonds?

A knock at the door broke made her shiver, but her heart slowed as she eyed her bed and the safe blue walls of Chevron Manor. "Come in."

Julia pressed inside. A smile lit her face.

Gaia's heart warmed. It seemed like forever since her sister seemed happy.

"Let me help you with your gown. You looked very pretty this evening, Gaia. See, you didn't need pink." Julia untied and unbuttoned the tail and waistband of the grey silk.

Well, the duke thought so. Smiling, she pivoted from the mirror and gave Julia a big hug. "You are always lovely."

Her sister drew her arms about Gaia's neck. "I was so worried that you wouldn't understand."

Gaia stepped back, breaking the embrace. "Understand what?"

Julia's voice lowered, "About Elliot."

Holding her breath, Gaia held her anger inside. "Then, you do remember how I feel."

"In London, he met me on Bond Street, and was so chivalrous, carrying my bundles." The girl looked down at the floorboards as she twisted her fingers in knots. "I helped to relieve his disappointment with Millicent. That's when I saw what you've always claimed. Elliot is the dearest of men. He'll not be deterred by my shyness."

Gaia let her silk dress fall to the floor. She stepped on her gown, trampling the pleats, as if it were her heart. Picking up her muslin robe, she covered her stays and pivoted to her sister.

Tears filled Julia's eyes. "I am so grateful to you."

Gripping the post of her bed, as if she'd fall in a faint, Gaia put her full weight against the footboard. "Has he declared his intentions?"

"No, but not a ball in London passed without him seeking me out for a dance. We know he's the marrying kind, with his mismatch with our cousin." Julia floated toward her. Her graceful movements imitated a swan gliding on the pond. "I'm sure if no one else catches his eye, he will come up to scratch. I won't be an old maid."

Was it that simple? Would Julia use guilt to remove rivals from the field of battle? Given Gaia's meek nature, her heart for her siblings, she grieved. How could Julia try to take advantage of her?

Even as she stared at her, another notion struck. Julia actually believed Gaia to be competition. Her sister was tall, with milky skin. Every man of sense desired that. Chest aching, as if she'd been stabbed, she lifted wet eyes to Julia. "Do you love him?"

A blank expression filled Julia's countenance as her mouth drew to a dot. "I respect him and his research."

Blood pulsing so hard, Gaia's ears throbbed. "Do you know what it is?"

Julia wiped her cheeks as her eyes zipped from side to

side. Then she tapped with her new sleek ballroom slippers and raised her head. "It's plants."

A sour taste, like bitter lemons, landed on Gaia's tongue. Her sister was going after Elliot because he was available, nothing more. How could that be fair to either? "Julia, you are lovely. You don't have to wed a man you don't love."

A hollow stream of laughter fell from Julia's lips. "Yes, and I'll be as happy as our mother and father were." More wretched chuckles descended, until nothing but a choked cry filled the air. She wiped her runny nose on her sleeve. "She found happiness once. I saw it."

"Tell me about him, my father."

Julia tugged at one of her blonde curls, wrapping it about her pinkie. "Then you know."

"Please, sister, tell me."

"He was a foreigner, a bard who strummed a violin. His voice felt like honey. I think Mama brought him here to teach singing lessons."

From the little Gaia could remember of her mother, the memories did have music. "How could she break her vows? They are a promise."

"I don't know. Maybe she felt trapped. Maybe Grandfather only approved of Father because of his land and because he was a gentleman. Maybe she didn't have a choice in marriage. So many good men are tradesmen or teachers... a dance master."

Who was she talking about, Mama or herself? "Julia, do you feel trapped?"

Her sister swiped at her eyes. Her usually-soft voice sounded harsh, like a screeching cat. "I am. I'm twenty-six. I want a comfortable home, and the respect marriage will bring. Elliot Whimple is my last chance."

Intending on shaking some sense into the girl, Gaia rushed to her sister and gripped her elbows. "How will it be good when you are acting out of fear? You don't love Elliot. Will the lack of love drive you to sin, just like our mother? That weakness wasn't fair to your father nor will it be to Elliot."

She pushed at Gaia's shoulder and broke free, sending Gaia crashing to the mattress. Her crown barely missed the footboard's post.

Julia stood over her. "Don't judge me. Don't let your childish feelings interfere."

"Interfere? Yes, I suppose loving Elliot for more years than I can count is interfering. I'm not going to slink away. And I *will* dance with him the next opportunity."

Backing away, Julia's hands shook. "Do you think he'd choose you if knew the truth of your birth?"

Gaia sat up and bottled the fear such whispers would conjure, but she was done with lies. "I will tell the man I marry. If he loves me, it will not matter."

"I don't want to hurt you, Gaia, but if the truth becomes known, Elliot won't be allowed to love you. His parents, the expectations of his family, will weigh heavy on him. He'll be like Mother, and won't be able to withstand the onslaught. We'll both lose him."

No. Elliot was different. He had to be made of tougher stuff. Yet Gaia couldn't remember a time when he went against common thinking. Wasn't it his father's tease about Millicent's money and looks that set their brief courtship into motion?

"Please, Gaia. Let him choose me. Don't add to my shame, and I won't add to yours."

The door slammed. The closeness to her sister was gone, all because of a man. Gaia wept and punched at the mattress. She wouldn't be guilted or frightened into giving up on Elliot, even if it meant the loss of her sister's love or being exposed to the world as a mulatto. But was she ready to be seen, truly seen by society as a mistake?

* * *

Shaved and stuffed into a cinnamon-colored waistcoat and breeches, William tried to close his eyes and rest. A few bounces of the carriage and a sway from a gulley in the road prevented it. His whole body ached, and his head felt full, as if it would burst.

Singling out a young woman at a ball had consequences. To not visit her the day after would be a slight. He'd do nothing to disparage Miss Gaia Telfair. Yet what better excuse could he have to show up at her doorstep in person? Gaining help from the Telfairs was only a few rituals away.

"So we are going to further a connection with the studious Miss Telfair." Stelford's wide, cat-like grin irritated William.

"Yes. I also hope they will soon be dining at Ontredale." He sat back, his lips lifting into a smile. "If Miss Telfair will spare some time to help Mary, or teach me how to communicate with my daughter, all this trouble would be worth it."

"A great honor you offer to them. Why not admit that this chit has caught your fancy?"

No. Fancy-catching meant a commitment to an honorable lady like Miss Telfair. Like a shaft of iron had pierced his chest, he wrestled with his cravat. That part of his heart no longer worked, crushed by Elizabeth and his own unrequited expectations. "I'm not dead, Stelford. I notice a pretty girl, but maybe you noticed the terror in my little girl's cries last night. That's my only concern."

"Well, sin starts with the eyes then works its way into ideas. Unless you've become your sainted father, there's no need to pretend you don't have needs."

Before William could lash out at the grinning fop, the carriage slowed. Head aching from lack of sleep, he crawled out, straightened his posture, and walked in step with Stelford. Long stalks of yellow gorse lined the flagstone pathway. The coconut scent of the flowering thicket filled his flared nostrils.

He whipped a handkerchief from his pocket and mopped his brow. Surely, his friend couldn't be right. There was a difference between friendship and amour.

He and Stelford stood under the soft Doulting stone fashioning the door hood, and knocked. No twin girls were about, so the carriage team was safe.

One of the devilish cherubs appeared and led them to the cheery parlor of light-colored lime-washed walls. No matches or looking glasses lined the child's fingers. "Are you playing more safely today, miss—"

"Helena Telfair." She looked down, her foot tapping. "Yes, Father has banned us from even looking at candlelight."

William stripped off his gloves, coat and hat, and offered a smile. "Good man, Mr. Telfair." The child scampered away, disappearing into Chevron.

Stelford dropped their cards into an empty bowl. They were the first visitors? It was well past noon.

Mrs. Telfair and Mrs. Monlin sat in chairs by the fireplace. A table spread with treats and teacups lay in front of them.

The ladies stood and made a short curtsy as Mr. Telfair waved them forward. "Do come in, gentlemen."

The older man with greying blond hair and a thin frame plopped back down into a chair by Mrs. Telfair. He was clad in a brocade robe and dressing gown, as if he didn't expect company.

William held his hand out to the man and shook his. "Are you feeling well, Mr. Telfair?"

The fellow eyed him with squinting brown eyes. "Well enough to attend you here at Chevron. To what do we owe the pleasure?"

His tone was low, almost harsh. Again, William admired the suspicion. "We are calling on few after the ball. 'Twas a lovely affair."

Still grimacing, the man nodded and waved them to sit.

What game was this? Surely the ladies had spoken of William's singling out Miss Gaia. Shouldn't a father be pleased? "I came to deepen my acquaintance with the Telfair family."

An off-pitch chord caught William's attention. He swiveled his neck, gaze trailing the low ceiling, slipping along a plaster-covered beam to a corner niche. He gaped at the majestic sight, the detailed moldings, the small pianoforte, the lovely Gaia instructing Master Timothy.

The chair railing and the plaster medallion decorating the curved wall surrounded her like a fanned headdress. She looked exotic, her graceful wrists rising and lowering to the soft notes of her tune. Lack of sleep must really have him flustered to have passed her at the entrance.

Note after note, Timothy mocked each sound with his soft voice. A little piece of his soul imagined the lady singing to Mary, and his daughter repeating. If he'd done it right, Mary might have responded last night.

"Your Grace."

"Yes?" He returned his attention to the old man.

Mr. Telfair leaned forward, his chin whipping between William and Gaia. "Are you here to speak of intentions? I must warn you that it is a Telfair tradition to not have the younger girls out before the eldest is settled."

Another harsh chord sounded from the corner.

Withholding a chuckle, he swallowed a cough growling in his throat. "I am following your other advice, and becoming more integrated into the community."

Mr. Telfair rubbed his jaw. "All my girls and Gaia are fine daughters. But I must warn you, the Hallows' Ball was a rare exception of my rules."

Stelford picked up a biscuit. "Rules are meant to be broken, and nothing better than a ball to test them." His friend's countenance was smooth and pleasant. Well, at least he was democratic in tweaking noses.

Mrs. Monlin picked up a set of knitting needles, her eyes rolling. "Don't mind my brother. Sarah and I will smooth his ruffled feathers. All the girls will have their share of amusement. How long will you gentlemen visit Devonshire?"

"I am at the Duke's disposal." Stelford shifted in his chair and adjusted a striped cushion.

Mrs. Monlin leaned over and drained the last of the tea. "Sarah, can you see about getting our guests some more refreshments?"

The spry Mrs. Telfair popped up. "Of course. Your Grace, please continue to share your plans for the season." She left the room.

Feeling the heat of the brother-sister team now beaming back at him, William took a quick breath then spoke up. "We will definitely be here through the summer. Might even winter here. Devonshire is one of my favorite places. I was born here, but it's been a long time since I've been here."

With a raise of his brow, Mr. Telfair leaned forward. His dull eyes seemed to bear down on William. "Who are your relations? We should know them."

"The St. Landons. My father held the living at the vicarage."

"Vicar St. Landon?" Mr. Telfair stared at him, as if this was a first meeting. "You're St. Landon's son, the one who went very early into the regiment?"

"Guilty."

Wiping crumbs from her mouth, Mrs. Monlin winced. "A St. Landon; you don't seem anything like him, well, a little in the height, but such a pleasant expression on your face."

Yes. Father wasn't known to smile. Kind expressions were wasteful, with so many for the vicar to condemn. "He was a very stern man," William swallowed, "but a good man."

The pinch gripping Mrs. Monlin's lips didn't falter, and creases folded her forehead. "You never visited before now, not even at the vicar's passing."

"Napoleon didn't set his battles to my life's journey. It was regrettable." Air slowly streamed from his tight lips as guilt pressed upon his lungs. "Very regrettable."

Mr. Telfair sat back and crossed his arms, skepticism seeming to flow from the tense set of his posture. "I didn't know St. Landon was related to persons in peerage. Why didn't you mention this before."

"We were distant cousins to the late Duke of Cheshire. After the death of his son, he made himself know to the St. Landons. He reclaimed Ontredale and restored it to a handsome house, a symbol of renewing the Devonshire branch of the family. He even purchased my first commission." The late duke was more like a doting uncle than cousin; encouraging, bolstering… nothing like his father.

William filled his lungs, trying to forget every reason he'd avoided mentioning his connections to the harsh vicar. "As for the Vicar St. Landon, I'd rather be known on my own merits. Some don't have fond memories of him."

Mrs. Monlin nodded in silent agreement. She fluffed the edges of her mobcap. "Enough of this morbid talk. Death frequents far too often. We should talk of music and celebration, the next celebration, the Masques Ball. It's the highlight of the country these past eight years. So many engagements have occurred because of such beautiful evenings."

William blinked at the mention of *engagements*, but his attention returned to the soft music playing from the niche. "I like beauty."

Both Stelford and Mrs. Monlin began to laugh, but he wasn't sure if the humor was from his statement or his careless glances at Gaia.

Mrs. Telfair returned. The elder sister, Julia, followed, bearing a fresh service of tea and biscuits. The prim girl adorned in pale, salmon-colored muslin offered him a delicate bone cup. She filled it, but he waved off the sugar and cream. No need to water down the richness of the chamomile.

The sister sat on the sofa, to the right of everyone. Her hem floated, sweeping across her thin ankles. She was quiet, though his friend looked her way a few times.

Another five minutes of Mrs. Monlin and Stelford's tidbits of the Hallows' Ball engulfed the seated party with laughs, but Miss Julia said nothing, and sipped her tea.

She reminded William of a pastel portrait, with her light hair and eyes, but like a canvas lacking dimension, without any detectable conversation.

Those with a voice should use it. What he wouldn't give to hear Mary's reciting words, and no longer given to hellish cries.

He stole a quick glance toward the pianoforte. His gaze locked with his spectacled dance partner, and he absorbed the neat, tawny chignon and the buttermilk gown hanging on her curvy frame.

A bite of biscuit did little to stop his tapping foot. Patience wasn't his virtue. He rounded back to his host and waited for a lull in Mrs. Monlin's noise about the length of lace she'd seen at the ball.

Finally, the woman took a breath and a piece of scone.

"I would like to invite you all to Ontredale Hall for dinner at the end of the week," William announced, as if the words burned his tongue. In a way, they had.

Mrs. Telfair beamed. "We have no other engagements. We would be honored."

Mr. Telfair grimaced, but then nodded. "For a respectable son of St. Landon, it would be an honor."

The statement sounded as if it were a question. Well, knowing the baggage he carried of Elizabeth's affairs and the blackmail, it might be a fair one, but William would never expose such concerns to the man who could block the prayer warrior's help. "Good, I shall expect you, Mrs. Telfair, and both elder Telfair daughters, Miss Julia Telfair and Miss Gaia Telfair."

The old man's lips pinched, as if he'd sucked on lemons. "My daughters?"

Mrs. Monlin's eyes blazed like fire and, if she'd sat closer, the way her fingers fisted, she might have given her brother a punch. "Yes, of course both girls will be there."

The calm Mrs. Telfair put a hand on her husband's arm. "It is quite an honor for our girls and the Telfair name to be thusly invited."

Mr. Telfair nodded. "Yes, it is."

At least he got the man's agreement, but what was the problem? Perhaps William should reassure the man that this was a social outing, and nothing romantic. Yet, if he voiced that, the coercion of Mrs. Monlin and Mrs. Telfair might dissipate. An easier sigh filled William. He was but a week to his goal. His Mary would be advised by the one woman who knew what to do.

Before he could sit back and relax his shoulders against the broadcloth of the chair, a maid brought another visitor to the door. Mr. Whimple.

The fellow stopped, and whispered something to Miss Gaia that made her cheeks darken.

An off-key note from her pianoforte followed.

William stood, turning away from the couple, and walked to the window. He gripped the sill to do something with his hands instead of clenching them. A man who only noticed a sapphire like Gaia Telfair because of another's attention couldn't be worthy of her. "Mr. Telfair, there seems to be a smallish park on this side of the house."

"I suppose you didn't get a chance to enjoy it the last time you rode through it."

He spun from the glass and lifted his chin to the pianoforte. "I'd like to examine it now, if you don't mind. Could Miss Gaia Telfair be my guide?"

The old man stared toward the two young people in the corner. Perhaps he didn't like Whimple either. "Yes, Gaia, you and Timothy show the Duke the grounds, while Mr. Whimple comes in and tells me and your sister of his London travels. Remember, Gaia, Timothy's your responsibility."

The man's tone was firm, bordering upon harsh. Why would it matter who watched the child? From all the lad's adventures, it would be better if both William and Gaia oversaw him.

The young woman stood. Her face blanked, as if she'd been slighted, but then lowered her head and closed up the music box. "Yes, sir. Come along, Timothy, let's get our coats."

William tried to ignore Stelford's cheeky smile, and followed them to the door. The prayer warrior might be mad at his intervention, but it was for her own good. Falling too quickly for the botanist's charm would spell disaster. Yes, that was a good story to tell himself. Interrupting Miss Gaia was for her good, not the twinge of unease simmering in his gut at seeing Whimple flirt with her.

CHAPTER EIGHT

Staking a Claim

Gaia knotted her bonnet under her chin before buttoning up Timothy's deep blue coat. She should be glad that the duke continued to show her favor in front of her family, yet she wasn't. Something heavy-handed had transpired, and she felt like a pawn.

But whose?

Mr. Telfair who reminded her of his plans for her to be Timothy's governess?

The duke who needed her to see the lawn when they'd ridden across it about a week ago?

Or even Elliot who now saw that she breathed because of the duke's attention?

What if Mr. Telfair subtly reminded her of her tenuous place in order to dissuade any designs she had on the duke? Her breath caught and trembled inside her lungs.

Mr. Telfair wouldn't tell; not without exposing his plans. Her pulse slowed. At least his pride was good for something.

Holding Timothy's hand, she moved past the parlor.

Elliot still stood near the piano. His charcoal trousers and buff waistcoat made him look very elegant, yet he wore gaiters on his shoes. A small leaf stuck out, caught between the leather and his low shoes. Had he been tramping around with his plants before coming to visit?

He lifted his head and caught her gaze.

Oh, who couldn't forgive penitent sky-blue eyes?

"Miss Telfair, shall we go?" The duke's baritone made her shiver, as if she'd been caught doing something naughty.

She adjusted the bow on her bonnet again and headed toward Chevron's entrance. "Yes, Lord Cheshire."

The duke stood in the way, his broad shoulders blocking a little of the sunlight spilling into the hall. He glowed and looked every inch a warrior. The glint in his eyes shined of humor.

He held his palm to her and lowered his other to Timothy. "Ready, little man?"

Forget the duke and his games. With the boy hooting like an owl, she traipsed past Lord Cheshire, out of the house.

The wind whistled, bringing the sweet smell of spring to her nostrils. She kept walking, following an undergrowth of anemone. Their solemn white petals lined the path. The drooping curve of their leaves looked like a hundred shrugs. The plantings were just as confused at what was happening.

Her glove slipped off with Timothy's fidgeting, and her bare olive hand clutched his small white one. A sigh fraught with frustration slipped past her pursed lips. She should be grateful for the duke's attention, for Mr. Telfair allowing her to partake in the duke's invitation. But why did gratitude feel like a kick in the stomach?

"Pleasant weather we're having," the duke caught up to her, stride for stride. His freshly-barbered face made it hard to miss his square jaw with a tiny cleft, or the flat spot on his nose. He must've taken the bad end of a punch. Still, he looked very handsome, with a smidgen of a pout on his lips.

Something in his boyish smile begged forgiveness.

Gaia swallowed, clearing her dry throat. This wasn't the

time to be charitable. "Why did you wish to see the park?"

"I thought it best to remove you from Chevron before you fawned over Mr. Whimple, ruining our good work." He bent down to Timothy and placed his big top hat on her brother's head. "Don't run off, young man. I'm not at my best today. It would be hard for me to retrieve you."

Timothy nodded as a toothy grin split his round face. He sat and gathered acorns from the massive tree offering shade from the noon sky.

She put a hand on her hip and stepped in front of the duke. "Fawn? I don't fawn."

A grin teased his mouth. "Yes, all young ladies do; particularly when they don't understand their appeal."

"Speaking in riddles again, your grace? Is that what you old men do?"

He frowned and put his hands behind his back. "I wouldn't know; I'm not that old."

She took a step closer to him, so he'd plainly get her meaning. "I didn't think you are more than a decade older, but manipulating me into a walk when Mr. Whimple obviously wanted to chat? That's something Mr. Telfair would do."

"You speak of your father in distant terms. Is there—"

"No." Panic and fury filled her bosom, and she struggled to lower her tone. "Don't change the subject. Elliot Whimple has noticed me, and you interfered."

Cheshire shook his head. "The botanist may be chatty now, but that was to reassess his position, to make sure you were still his champion. Once he determines you still like him, his attention will turn away again."

It sounded true. It felt true. Her breath caught. She put her face into her hands. "Then how is he to love me?"

A strong palm gripped her shoulder. "Give him something to chase. Every man wants to win love, and know that it's his alone. It'll be his greatest treasure."

The buttery-soft leather of his glove stroked her chin. She lifted her gaze to his. His eyes held streaks of red, like the sea after a storm. What raged in him, and why did she feel compelled to help? "You didn't get much sleep last night?"

Still holding her hand, the duke tugged Gaia with him as he leaned against the trunk. His skin looked flushed.

Maybe the hot sun beat upon him too hard. He yanked a brilliant white cloth from his pocket, but it slipped to the ground.

She scooped the monogramed handkerchief from the tall pea- green grasses, and almost mopped his brow. Her fingers hovered, frozen in the air. This wasn't Timothy. She had no right mothering this grown man.

His palms covered hers and pushed the union to his forehead. "My meek girl. If you decide upon something, commit to it. Unwarranted deference or wavering will not gain you anything."

Images of wanting to say something to Elliot and stopping filled her brain. Other pictures of him sailing past her danced there, too. Why did the duke have to be right again? Balling the handkerchief, she took a step backward. "I don't want anything from you."

He released her hand. His eyes widened then a few chuckles left his mouth. "No, it is I who need something of you. I guess God loves the humor. I have everything but a way to make my daughter whole. And you want a man who may never deserve you. Maybe you should adjust your petitions. They are still amiss, prayer warrior."

A harsh sigh left her nostrils. "Why do you joke so much, especially about God?"

He dabbed his wrist to his temple. "Pity, it's hot today. I don't mean to make light. You've just made an impression upon me with your prayers."

"Being a vicar's son, does that make you used to them?"

"Not authentic ones." He swiped at his mouth. "You call upon the Lord, and I'd wager He answers."

The man seemed sincere, but it was so difficult to tell when his lips thinned to a line.

"God does answer when you cry out to Him. He's everywhere, waiting for an appeal. However, it has to be honest, not a jest. I think He responds to an open heart."

The duke bent down, picked up a smooth stone, and rolled it in his palm. "He's not the only one."

"Are you cynical because of the notes, or because of Lady Mary's struggles?"

The pebble flew from his hand. The duke then fanned his face. His cheeks held a full blush. "Life has a way of testing convictions. Please tell no one what you overheard."

"But what is this note? Why are you so afraid?"

"I don't fear for my person, but for my daughter. There are things." His lips pressed together again. The frown deepened, threatening to swallow his face. Whatever the problem, he struggled mightily over it.

His tone, the slump of his powerful shoulders made her sad. Gaia wanted nothing more than to reassure him. "I won't tell; you can trust me. I want to help."

"I'll keep that in mind."

She reached out and put a hand to his arm. "If not me, go to God. He's available to everyone. I feel that He hears me, knows the sound of my voice, like a good father." For a moment, her heart smiled. If she could always remember God's fatherly love, then maybe the absence of Mr. Telfair's wouldn't hurt so much. "I like to think he accepts me, warts and all.

If eyes could smile, the duke's stormy eyes smiled like the lifting of a storm. "I don't see any flaws, Miss Gaia."

Something warm filled her middle and spread to her cold

cheeks. They burned now. "That's your fatigue talking. You should go home and get some sleep."

He stretched against the deeply creviced bark, as if it were a mattress, and closed his eyes. Would he nap there?

"Gaia Telfair, you're very good at taking care of others."

"Having siblings is training." Like a magnet, she let her fingers trace the weave of the handkerchief. Very fine cloth. "Why did you risk your health to come today? Surely, you could've sent a note."

He straightened, as if he remembered his sagging posture. "I am not fond of notes right now, and you saw how I had to ask your father to secure your coming to dinner. But maybe I came because I had to see you."

"Sounds as if you haven't made up your mind." Filled with concern, maybe even a tiny bit liberated by his foolish talk, she put one hand to his temple, and then tapped his ear. "You are a little warm. You should go home."

He laced his fingers with hers. "I think I've come to stake a claim; wouldn't want to make things easy for Whimple."

Her hazel eyes flared, and she wrenched her fingers away from William. He regretted his words as her smooth gloves left his skin, but he had to know her thoughts. Was she partial to him, even a little?

He folded his arms and again gazed at her at her smooth, even complexion. No youthful blemishes marred her perfect, tanned countenance, and he couldn't look away from her questioning eyes.

A single man who wished to remain such would do better to remain quiet than to stir calm waters. Why had he risked elevating her marital hopes, when he had no intentions of ever wedding again? He cleared his throat. "It was a poor joke. I shouldn't have said anything."

She licked her lips as she removed her spectacles, cleaning

the lenses with his handkerchief.

With a quick swallow, he soothed his raw throat and scanned her long neck framed by the pleated frill peaking her short, tobacco-colored spencer. Buttermilk and brown spice. The blend would make an excellent tea, his favorite beverage since giving up spirits. "Let's change the subject. How did you know your tactics were working with your brother?"

"I watched him most carefully, and saw he enjoyed repetitive tones and lots of attention." As if trying to choose her words with care, she looked down at her fingers and traced the warp of the linen threads. "I'd like to believe you and I are friends."

A nice safe answer, but a tiny part of him wanted more sentiment.

His stomach rolled, but it wasn't from sickness. Stelford was so right. William was attracted to Gaia. Magnus should kick him in the rear for traipsing about like a jealous court jester.

The young lady smiled as her gaze lifted. "Yes, you are my *friend*."

Something about the way she said *friend*, with her brow cocking and her gentle full lips parting, made him covet each word. Unlike Elizabeth's artificially brightened eyes created by drops of belladonna, the genuine light of Gaia's made his cold fingertips vibrate. "Friends? Similar to you and Mr. Whimple?"

Her cheeks reddened, and she pivoted in Timothy's direction near a thick hedge of dead nettles. The white sand-colored bulbs shook their hairy upper lips in the slight breeze, calling the boy to come close and pluck them.

Timothy made a loud hum then filled his small hands with the flowers.

William pulled away from the oak and reached her. Even as he chided himself for acting like a schoolboy, a charge of energy swept through him as his thumb caught her cloak, burning like a fever. "I didn't mean to embarrass you."

"You, who caught me in the woods, know my feelings." She slipped on her lenses and rotated to face William. "It seems Mr. Whimple only notices me when you are near."

"Then perhaps I should be near you always." He covered the words with a quick laugh. She didn't need to know the warring thoughts in his head.

He looked down again at the sparkle in her clear eyes, brightened by the prism of her lenses. She'd put the handkerchief into her pocket and stooped to help Master Timothy's pursuit of the acorns. The woman was forthright; utterly beguiling.

Shouldn't he have the good sense to tame his thinking? What was he doing pursuing another man's lady, or any for that matter?

He shook his head, as if the motion would order his wandering mind. "I want your friendship, and I need your assistance. We must convince your father to let you help my Mary. I will press him when you come to dinner."

Those lovely eyes widened as she stood and came near. "When I said I wish to help, I meant it, but not just with Lady Mary; but with you too. The notes, the she, tell me the whole of it. Trust me."

His trust? Is that what she wanted? And how could she tell he hadn't fully offered it? He tucked his arms behind his back again. With a tortured sniff of air passing his nostrils, he lowered his gaze to his boots and her worn slippers. "More will be explained when we gain Mr. Telfair's permission."

She motioned to Timothy, which made the lad leap up. Gaia brushed the knees of his breeches, gripped her brother's hand, and tossed the beaver hat back to the duke. "Then there is nothing more to say now. We are heading back to Chevron."

William watched her for a moment, her curvy hips floating along the terrain. She didn't look so young. No, she was beginning to seem the right age.

Sending Timothy into Chevron, Gaia waited at the door and waved at the sleek onyx carriage carrying the duke. She tucked a loose curl behind her ear and allowed her pique to cool. Bothersome man. How could he be both secretive of whatever was going on and so certain she could help?

She shook her head, turned, and rammed into Elliott.

He caught her. His hands went about her shoulders for a second before dropping away. "In a hurry, little one?"

Heart in her throat, all she could do was nod and count the familiar flecks of gold in his blue eyes.

Arms folded, lazy smile on his lips, he cleared his throat. "Seems Cheshire is consuming your time these days. Do you like him?"

No. Elliot couldn't think that. "Mr.—"

"Come along, Julia." Aunt marched out of the parlor. "We can't keep Mr. Whimple waiting."

As they moved to the door, her aunt tilted her head toward the parlor. "Dear, your stepmother needs you. I'm chaperoning Julia and Mr. Whimple today."

Tipping her straw bonnet, she came close to Gaia. "Go on, girl. You've interested a duke. Leave something for your poor sister."

With a frown, Elliot extended his arm to the ladies. "Miss Gaia, I wish there was room. I did want to talk with you. Seems we haven't done that—"

Aunt tugged him out the door. "Come on, Mr. Whimple."

Gaia's feet felt cold. Elliot missed talking with her. She leaned against the wall. Her dreams were coming true. A hum bubbled inside until Julia drew near.

"Don't go hoping for something that can never be. Elliot's

not strong enough to handle the truth about you, but maybe the duke is."

Julia's angelic face with big wide eyes loomed close, but that wasn't concern filling them. It had to be jealousy.

Gaia wouldn't be frightened. With a hand to her hip, she pivoted, putting her back to her sister. "You're just saying that to make me give up on Elliot. I won't." She stormed away, not waiting for Julia's coercive pout.

Head ringing, she pushed closed the parlor door, waiting in its shadow for all the noise to disappear from the hall. Alone, she allowed the confidence she'd displayed for her sister to disappear. Slouching against the wall, she willed away the urge to cry. Julia should be helping Gaia, not using every moment to remind her of their mother's failings.

Yet was her sister right about Elliot? Was he not as strong of mind as the duke? Why else would he drift from Cousin Millicent to Julia, then possibly to Gaia?

The man she loved would have to be strong to love all of her, both the black and white halves. Elliot had to be. He just had to be.

Timothy yanked on her skirt. "Duke. Duke. Duke." He went on into the parlor.

The nerve of Julia, trying to bring the duke into this. The man had his own problems. Cheshire was in trouble, serious trouble. Why else would he act so oddly and be so secretive?

And his poor daughter…would Gaia's methods work? Could she restore the child's voice?

Leaning against the cream-painted threshold of the parlor, she readied to bang her head against the molding.

Cheshire put his hopes in her. If her methods failed, she would disappoint him terribly. Somehow, disappointing him pricked like a thorn along her insides. Lady Mary had to respond. She just had to.

Her gaze fell upon the bowl brimming with cards. More

than one neighbor had called while she walked with the duke; no doubt to see whether the duke attended the Telfairs. Nosiness was madness.

Steadying herself, she stalked into the parlor. Only quietness remained; the room empty now, save Sarah, and little Timothy at her slippers. The woman sat in her chair by the fire. Her lap held an open Bible.

Gaia hovered at the door. She wanted advice but didn't know how to ask. Deciding to return to her room, she pivoted toward the exit. "I didn't mean to disturb you."

Her stepmother spread her arms wide. "I've been praying you would. Come, child; sit with us"

Running, Gaia could think of no other place to be. She snuggled her head against the lady and welcomed her embrace.

Sarah stroked Gaia's hair and let her have a good cry before pushing at her shoulder. "What has happened? Has the duke's attention upset you?"

Attention? Gaia pulled a handkerchief from her pocket, wiped her eyes, and blew her nose. "I just feel overwhelmed."

The woman lifted Gaia's chin. "Why shouldn't it? You've attracted the interest of a very powerful man, but don't go thinking too hard; we don't know whether he'll make an offer."

An offer from the duke? Preposterous. Gaia lifted her head, squinting with incredulity. He didn't want someone like her; dark, poor, hiding a scandalous secret. No, he wanted her talents. "The duke has a daughter with challenges, and he wants my help. What if what I did with Timothy doesn't work? It seems that he's putting too much faith in me."

"God will help you know what to do." She tucked a frizzy strand into Gaia's bun. "His will for you is perfect."

How could it be perfect with so many questions, so many secrets? No, it was almost perfect, allowing mistakes like Gaia to exist.

Sarah released a breath, "You are so caring. God has given you a special gift with children. No child can help but to be drawn to you. You will be able to help the duke with his daughter."

"But what if the girl doesn't understand I want only good for her?" Gaia swallowed hard. "And if she treats me as I did you, standoffish and aloof, I'll be of no use to the duke. I am so sorry."

A low weeping sound caught her attention. Gaia glanced up.

Sarah cried, "At least you now know, my love. And my independent Gaia is finally letting me help."

"How could you do it? What made you want to be a mother to Julia and me? Was Father's love that strong?"

With eyes drifting to the right, Sarah smoothed Gaia's cheek. "I remember reading of a man whose intended came to him a few weeks before their wedding and told him she was pregnant. And the babe wasn't his."

"Oh, the scandal must've made Aunt's papers." Gaia wiped her eyes again on the soft fawn linen she held betwixt her palms. She'd kept the duke's handkerchief. The hint of spice, tarragon, made her lips curl into a smile, even as a wave of guilt hit her for not returning it. Well, at least she could launder this one. "Did the man abandon the woman?"

Sarah's creamy mobcap fluttered as she shook her head. The tiny crimson rosettes the lady spent days stitching floated like rubies on a crown. Such a decent, dedicated woman. "On the contrary; he had compassion on her, marrying her and becoming a father to that son."

Gaia shivered. "Like Mr. Telfair to me. No, Mr. Telfair wanted a servant for his heir."

"He's not a villain, Gaia. And deep down, there is love and admiration."

No. There couldn't be. Mr. Telfair didn't want to be disgraced, liked the Olivers. Such pain they endured when their eldest daughter compromised her virtue. No one associated with them, let alone married her or wanted to become a father to her babe.

And was it not Vicar St. Landon, a large man sharing Cheshire's build pounding the altar, rebuking them in church? A sermon, heated like fire, spewed from his mouth. Big words, evil ones she wouldn't know the meaning of until years later, sailed from his mouth.

Head hurting, Gaia rubbed her temples. "Sarah, that fiancé was an extraordinary man."

Timothy tugged at the bow on her slipper. "Duke. Duke."

Sarah patted her son's thick mop of hair. "Cheshire, maybe; that remains to be seen. But Joseph of Nazareth was. He decided to be a stepfather, though he could never compete with the babe's true father."

She pulled Gaia to her feet and towed her to the silver tray on the side table, angling their faces so both Sarah's and Gaia's showed. White and ruddy was Sarah's, tanned and slim was Gaia's; but somehow the differences didn't seem so stark. In that instance, it seemed as if they belonged together. Maybe since they were both Telfairs by marriage, not blood, they possessed a bond. One Gaia had been too prejudiced to see.

"Joseph would have missed the opportunity to be the earthly father of the Christ if he'd let fear or pride stand in his way. I knew I would never replace your mother, but I wouldn't miss the opportunity to befriend you and Julia. How empty my heart would be without you girls."

Rotating, Gaia threw her arms about the woman, her anchor. "You are more of a mother to me than my memories. If only...."

"If only what?

"If I knew who my father was, that might explain—"

Sarah held her fast. "Mr. Telfair raised you, clothed you, and kept you safe. *He* is your father. Be easier on him. It's hard to deal with disappointments. And he was so hurt by your mother's unfaithfulness."

Gaia would like to believe Mr. Telfair loved her, but she knew now the distance she felt from him was deeply-rooted. He'd never looked at her as anything but a disappointment. She'd proved convenient by helping his only remaining male heir. Mr. Telfair wasn't Joseph, and probably thought of Gaia the same as he regarded the disgraced Miss Oliver.

CHAPTER NINE

Dinner and a Miss

William smiled to himself. Everything at Ontredale flowed well. The aroma of the cook's white soup filled the hall. Ordinarily, smells weren't wanted, but it made the place feel like a comfortable blanket, very much like a home.

The brass and crystal fixtures sparkled and shined. In the five days since leaving Chevron, he'd been on a terror to make everything glow. Now, no nail head or crevice of gilded trim in the entire house held dust. And best of all, no new notes. William was right to do nothing to draw attention. Hopefully, the fiend would think the last note was amiss and look elsewhere, or give up.

Slapping his head before he began wishing on stars or grasping clovers, William spied the spotless marble floor. Mr. Telfair would find no offense at Ontredale. Nothing should prevent him from lending his daughter's help. If all the hints of scandal stayed hidden behind starch and lemon polish, Mary would get the help she needed.

Marching into the dining room, William ran his fingers over the frost-colored linen tablecloths pressed with perfect creases. Dinner would be wonderful. Would Miss Gaia be impressed, too?

Of course she would. Who wouldn't?

With pep in his step, he jaunted up the long flight of stairs to check on Mary. The girl lifted sleepy eyes to him. Her little arms hugged her Spanish senorita. He kissed Mary then headed back to the drawing room. With the father's consent, he'd take Miss Telfair to meet his daughter after dinner. Would the young lady's tactics work right away?

When Mary regained her voice, would she be able to tell what happened the horrible night her mother died?

Shrugging, William sat on the sofa. One step at a time; first the talking, then the syllables, then maybe whole sentences, like who was her mother's amour. Was he there when Elizabeth tumbled down the steps?

He slapped at his skull. The child shouldn't waste words on the evil of the past. Though the blackmail notes might very well come from the adulterous dandy who stole Elizabeth's loyalty, this wasn't his daughter's burden. The sin, everything, died the night her mother fell.

Pushing away from his anger, he opened *The Monk*, the book he'd been reading the past week. Though fitting, the path his life seemed to have chosen, the words couldn't seep into his skull. Mary's healing was too close. With a sharp intake of breath, he settled down, plopped the pages on his lap, and waited for the clock to strike six.

When the housekeeper announced a visitor at four, two hours early, his heart lurched. Was Mrs. Wingate's roast duck even finished? He stood and brushed his ocean-blue waistcoat.

The door opened, and his mouth fell open.

"Cousin, you are a hard man to find," Deborah Smythen curtsied then rushed forward and gripped him in a bear hug.

Nausea flooded his stomach as her over-perfumed wrists held him fast…lavender. Too sweet a fragrance, too fresh a scent on the disagreeable old maid.

He pried out of her bronzed-draped arms. "Why didn't you send a note? I could've told you that tonight was not good."

She chuckled, the notes sounding nervous. "I think you've been avoiding me. And I didn't want you to run away again."

Her green eyes tilted toward the door. "Where's my cousin, Mary? I miss her so."

William folded his arms, his ire simmering to a boil. The woman didn't seem to like children, especially a fussy child, like Mary. "She's with her nurse. Why have you come?"

"Can't family come to see family?" She moved to him again, her reddish hair bouncing with her speedy gait. Taking her pinkie, she traced the lines of the revers on his charcoal tailcoat. "You look well. Can't my Abigail and I stay, Cousin; or is there no room in your very large inn?"

He couldn't very well throw family out, though he'd like to. The word *problem* must be matted to Deborah's rouged cheeks. "I'm not in the mood for your tricks. I have friends dining at Ontredale today. It's very important to me."

"It was an accident, my ending up in your bedchamber. Can't you forgive my walking in my sleep?" She batted her eyes at him. "You weren't even in there when your valet came upon me."

Thank goodness for Mary's nightmares. If the shrew had been found with him, dressed as she was.... A shudder traversed his spine.

"Well, you'll need a hostess. I know exactly what to wear." She started unbuttoning her walking dress, lingering on the large bone button at her bosom. With a wink, she sailed from the room and closed the doors behind her.

William smacked his skull. She fled without him extracting the promise. What manner of chaos had he just unleashed on his household?

The doors to the drawing room opened again. Stelford walked inside. "I saw the winds of a tornado blowing up the stairs. Miss Smythen found us."

Legs tight, William bent, scooped up his novel, and tossed it into the fire. The burst of flames mirrored his fouled mood. "I know you rationalized things, but I'm convinced my cousin is trying to compromise me. My rooms will be locked night and day."

Stelford chuckled, "Miss Smythen's not the most handsome woman, but she is devoted to you."

William grimaced. He was an honorable widower, not some rake looking for comfort. Another marriage was out of the question, especially to someone who couldn't love Mary as he did. "Whatever you do, don't leave me alone with Deborah."

"You have my word." Stelford moved to the fireplace and used the poker to move the ashes about, calming the spitting embers. "Perhaps your new girl will help."

Taking a deep breath, William dropped onto the sofa. He'd been good at keeping his temper tamed, even against his friend's jokes, but a few minutes with his cousin renewed his old fiery nature. With taut fingers, he visualized strangling both Stelford and Deborah.

The evening was doomed and, with it, Mary's hope. Only a miracle would save this dinner. Looking into the flames, something inside taunted of peace. His knees wanted to buckle and force him to kneel and pray, but his military discipline kept him upright, and prepared him to face disaster head-on.

Gaia had never seen a table so covered with Wedgewood platters. Roast fowl, poached salmon, and jellies the colors of the rainbow covered the duke's pristine, white table linen. With a shy glance, she savored the room clad in gold-framed pictures and thick moldings running from ceiling to chair height. She'd never seen so much trim and fidgeted with her long sleeves, an inch too long, covering her palms.

Two servers dressed in snowy stockings and shiny blue coats stood on either side of the grand table, refilling glasses, moving dishes within reach. A rounded pass-through cut in the bright carmine-red wall exposed a servants' entrance. Every few minutes, a different person came or exited through the passage, ferrying more rich food, clearing half-empty platters. How many people stayed in the duke's kitchen? It had to be much larger than the Telfair's meager one.

When the tall black came from the foyer and handed the duke a note, Gaia couldn't help glaring at him.

The duke nodded. For the first time, he allowed a smile. "Thank you, Albert."

Mr. Telfair dipped his powdered head, as if in silent prayer, but Gaia sensed he, too, stared. Her mother had died years ago. Would he be forever angry with her straying? Did he blame all blacks for it?

Didn't he look at Gaia daily as a constant reminder of her mother's sin?

Sarah scooped salmon and a dollop of potatoes onto his plate. "Your favorite, Mr. Telfair."

He waved at her, his hand swaying quickly, stopping her in mid-scoop. "You let your servants have free rein in the main house, Your Grace? Something your father wouldn't do."

The duke looked up from his bowl of soup. "There are many things I do he would never consider. It's a son's prerogative."

The pleasant tone of the duke's voice didn't match the hardening line of his jaw. He quickly shoved a spoonful of the delicious soup into his mouth, masking it.

But Gaia saw it. Did he possess anger at his father? Could the mystery involve the late vicar?

Sarah shifted in her seat, fluttering the feather in her

headdress. This time, the ostrich plume of her hat stood tall, as if starched for the occasion. Her willow-green dress with its half-sheer sleeves matched the color of the bowls holding the white soup. Though Aunt called the style with its fuller skirt *a season long passed*, there was no doubt it was a good season for Sarah. She looked very well, very elegant.

"Everything is delightful," Sarah said.

"Your Grace, the jellies. I must compliment your cook on the jellies; so many and so colorful." Aunt poked a sunburst-colored one with strawberries suspended inside the dessert. It jiggled as much as Aunt in her shimmering copper gown with cap sleeves. "So nice to have your cousin, Miss Smythen, with you tonight; family is so important."

The fancy lady leaned forward and smiled at the duke. "It is my pleasure to be at his disposal."

Cheshire nodded, but no words left his mouth. Not even a joke. Something seemed amiss. What else could be wrong?

Gaia's heart beat fast. Was the problem with his daughter worse? Or the blackmail letters? Was his cousin's arrival involved?

He caught Gaia's gaze and held it. A sense of pleading colored his eyes. The grim lines framing his face intensified. A jolt went through her. *Oh, please, let nothing ill have happened.*

After a servant refilled his glass, Mr. Stelford sat back in his chair. "Your Grace, I see you like this vintage; so sweet and yet reserved." He glanced at Gaia's end of the table. "Yes, a fine young combination."

Gaia's cheeks felt hot. The man insinuated that the duke liked her, but not in a good way. She struggled to finish her soup, trying hard to focus on the cream and the hint of almonds in each spoonful.

"Reservation is something everyone should have," the haughty tone of Miss Smythen's voice forced Gaia to level her shoulder and accept the forthcoming remark, or slap. "I think it a virtue," the fancy woman continued, "to cautiously approach one's station in life and to think twice before changing it."

What did she mean? The woman kept spying over her long nose at Gaia. Did Miss Smythen think she had designs on Cheshire, too?

It was obvious Miss Smythen did. She rushed to take the seat next to the duke, only to be routed by Mr. Stelford. He plopped between them while Aunt took the other side.

Miss Smythen leaned Cheshire's direction and lifted a napkin. "Your Grace, you should eat. I think you need someone to help take better care of you." If the lady had been closer, she'd probably try to wipe his chin of imagined droppings.

Serendip was bold in her flirting, an expert in her 'come hither' expressions and fan movement. Miss Smythen seemed clumsy or desperate. An image of Julia came to Gaia's mind, as well as the force of the girl's tears after the Hallows' Ball.

A lump welled in Gaia's throat, and she sipped from her glass. The world could be very cruel to women, making them seek matches they didn't want, just for comfort or respect.

That wouldn't be Gaia's fate, now that Elliot missed her. Maybe he thought of her right now.

Putting down her drink, she turned her attention back to her own silverware. Her knife reflected the sage color of the gown Julia lent her. Her sister seemed very happy to stay with the younger girls and help with their dance lesson. Did she think her generosity would make amends for their quarrels? Julia was transparent. She wanted Gaia to give up Elliot for the duke, but how could a few weeks of one man's attention erase a lifetime of seeking Mr. Whimple?

The duke wasn't interested in her, was he? Her pulse rose when she peered up and spied him looking her direction.

Miss Smythen tapped her nails on her water glass. "So, it is very good of you Telfairs to join us at Ontredale Lodge. I think it very democratic to know all neighbors, rich or poor." Her gaze lingered on the duke, and then skipped back in Gaia's direction.

William dropped his fork. His lips flattened to a tight line. "I am honored to have you all dine with us. My cousin arrived today for a visit. It was unexpected."

"It is our pleasure, Your Grace. I understand," Mr. Telfair nodded. His eyes crinkled with a smile, probably the first time he looked upon the duke with sympathy.

Aunt placed another portion of the blueberry-colored jelly onto her plate. "Well, if you are staying, you must make your visit a few weeks to attend the Masked Ball. It's the highlight of spring."

The loud cousin clapped her hands and batted her lashes at the duke. "A ball; oh, William, a ball will be lovely. I must stay until then."

He said nothing, and lifted an apple to his mouth. His eyes rolled, and he appeared to mouth the word, 'help'.

Miss Smythen's familiarity with the duke grated on Gaia's nerves. Something burned in her chest when the woman used his given name.

Mr. Stelford leaned forward, as if rubbing his leg under the pristine linen covering the table. "I don't think you should stay that long. All Cheshire is probably missing attendance in your salon."

"Nothing means more to me than Cousin William and little Mary. I'd turn away strangers for family any day." Miss Smythen passed a tray of expensive sliced pineapples directly to the duke.

His fingers gripped it, exposing tight white knuckles. The man seemed very agitated, but what could be done with obnoxious family members?

Sarah sipped her glass of lemonade. "Your Grace,

everything is so wonderful. You must give your cook my compliments."

"I'm sure the servants will enjoy your words. With your simple country fashions, you're obviously well-travelled enough to know such differences," Miss Smythen chuckled and turned toward Mr. Stelford. "I'm teasing."

It wasn't nice to joke at others' expense. "Your humor is very enlightening. It shows how one could travel and be unmoved by the experience," the words popped out of Gaia's mouth before she could stop them.

Cheshire looked up from his plate. A smile briefly passed his lips. "Stelford, lead everyone to the drawing room. Mr. Telfair, with your permission, I'd like to show Miss Telfair my daughter, if she'd please remain behind."

"May I witness? I so miss the little dear," Miss Smythen leapt up and smoothed her Sardinian-blue bodice and its yards of sprigged Mechlin lace.

"Cousin, you said you would assist with my guests. A good hostess should play something on the piano."

"I will," Miss Smythen's cheeks brightened.

Gaia doubted it was from modesty. The lady took Stelford's extended arm and walked away.

Everyone else rose and headed down the polished hall, but the duke grasped Gaia's hand, placing it on his arm, and then led her to the stairs. Her irritation slipped away at the touch of his palm. Why did it feel right to follow him?

The dinner he'd fretted was done. It had been a long time since William was this on-edge. He patted Gaia's fingers and enjoyed the calming hint of honeysuckle in her hair. "I apologize for my cousin. She's difficult to take in long increments."

A gentle smile curved the young lady's lips as she nodded. "Some people can't help making mischief. There is no need to be uneasy."

A sigh of relief released from his lungs, as he and Gaia took to the treads. Though he hoped his emotions weren't so detectable, the last thing he wanted was for the Telfairs to feel uncomfortable, or, worse, belittled. It didn't matter to him their class or wealth, not with such kindness brimming in his young friend's eyes. Such beautiful eyes. "You look very pretty today. This is a new color?"

"My sister loaned it to me. I'm glad she did. My other dresses might expose me to be too-little travelled."

He chuckled and laced his fingers with hers. Bare palm to bare palm, something felt right having this woman at his side, checking on Mary.

Up one flight and turning for the next, Gaia tripped on her hem, but he caught her. His arms went about her so tight he felt her strong heart beating against his ribs. "I've got you. Did you twist your ankle?"

"No, but, thank you," she clasped his waist, clinging to him as if she were dizzy.

Something in his chest tightened; again, the feeling of peace, of the rightness of having her within his embrace, swept over him.

"Julia's taller than I."

His pulse raced as his once-cold heart thudded in his ears. Think friend, Mary, another man's prize. It didn't help. His mind blanked, and he strengthened his arms about her shoulders.

As if time froze, they held each other in the silent entry within the shadow of the twisting treads. "Thank you for keeping me upright," her voice was breathless and soft. "A person could hurt themselves tumbling down these ornate stairs."

"Or worse. My Elizabeth fell. That's how my late wife died," he couldn't say anymore, as his throat thickened. A deluge of memories hit him. Their last argument…he broke a chair when she shouted she hated him…the sting of receiving Stelford's awful note of her death.

Closing his eyes, he saw the overcast day of Elizabeth's funeral, standing with Stelford at her graveside. The clanging of the church's wrought-iron gate blocked the moans of his conscience of what he should've said to her if he'd known their conversation would be the last.

His voice sounded small, as if he were a lad lost in the woods. "If I'd been home, I might've saved her, kept her from whatever irrational bend made her rush down the stairs."

Arms tightened about him as if to lead him from a dark forest. Gaia's soft voice became an anchor, "Accidents happen. It's not your fault."

A small press on his shoulders shook him free from his paralysis. "We should see about Lady Mary."

This wasn't his wife or even a lover within his embrace. Gaia Telfair was a friend, a friend to aid Mary. He released her and again tucked her arm within his.

With her free hand, she pulled from her pocket a starched square tied with a pale pink ribbon. "Your handkerchief, Your Grace. It is too fine to keep, and I shouldn't impose."

Slipping it into his jacket, he lifted a brow. Such a thoughtful woman. "Don't make yourself uneasy. I have—"

She lifted her skirt an inch and exposed worn slippers.

"I have many." What a daft thing to say as he pretended not to notice her shoes, but the contrast between the new herb-green-colored satin and the water-stained slippers puzzled him. With an estate the size of Mr. Telfair's, surely there was enough to keep both elder daughters in finery. Maybe it did not. How horrid to choose which child would be favored. The way William fiercely loved Mary, his heart would cleave in two if the babe had been twins and he could only give to one.

He pushed open the door to the nursery. Mary and her

nurse sat in the corner, stacking blocks. As the child lifted her gaze, she held out her arms to him.

Picking up the little girl and swinging her about, he tucked her close. "This is my daughter, Mary. Lady Mary, this is Miss Gaia Telfair."

His daughter tugged on his coat and squirmed in Gaia's direction, as if to inspect at what he pointed.

The maid withdrew, closing the door behind her. They were alone, the three of them, and could speak freely.

Gaia put her hand on the baby's cheek. "She doesn't have your wide ears."

A dangerous compliment to a man being blackmailed about an unfaithful wife. He swallowed. "Lucky girl?"

Mary leaned forward and gripped a lock of Gaia's hair.

"May I?" she slipped her palms about Mary's waist.

He hesitated for a moment then released the child to her.

Mary went easily. No fuss or cries.

"I'm impressed, Miss Telfair."

Gaia smiled at him. Her sweet lips hummed a tune, maybe the reel they'd danced at the Hallows' Ball.

That heart of his had a mind of its own, skipping with the rhythm. "They say children know a kind spirit."

Again, Gaia beamed at him then lowered her gaze to Mary. "So, tell me how old you are."

Oh, how he'd wish his girl would answer. Nevertheless, she wouldn't until this young lady, this beautiful, kind-hearted woman, drew Mary from her silent shell.

And Gaia, sweet Gaia, would keep the secrets his daughter's returned voice would bring. He was sure of it.

The babe tugged hard on the frizzy lock of Gaia's hair as she pivoted to the window to get a better look at the child. "Tell me, Lady Mary, how can I help you?"

His jaw tense, the nervous papa held out his hands as if

she'd drop the babe.

Gaia had been handling children longer than anything, from the twins and Timothy, to some of the neighbors. She shook her head. The duke would have to learn to trust her if she were going to help his daughter. "Be at ease, Papa. I will not harm this little one."

A smile briefly lifted his lips.

She looked into the child's greenish-blue eyes, then back to Cheshire. "Does Lady Mary grunt or annunciate a syllable?"

His mouth opened then closed, as if he'd changed his mind on how to respond. "Sometimes; when I tried your song idea, she seemed to try to mimic."

Releasing Mary's tight fist from her hair, Gaia tickled the girl's thumb and spun again in the salmon-pink room. "Has she ever spoken?"

"Yes; I remember the sound of her voice like my own name. Right before I left to go to Parliament, she said 'Papa'." A sigh left him, as if the memory weighed on his lungs. He rotated on the thick puce rug, then, as if he couldn't stay away, moved closer and clung to the white-trimmed window.

His scent, warm tarragon, swept about Gaia. Her mind should be on Lady Mary, not how nice it felt to be in his bold, strong arms. She looked away and made eyes at the child, causing the girl's smile to widen. "I remember how sad my stepmother was when we discovered little Timothy's troubles. She thought it was her fault. But what mother or father could change God's design?"

He bolted up from leaning against the sill and spun to her. The sun shining through the mullions fell upon his dark jacket and the deep shadows lining his face. "And why would a *good* God allow this? If sins should fall upon anyone, shouldn't it be on one whose shoulder can bear the stripes?" He touched a lock of the girl's hair. "I should suffer, keep suffering; not Mary."

Gaia had questions, too. Why couldn't she know who her true father was? Would the man she loved accept the truth of her birth? But she kept these thoughts to herself. "Why things happen, I don't know. My lack of understanding doesn't change things. And I choose to believe the God Who set the world in orbit, clothes the sparrow, and decorates every corner of the moors in beauty, has a plan."

His brows furrowed as his arms folded across his deep-blue waistcoat. "A plan?"

"Timothy has such understanding. His friendship, though the world has called him slow-witted, or knocked in the cradle, has helped me through my awkward years. I am sure that your little one is only beginning. Someday, she'll set the world aflame."

His gaze swept over Gaia as his raw tone lifted. "Is that even possible?"

She gazed into the babe's expressive eyes. "Yes. Her world might just be the moors, or the run of your house, but she will make a difference to those blessed to know her."

He leaned down and kissed Mary's forehead. "I wish I could believe like you."

Returning the babe to his arms, she brushed his sleeve. Her touching him seemed so natural. "Give this child support and unconditional love, and then you'll see and believe."

"How will we begin, dear Gaia?"

The way he said her name, almost breathless, lingering on the second syllable, made her pulse race. She must still be undone by nearly falling down the stairs.

Her palm floated to his arm as her other straightened the lacy collar of Mary's pinafore. "Father should let me visit once a week. Timothy and I will come."

His full lips folded into a smile, but he looked to the floor, as if to hide the expressions crossing his face. "I'll send a carriage for you two. Magnus hasn't quite gotten over his last ride with Master Timothy. You don't know what this means."

He looked down and shifted his sleek slippers. "I could even pay you for your trouble."

"Pay me?" Heat crept up her neck. Her beating heart shriveled. "You mean like a governess, and teach Lady Mary lessons?"

"Yes... No... I just want to thank..."

Her feet started moving, and she gripped the crystal doorknob. "There are many things I do for friends, but if I was ready to put myself on the shelf, I wouldn't need Your Grace's assistance."

The door flung wide, and Miss Smythen pranced in. "Oh, that's what this night was about; you're interviewing the family of the new governess for our Mary."

The little girl screamed, as if seeing the duke's cousin upset her. For a moment, Gaia wanted to turn back to settle her, but she couldn't let Cheshire or Miss Smythen see the tears in her eyes. "Tell my party I'm at the Hallows'."

His footfalls and Lady Mary's moans came closer. "Don't go; Southborne is two miles away," his voice sounded strained, but he hadn't been injured. He just let his true motives be known—a lowly governess for the rich man's daughter. That's why he'd been so secretive, to draw her in.

She walked to the stairs.

"Please, Miss Telfair. Wait. Take the steps slowly."

She gripped the banister and charged forward. When her slippers met the mahogany planks of the first level, she slowed, raised her chin, and walked to the front door.

Albert, the brooding groomsman, blocked her path.

She wasn't employed by the duke. No one but Mr. Telfair could control her actions. "Open the door for me."

The servant looked toward the stairs then opened the door for her.

When the door shut behind her, she started running, and

let the air dry her face.

With a mile behind her, taking its toll on her lungs, she stopped and gasped for air. The closeness and growing warmth she'd felt for Cheshire had been so misguided.

Almost slipping on wet grasses, she steadied herself at the edge of a lily pond. It was too early for the white and yellow flowers to bloom, but the heavily-veined leaves floated on the surface, staking their positions for the summer. At least they knew where they belonged.

She looked at her reflection in the clear water, hair falling, smudges on her glasses. Cheshire's family and the Telfairs weren't of the same class. She was poor. He was rich. She thought him a friend, and he made her a governess. Tears fell again, blinding her to the setting sun or the sentiment awakening in her heart when the duke held her close on the stairs.

She liked him, really liked him. How could she have been so mistaken?

Stooping low, she pushed a lone leaf, forcing it to join the cluster of leathery greens in the middle of the water. Maybe she should just do as Mr. Telfair wanted. Maybe he knew what was best for her.

Yes, Mr. Telfair was right to think of her as a governess. At least she'd be given a place of honor and influence at Chevron. What more could a scandal-ridden girl want?

If it weren't so far, she should make for home and read to Timothy. She needed one of his big hugs right now.

"That is Nuphar Lutea Aquatic." A crop of willowherb parted its hairy, oval leaves, and allowed Elliot Whimple to forge through the brush. "That is you, Miss Gaia."

The lowering sun bathed Elliot, adding a glow to his lightly-tanned skin. His crowned felt hat lay cocked to the side, making his smile seem wider. The short cut of the caped greatcoat meant he'd been stalking the woods for his treasured plantings. His patent gaiters had smudges, and the smell of raw mud hovered about him. Yes, he'd been with his first love…nature.

How could she look at Elliot, knowing her traitorous heart had started to favor the duke?

CHAPTER TEN

The Wrong Man

When Elliot held out his palm to Gaia, she hesitated to claim it. How could she, with her arms barely cold from the duke's touch?

Elliot extended his hand again. "Miss Telfair, I admire your reserve, but I won't bite. What are you doing walking alone?"

This time she took it. "I needed some air." She whipped her head toward the dirt trail, then began to pin her hair; so many fallen tendrils. "I was on my way to see Serendip Hallow. Oh, I must look horrid."

His gaze swept over her. "You look charming, but I've never known you to be caring of your appearance. You always seem at ease with nature."

Charming. Did he say *charming*? She kept a sigh from leaping from her lips.

"It's not safe being here alone. I shall accompany you. I've just left my brother's. I, too, needed to walk."

In her haste, she'd forgotten her gloves, but now her bare hand could feel the taut muscles in his lean forearm. All the memories of admiring Elliot Whimple flooded back to her mind.

He stopped and parked in front of her. "Are you well, Miss

Telfair?"

His Spanish-blue waistcoat and buff breeches hung well on his thin frame. This was Elliot, so kind, and concerned with the feelings of others. He was what she wanted, not someone ashamed of her and her family. She'd just been confused since the Hallows' Ball.

"Miss Telfair," he gripped her hand, tugging it to his chest, "should I carry you to the Hallows'?"

The thought of being that close to Elliot made her cheeks feel hot. "No, I'm well. How is your brother doing?"

Elliot looked up to the thick tree grove. "He's not improving. The injuries to his amputated leg bother him. Horrid war. Most days, he doesn't have the strength to play with my niece. I take it as my duty to roll hoops with the active child."

She picked a leaf stuck in the tiered woolen cape of his coat. "You were rolling hoops, not skulking about the woods?"

He bent and dusted his knees. "I did both. My niece is a brilliant child, and I'm not so old as to forget what it's like to have fun. From what I recall, you liked hoops."

Now Gaia was sure her face had caught fire.

With a gentle tug on her hand, Elliot led her forward. "My niece is learning plants, too. I'm a very proud uncle. But enough of my ramblings… what are you doing so close to Ontredale?"

She swallowed. There was no other explanation but the truth. "My family and I just dined with the duke and his friends."

He squinted at her. "And you're out walking to the Hallows' alone? The number of social engagements you young ladies keep."

Yes, she'd let him think she'd planned all this and hadn't stormed out upset and insulted. "I like walking, Mr.

Whimple. It helps me think. Right now, I'm contemplating life choices. What do you want out of it?"

For a moment, he closed his eyes. The edges of his thin lips curled, highlighting his prized dimples. If she kept looking at him, she'd surely melt into a heaving puddle.

With her arm firmly set in the crook of his, she fell in step with him. "You don't have to answer my impertinent question. Let's be on our way to the Hallows'."

A chuckle fell from his mouth then his tone became somber. "I want what any man wants; a happy home, maybe to make a difference with my research."

"I have always loved..." Fear gripped her heart, and she clamped her teeth together. Her resolve disappeared. She couldn't speak her mind and ruin this moment. Fouling up things with two men was too much to bear.

He stopped and gazed down at her. "You were saying, Miss Telfair?"

She licked her lips. "I've always loved your dedication to science."

"I hope my studies will lead to more plentiful corn. Then, Mother England will end famine worldwide. Oh, look at me running on." He patted her fingers. "Are you chilled?"

"No. Tell me more of your research." She was quite warm, listening to the resonance in his low voice. The walk to Seren's should last forever.

"Nonsense." Elliot took off his coat and draped it about her shoulders, then continued telling her things she couldn't understand.

Gaia didn't care. Her horrible evening had restored her to a man who would never think her too poor with whom to associate, but would that sentiment remain if he knew the truth of her origin? Julia didn't think so.

Elliot took the time to point out tall stalks of flowering yellow gorse, and the green twigs and seedpods of the broom bushes. His description of the three-lobed leaves of the wild strawberry runners made the common seem exciting.

The more she listened, the more he seemed to want to say. If they married, would this be how their evenings would flow? How wonderful. It didn't even matter so much that he hadn't asked what she wanted. At least he didn't insinuate that she'd be content being a governess to his niece, or servant to his future children.

Arrival at the Hallows' gate came too soon. Elliot released her hand and pressed on the wrought-iron spindles to open it.

After folding his coat over his extended arm, she curtsied to him. "Thank you for a lovely stroll."

He took her hands within his. His breathing seemed a bit labored, like the duke's. "The pleasure was mine; however, I do have a request."

Her gaze floated over the tall man, the hero of whom she'd been dreaming, save the last three weeks. It felt normal and safe to be with Elliot. She smiled at him. "What would that be, sir?"

He bit his lip, as if hesitating or hunting for the right words. "I request your first dance at the Masked Ball. I don't want to contend with any duke."

Her pulse seemed steady, despite hearing such sweet words from Elliot. Was it so because of the hint of jealousy blended in his plea?

She lowered her gaze. "Everyone will be hidden by masks. How will we find each other? I don't intend to miss any dances."

He shifted his stance, knocking a rock with low shoes. "Then let's meet at one of the salons at the rear of the hall, say, nine-thirty."

She nodded as he kissed her hand. The feel of his warm lips against her skin made her float up the drive. *Oh, to tell*

Seren!

Mary finally settled. William set her in her bed and pulled the blankets to her chin. She looked like a sweet flower, but for the last forty minutes, her banshee-like cries rattled the walls. Tiptoeing out of the room, he took a deep breath then closed the door. The handle felt loose. He'd mention it to his steward tomorrow. Now, to face his remaining guests...

How could he have bungled things so badly? Gaia ran off, thinking him some callous rich man, wanting her for a governess. He wanted her friendship, needed her help. Oh, God, this was horrid.

Heading for the stairs, he envisioned Miss Telfair's flight down the treads. His heart stopped beating until her slippers hit the floor. If she'd taken a tumble...

He punched at his chest and took a deep, filling breath. What a time to realize that his feelings for Gaia had deepened, now that she hated him.

With a final blow, he pounded down the stairs.

Albert stopped him at the bottom. As his man straightened his livery, he whispered, "Miss Telfair made it safely to Southborne. A gentleman escorted her halfway to the Hallows' gate. Young Mr. Whimple."

William nodded. His gut twisted. Did the man comfort her in her distress?

Steadying himself against a tide of angst building in his stomach, he stomped to the drawing room. He planted his palms on the show table next to the doors. Two miles is a long stretch of the legs, particularly if one is upset, maybe crying. Did Whimple shelter her in his arms? Useful Mr. Whimple.

Fist balling, William let out a deep breath and focused on Gaia, not the botanist, or the desire to smash the Dresden rhinoceros so close to his fingers.

Despite his ire at Whimple's interference, William would

never forgive himself if any harm came to Gaia. Moreover, he wasn't likely to forgive himself for allowing her to be belittled. With a houseful of guests, he couldn't jump on a horse and follow her. No, it wouldn't be wise; he'd say or admit to something a bachelor would regret. He straightened and eyed himself in the hanging mirror. His snowy cravat held wrinkles. Shadows of regret hovered about his eyes. He hated this helpless feeling.

Maybe he should go get Magnus. What would he say to Gaia if he went to retrieve her? *"Sorry. I do want your help. And ignore my clumsy talk and any hint of sentiment."* No, that wouldn't do. Maybe it was better she thought him callous than an out-of- practice admirer.

Meek as she was, the hornet sting in her stride forewarned it would not be easy to make amends. He stopped chasing after Elizabeth. That woman found fault with everything, intentionally provoking William in order to isolate him and stay true to her lover. His late wife had no want of peace in their marriage. Would he have peace chasing a friend?

The temptation to crash the porcelain animal on the table again plagued his spirit. He took a breath and suppressed all the feelings raging within; anger, loneliness, jealousy. Driving one fist into the palm of the other, he released another belly full of steam. Anger never solved anything. He wasn't that man anymore, and he wouldn't run after another woman; not even a friend.

With a lift of his head, he sidestepped the breakable objects and pushed on the doors to the drawing room.

His cousin played Chopin. She raised her head and showed off her alligator teeth. Anyone who could find beauty in her pale, close-set eyes, hawk-like nose, or haughty character, had to be drunk on her money.

Yet he couldn't take away from her playing. At least she possessed the good sense to come back down and entertain his guests. The sweet notes from the horrible woman circled the room, moving Mrs. Monlin's hands to the rhythm. Stelford and Mr. Telfair stood by the fireplace, steeped in conversation.

The sweet scent of burning hickory fell on William. Maybe the memory of the hurt in Gaia's eyes would burn, too.

The stepmother sat alone on the sofa. Her gaze locked with his as soon as he stepped inside.

He strode across the tapestry, and dropped beside her. "Miss Telfair has left, and is visiting the Hallows'."

Her eyes narrowed, and she leaned closer. "It takes a great deal to frighten my daughter away. What has happened?"

"A misunderstanding, indeed, and it is my fault."

Mrs. Telfair pushed out a sigh and eased her stiff posture against a tufted pillow. "I see."

"Let her know my sorrow. Let her know she is highly esteemed, nothing less."

A smile set in the woman's brown eyes. "My Gaia is not easy with words; it may take a long time to convince her of your sentiments."

But what sentiment would he convey; friendship, the desperation of a father, or the foolhardiness of a smitten suitor?

Two weeks since his ill-fated dinner with the Telfairs, and Gaia Telfair hadn't forgiven him or spoken to him. William even went to church, his father's old chapel, only to watch her whip past him. To witness that gentle countenance lift and turn from his direction was worse than the squeamish feeling settling in his stomach, sitting in the cold pew. Luckily, his father's ghost didn't appear and taunt him from the pulpit.

Blinking, he hefted his flintlock. The scent of fresh- clipped heather blew across Ontredale's lawn as William aimed at the target. His thumb ran along the barrel of the gun. The cold metal teased his palm. Soon, the fire squelching from the long shaft would bring the heat and the heady smell of gunpowder. It had been too long since he'd held a rifle. Being a warrior at a time of peace seemed more difficult than he thought it should. Being at war with his head wasn't much better either.

With a quick squeeze of the trigger, he forced the flint to spark and explode. The bullet flew and pierced the center of the paper target.

The tension in his shoulders lessened. His accuracy was dead-on. Things weren't so easy with a live target. What else could be done to get Gaia to accept his apology, without slipping back into that dangerous area of suitor? He'd sent a note, but received no answer. A showy bouquet would get a response, but was he ready for the response; a girl delighted, hoping for love, or one indifferent, decidedly against him?

He'd been so close to getting Mary help. Why did she have to be in his arms, embracing him, making him hope for something he couldn't possess? The awareness of her, her curves, his loneliness, all made his speech clumsy. He could've agreed to nearly anything the way those hazel eyes pierced him. And what was so wrong at wanting to reward her, so she could buy shoes? He couldn't buy such a personal gift for her. Only a father or fiancé could.

Well, he didn't want to be Gaia's father, and, after Elizabeth, being a fiancé or husband was out of the question. With the shake of his head, he peppered his gun, set the flint, and aimed. The trigger compressed with ease. The released bullet sailed into the same bullet hole. What was he going to do about getting Mary help now?

"Well done," Stelford clapped, marching toward him, his boots scuffing a path down the lawn. He wasn't very steady. Too much drink this early? It was barely past nine in the morning. What had happened to his disciplined friend?

William slung the gun down to his side. "Have you gotten my cousin to agree to leave?"

Stelford adjusted his cravat. "Not exactly."

Pivoting back to the targets, William nodded to a groom to set up another target. "Explain."

"She won't leave until after the Masked Ball. That's the best I could do."

Another two weeks of suffering the woman's voice and her awful flirtations--horrible. With a shake of his head, William weighed his pockets of lead shot. Enough for a few more kills. "Why won't Deborah leave me?"

Stelford broke into a steady stream of chuckles. "She wants to be a duchess. I think she loves you."

"Humph." William fired another shot. This one hit off-center. Waving for a fresh target, he took aim again.

"Maybe Miss Smythen is the answer." Stelford pounded closer. "She would make sure Mary is unharmed, and kept respectable if Elizabeth's scandal is exposed."

William lowered his gun. "The letters have stopped again. The storm may have passed. Why would I marry someone I don't love? I can barely stand her."

"She's inarticulate, and pompous, but at least she loves you. Why are you drawn to the ones who don't?"

With fingers tightening about the handle, he turned to his friend. "What are you talking about? Elizabeth loved me."

Stelford pointed the barrel toward the ground. "Did she?"

"Be very careful, Stelford." He pulled the weapon away, spun back to his target and raised the gun. This time, he perfected his aim. The shot hit dead-center.

An audible swallow came from his friend. "And what of Miss Telfair? We have seen neither *hind*, nor hair of her since your big dinner.

He squinted at his lecherous friend. William needed no reminder of Gaia's curves. "Careful, Stelford; she's an honorable woman."

"The Telfair cook says she's been spending her days stitching an onyx domino, not with another man."

So, Whimple hasn't been chasing her. William cocked the brow of his hat. "I didn't ask to you to set your spies on her."

"The first girl in ages to bring joy to you, and you'd think I'd let you lose out. So send the chit some roses to impress her."

Torn between gratitude for the intelligence and annoyance at his friend's take at managing William's life, he called out to Albert, "I'm done for today."

Stelford took the gun from him and tapped the holder against his boot. "Well, you want the miss, don't you? She's too refined to come to you, but all fresh targets can be tamed if you aim for them."

If he repeated, 'Stelford is my friend' a few times, maybe the notion would stick. "I need Miss Telfair's help with Mary. How many times must I explain it to you?"

Rubbing his freshly-shaved chin, Stelford offered a sympathetic tone. "Fine; pretend she doesn't interest you, but it's obvious she's mad at you. And where there are fumes, there is fire. A little skillful cultivation will make it blaze."

Could it be true? Could Gaia want more than friendship? Is that why she became so angered when it sounded as if William wanted her to be a governess? He looked down and kicked at a rock. "You are ridiculous."

"If only you knew what the unusual chit liked; then you'd get the response you seek, Your Grace. That's what I've always done."

What did Gaia like? A vision of her praying in the moors in the grassy knoll leapt in his head. Maybe she was there now, just as miserable as he about their disagreement. He pushed the thought out of his mind. To figure out what she liked would be the equivalent of targeting and pursuing her, as

Stelford had said. Wasn't there a middle ground? How could he restore their friendship, eradicating the misunderstanding between them, without going back to that dangerous area of wanting more?

A knock at Chevron's door gave Gaia an excellent excuse for abandoning dance practice. Though she wanted to be perfect for Elliot tonight at the grand Masque Ball, Julia and the dance master were too demanding. The couple was in each other's confidence, laughing and torturing Gaia and the other girls.

On the other side of the library door, Gaia took a moment to collect herself. The hall held an air of peace. What would she say to Elliot when they danced? She would have to be bold, as Seren said. This would be her one and only chance. Since he hadn't been to Chevron in over a month, maybe his attachment to Julia had waned. Gaia surely had a chance.

Yet dancing with Elliot didn't give her as much concern as did running into Cheshire. She'd been good to avoid him, his sea-blue eyes, and the guilt of not helping his daughter. Well, not so much on the last point. Perhaps, if she saw the duke, she could ask of Lady Mary and offer more suggestions.

Another loud knock brought her running to the entry. Breathing heavily, she smoothed her wild hair and opened the door. Her mouth dropped.

Cheshire stood there, a bouquet wrapped in peach-colored paper planted within his fist. "May I have a moment of your time, Miss Gaia Telfair? You've all but abandoned our meeting place in the woods."

Her heart started to pound, but she refused to be swayed by the lost look in his sad eyes, or his admission of searching for her at her oak. "I've been avoiding the sun, in order to look perfect tonight."

His brow scrunched. "So it's the sun, and not me, you're

hiding from?"

She couldn't admit to either or the fear of looking browner and coarse. "It would be rude to turn you away. Mrs. Monlin and Mrs. Telfair are in the parlor. I'm sure they'd like to see you."

He shoved the flowers into her hand. "I am here to see you, Gaia. No one else will do."

His saying of her given name gave her a shiver, so personal and yet sounding so dear from the austere press of his lips. Towering above her, his tall, muscular frame blocking the door, he rent his chocolate greatcoat and tugged on his silken waistcoat. "I will not be deterred. Too much time has passed, and my stubbornness and yours can't coexist. There is too much at stake. My daughter's happiness is at stake."

Garlic fragrance assaulted her nose. Peaking at the flowers, she gaped at the lovely sight. Wildflowers, stalks of buttercups, white ransoms, and lousewort. The golden-yellow cones peered to the ceiling as the feathery lousewort guarded the buttercups' stems. This arrangement was so different from expensive hothouse roses she'd seen Seren receive.

And her best friend's suitors were not as wealthy as the duke. Gaia spied dirt stains on his gloves as she took another sniff. He'd made it himself. It was a perfect gift. "Why have you done this?"

He took her hand and towed her from Chevron's door. Releasing her, he pulled his arms behind his back and leaned against the framing limestone. "I am a desperate father who lost a friend over a misunderstanding."

"Go inside and speak with my family. I can't be out here with you. It's not proper."

His frown deepened. "All these rules to remain respectable and I still lose. I keep losing."

What was he talking about? He wasn't the one deemed a

servant. Still clutching his flowers, she put a hand to her hip. "You are wounded? I'm just glad to have found out your game before.... Oh, never mind."

His eyes widened. He reached out, as if he wanted to touch her, but stopped and lowered his hand to the side. His voice sounded raw and tight. "Before what?"

Her pulse ramped, and she found it hard to swallow. She wasn't intimidated. No, something intangible filled her, making her almost breathless. "It doesn't matter, and if you will not speak with my family, I suggest you leave."

"Then, we will speak tonight at the Masked Ball."

He wouldn't stop pursuing her for his employment, and the month of not seeing him didn't lessen his dizzying effect upon her. She swallowed and looked up at him again. "Everyone will be in disguise. How will you know me?"

A grin filled his countenance before he cleared his throat. "I will find you. This misunderstanding will end tonight, and I will have my friend back."

He bowed stiffly and marched to his horse. "Tonight, Miss Telfair."

Not knowing what to say or do, she stood there, watching the image of man and beast growing smaller until gone from her sight.

Shoulders drooping, she walked into Chevron. Dropping the fine paper and wild flowers on to the show table, Gaia stopped and looked at her reflection in the mirror. No sun for a month had left her very pale. Perfect. A smile of expectation set on her lips. But what drove this feeling; the chance to dance with Elliot, or the duke saying he could find her in a room of masked people?

What would he say this time; another apology, another tortured explanation?

"Gaia," Telfair's voice sounded behind her, "was that Cheshire?"

"It was."

A sigh left him, as if someone had put a hole in him. "I raised you to be respectable."

Surely he didn't think the duke's visit was her fault. She glared at Mr. Telfair. "Yes, to be a respectable governess."

His mouth parted, as if to say something, but the noise of her siblings' prancing, coming closer, seemed to stop him for a moment. He coughed. "I depend on you to care for them."

Depend? What of love, or even a little smudge of respect? She shook her head as the children gathered about her. "Come along; I have something special for you."

Like a good governess, she leveled her shoulders and turned from Mr. Telfair, shuttling her young siblings up the stairs and into her room.

A sigh left her lips. She should be grateful that Mr. Telfair hadn't tossed her to the streets or forced her mother to give her up. Her heart sank to the pit of her stomach as fingers curled around the knob on her door.

It wasn't enough. It would never be enough. Elliot would have to come to his senses and marry her soon. Gaia needed to be where the man whose name she bore loved her, truly loved all of her.

She glanced at the beautiful domino she'd created from an old carriage dress and some morning garbs. She could even wear the pink dress she'd made beneath. She'd stand out, and dance with the man she loved. Tonight he'd realize he loved her, too, and would settle it all with a kiss.

"Gaia," Lydia tossed her head back and caught Gaia's gaze, "have you come up with a new torture for us?"

Helena folded her arms over her blue-checked skirt. "We're sorry. A thousand times sorry for setting fire to the duke's horse. How long will it take for you to accept what we say is true?"

Timothy's face bloomed. "Duke. Duke. Duke. He's no

mad."

Was Gaia slow to forgive? She suddenly felt queasy at how long she'd offered her stepmother nothing but politeness, and no warmth. That was so wrong.

With a heavy blink, she couldn't push away Cheshire's frown, the determined sound of his voice. Was she punishing him like the girls?

But the duke wanted her as a servant like Mr. Telfair. They deserved.... She deserved.... She was in the wrong harboring bitterness.

Abstaining from forgiveness was dangerous. *Oh, God, deal with my heart*. "Come here, Helena, Lydia." She dropped to her knees and threw her arms about the twins. "I was so angry, but you're just children. Everyone needs to know they are forgiven. I love you all."

A healthy dose of tears and squirming limbs filled Gaia's arms. Swiping at her eyes, she stood and directed the girls and Timothy to sit on the floor. Gaia picked up her craft box and laid out paper and paste and feathers and other materials.

Lydia picked up a sand-colored feather. "This is so pretty."

Timothy ran his hands through the pile of scrap cloth. He lighted on a deep-blue piece that matched his waistcoat.

Helena made a series of heavy blinks then looked at the jeweled rocks Gaia had collected. "I don't understand."

Soaking up the joy beaming from their faces, Gaia sat with them. "I thought we all might make masks. That way, no one will have to share."

A noisy set of voices and hurried footfalls boomed outside her door. Mr. Telfair, coughing, with a grim look set on his wrinkled countenance, stormed into the room. Lydia and Helena scooted out the threshold. Timothy shrank back into the corner near the bed table.

Sarah and Julia followed Telfair.

Sarah looked flushed, with plum-red cheeks. "This is not Gaia's fault."

In her father's hands were the wildflowers Cheshire gave her; the ones she'd left on the show table. He waved them like a sword. "I will not have you made into a doxy by a rich man. I knew wantonness stirred in you."

Gaia shook her head. "No one is making me into anything."

His glasses slipped down his nose. He shoved them back up the incline of his duck's bill. "So you're willing? He hasn't spoken with me of any intentions. I must deduce this is underhanded."

She couldn't very well let him know the man just needed a governess for his daughter. "I believe he wants my friendship."

"That proves my point. You are too young. Obviously, the duke did something untoward, or you never would have stalked out of Ontredale. I didn't believe your explanation, Sarah." He shook the flowers. "This explains it. We may be poor, but the Telfair name is respectable. You should remember that. I won't have you used like the Olivers' chit."

"Tsk. You sound harsh, like the old vicar, God rest his soul." Sarah put her hands on Gaia's shoulders. "Yes, she has caught the duke's eye, but we have taught her values. You do her a disservice by not trusting her."

"Enough of your reasoning, woman. Gaia, you will not go to the Masked Ball." He gave her the flowers.

Gaia shook so hard, leaves from the arrangement started to fall. "No, please; I've been working so hard on my costume."

He stomped over to her bed. His charcoal morning coat billowed with each angry step. With a whip of his hands, he tugged the domino off the bedpost. "Here, Julia."

He shoved the cape into her sister's hands.

"But…" Gaia's heart was in her throat.

"This is for your own good. We must fight the foulness of

your blood. No Telfair daughter will be led astray."

Daughter? This must be a joke; a horrid joke. "It's just flowers."

He folded his arms. "And they're not from the one you proclaimed to want. Be grateful for the opportunities I've given."

"Yes, passed-down clothes, worn-thin shoes, pretending in public that I am a good Telfair girl, only to remind me in Chevron that I'm not." Gaia stepped away, clutching her bedpost. "Your plans of isolating me won't work. If it weren't the duke, it would be someone else. You want no happiness for me."

He stepped beside her and stretched his hands out, as if he wanted to embrace her, but he'd never touched her more than a pat on the head, or when he raised her hands to show his superiority. "Someday, you'll understand that I am protecting you from the weakness of your mother. She put herself in a position in which she was taken advantage. I won't let you do that."

Was he now suggesting Mama's straying was coercion, rape? Could she be a child of rape? Anger burnt a hole in Gaia's gut. She stiffened, moving away from the lies. "It's not true."

He lowered his voice. "It is. And Julia will wear this outfit to the ball. Someday, you will understand it's for the best. The duke couldn't want anyone like you but for a plaything. His blood is too pure for the likes of you. His motives aren't pure at all."

Hinting at rape would be the harshest thing Mr. Telfair ever said. Why did he put to words how unworthy Gaia was?

Plodding to the corner, he grabbed Timothy's hand. Taking the boy in his rail-thin limbs, he headed for the door. "You know I am right."

Julia put the domino on the bed. "I can't. I've been working on one, but it's not quite as grand." Was the lilt in her voice admiration for Gaia's sewing, or joy from Mr. Telfair's edict?

Numb with unworthy blood sloshing in her veins, Gaia picked up the outfit and the mask she'd labored on for so long. "No, you wear it, as your father demanded." She pushed her sister out the door.

Tears leaking down her face, Gaia felt like falling to the floor. Her innards stung, as if Mr. Telfair took his knife and pierced her through her middle. If her birth was formed from stolen virtue, she might as well have been stillborn. "This can't be true."

Her door opened. Soft footsteps followed. Then arms went about her, but she pried free. Gaia felt so different from the white flesh closing about her. "Is it true? Am I a child of rape?"

Mobcap fluttering, Sarah shrugged. "I don't know… Mrs. Monlin was your mother's best friend; she would know. I'll ask her."

All the ways her head euphemized her mother's affair, the blame she'd been pointing at the grave came back to Gaia. She'd hoped the woman had lost her way and that love had made her break her vows. Now, Gaia couldn't cling to that, not even lust. A wave of vomit coursed into Gaia's throat, burning her soul. "How can anyone love me now? Elliot wanted the first dance with me, but he'll never love me. I don't even love me. I can't be here anymore."

"You won't run away. Don't break my or Timothy's heart." Sarah took a strand of coral beads from her neck. "Take these. Sell them in the village for a new costume, or go to your friend, Miss Hallow. She seems a bit of a schemer. Have her help you with a different costume, and go to the ball tonight for your dance with Elliot. I'll make Mr. Telfair understand."

"But this is your special necklace, something for your own daughters; not someone like me."

Sarah kissed Gaia's forehead. "You *are* my daughter. Now go."

Gaia couldn't accept or feel Sarah's love. Mr. Telfair's words haunted each breath. She started down the steps and bounded through the kitchen to the world outside of Chevron. She pointed her feet toward the Hallows', and let her bitter tears flow. What possible reason could God have allowed this? How could she look anyone in the eye, as she was now so beneath everyone?

Serendip Hallow, would she be her friend through this? Would she associate with a black born of rape?

Soon, the tang of salty air enveloped her. Lifting her gaze, she saw the cliffs of Devonshire before her, the grey and brown rocks forming the low hedge separating earth from endless water. Six miles. She'd walked six miles past the Hallows' home. Even the duke's Ontredale sat away off.

Gaia didn't feel tired, just empty. Gasping, she stretched out her hands in the light mist. "God, can You work good from this?"

She couldn't hear His voice or feel His presence, not now, with all her hopes crumbling. The sound of water crashing on the rocks below called to her. For a moment, the pain inside screamed for release. Taking her useless life…wouldn't that stop the ache?

The sea moaned, slapping at the cliff. It was crying out to every weak place inside; the black parts, the white parts, too.

But Gaia couldn't answer. She'd rather let the shame kill her than give into cowardice. She stepped away from the edge.

Turning, she headed to her friend. Serendip would know what to do. She had to.

CHAPTER ELEVEN

The Wrong Kiss

Gaia sank into the darkness of the Hallows' carriage as it moved to the estate hosting the Masked Ball. Clutching the delicate coral beads her stepmother gave her for strength, she stared at her smiling Serendip. Her friend refused to take them as payment. "You should let me give these to your brother as a bribe, not use your pocket money to get him to ride with your parents."

Seren smoothed her silky curls. "See, you give my brother a fiver, and he gives us privacy."

The beautiful ivory satin of the domino Seren loaned her boasted a lacy, almost bridal-like gown beneath. Gaia didn't feel a fairy princess, just a pretender. People like her didn't attend fancy balls. No, they waited on gentry. Though raised as a gentle daughter, she didn't belong. She knew that now. "I shouldn't be doing this, but I promised Elliot a dance. I won't be a liar, too."

Seren stroked the gilded netting of her skirts. She plopped her iron scale on the bench beside her. "You can't miss it. I'd never forgive myself if you missed this night because of things you cannot control. You need a name of your own. It won't happen playing governess at Chevron or abandoning

Mr. Whimple tonight."

Peeking out the window, Gaia concentrated on the carriage ahead. The Hallows, Seren's parents, had held hands as they'd departed Southborne.

"Your parents are an affectionate lot." That is how love should be; ever wanting to be with each other, even when old and grey. I hope Sarah didn't earn too much trouble fighting for me."

Gaia wasn't worth it. The lump in her throat grew larger.

With shaking hands, she fingered the pearls sewn onto the edges of the sheer veil draping her head. "Seren, I'll only stay for my dance."

Her friend toggled the scale, making it clink with her thumbs. "Yes, yes, and the driver will take you back to the house. That's if you want to leave."

"I made a promise to Elliot. That should be worth something. I'm not untrustworthy like Millicent." Or like Gaia's mother.

Seren leaned over and gripped Gaia's hand. "You didn't put the blood in your veins, so you are not responsible. We don't know what happened. Gaia Telfair has to make up her own mind as to who she is. I just hope you really know what you want."

What did she want? To know the truth of her origins? To dance in the arms of the man she'd always loved, and gain a name, a true one that couldn't be taken from her? Or to find Cheshire and accept his apology?

No, she would remain angry with the duke. It was his flowers that caused this. Yet, if not for his overture, she wouldn't know the rest of the lies. The duke was a wise man who could see the truth. Gaia Telfair was a fraud, someone who should be lucky to be a servant to Timothy, or the duke's daughter.

The tension in her neck now pressed her temples. It grew

worse as the carriage stopped. "I can't do this, Seren. My head is hurting."

"I think your spectacles are smudged. Take them off and put them in your reticule. You couldn't manage them with your mask anyway."

Seren was right. The soft egret-feather-mask fit close to Gaia's eyes. She let her thumbs trail the crystals lining the paper. "Everything will be blurry."

"Only for a moment; then things will adjust. You're not trying to read. I'll situate you in a salon. And the face of the man you dance with will be in view." Seren reached and took the lenses, pushing them into Gaia's bag.

Viewing things in a haze did seem to lessen the pain. With her silver mask rod, she wore her mask and held onto Seren's arm as they descended the carriage.

Large purple and gold blobs hung from the ceiling of the public assembly hall. The royal colors wrapped about the columns, as if it were a decadent Roman temple. Smells of a feast overwhelmed her as she entered. It had to be roast duck, with every savory herb in the country. Would it taste better than dining at the duke's?

With a deep breath, she rubbed her stomach and followed Seren deeper into the main hall. It was a little frightening. Colored objects would come into focus only a foot or two from her face.

Gaia turned in the path of a tiger, rather two people dressed as tiger, the front, a real animal's head.

Unnerved by the sudden appearance of costumed beasts, she gripped Seren's hand tighter. They moved deeper into the hall as the quartet's music encircled Gaia. The sway of the bewitching tune eased her nerves, blending jackal, sultans, and otherworldly demonstrations into a sea of happy dancers.

With a scan of the room, she spied the outlines of the

musician's box two stories up. For a moment, Gaia stopped and let her feet tap to the swirling tunes.

A young man stopped in front of her. "Do I know you?" Though his face remained a shadow, his costume suggested he imitated a merchant from China, with a wide bowl-shaped hat and tapestries fashioned into a robe. He put his hand forward, as if to ask her for a dance.

"Excuse us." Seren towed her away. "You have an appointment, remember?"

They walked down a long hall. Seren tugged at doorknobs, peeking into rooms. "Gaia, this one is vacant. Let's set you up here."

She helped Gaia sit on a settee covered in lime-colored Tammies fabric. The glazed cotton shined. Even as she smoothed the fabric beneath her palm, her fingers shook.

Seren adjusted the delicate gauzy silk flowers lining the edges of Gaia's cape. "Wait here until your Elliot arrives. Don't leave this room; I'll come back to find you."

Part of Gaia didn't want to release Seren's hand. Half-seeing things made the room frightening. Her pulse raced. "What if someone else arrives?"

"Tell them the room is occupied. They'll understand." Seren adjusted her silvery sarsenet cape, balanced the scales she hung on a cord in place of a reticule, and smoothed her wide skirts.

Grasping hold of the armrest, Gaia forced her lips to smile. "Good luck to you, Lady Justice. I hope you have fun."

"If you find the love you seek, I'll be happy. You deserve happiness for being you, not someone's daughter. Tell Elliot of your love. Gaia, you need a name and a household of your own, where secrets can't harm you." She gave Gaia a hug. "I want your cup filled with joy."

"Even if my cup isn't pure."

"Your heart is untainted by the past, made pure by

salvation. That's what matters." Seren put a hand to Gaia's face. In the candlelight, she and Seren, their skin, looked the same. "Live free tonight."

Seren moved out of focus and left the room, closing the door behind her.

The lime blur of the settee was as comfortable as it was big, but Gaia couldn't sit still. She fidgeted and tapped her slippers on the floor. The ticking of the mantle clock filled the quiet room.

Trying to ignore it, she clutched the ribbons of her papier-mâché mask and straightened its creamy feathers. She stood and, with the pace of a turtle, she moved to the fireplace and strained to see where the limbs of timepiece pointed. Nine-fifteen.

Elliot would be here soon. What would she say to him? Would she remain silent and just dance with him?

She leveled her shoulders. How could she not say her peace, as she looked into his blue eyes? How ironic to unmask her heart at a masquerade ball.

The moon finally broke through the clouds and cast its light into the salon. Whether from the fuzziness of her vision or the beauty of the glow, the window glass sparkled, as did the mirrors and polished candleholders of the small room.

The low tones of the musicians started up again. The jaunty steps of a reel sounded. The tone called to her feet again, and she danced as if she were in someone's arms. The beechnut- colored walls and white moldings swirled as she did.

That set ended and then another and another. She paced in front of the mantle clock. It tolled a low moan as it struck ten. Elliot had missed their appointment. Heaviness weighed upon Gaia, from the crown of her costume's veils to the thick folds of her opal domino.

How ironic to stand in such finery, when Mr. Telfair told

her she wasn't worthy. Yet hadn't she schemed with her stepmother and Seren to be here? Gaia should leave. Too many wrongs would never equal righteousness.

Movement outside the room sent her pulse racing. Maybe Elliot had been detained, but was still coming. She wrung her hands and looked to the shining circle on the door, its crystal knob.

The footsteps passed by, the sound diminishing, as did her dreams.

Elliot wouldn't show. He must still think of her as a child, as Julia's hapless sister, as Millicent's plain cousin. Or maybe Julia had told him. They could be laughing about it now.

Sighs and a misguided tear leaked out. She leaned against the burnished mantle. The warmth of the hearth did nothing to thaw her suddenly-cold feet. It was best he didn't show. He'd saved her the embarrassment of his rejection. A mulatto's dance or kiss could never do for him.

The rhythm of a dance set crept beneath the ivory doorframe. Maybe Elliot found a new young lady, whose large dowry like Millicent's made her irresistible to men. Was she in his arms, basking in the glow of his smile, his fun conversation?

The ache in her bosom swelled. Gaia released her breath, stilling her trembling fingers against the sheer veil of her fairy costume. Perhaps she should slip from the room and run into the moonlight of the moors.

The door opened. The strains of violin-play seeped into the salon.

Elliot in his domino cape and ebony half-mask entered the room. "Excuse me," his voice was low, hoarse. He whipped a handkerchief from his pocket and wiped his mouth as he bowed.

Always so formal, but what a pity his melodious voice sounded raspy.

Now or never. She cleared her throat and, in her most sultry manner, she placed her hands to her hips and curtsied. "I've been waiting for you."

"Excuse me, do I know you?" He tugged at the ribbons of his mask.

Waving her arms, she caught his gaze. "Please don't take it off. I won't be able to get through this if you expose your handsome face."

"I see." He stopped, his strong hands lowering beneath the cape of his domino. "Miss Telfair?"

With a quick motion, she whipped up her airy silk skirts and moved closer, but maintained an easy distance on the other side of the settee. "Call me Gaia. We needn't be so formal."

His head moved from side-to-side, as if to scan the room.

"You needn't fret, sir. We are quite alone. That's why I decided to confess my feelings."

"I see."

Must he continue to act as if he didn't know her? The moonbeams streaming through the thick window mullions surrounded him, and reflected in the shiny black silk of his cape. Could he be taller, more intimidating?

Elliot had to think of her as a woman. She straightened her shoulders. "I'm so glad you've come. I know I'm young, but not too young to know my heart."

"Miss Telfair, I think this is some sort of mistake."

Blood pounding in her ears, she swept past the settee and stood within six feet of him. "Please call me Gaia."

"I'll not trespass on your privacy any longer." He spun, as if to flee.

She shortened the distance and caught his shoulder. "Please don't go. It took a lot to garner the courage to meet you here."

With a hesitance she'd never seen from confident Elliot, he

gripped her palm and kissed her satin glove. "I know it takes a great amount of courage to make a fool of one's self."

"There's no better fool than one in love." She slipped his hand to her cheek. "Why hide behind mocking? I know you. I've seen your heart. The way you take care of that precious little girl as if she were your own." It touched Gaia, witnessing Elliot helping his brother's household as if it were his own.

"How did you know my fear?" He drew his hand to his mouth. "You see too much."

Squinting, he still wasn't quite in focus. He shifted his weight and rubbed his neck, as if her compliments made him nervous.

"This is a mistake. We should forget this conversation. A man shouldn't be alone with such a forthright young lady. I will return to the ball." He leveled his broad shoulders and marched to the door, his heels clicking the short distance.

Maybe being so low was freeing. "Why leave?" she let her voice sound clear, no longer cautioned with shyness or regret. "Here can be no worse than out there, with the other ladies readying to weigh your pockets."

His feet didn't move, but he closed the door, slamming it hard. Had she struck a nerve?

He pivoted to face her. "Aren't you just like them, my dear? Weren't all gentle women instructed to follow a man's purse? No? Perhaps torturing is your suit, demanding more and more until nothing remains of his soul."

"Men hunt for dowries, and they know best how to torture someone; ignoring people who want their best; separating friends, even sisters, in their pursuits. The man who raised me did so begrudgingly, just to make me a governess to my brother. Is there no worse torture than to yearn to be loved and no one care?"

"A governess? I think I understand."

This wasn't how she'd expected this conversation to go. Elliot's graveled words possessed an edge as sharp as a sword. He seemed different, both strong and vulnerable. It must be the costumes, freeing them both from the confining roles they lived.

Yet he didn't move. He didn't feel the same.

She fanned her shimmering veil. Half-seeing and disguised, she could be as bold and as direct as Millicent or Seren. Gaia could even face the truth. "I forgive you for not feeling the same."

She'd said it, and didn't crumble when he didn't respond in kind. Maybe this was best. With the release of a pent-up breath, she added, "I wish you well."

He chuckled, the notes sounding odd for Elliot's laugh. "Has a prayer wrought this transformation? Well, He works in mysterious ways."

Maybe it was all the prayers over the years that built up her strength. Amazing. Elliot didn't love her, and no tears came to her. Well, numbness had its benefit. "Good evening. You can go; my friend Seren will be back soon."

When he finally moved, it was to come closer, near enough she trail her pinkie along the edgings of his domino, but that, too, was a cliff she wasn't ready to jump.

"Gaia, what if I'm not ready to leave?"

Her ears warmed, throbbing with the possibilities of his meaning.

"If I am trapped," his voice dropped to a whisper, "it is by your hands."

Her heart clenched at his words. Elliot never seemed more powerful or more dangerous. "I'd hope I, ah, maybe I should be leaving."

He took a half-step, as if to block her path. His outline remained a blur; a tall, powerful blur. "You've had your say, sweet Gaia. Now it is my turn."

This near, she could smell the sweet starch of his thick cravat and a bit of spice. Her heart beat so loudly. Could he hear it?

He drew a thumb down her cheek. "Pretty lady, your eyes are red. Your cheeks are swollen. What made you cry so hard? And why didn't you find me?"

Something was different about the tone of his hushed voice. There was pain in it. Did he hurt because Gaia had? Could she have discounted the possibility of Elliot returning affections too quickly?

Something dark and formidable drew her to him like never before. "How could I find you? I didn't know you cared, not until this moment."

His arms went about her, and he cradled her against his side. His fingers lighted in her bun. "I'm fascinated with the curl and color of your hair."

Too many thoughts pressed as a familiar tarragon scent tightened its grip about her heart. "Not course or common—"

His lips met her forehead. His hot breath made her shiver and lean more into him. "Never; that's what I've been trying to tell you."

Heady, and a little intoxicated by the feel of his palms on her waist, she released her mask. It fluttered to the floor. Its pole drummed then went silent on the wood floor. She dropped her lids and raised her chin. "I guess this is when you kiss me. Know the lips of someone who esteems you, not your means or connections."

"A lass as beautiful as you needn't ask or wait for a buffoon to find you alone in a library." His arm tightened about her, and he pulled her beneath his cape. The heat of him made her swoon, dipping her head against his broad chest. He tugged a strand of her curls, forcing her chignon to unravel and trail her back. "Now you look the part of a fairy, an all-knowing auburn-haired Gypsy."

He lifted her chin and pressed his mouth against her sealed lips. However, with less than a few seconds of rapture, he relented and released her shoulders.

She wrapped her arms about his neck and wouldn't release him. "I'm horrible. This is my first kiss. I'm sorry." She buried her face against his waistcoat.

His quickened breath warmed her cheek. "Then it should be memorable." His head dipped forward, with the point of his mask, the delicate paper nose, trailing her brows, nudging her face to his. Slowly drawing a finger across her lips, his smooth nail, the feel of his rough warm skin, made them vibrate, relax, then part. "Trust me, Gaia."

She wanted to nod her consent, but didn't dare move from his sensuous touch.

"Let a real kiss come from a man who covets your friendship, who thinks you are beautiful." He dropped his domino to the floor.

His bare face came into focus seconds before his mouth claimed her. It wasn't Elliot melting every bone in her body. It wasn't Elliot she linked her arms about, holding him tighter until their hearts beat as one. The duke hauled her higher into his embrace.

She willed her limp arms to cling to his shoulders.

His fingers wandered the length of her back, encouraging her to surrender, but to what; a moment of passion, or love?

Too much thinking. She stopped trying to discern what this meant, or the consequences, and held on to him. He was solid, not a fantasy. And he was here. Head spinning, she allowed him to kiss her more deeply. A hunger burst inside. She wanted everything he could offer in this embrace.

Cheshire, the first man she could tease; the one who saved her at her first ball, the first to send her flowers, and now, the first, the only, to send a tremble down her spine.

When no air could possibly remain in her lungs, he

relented, and she caught a boyish grin on his countenance before he stepped out of focus. "There, that's one to remember. I won't forget it, my dear fairy."

Overwhelmed and dizzy, she staggered, and the duke scooped her up, holding her against his firm chest. A feeling of safety washed over her, as it did when he saved her from a tumble on the stairs.

Her arms were about his neck again, and he seemed hesitant to put her down.

Releasing a breath, he lowered her to the settee. "You really should wear your glasses to avoid kissing the wrong man."

Not knowing what to say, she sat up and drew her knees to her chin. "I don't know if it was the wrong man." She bit her puffy lip. "What you must think of me; professing love to one, but kissing another."

He shrugged. "It is I who is in the wrong. I must apologize."

How could he apologize for a kiss like that? Plays should be written of it, but would it be a tragedy or a comedy? She reached for his hand and leaned close to see his face. "You did say you'd find me. What does this mean?"

The door swung wide. "Sorry I'm late, but.... Miss Telfair, are you well?"

That voice. Elliot's? Her face fevered, she released Cheshire's palm.

"The young lady seemed a bit out of sorts, so I kept her company until her senses returned. My dear, we must finish this conversation. I will visit you tomorrow."

Unable to speak, and fighting the heat of shame, she nodded.

Side by side, the hazy figure stood. The duke's outline appeared thicker, more muscular than Elliot's did, and his overshadowed the scholar's by an inch. She dipped her head. She should've known the difference, but ignorance brought bliss.

She drew her fingers to her mouth. Cheshire must think her a tart, just like Mr. Telfair said, just like her mother. Yet, if she weren't a tart, why did she long to be back in his arms, feeling his heart thumping in her ear, his lips caressing hers, over and over again?

The duke scooped up his domino, then took out a handkerchief and tapped his lips. "Miss Gaia, feel better. I will call upon you at noon. We'll go for a drive.'Til tomorrow."

He left, whistling.

No words filtered into her mind. She pulled her arms tight about her. She'd vowed to kiss only Elliot, the man she hoped to marry, but her lips still tingled from meeting the duke's. What was she going to do?

Elliot pulled a chair near. "Such a serious look on your face, but I assume that the duke took the first dance. What is left for me?"

Nothing. She'd just given her fancy speech and her kiss to the duke. "I am not well. Can you help me to my carriage? I need to leave."

His face held a frown, but he wasn't the man of Gaia's concern. No, the duke could now claim sole possession of it. And what would happen when a man so high in peerage discovered he'd kissed a mulatto?

CHAPTER TWELVE

The Consequences of a Kiss

William held his breath and ducked into the shadows of the pollen-dusted portico of the Masked Ball. Restringing his domino, he watched Mr. Whimple escort Gaia to a carriage. She clutched her shimmering mask, and the moonlight reflecting from it made her glow.

Whimple handed her into the carriage, without attempting anything untoward. The young man seemed an honorable lot, and didn't try to take advantage of the confused woman.

Not as William had. He pounded his skull, slightly cracking his stiff papier-mâché mask. Knowing that the lass was bewildered didn't stop him from kissing her. His lips still pulsed with the taste of her, and his palms remained warm in the chilly air. The memory of holding her, of feeling her soft curves melting in his arms, would last long into the night. What happened to his bachelor calling? If Stelford knew, he'd chide him so.

The sleek onyx carriage slipped down the lane. He almost wished she'd peek out the sleek rear window, but who would she seek? Whimple, no doubt. A sigh left William as he slunk back inside the hall.

The musician played a jaunty tune, but it was absorbed by

the fabric-draped walls and the throng of costumed people.

A woman clothed as a milkmaid approached. "Do I know you?"

"No, you do not. Excuse me," he bowed and stalked away to stand by the long refreshment table. The half-empty brass bowl of Negus sat dangerously near the edge. The picked-over cuts of meat on the earthen platter looked even less appetizing.

Another lady came his way, and he waved her off. He'd already danced with six girls, all Gaia's height, wearing dark dominos. Who knew he'd find the right lass in ivory and sheers in a salon?

How much time had he wasted on Stelford's fowled bribe? The Telfair's cook said Gaia had worked for days on a black satin domino. Of the girls fitting the demure build and attire, only Miss Julia Telfair made for a pleasant waltz.

The sister spun past him, again in the arms of a sleek shepherd. Draped in burlap and hoisting a crooked staff, the fellow turned her with great ease. This would make four dances. How many had they taken while he visited with his fairy?

At first, the sight of them piqued his ire. He'd assumed it was Gaia and Whimple. It was neither. Now William's brows rose in concern. Though society's rules loosened at a masked ball, out in the open, a young miss should take care.

He sighed as another wave of guilt washed over him, nearly drowning him. William was hardly one to make judgments. He'd just risked Miss Gaia's reputation, kissing her like an unthinking schoolboy. If they'd been discovered, he'd have to marry her to protect her. A smile curled beneath his mask, then faded. It would be a disaster to marry another woman who loved someone else.

Yet would she kiss William if her love for Whimple held strength? After announcing himself, did she not lock her arms about his neck? For a moment, he allowed his lonely heart to remember Gaia's softness, the warmth of her touch. The fever she created within stirred anew. Part of him wanted Gaia Telfair for his own.

A tap on his shoulder made him turn.

Stelford stood near. "I don't think the curvy Telfair came. Sorry, old man."

What! Stelford didn't have new intelligence. William chuckled, "She was here, and now she's gone."

Adjusting his mask about his face, Stelford grunted, then stretched. His domino fluttered with the swings of his arms. "Well, did you convince her to forgive you?"

Oh, he hoped she didn't kiss like that if she were angry with him. Well, maybe that would be a fun result to an argument. He rubbed his chin. "I'm to visit the Telfairs tomorrow."

The man started to chuckle and slapped William on the back. "I knew you just needed to find her. Ah, there's the one I've been looking for. Excuse me."

Stelford moved away after a princess dressed in silver. A flock of admirers followed in her wake. Pretty, but nothing could compare to his fairy.

Humph. He'd never seen Stelford take an interest in anyone since he'd lost his great love, some mysterious woman from his youth. Hopefully, the princess was unattached.

But what of William's masked fairy and her love for Mr. Whimple? William backed into the corner to lean against a column, and resisted bashing his skull against the cold marble.

How did Gaia guess his real fear wasn't the exposure of Elizabeth's infidelity, but his daughter's paternity? Was it Mary's ears, or had he given her a clue to the dilemma? Had the gossip reached his beloved Devonshire?

He shook his head. Legally, she was his daughter, born during their wedlock. It wouldn't change his love for the girl, but it would take away all illusion of his marriage. Then he'd know Elizabeth never loved him. That would be a stab to his gut.

Why had Gaia been crying, and what of this business of her father wanting to make her a governess? Something other than unrequited feelings had hurt her deeply, and that made his blood boil again.

"Cousin, you must dance with me," Deborah curtsied before him.

He took her lace-draped hand and escorted her to start a reel. She didn't look so awful, with an ivory mask covering her face, and the noise of the crowds drowning the high pitch of her voice.

She tapped her snowy fan on his shoulder. "Are you enjoying yourself?"

He spun her and moved apart as the dance required. This was good, because he couldn't decide how to respond. Jealous. Lost. Unsure.

She swayed back to him. Her salmon domino swished like a fish tail.

He came in to step with her as they moved in unison to the edge of the floor, and lifted hands. "And what are you supposed to be this evening?"

She grinned a shy smile. "I am virtue tonight."

A chuckle bubbled in the back of his throat. "Well, I suppose on a night like this, anyone could be anything."

Her lips curled down. "What did Miss Telfair come as, a dairy maid or a governess?" Venom sounded behind the s-sounds.

Something protective, more than paternal, rose up in him. He stopped, his gaze unflinching. "Don't hurt my friend."

Deborah's cheeks turned bright red, and she stammered, "I

didn't mean anything. Is she here?"

If he answered, it would either expose his interests in Gaia or hurt Deborah's feelings. Neither felt like the right thing to do. He patted his cousin's fingers and led her from the floor. "Have you seen her?"

The tension in the woman's jaw eased. Her smile returned. "I suppose she hasn't showed. Now, maybe I'll have your attention."

A measure of sympathy hit him. It was horrible not to have your love returned. Knowing the pain he held in his own heart, he should be more sensitive. He smiled down at Deborah. "Come, let's try one more dance."

She took hold of his hand. "Cousin William, dear man, I know you are lonely. And certain women will take advantage to better their lot. Take care. For Mary's sake, she needs a well-connected woman to mother her."

"I'll keep that in mind, if I ever remarry."

She tugged on his domino, stopping him from spinning her in the reel. "You need to think of remarrying, for nothing more than producing a male heir who will inherit your title and who'll be able to protect Mary all her days. You may not always be able."

William didn't respond. The lump in his throat was too big. His selfishness could leave Mary unprotected. He bowed to Deborah and walked out into the cool night air.

Gaia released a yawn and glanced out her bedchamber window. After a sleepless night, Seren dropped her to Chevron at the crack of dawn. Her lack of rest didn't dim her anxiousness. Cheshire said he would call today. Her face dipped and her brow pressed against the cold glass. She closed her eyes.

A pat to her shoulder made her bolt upright.

Sarah stood behind her. "Did you dance and have fun?"

She waved the cream mask Seren forced Gaia to keep. "I didn't see you until Mr. Whimple escorted you to your carriage."

"Is Mr. Telfair ready to send me away to a convent?" That is, if one would take her.

"He didn't attend. The tirade up here left him too tired, or maybe it was the warm milk. So, was your dance with Mr. Whimple extraordinary?"

Half-shamed, half-enraptured, all confused, Gaia fingered the brown buckle at her waistband. "I didn't dance, but I kissed a duke."

"Oh, I see." Sarah sank against the bedpost with a thud.

Gasping, Gaia stepped closer. "Are you all right, Mother?"

She raised a hand to Gaia's cheek. "My heart sings when you call me that."

"Please, Mother, tell me what to do. Serendip couldn't stop laughing. She thinks I might love the duke, but that can't be right."

Sarah lifted her chin, exposing misty almond eyes. "Can't it be?"

Gaia shook her head so hard it hurt. "Oh, how could I be so faithless? I am just like the woman who birthed me. At least I am no victim; I caused this travesty with my own hands."

Taking Gaia's palms in hers, Sarah shook her head. "You are your own woman. If your feelings have changed from Elliot to the duke, it's fine. And we don't know what happened with your mother."

How could it ever be fine? With Elliot, there was a chance at love. The years they'd known each could outweigh her impure blood. Gaia stiffened her posture. "Why has my heart changed? It should be set on Elliot. He was attainable. He, more so than the duke, could accept a by-blow."

Sarah sighed. "Don't call yourself that. You are bright, pretty Gaia Telfair. I know Cheshire cares for you."

Caring for was very different from love, or even acceptance. Gaia shook her head. "Mr. Telfair has cared for me these twenty years. It's not love. It carries no more weight than how useful I am to him. And if my wanton behavior is found out, how much care will he have for me then?"

The neighing of horses sounded through the window. Gaia looked out and caught sight of the duke in an obsidian carriage pulled by a team of four handsome walnut roans. Several grooms surrounded the open carriage. Was that his daughter by his side?

"What's happening, Gaia?"

"It's him, in a landau. The duke wants to take me for a drive."

Aunt rushed into the room. Curling papers still sat in her auburn hair. "Well, she'll need a chaperone. I tell you, Sarah, this is the one I should have had for a season. This meek one's going to get the duke to come up to scratch in no time. You may not have Julia's beauty, but your wit has snared him. My dear friend, the first Mrs. Telfair would be so proud."

All the air left from Gaia's lungs. How could that woman, faithless or victim, ever be proud?

Sarah bounced to her feet. "Hush, Tabitha, and go get dressed. Gaia, we'll need to go downstairs."

Aunt grabbed Gaia by the shoulders. "And you come. Maybe we can get you into one the gowns I had made for your sister. She's only an inch or two taller."

Gaia shook free, but kissed Aunt's hand. "No; if he's come to visit me, it will be plain old me." No more dressing like Julia or Seren. Her brown-checked gown would have to do.

Aunt shook her head then marched to the door. "When did she become willful?"

The transformation started when Gaia met Cheshire by her tree. It became more real when he kissed her. Pity, it would all be for naught when she explained her true upbringing; even a man as kind as the duke wouldn't want such a dark, scandalous girl.

The doors to the parlor opened.

Sarah and Gaia curtsied as Cheshire entered with his daughter. The little darling held his hand. Her eyes seemed wide as her head whipped from side to side.

The pair wore coats in matching shades of blue; his, a slim waistcoat over buff breeches, and the tot wore a miniature carriage dress. He'd combed his dark hair back, except for the errant curl falling over his brow. It had to be her sleep-deprivation that kept her gaze lingering on his pleasant smile.

He took a long-stemmed buttercup from behind his back and handed it to Gaia. "Are you ready for our drive?"

Aunt walked back into the room, her chignon stuffed into one of Sarah's embroidered turbans; a rose-colored one with tiny stitched flowers at the seam. "Your chaperone is ready."

Gaia swallowed, trying to force moisture into her dry throat. "What if we just take a walk? I'm fond of walking, and we won't need a chaperone."

"I could watch the child," Aunt attempted to pick up Lady Mary, but the child ran to her father.

He scooped up the little girl, and she pulled at his finely-knotted cravat. "She's not very sociable."

Gaia bent and played with Lady Mary's fingers. "Let's take her with us, and my little brother can come, too."

His eyes darted, as if he didn't agree, but then he nodded. "Let us go. We need to finish our talk."

Yes, she'd savor this talk. It would have to be their last.

CHAPTER THIRTEEN

A Mistake or An Opportunity

Waiting for Gaia to collect her brother and a pelisse, William stood in the lime-washed hall of Chevron Manor, tapping one boot on the dark-stained floorboards while Mary latched onto the buckle of the other. A servant passed in front of him and curtsied. Then a set of giggling girls stepped around him to enter a large room… probably a dining room with a table missing.

He lumbered an inch or two, with Mary smiling up at him, and peered through the crack in the door to the dining room. Julia Telfair performed the steps of a reel with someone. A dance master?

She was all smiles, and the young man was, too; even as the bouncy twins and four other girls popped up and down on the bare hardwoods.

A lesson? William leaned a little closer to the door, gripping the dulled brass knob. There was something familiar about the couple's form, the way they moved in unison. Was that the shepherd from the night before?

The sister glowed as she linked arms with the young man. Oh, my; someone has made the flower bloom. Moreover, it wasn't the shared botanist.

William scratched his chin. Perhaps he should warn Mr. Telfair of the attachment.

One of his father's fiery sermons about temptation leapt to William's head. While the parishioners seemed roused by his father's oration, William could only cringe at the man's illustration of a near-elopement of an under-gardener and pretty young parishioner. His father humiliated the girl, telling of her pregnancy out of wedlock. Fully sobbing, Miss Oliver hung her head through the sermon. The family moved a few months later.

The shame had to be unbearable, and it killed the fortunes of the younger sisters. Yes, he should warn Mr. Telfair.

"We are ready, my lord." Gaia held her little brother's hand. A grimace painted her high cheekbones, as if this stroll would be torture.

He deposited Mary onto his shoulder and extended his arm.

When Gaia's chocolate-colored sleeve merged with his, his mind cleared of everything save her frown, and what it would take to lift it.

With a tug, she walked forward. "Let me lead the way."

He swayed but kept his feet planted, not moving. "Giving orders to a military man?"

She bit her lip but raised her gaze to his, the first time today. "Please follow me."

Her eyes radiated even more so than they did with her ball mask. Right now, it wouldn't take much for him to follow wherever she wanted to take him. Hadn't she led him by the nose these past weeks?

Acquiescing, he fell in to step with her.

Further away from the house, William followed the beauty to a grove of beechnut trees. The sweet smell of clover hung in the slight breeze.

A strand of her curly brown hair fell across her scrunched

brow. Gaia seemed in anguish.

His apologies went nowhere with the lass, and Stelford's advice seemed to dig a deeper hole. William even prayed this morning to find the right words to say. But what was prayer? Merely an incantation to get God to force others to do what you wanted.

That was what his father's prayers were. Vicar St. Landon prayed William would choose the church, that another heir be found; nothing of wanting his son to be happy.

Swatting at an insect with a little too much force, he forced his hand to lower. He needn't remember that horrible time, father versus son... or the guilt.

Gaia didn't look at him. She held her brother's hand and stared at the rich, emerald ground. Her worn slippers now bore hints of mud stains. They must be freshly-scrubbed, but still not as good as new shoes. Very few women were as resilient as this young lady. Elizabeth wouldn't stand for such.

William put an arm tighter about Mary's middle. She latched to it as if it were reins, and his shoulder a saddle. One day, he'd have to say or write something good about Elizabeth for Mary. How was he to do that?

Hadn't he bowed his head feverishly for the restoration of his marriage? Yet if he'd known of her deceit, could their marriage have been repaired if she hadn't died?

A sigh breathed from his soul. No. He wasn't that big a man. Forgiving such debts wasn't in his cup.

With the silence shredding what little composure he still possessed, he stopped and turned to Gaia. "Did you sleep well?"

Her hazel eyes slimmed to dots and, like focused sunrays, would soon burn through his favorite coat, straight to his chest.

He placed Mary on the ground and pointed to Timothy to

sit beside her. "Guard her for me, young man."

The boy nodded and settled near the little girl. She'd already grabbed fistfuls of tall grasses.

Taking Gaia's arm, he towed her a few feet from the children. "I'm at a loss as to how to begin this, but why are you angry?"

She balled her fists. "You let me run on like some ninny. You could have stopped me."

"Your speech was too beautiful to interrupt." He rubbed a patch of marigolds with his boot, and tried to hide the smile lifting his lips. Last night, she'd dazzled him with her boldness, just as with her misery prayer. "Shakespeare would be proud. Such tragedy and mystery wrapped in your words."

She started pacing, flattening the low heather and the poor yellow flowers. "You didn't have to kiss me."

He gripped her shoulder to stop her. "Oh, yes I did. I couldn't let you ask some other fool, one who might try to take more advantage of a girl alone at a Masked Ball, or worse, you could've shared your feelings with the botanist, only to have him say no to your heart."

With his finger, he traced her jaw. "Trust me, my dear; there is no greater pain than heartache blended with humiliation."

Her chin dropped, and wind sighed out of her like a hole in a hot air balloon. "He might've agreed."

"Isn't it better to kiss a friend, one who sees you when the world thinks you're invisible? Shouldn't I have a claim to those pert lips?"

He drew her near and cupped her cheek. "It's the light of day, Gaia Telfair. You see William St. Landon standing before you. And he thinks you are beautiful, and gifted with wit, and he wants to kiss you now."

Her eyes widened as her cheeks brightened. "Now? Am I not too brown?"

He gazed over her braided chignon. The children passed a pinecone between them, seemingly oblivious to the adults' conversation. "You glow, and, right now, I *will* kiss you."

He dipped his head and claimed her. His mouth hummed as she allowed him the liberty. Warm and sweet, it was even better than last night. He trailed his hands down her shoulders. A hint of honeysuckle from her tresses hit his nose, and then blended with the light perfume of the marigolds. Oh, this was better than the Masked Ball, and she knew it was William, not a figment of Whimple.

When her arms rounded his waist, a tingle coursed through his spine.

This wasn't what he'd planned, but he surely didn't mind. He didn't realize how alone he'd felt until he shared this moment with Gaia.

She pried herself free and, with the back of her hand, wiped at her mouth. "We must stop this."

"You are right. I can't keep going around kissing you." He again scanned the area to ensure they'd maintained their privacy. "Someone will talk if I lunge at you every minute. Though I wish it were Mary talking, I don't know what to do to help her. She's trapped in silence. I'm helpless."

Gaia slipped her palm into his, and led him back to the children. "Tell me, have you been singing to her?"

"Yes, 'til I'm almost hoarse. Mary's very fussy. I haven't found good caregivers who understand what to do. The last thought me silly."

"William, you probably looked silly singing with blocks, but that can't matter; it's how she'll learn to read or know her letters."

She'd used his given name. He swallowed instead of kissing her again. "I'd listen to a friend, if she still wanted to be mine after my behavior last night. I took advantage of you."

After straightening the ribbons to Mary's straw bonnet, Gaia pivoted to him. "I was alone, half-seeing. I am to blame."

"Why had you been crying? Why were you away from your family? Had I interrupted a lovers' moment; one belonging to Whimple?"

"'Twas no moment; a month ago, he asked me to wait there for a first dance, but he forgot, or someone lovelier took his attention."

Then he was a bigger dunce than William had expected. "Is that why you'd been crying? Did he break your heart?"

She squinted at him, a crinkle settling on her forehead. Her eyes held a secret but her reddened lips said no. "It was some bad news from home; something of no consequence now."

She looked away, but the hurt lingered in her voice. Something evil had happened, and it took something from her. If not the loss of Whimple, what?

"William, let's discuss how I can help Lady Mary. I don't want compensation or charity. I would do it as a friend. My aunt's here for a full month. She won't mind chaperoning. This is a small village… I wouldn't want anyone forming the wrong idea of my helping you. I'm not Mary's governess or your... doxie."

Oh, he'd make sure on both counts, even pounding Stelford if he insinuated anything. "Of course your aunt can come, and we'll take care with your reputation. I suppose that means no more kisses?"

She nodded.

It was for the best, though the notion of a goodbye kiss held an appeal. "Well, you can't blame a man for asking, but I am grateful. I just want to do something to show my gratitude."

He glanced at her stained shoes. "Your father can't afford all the fine things that you and your siblings deserve, but I can."

She shook her head. "No. I want to be a benefit to your little girl. Some of the things I've tried with Timothy should work."

Fine, he'd figure out some way to show his appreciation for her efforts with Mary. "You don't know what it means to me for you to accept. Your kindness—"

"You accepted the Duke?" A dense patch of winter aconite, deep jonquil flowers were torn asunder, and one of the small Telfair girls jumped out. Her brown eyes were large like walnuts.

Gaia paled. Her voice sounded strained. "No, Helena, you don't understand."

"I saw him kiss you. He must've proposed. The Duke made an offer to my sister!" The younger Miss Telfair ran like a firecracker toward the house. Her deep-brown chignon unraveled and flopped at her high speed.

"Helena!" Gaia attempted to go after her, but he grabbed her around the waist and held her in place.

"No, let her go. It's perfect. Let's agree to marry."

The duke had surely lost his mind.

Gaia struggled within his strong arms, but he wouldn't release her. Near tears, she gave up and withered against him. "This is terrible. How am I to explain this? You can't want me as a wife. No one can."

His low voice stroked her ear. "You're speaking nonsense. As my intended, no one will think anything untoward if you visit Ontredale. With a proper chaperone like that aunt of yours, you can visit as much as you like. If I send you a gift, as my fiancée, you can accept it. A proper fiancé is bound to protect his future wife. I shall always protect you."

"How is this proper?" She shook her head as her slippers sank into the creeping wave of marigolds. They needed to just take hold of her ankles and pull her free. "My dearest friend says that you only wed for love."

"No." He cradled her shoulders until all her weight fell on him. "Some marriages are practical, built on a foundation of respect and honor. You have mine."

The smooth feel of his damask waistcoat coddled her cheek. The scent of his skin, spicy tarragon, swept over her, weakening her resolve. "I respect you, too. You seem an honorable man, and a good father, but this is too much. You don't know anything about me. I could have secrets."

"Don't you want to marry?"

"Yes; a name of my own is a dream."

He kissed the crown of her head. "You would actually have three; Duchess, the Duchess of Cheshire, and Gaia St. Landon. I know enough about you to know this is right. Think of the utility of this marriage; two friends bonded by respect and faithfulness, sharing a mission to protect our families."

How could Gaia be faithful? Kissing the wrong man and her own wanton heritage should be enough proof that she couldn't. She dropped her chin. "This is madness."

"It would be perfect: you helping Mary, me protecting and aiding the Telfairs. You'd never become a governess to Master Timothy or anyone."

Oh, why did she prattle on about Mr. Telfair's plans? Now William could use her fears to sway her. She should just tell him she wanted to marry a black like his servant Albert. She opened her mouth, but those words wouldn't come out.

"Agree, Gaia."

"We can't. You should marry someone beautiful, with milky skin like Julia."

"I don't want your sister and, as for you, dearest Gaia, let me see thy countenance, let me hear thy sweet voice, and thy countenance is comely."

"Song of Solomon?"

His smile widened. "You can't be a vicar's son and be unscathed."

That passage also talked about being black and comely; the duke couldn't have meant that. She squirmed again, but her strength lessened within his firm grip. "Why me?"

"Why not you? Gaia, this alliance will help your sisters. Don't you want to make sure they have the best opportunities? How could they not, with a sister who became a duchess?"

With no one, not even Elliot, closer to proposing to Julia, the girl might as well be fitted with a spinster's cloak.

Though she wanted to yank Helena's braids, all her sisters, Helena, Lydia, and even Julia would be elevated. That had to be good. They were all sisters, despite the foulness of Gaia's blood.

"When I speak with your father, I will let him know it will be a long engagement, lasting through the summer."

Her father? Oh, he meant Mr. Telfair. She clasped the duke's arm, tapping it in protest. "How does that make it better?"

He leaned down, and his warm breath caressed her neck. "Given enough time, you'll see the rightness of our match, and, if not, you can break the engagement. It's a woman's right, but I can think of no one else who should possess my name."

A name. He wanted to give her a name. Pulse throbbing, her chin lifted of its own volition, as if to give the duke full access to her jaw, to allow his pant to cascade her bare neck, unprotected by the collar of her pelisse. She stiffened, throwing off the delusional thought. "You're rich and handsome. You don't need an arranged marriage."

"I do need a wife, someone who I trust to help raise Mary. I'd rather wed a friend than a careless smile that pretends to love me. Gaia, I don't believe you'd break vows and scandalize my name with affairs." An edge settled in his voice, then cleared as he released her. "What say you?"

Her mind swam in a sea of conflicts. Engaged to the duke? If their marriage weren't based on love, wouldn't she stray just like her mother? Did wantonness swim in her blood? She blinked, hoping clarity would enter her vision. It wouldn't.

"You will be protecting me from the throngs of ladies... Oh, how did you put it... Weighing my pockets... or, worse, attempting to compromise me? It happens to men, you know."

Timothy gave a hoot, and Lady Mary waddled to chase him. They stopped in front of Gaia, each child eyeing her, as if they knew she had a big decision.

The little girl looked at her with a wide, silent grin. Her heart fluttered as she remembered Timothy's first clear words. God gave Gaia a talent to care for His little ones. If she didn't try, how much time would be wasted, before Mary received help? Maybe this was why Gaia existed.

"This will solve all our problems, Gaia… lovely Gaia."

His voice sounded so confident, as if this had been his plan all along, not Helena's creation.

His hands tightened on her elbows, and he eased the tension in her limbs. "Trust me. Take a chance. Share my name."

She must be dizzy, but his arguments swayed her. This could help a little girl, and keep Gaia from being a governess. Their union would improve the lot of her family. And at last she'd have a name. How could she not?

She licked her lips. "Shouldn't you be on bended knee or something?"

He spun her in the circle of his arms. "Let's just say I did, and we skip to a congratulatory kiss."

Before she weakened anymore to the glint in his sea-blue eyes, she pushed on his chest. "Go see Mr. Telfair."

* * *

William stepped away from Gaia. This was perfect. The unbearable memories of his wedded bliss had blinded him to the obvious solution... a marriage of convenience. He shuffled down the path, inhaling the spring scent of the gilded flowers: marigolds, aconite, and buttercups; the perfect nectar for an almost perfect morn.

Gaia would be the best wife, pretty and funny. An attraction simmered between them that, given time, would solve the heir issue.

With a wave, he turned for a last glimpse. Gaia leaned over Mary. His heart clenched when the child went easily into her arms. She'd take care of his Mary. They'd have a quiet, honorable life. Why hadn't he seen it before?

One foot after the other, he walked the trail. This felt right. Gaia would help his girl, and give his daughter the love and affection Elizabeth denied.

But what of Gaia's affection for Whimple? He fisted one hand into the other. Had he just placed himself in jeopardy? Like Elizabeth, would she eventually stray, too?

Gaia wasn't immune to William. He could keep her so, right? Possessing a natural amount of male vanity didn't stop his gut from burning at the notion of Gaia turning cold to his touch.

Shuddering inwardly, he entered the threshold. The house was in an uproar: Mrs. Monlin crying, dancing children; too late to beg off now. He wiped his brow, and pulled off his gloves.

Mrs. Monlin swiped at her eyes and shoved him into the parlor. "My brother will be down in a few moments. The cold night air has taken a toll on his strength this morning."

She sat him on the burgundy sofa, but kept fidgeting until she popped up. Her puce gown floated like a bell, swishing about her ankles. "I'll go see what's keeping Mr. Telfair."

As she left, Mrs. Telfair entered, bearing a tray of scones and a pot of steaming tea. Her forehead held crinkled lines.

He might as well ease the mother's mind. "I know this is sudden, but I would be honored to receive Miss Telfair's hand."

Mrs. Telfair slipped into her chair, but a strain stayed on her face. Even her eyes looked weak, as if they'd leak at any moment. "It's not mine to give. She agreed to this?"

He nodded.

She put a hand to her jaw. "You know she has feelings... Her opinions.... She claims to love—"

"I know about the plant-loving Mr. Whimple. I love plants, too. Gaia is smart enough to know the difference between an infatuation and lifelong security."

The woman righted herself in her seat. The buxom, but pretty, Mrs. Telfair pushed a red curl up into her mobcap as she leaned closer. "Do you really care for her?"

His throat dried. A joke or vagueness wouldn't do for the honest, almond-shaped eyes blinking at him. He left the sofa and stalked to the creamy mantle. Moving the fine garniture vases stationed on the right to the center, he formed the words on his tongue; careful ones. "I respect her very much. And her direction will benefit my daughter. My Mary is mute."

Mrs. Telfair's voice was laced with sorrow. "I see, but love is important."

Tracing the pink porcelain of the tallest of the three vases with his thumb, he shifted his stance. "It's best to focus on the benefits of this arrangement. It will serve both families well."

A hand, soft and pudgy, tugged at his shoulder. "What if Gaia decides she wants love?"

He turned to Mrs. Telfair and caught a wide-eyed, sympathetic gaze. "I shall do my hardest to spoil her with the comfort and security of my position. My care and concern are not fleeting, not tossed aside for new or old passions." The years had taught him how to be indulgent, even doting; and he wasn't away to war this time to strain relations.

Fussing noises of warring siblings, older adult siblings, filtered into the parlor. Mrs. Monlin and Mr. Telfair entered. His hair held a little grey powder, as did the edges of his dark coat. He straightened his glasses and shook free from his sister's tucking and brushing of his attire. "Everyone, leave me and the Duke. Sarah, make sure my sister is away from the keyhole."

The door slammed shut behind the ladies' hasty exit. Mr. Telfair tapped the pianoforte as he continued a slow effort across the room. "Take a seat and say your piece."

"I'd rather stand." William crossed in front of him. "I'd like your permission to wed your daughter, Gaia Telfair."

"She has no dowry. We have few connections. I don't want her subjected to the cruelty of joining a higher class."

William's posture stiffened, as if he were giving a report to his military superiors. "No one who has met Miss Telfair, who has seen the wit, her sharpness of mind, would think less of her. I certainly wouldn't allow it."

The man nodded, as if the verbal parry were acceptable. Then he tugged on the wide revers of his midnight coat. "I haven't seen you but a few times at the church, your father's church. I can't give her to heathens. Pagan blood is catching."

This was a new route of interrogation, one with a sinister bent. Why? William straightened his shoulders. "My lack of attendance is an oversight. It will be corrected."

Mr. Telfair nodded, even as a grimace filled his face. Did Gaia's father not want his daughter to marry well? Didn't all men want security for their daughters?

"Your father was a good man. He did me a valuable favor a year before Gaia's birth. It would be ironic for our families to have a connection now. Hasn't he told you of our friendship?"

What was the bird driving at? And why would this keep William from Gaia? "If my father did you a favor, then this union is repayment."

Telfair sank into a chair near the fireplace and adjusted his low heel. "I don't think he'd want that, not this bargain." He coughed, as if to hide something. "It is our custom that the elder girl marries before a younger."

"I'm not Jacob of the Bible." William tucked his arms behind his back. "I have no intentions of waiting seven years, or committing the crime of bigamy."

This brought a chuckle to Telfair's lips. "So, you *are* conversant in the ways of God. A point in your favor. She will need a strong hand to keep her well-grounded."

Papa's training was good for something, but why did it seem Telfair's opinion of Gaia was so low? Had she done something in her younger years? Nonsense. William leaned forward. "Telfair, what is your true objection? I am a man of some means. This elevation will help all your daughters."

"I had my own expectations for Gaia. My son will need her always. I want her to take care of him when I'm no longer able."

Ah, the governess business. "As her husband, I will make it my responsibility to make sure Master Timothy is well cared for. If you give me the honor of her hand, I will be a doting older brother to all the Telfairs."

"And what if scandal comes and nasty things are said of Gaia? Her skin is darker than most. It's been fodder for the mean-spirited. I don't want the Telfair name disparaged, or that you say later that you are injured by some means of deceit."

What was he insinuating? There was another story here, probably the thing that had made Gaia cry. A fierce sense of protection filled William, puffing out his chest. "I will protect her and the Telfair name with my life."

"I'll trust you are a man of your word. I don't know how she could be what you want, especially with my first wife's ideas about marriage."

So, Telfair's first marriage wasn't good. Join his personal club. Yet how could he besmirch Gaia? There was something evil about the man's smile, but, being plagued by his own scandals, William wasn't hunting for others. He drew his arms behind his back. The tightness of his stance should tell Mr. Telfair the seriousness of his commitment. "We will have a long engagement, and if she decides that she must break our engagement, I'll let her."

The old man shook his head. "Cheshire, you have thought of everything."

Telfair must believe Gaia's feelings for Whimple were strong. If she couldn't keep her vows, yearning for the botanist, William would gladly let her go and spare himself the misery of another scandal. He cleared his throat. "If there is a break, I'll even give you four thousand pounds as a dowry for her. I need an answer, plain and simple. Do I have your consent?"

Telfair rose up on wobbly legs and held out his hand. "Only a fool could turn away a man so rich. You have my consent. Send her in to see me."

He swiped his damp palm on his coat, shook Telfair's hand, and then walked out of the parlor. Part of William wanted to wipe his hands again from dealing with the old man.

Gaia sat on the floor near the show table, with her back against the wall and Mary on her lap. In low tones, she counted the child's fingers.

Mary must've thought it a game. She tried to wiggle her hands, as if to avoid the numbering.

"So Mr. Telfair said no? I didn't think—"

"On the contrary." He bent and took Mary from Gaia, then

helped the lady stand. "He's given his consent, and wishes to see you."

Gaia's face paled. She reached for her lenses, as if to clean them, but he suspected she hid a tear. "Well, I'll go to him."

"Come to Ontredale tomorrow."

Her eyes widened. "That's too soon. I won't be ready to see you."

He tugged on his gloves and hoped to appear indifferent. "Won't be ready to spend time with Mary? How about the week's end?"

She nodded and slipped away, as if his breath held fire.

What made her so fearful? Maybe her attachment to Whimple was stronger than he'd assessed. A practical marriage of friends was for the best. God opened blind eyes. What of near-sighted ones? Maybe he needed to start praying again for things like that.

He climbed into his landau and waited for the horses to move and the wind to wash his mind of defeat. No, he wouldn't lose this time, so he had to be sure Gaia understood his offer and his requirements for fidelity. If she did, this could be a good marriage. But had he learned enough since Elizabeth to make a second one work?

CHAPTER FOURTEEN

The Consequences of Yes

"Wake up, sleepy head," Aunt shook the mattress.

Gaia lifted her heavy lids then sat up in her bed. Engaged for five days, and already the world was different, except for Mr. Telfair. No words of congratulations, just of warning to forget her origin. How could she do that? What type of person would that make her if she wed William in deceit?

Aunt shifted the pillows and plucked curl papers from Gaia's head. "Time is wasting."

"What am I late for now?"

"Just one more fitting," Aunt tugged on Gaia's shoulder then gave her a hug. Could the woman be any happier, even sending for her mantua-maker from London? Well, at least someone enjoyed this engagement.

Casting a longing glance to her old muted dresses, Gaia pulled on her robe, tangling her fingers in the drawstring. "Is there nothing suitable in my wardrobe? Surely, the brown-checked one is fine. What of the new dress I started? The lovely pink."

"Those rags." Aunt sashayed to the furnishing. The ruffles in her fancy burgundy-striped gown fluttered as she yanked Gaia's pale muslin garbs off the shelves and onto the floor.

"Why dress like a peasant when the duke can send you yards of sarsenet?" She pulled the lace and a bolt of light-blue fabric, sunnier than Gaia's bedchamber walls, from a bundle of other silks William had sent. Aunt wrapped it about her apple-shaped head.

Gaia looked at the woman, her mother's best friend. The questions couldn't wait anymore, not with this farce of an engagement readying to be announced to the world. "I call you Aunt, because you always loved me, took time with me when my mother died, but we both know that I share no Telfair blood. Who is my father?"

Mrs. Monlin's cheerfulness shattered. The sheepish grin disappeared, and she paled lighter than a sheet. "No one was closer to Delilah than I. You are my brother's daughter, a Telfair."

Gaia's hands shook beneath the bedcovers. "A lesser Telfair, who is now getting to wear finery like my sisters because a duke sent them. No more denials to the black Telfair. Your brother says I'm not his. He wouldn't lie about something so important. I have to know. Was I conceived in rape?"

Aunt put her hand to her ears, as if that would end the questions. "Don't ruin this, Gaia. You are my brother's daughter. The world knows you as such. Soon, you will be a duchess. That will end all questions."

Sarah opened the door. "What is going on in here?"

"I'm trying to make a duchess, and I'm not getting very much help. Speak with her, get her to understand to leave the past in the past." Still draped in the fabric, Aunt moved from the room like a fashionable shepherdess.

Gaia lay back down and *pretended* her world hadn't changed, and that one careless word couldn't set everything aflame.

Sarah straightened the rolls of cloth; such soft vibrant colors. "What is the problem? Do you disapprove of the duke's taste?"

William did have a fine sense of fashion. Fabrics Gaia had only dreamed of wearing now sat on her bed. Her neck heated, thinking of him selecting things for her. Yet again, he claimed another first, the first to make her blush with his attention. The creamy leather shoes he sent yesterday sat wrapped in paper on her bed table. Her heart slowed. All this would go away when he learned the truth. "I am a lie. I can't create another. I have to tell him."

Her stepmother looked up. "You have to do what you think is best, but, before you do something that could affect our family, make sure you give him a chance to know the whole of it."

Sarah marched closer and dug inside the covers, grabbed Gaia's arm, and towed her to the vanity. "He won't understand if you hide."

How could he know all, when Gaia didn't? She put a hand to each cheek and leaned over the flat oak surface, bearing her brush and the duke's jewelry gifts. "Everything is changing. Why did I accept?"

Sarah picked up the pewter comb, and began smoothing a section of Gaia's crumpled curls. "He made you an offer you couldn't refuse. You are not still thinking of Elliot?"

"Not really. And he's not thinking of me." Elliot hadn't stopped by. His parents visited yesterday. They said he was busy, surveying a section of a bog. Swampy soup was more important than questioning her engagement.

When Sarah snapped a knotted tress too hard, Gaia reared up. "Ouch. My frizzy hair. It's nothing like Julia's. She should be the duchess, not a... Mulatto, black, servant, governess. I'm so beneath the duke."

"Hush," Sarah made a sympathetic *tsk* sound with her tongue. "You are a sweet, beautiful gift of God. This family, my Timothy, we would suffer so without you. Don't you know your worth?"

How could Gaia, with all the falsehoods and secrets? She buried her face against Sarah's soft middle. "I can't marry like this. How will he handle hearing the truth from someone other than me? At least with Elliot, he had the benefit of knowing my character these twenty years."

"Dear, all the best and some of the so-so of the genteel population have visited and offered congratulations, but not Elliot. You are not a priority to him, Gaia. Measure a man by what he does, not his words or a vision you've painted in your head."

Gaia pushed hot air out of her lungs. "You must think I'm a ninny. Cheshire is handsome and rich. Any girl would be lucky to have him."

"You are lucky, but so is he. You're not like others."

"That's the problem, Sarah."

"Gaia, whether right or wrong, you follow your heart. You always have. It takes the right man, a God-sent man, to see the beauty of your spirit, and you can't think of Elliot. You've outgrown the need for a one-sided love."

Loving Elliot held safety. She knew her place. They were neighbors. Her heart withered within her chest as fear of being shunned or hated by William invaded her mind. That was it. The loss of William frightened her more than anything.

She slumped at the vanity. The cold wood top with its rough grain reminded her of strength and provision and truth. "I must tell Cheshire. No matter what happens, he must know, and it must be said by me."

"Give him the opportunity to respond wrongly and make mistakes. Be willing to forgive, if you expect understanding. I wouldn't be surprised if he has secrets, too, or opinions that will require your understanding. I know he cares for you. He's promised a long engagement. Find the right time to tell him."

Her stepmother's words vibrated within Gaia's head, as did what she'd overheard from the duke and his friend on the Hallows' balcony. The *she,* the blackmail notes. Maybe Gaia and the duke were equally yoked, both steeped in dark mysteries.

Trying to sweep aside her concerns, she looked on the vanity for a necklace to wear, something to clasp jittery finger to. She avoided the fine gold locket William had sent, and picked up Sarah's coral strand. "I'd like to wear this, Mother. It will remind me that someone believes in me."

"Of course, dear," with a kiss to Gaia's cheek, Sarah prayed. "God, give my daughter the courage to be happy, to enjoy a bright future."

The only way to get this bright future to happen was to survive the dark patches. Was the friendship she shared with William enough to withstand all the secrets being exposed?

The afternoon came too soon for Gaia. As the carriage arrived at Ontredale, her pulse started to race. Aunt Tabby held her hand, as if she'd escape or fling herself through the opening. Nothing was further from the truth. She'd rather hide in the dark seats, and let the quilted silk-lined walls envelope her and escape everyone's notice.

Aunt pretended as if Gaia had never asked about her true paternity, and Gaia didn't have the heart to try again. Aunt bubbled, overflowing with joy at this engagement. No one should take her joy away, not even a pretend niece desperate for the truth.

She hadn't quite worked out how to tell her intended he was marrying someone passing for white. How did that get brought up? Excuse me, my lord, but I'm not what I seem. A funny thing happened when I told *my father* I wanted to marry.

With a rub of her temples, she filled her lungs and smoothed her cream gloves. In the past, she'd only been this nervous to see Elliot, and that longing had faded. When Sarah said he'd sent a note announcing he'd be visiting today, Gaia didn't flinch. She wouldn't change her plans to spend the day with Mary or William for anything.

A footman arrived and opened the door. Albert and one other servant stood at the entry, as did William. Did they suspect that the duke's betrothed was no higher than they?

Stop it, Gaia. No one can tell her secret. No one would know, not until she told.

Cheshire walked down the steps. The handsome man wore a bottle-green waistcoat and olive breeches. His chestnut tailcoat whipped from side to side as he launched down the final step. Taking her hand, he secured it on his well-muscled arm, and then gave Aunt his other.

"You ladies look very well today."

"Thank you. My niece looks particularly sweet in the mint-green silk you sent, but there wasn't enough for matching gloves."

Wanting to jump off the steps and into a hole, Gaia stopped in place, prohibiting their procession. "Aunt, Cheshire has been too generous."

A smile bloomed on William's countenance. Must he take pleasure in her discomfort? Wicked man.

"An oversight I'll correct with my next gift. A man should be generous to the woman he wishes to marry."

Aunt giggled, and Gaia's breath faltered. The glint in his eyes spoke volumes. He meant it. Why did it feel as if the 'of convenience' part of their arrangement was slipping away? Did he want a full marriage, one with love and tenderness?

He marshaled them into the main hall. "Ladies, let me take you on a tour of Ontredale."

Aunt Tabby raised her head and peered toward the

daunting stairs. "Might we just view the first level and enjoy some refreshments?"

"Of course; wouldn't want you to become winded. You've seen the drawing room and dining room. This way to the library and the grand balcony."

Letting Aunt and the duke continue forward, Gaia stopped and admired the marble floor.

Passing a few more servants, one polishing brass hardware, another arranging fresh flowers on the round table by the massive stairs, another dusting porcelain sculptures, she lifted her head high even as a shiver skirted her spine. The duke must possess great riches. Under normal circumstances, he wouldn't associate with the Telfairs, a family of such low connections. And now a woman with a dark secret was marrying him.

Albert walked past. His deeply bronzed face held a smile. "Do you need something, miss?"

She shook her head at the only other person like her, one serving this good man, and rushed to catch up with the duke.

William's countenance held a pleasant smile. He seemed to enjoy showing Aunt his collection of Dresdens or describing the number of looms it took to weave the fancy silver tapestry filling the library, or the lengths the late duke and some great-grandfather went to secure the wall of books.

Gaia's fingers fidgeted, and she made a death grip on the fat water pearl centered in the coral beads. Not looking, she tripped over the gold and cream fringe of a burgundy rug running the length of the long hall.

A massive arm went around her, steadying her.

Her heart beat hard, and for a moment she became lost in William's sea-blue eyes. It was as if he were saying everything would be well, to trust him.

But how could he trust her if he didn't know her secret, if she didn't share it?

William's voice remained smooth, as though nothing had happened. "Now, let me show you the balcony views from the back of the house."

Aunt clapped her hands. Her wide bonnet with the silky crimson ribbon on its brim was one of Sarah's creations. It billowed with the breeze, and she disengaged with William to clamp it down. "Simply beautiful grounds, your lordship."

Gaia gripped the rail and looked out at the sight. Beautiful wasn't the word. In awe, she opened her mouth. The greenery spread far and wide. As the cliffs dropped away, blue-green waters the color of William's eyes became visible, filling the space between man and heaven.

They stood too far to hear the foamy waves crest against the rocks. Yet she could hear it in her mind, could imagine the coolness of the sea wetting her bare feet. It would be worth ruining her shoes just for a dip. When she inhaled deeply, she sniffed a hint of the salt.

"What say you, *my* lady?"

His emphasis on the word 'my' started Gaia's pulse racing.

He stepped from behind to her side, grasping her palm. "Is the view to your liking?"

As a tangle of words flooded her throat, all she could do was nod. She pulled away and rubbed her arms, as if the air were cool enough to give her a chill. He couldn't know it was her fear of liking him too much making her feet cold. Glancing over the rail again, Gaia noted the curve of the massive stone stairs leading below. At the bottom lay a path of woven bricks. The line of them surrounded three circular gardens. Roses and other plantings gave the floral gardens a varying height of pinks and yellows. Elliot would know the names of the flowers, but it was unnecessary to distinguish them to enjoy the tranquil paradise.

"In the distance, you can spy a ship coming to England." A deep sigh left William. "I know I often looked for cliffs and hoped to catch a glimpse of Ontredale when we returned from Spain. It was rare to come here as a lad, but those times were memorable."

Aunt came to Gaia's left. "Yes, Your Grace went to war in the Regiments. Gaia, can you imagine our dear Duke in regimentals?"

Gaia's face fevered thinking of anything touching William's broad shoulders.

Pushing a smile from his lips, he moved to Aunt, offering her his arm. "Mrs. Monlin, lunch should be ready in the drawing room. Miss Telfair, if you'd like to stay and enjoy the view a little longer, I'll return for you."

Alone with William, in paradise. "No, I'll follow."

As they walked down the hallway covered in fleur de lis stampings, Gaia studied the grand portraits of women and men. Large gilded frames at least eight feet wide and nine or ten feet long hung every few inches; men and women, all ages, captured on canvas. Some were dressed in military garb with strawberry red coats. Some were genteel woman sitting with their children. Others were old, stern-looking men. What relation were they to William? Would they approve of the association he formed with the poor mulatto?

Never.

The eyes of the stills all now seemed to bear down upon her.

She stamped her foot against the dark-chocolate-stained floor. "God, why can't I feel worthy?"

William appeared, almost out of thin air. His brow popped up as his gaze swept over her. "Are you well, Gaia?" his voice lowered to a whispery kiss just for her ear. "More misery prayers? I must not being doing a good job of keeping your smile."

Her breath faltered. "I think I just need some air."

"Stay here. Mrs. Monlin, and let me situate you in the

drawing room. Then I'll return to take my fiancée for a stroll in the park below. Would that be all right?"

Aunt Tabby cocked her head. "I don't know."

"I'll be on my best behavior, and you'll get to enjoy Mrs. Wingate's latest pastries. She might even have a jelly prepared just for you."

An alligator-sized grin filled her oval face. "You'll not get in too much trouble by yourselves. Lead the way, sir."

They left Gaia by a pristine white sculpture of some Grecian goddess. Aunt giggled all the way down the hall.

Gaia leaned back against the wall and absorbed the quiet, so different from noisy Chevron. No siblings to watch out for. No terrors running and screaming their heads off.

But no Timothy. To be here meant missing their lessons. If she were to wed anyone, how would that change her relationship with her brother?

She stopped, twiddling her fingers. Why was she getting so bothered? She closed her eyes and chanted, "He's my friend. Just a friend. There is equality in that."

"You called?"

Lids slitting to a hair, she viewed William hovering over her. One of his hands pressed the wall above her. He leaned in close, near enough for his lips to be an inch from hers.

Before his tarragon scent weakened her resistance to his charm, she stepped from him.

His laugh sounded, as if it held a secret. "I didn't think you scared so easily."

Before she could retort, he brought his other palm into view. A creamy shawl with tiny rosettes about the trim hung from his fingers. "It's a little windy outside."

"Another gift? I can't."

"This was my cousin's late wife's, the former lady of this manor. I found it when we opened the house. Neither the house nor the shawl had been used in a long time. Something we shall change."

"Then I definitely couldn't. That is something that should be passed down to Mary."

"In due time. I shall let my friend, my fiancée, wear it." He slipped the fabric over her shoulders.

"Would your great-grandmother approve? Would any of your relations approve of us? Miss Smythen thinks I should be a servant. I can't say I disagree."

A blast of hot air huffed from his nostrils. "Our age difference is not so much. And my cousin has a limited understanding. She thinks goodness and wealth are mutually exclusive."

"When she learns of this *engagement,* she'll be livid."

"I don't care what *she* thinks." He spun Gaia and pointed to the painting. The golden trim shimmered with candlelight from the wall sconces. "And any of these St. Landons, captured in oils or watercolors, seeing your sweetness and intelligence, would approve too. But shouldn't it matter most what we think?"

Gaia stared into his sea-blue eyes and wanted to scream 'you're marrying a mulatto'. But those precious windows into his soul silenced her, speaking of things she couldn't discern. Was it tenderness, kinship, or something else?

Overwhelmed, she fingered the delicate tassels of his gift and remembered how he'd said *she*. "Is Miss Smythen the *she* you and Mr. Stelford talked of the night of the Hallows' ball?"

He blinked a few times, and a smile started from his cheeks. Dimples? "Our walk awaits."

She shook her head. They were to be married, and he didn't trust her with his secrets. Well she shouldn't judge, because she couldn't tell him her truth. Settling her nerves, she gripped his arm a little tighter and let him lead.

As he helped her down the sandstone stairs, she enjoyed the whistle in the breeze and the mixture of sweet fragrances erupting from the sculpted hedges. Perfect rectangles of henna and purples lined their path. Her arms pimpled. How could she be the mistress of such a place?

"See, I knew it was a little chilly." He patted her hand, his gloveless fingers interlocking with hers. "What are you thinking? I understand shy Gaia and nervous Gaia. I treasure forthright Gaia, but this version I don't know."

She looked to the stone path, for she couldn't tell him her thoughts. She wasn't ready to be shunned by him. "Where are your friend and your cousin?"

He lifted her chin. The rough skin of his knuckles jarred, making her stop and seek his face.

His gaze settled upon her, even as his lips formed a grimace. "Off in town. I won't have any third parties causing misunderstandings between us. Miss Smythen will be leaving soon. She is the *she*. My cousin has made a pest of herself, trying to coerce me into marrying her, even to the point of compromise. Our engagement now protects me from her tricks."

He exposed a secret to Gaia. Her heart thumped a little harder. "Why not just toss her out, make her go away, if she's bothering you?"

"Even as annoying as she is, she's family. Family is everything. Our family will be everything." He looked back at the house, and then nudged her forward. They walked a little farther. "So, there; have I passed one test?"

"I wasn't testing you much." She leveled her shoulders. "So far."

An ease settled on his countenance and he siphoned a deep breath. "Good. I like goals. Making you comfortable in St. Landon territory is a priority."

To be a priority to anyone was an enigma. She bundled deeper into the shawl and kept up with his long stride, deeper into the garden.

"I have always missed Devonshire. Spring makes it beautiful, with the flowers forming their buds." He bent and picked a buttercup and put it behind her ear. "Gaia means 'Mother Earth'. Seems this place is made for your enjoyment."

Great. Mr. Telfair named her dirt. How fitting.

"Sweet Gaia. Beautiful Gaia." The feel of his hand tracing her jaw to smooth away a lock of hair made her pulse speed. "You're still in your old shoes."

She licked her lip and tried to hide the turbulence stirring in her bosom. "They are so very fine. I didn't want to ruin things so soon."

"I see." His voice lowered and held a bit of sadness. "It's so hard to know what pleases. Well, that's a St. Landon tradition."

"What do you mean?"

He lifted his chin to the sky. "I wasn't a good son to the great reverend."

That didn't sound right. The late vicar seemed stern, pounding his pulpit, but how could he not approve of William? "I don't understand."

"He never wanted me to become a peer. He'd rather I follow in the church, not the military."

"I can't quite see you making sermons."

A smirk popped onto his countenance. "You'd be surprised how much scripture I know, taught to me by the great man, though I don't think he knew I'd be swaying my fiancée with King Solomon's words. Maybe you should quote it. *Let him kiss me with the kisses of his mouth.*"

Those weren't the verses that came to her head. No, the ones that quoted being black and comely repeated in her mind. She shook her head. "We promised Aunt to behave."

He patted her arm and led her a little farther. His tone sounded distant, "A man can try."

Gaia didn't like him downcast because of her ambivalence,

but what could she say, except ugly truths that would drive this good man away? "Did you and the late duchess visit?"

"Never." His shoulders shrugged. "I was away in the Peninsula, or caught up in Parliament, handling my uncle's affairs. Always something."

"She would have loved it."

He scuffed his boot and turned over a rock. "I don't think so. Close to the end, nothing I did seemed to garner favor."

William seemed uncomfortable, like a flame of anger existed beneath his cool exterior, but Gaia needed to press to satisfy her curiosity. "Will our arranged marriage be similar?"

"Dear Lord, no." He released her and rubbed a hand through his hair. A dark curl flopped onto his brow.

Knowing it could cause strife, but not able to stop, she asked, "Was there much sentiment?"

"Ah, forthright Gaia, my friend with the impertinent questions has returned." He stared out toward the cliffs. "Oh, fool that I was, I fell in love. Sadly, she did not. I blame myself. I should've done more to please her."

"It is difficult to know what pleases anyone."

A harsh, deep sigh blasted from his nostrils. "But one has to take time to build strong relationships. It's why I promised a long engagement. You are nothing like her, so this marriage will be better."

She adjusted her spectacles, as if that would help decipher his meanings. "Are you still angry with her and your father?"

His mouth twitched, as if he debated responding. How deep was his well of resentment, and would it spill into other areas of his life?

"You must free yourself of anger. You can't wish a memory or live person to change. You can't keep hoping for them to become pleased or supportive." Dressing differently, hiding behind a mask, or even marrying well, changed nothing. Mr. Telfair still didn't seem pleased with Gaia, as if marrying a peer brought no honor to the Telfairs.

Heart dipping low, she cleared her throat and pushed her disappointment to the back of her mind. "What will make our marriage, if we go through with it, different?"

His lips thinned. Maybe he didn't know either, and that frightened her to her core.

"Gaia, I'm wiser now. I'll never take another day for granted with someone I care for."

Care for? She could feel her face trying to form a smile at the thought of him caring for her. Could he learn to love her? And her him? Did he care enough now that her race didn't matter? "We all have shortcomings. Maybe we should pray each day for His blessings to guide us."

"So the lack of prayer wrought so much unhappiness in my first marriage? I'd expect that type of answer from my father, the late *Reverend St. Landon*." He tipped an imaginary top hat to accent the flourish he did with the pronouncement of the name.

"You like to joke, but guilt is no joke."

He walked behind her and pulled her against his chest. His head rested on hers as they watched the tide. "I'll pretend to agree, if it means I can keep you out here a little longer."

She pulled her shawl closer and fought the urge to turn and burrow beneath his jacket. "So we will be happy?"

"You wouldn't betray ... our commitment." The muscles in his forearm stiffened. "A new subject. Let's pretend my gifts pleased you."

Chilled, she rubbed her hands together. "There's no need for pretense. I like them all, but I haven't started helping Mary yet. That makes me feel guilty."

He bundled her fingers with his. "Well, aren't we a pair."

Even with the wind stirring, having him about her, warming her strengthened her. If one couldn't be loved, maybe friendship was the answer.

A sigh left him. "Tell me, why do you think so much of Mr. Whimple?"

"I don't know. It's a hundred little reasons. His family and the Hallows always looked in on us the year we lost my mother. At first, Elliot was like an older brother to Julia and me. I suppose I have always fancied him. He was so kind and strong, and then he rescued Timothy. Yes, that had to be when it changed."

"Being a hero can definitely make a heart swoon." William grunted, as if he disapproved of something. "Didn't I rescue Master Timothy twice? You should admire me greatly."

She was about to laugh when she felt the pressure of his hands sliding from her shoulders to crest at her waist, then planting at her hips. Wriggling, she took a step away.

He hefted his palms in the air. "Sorry; they have a mind of their own, especially with such feminine curves so near."

She bunched the lace about her neck. "This will be a marriage of convenience. Has something changed?"

"A week, Gaia. Days of remembering the smell of your hair, the deepening color of your irises right before I kiss you, and going to sleep in an empty bedchamber, all make me want more."

Her cheeks felt hot, but his words left her speechless.

"I need you to know that I desire you, Gaia. A marriage of convenience is how things start, not how they end."

Gaia swallowed as her pulse raced. "But this was for Lady Mary, to benefit my sisters, to keep me from becoming a governess, a name."

He stepped closer, his hand nestling her ear, smoothing a frizzing lock. "I've hidden my attraction, even denying it to myself for the longest time. If we are to be man and wife, you need to understand that this will be a real marriage, with arguments and expectations. You must be sure when you say your vows."

"Are you that sure? There is nothing that worries you? We barely know each other."

He slipped his hand away, tucking it to his side. His eyes flashed like a turbulent sea. "How did the botanist take the news of our engagement?"

Peering to the cobbles lining the path, she twisted her fingers beneath the soft shawl. "Doesn't seem to have bothered him. He hasn't showed at Chevron, but I was never a priority to him."

"Sounds as if you're over being tempted by him. Good." Gently, William pulled her close, rocking her. The motion was slow, like a soft, foaming wave. "I will be faithful to you always, and I demand the same. If you can't, or have any doubts, you must beg off and end this engagement. Infidelity hurts too many lives."

Didn't Gaia know that? If her mother had been faithful, Gaia could have had a father's love, not the dread of always missing it.

"Can you be faithful, sweet Gaia? Do you like me well enough?"

He was so serious in his words, but how could she concentrate with his thumb tracing her neck. "Yes, I like you."

"Then you will make a fine duchess, a wonderful mistress to Ontredale. What will you change when you have the run of the house?"

Mistress of Ontredale. A place to belong and a name, a worthy name. A smile bloomed in her heart. "Nothing. It's spectacular. There seem to be many servants, but I suppose you need them for the running of such a place."

"I suspect you like it quiet and more intimate like this. Maybe a spot for your audacious prayers." His voice caressed her, easing the tension in her spine. If he kept at it, she'd become rubbery, like one of those jellies Aunt loved.

His breath warmed her ear. "Have you prayed for anything

special of late?"

Except for empty words at mealtime, not a syllable had she uttered in reverence, not since the day near cliff. She was distant from God. So far from Him. She knew that now. "Nothing."

"None in general, or nothing special?"

"Nothing. Maybe your jokes have rubbed off on me, William."

His fingers stilled, locking about her abdomen. "When did you stop? I rather fancied them. Kind of wondered what you'd pray for us."

She glanced up to the clouds and wished with all her might he'd ask no more. It was hard enough finding her way through this day, their first meeting as an engaged couple. A man of almost royal blood and she…

It hadn't settled in her mind why God would allow so much bad to happen, her older brother and the twin boys' deaths, Timothy's challenges, and her mother, a victim or outright sinner? Why pray?

His lips bussed the crown of her surely-frizzing hair. "It would be hard for me to talk to you about journeying with God when I'm so wayward. I just recommend holding on to the bits of peace He offers. There's no more when you let go."

He slipped his palms to up to her elbows. "Someday you will share your thoughts with me fully."

"And you will do the same?"

A raspy acknowledgement sounded. "Well, today, just tell me what at Ontredale would please you. You can add anything."

What about saying anything? Would he still want to marry her if he knew of her scandalous birth? Would he still look at her as someone worthy to bear his name? Would his eyes darken with the passion of desiring her or fury at her deception?

Yes, standing with him, allowing him to draw her closer, as if nothing was wrong, as if they shared the same race—it was lying.

"Gaia, you are too quiet. No forthright statements. No prayers. Something is very wrong."

Her heart thumped louder. "What about a big classroom, where Timothy could come and learn?"

"Your brother would always be welcome. He'd have his own room, too, if he wanted to stay the night. And there's a big nursery on the third floor that could suit your teaching now."

"Nursery? A place for children?" The thought of a babe, another little person who would uniquely be hers, felt good, but then panic shuttled her spine. What would their child look like? Would he look like William, or be a brown baby, one whose paternity would be questioned? "Well, Lady Mary and Timothy can study there. They are children."

"So they are." He spun her from viewing the coast and waves to the folds of his cravat. "What color will your private rooms be?"

"Mine?"

"I'm not rushing you, Gaia, and I'm not planning the next few months, but a lifetime. We'll have separate bedchambers, and yours should be special." He kissed her forehead, and then leaned further to peck her cheek. "Imagine the color."

"Blue, a sunny blue, like my room now. Sarah had some left- over paint, and I thinned it to make my place special."

"I like blue. The day you invite me in will be one I treasure. You needed to know everything, all my intentions and expectations." His mouth hung dangerously close, but he didn't move. It was as if a line lay etched between them. "Is it acceptable to you?"

"I don't know. You've said a lot."

His arm stiffened as he released her. He started to pivot

toward the house. "We should go to Mary."

The second his warmth disappeared she missed him, and the openness of his eyes disappeared, too. She'd disappointed him. "Wait."

"Yes, Gaia?"

"I've never been kissed in a garden. I think that you should add this to the list of firsts."

As he rotated, she leaned into him on tiptoes and claimed his kiss.

Unlike the other times, she wasn't overwhelmed or surprised. No, she wanted William St. Landon to hold her, to partake in the power of his affection, and to make sure she hadn't ruined things. If they were going to be wed, she would tell him of her birth, but not until she was surer of herself, that the wantonness of her mother didn't lay hidden in her bones, waiting for a chance to ruin things. As quickly as her heart was turning from Elliot to William, she wasn't sure.

William folded Gaia deeper into his arms as the kiss exploded into a heated tangle of her hands clutching the folds of his cravat, a button on his waistcoat, his fingers looping into her thick chignon.

She did desire him. He hadn't misread the attraction, but what caused her reticence? What took away her prayers?

A moan left her as he nibbled along her jaw. "William. I like the smell of you."

She'd panted his name; his name, not the botanist's.

"Good."

The woman shivered and burrowed beneath his jacket. Her nails clutched his shirt fabric. He savored the plumpness of her lower lip, and teased it until Gaia opened her mouth a little wider. Only for a second did he intend to indulge in the sweetness of a deeper kiss. His heart thundered as the second stretched to minutes.

Before his thumbs ruined her chignon, he stopped and just held her close. He needed to slow down before his thoughts wandered to the long list of firsts he'd begun to create, like the first time to make love to Gaia in a garden.

Oh, things would be very well for them if she committed to the marriage, just as she'd committed to his kiss. Could she be happy with him?

Though she fit his chest as if she was meant to belong there, he couldn't risk opening up his heart completely; not until the Whimple business was done.

Yet as Elizabeth taught him, attraction, love, and faithfulness were three different things. As long as there was faithfulness and attraction, love didn't need to coexist.

Gaia wiped at her eyes. "You must think me wild to allow such liberties. I'm not a good example of a demure duchess."

How could she be so unsure of herself or the pleasure he took in being the one to lead her into folly? The change in the wind cooled his neck, prickled her forearm. He stepped back, wrenched off his jacket, and placed it on her shoulders. "We are alone, and you should be free to do and be."

"If only you'd always feel that way."

There was something in her voice. Was it fear? Ridiculous. A little more time and Gaia would settle into their engagement and forget about Whimple. This time William wouldn't lose.

CHAPTER FIFTEEN

A Routine of Hope

A second week of lessons with Mary hadn't produced much progress, but coming to Ontredale every other day, having tea with William and Aunt, and then escaping with him for a walk in the garden, had become a routine for Gaia; a nice routine, something to look forward to, as was sitting with this sweet girl in her room.

His charm and patience and Mary's exuberance were infectious.

The child looked up at her, offering a silent, toothy grin. The initial dread of everything — being engaged, working with Mary, all had lessened, almost disappeared.

Gaia could be happy in this life. If she helped the child to speak, maybe she could feel worthy of all of it.

Mary wrapped her tiny palm about Gaia's finger. With another chubby grip, she tugged on Gaia's frizzing hair.

The sea air encompassing Ontredale made it a challenge to keep a tidy bun. Williams hands in it as he soundly kissed her didn't help either. "Let's pass the toy, Mary."

The little girl's cheeks flushed as she pushed the wooden horse to Gaia. The wheels of the toy offered a muffled squeak against the thick puce carpet.

William, who stood at the door, watching, had the oddest look on his face. As if to keep his palms still, he put them behind his back. The ash-colored waistcoat puffed out of his olive tailcoat. He was large and well-built. How could she have ever mixed up him and Elliot at the ball?

"Should I sit with you ladies? I so want to help."

"The sweet child spent the past thirty minutes shifting her head betwixt you, me, and the toy. Your anxious grimace surely isn't helping."

Well that comment made his handsome face frown. "William, why don't you go down to my aunt? Let me have some time alone with this pretty girl."

His brow furrowed, but he nodded. He stalked over and closed the window above the child's trunk. "If you think it will help."

"I do. Lady Mary has to become used to me and learn to trust me. I don't think it will happen if she's looking to you for permission. And since I am to be her stepmother…" Gaia swallowed as the weight of her new responsibilities fell upon her. "You must trust me."

He leaned down and kissed the child's head. "Fine. Thirty more minutes, then put her down for her nap." He lifted Gaia's hand and put his lips to her knuckles. "Then you'll join us in the drawing room."

With a final glance in Mary's direction, he walked to the door and wiggled the sticking doorknob. "I'll have the steward look at this. Don't pull it tight." With another jerk, he opened the paneled thing, exiting.

"Well, Mary, it's just the two of us. Tell me about yourself."

The little girl's luminous green eyes seemed to study her. Then she pushed the toy to Gaia.

"This is an exercise in patience. My own stepmother has been the greatest example of patience." She fingered the coral necklace along her throat. I'm going to try to be like her for you. I hope you will show me how to talk with you."

Clasping the horse and spinning the wheels with her finger, Gaia sent it roaring to the girl. The child smiled big and imitated what Gaia did, turning the doweled circles with her pinkie.

That might be the way Mary could learn, by repetition and example. *Oh, God, help me teach this little girl.*

They played like this, back and forth; each time, Gaia made the actions a little more difficult, a couple of pats, turning of the toy. Mary did each action, making Gaia's heart soar.

Like clockwork, thirty minutes later, the tot began blinking her eyes. It was time to nap.

Gaia scooped the child up, cradled her, and hummed low in her ear. Leaning over the crib, she put Mary down, but found no blanket to cover her.

A quick look in the closet didn't produce anything but very heavy woolens. Something lighter would do.

Nothing on the shelves. Maybe the trunk? She eased over to it and lifted the heavy lid. Beneath baby caps and a few more toys, there looked to be a woolen blanket. She stuck both hands inside and snagged the Indian silk lining the sides with her thumb. The vermilion red fabric split and two letters fell out.

Pushing up her spectacles, she stared at the blue-tinted paper. It called to her as all good quality foolscap did. She picked it up. It was wrong to read other people's thoughts, but she couldn't help allowing her pinkie to pop the seal.

Undying....

My heart beats only...

Seconds from your side are a torture....

The words of love scribbled on the paper flowed. This must be a love letter from William to his wife. He really did love her as he'd claimed. She must have loved him, for why would she have kept these if they meant nothing?

Yet how could the late duchess not love someone who wrote poignantly of his feelings? Smoothing the letter, she tucked it back into the trunk and made the seam where the papers had fallen out appear untouched.

She lifted a soft pink blanket out and laid it on the child.

A small snore left Mary. She seemed so peaceful. It was good to know this child was born of love, no matter how things ended.

Would William ever write Gaia such a note? Would friendship be all they had?

Easing from the room, she left the door cracked. After church on Sunday, she'd be back to give it another go with the girl. "Lord, let each time be easier with Mary."

She put her fingers to her lips. Her habit of crying out to God had become second-nature. Maybe on the small things, He'd answer. And this small thing felt good to ask. A part of her missed the freedom of her prayers. Maybe William was right about not losing peace.

As she tiptoed from the room, she saw Albert standing in the hallway.

"Miss." His dark face swiveled left and then right. "I would suggest you braid your chignon tighter if you go into the sea air."

Gaia touched at her frizzy hair, but kept her eyes on the chocolate-colored man standing at the edge of the stairs. "Why do you suggest such?"

"I have a niece of mixed blood. Her hair feathers like yours in the fog. As the future duchess, you should always look well." Albert nodded and slogged down the steps.

Breathless, Gaia sank against the wall, out of sight of the stairs below.

Albert could tell.

How many others could?

And would they expose her secret to William before she

did?

Stelford shook his head. "You are serious. You and the Telfair chit are engaged. She's…"

William helped his old friend onto his horse as he tried to choose careful words. "Young is the word you are searching for?"

His friend leaned back in his saddle. "Wholesome. I told you to gain comfort, but a wife, a mouse-poor, brown wife?"

Ire burning, William balled his fist. "Do you think I chose a diamond of the first water the first time?"

Mouth pinching as if he was going to spit, Stelford shook his head. "Are you ever going to forgive Lizzy for her mistakes?"

Folding his arms and glancing back toward Ontredale, William tried to hide his anger. "Are you sure you don't want to come to church with us? I suspect that if you spend time with us, you would see that my fiancée is one of the most beautiful women I've ever met."

"More so than Elizabeth? Your duchess had a flawless complexion."

"But not a flawless character; Gaia Telfair is beautiful inside and out."

Saluting, Mr. Stelford turned his mount toward the village. "Until she shows you she is human. Then how mad will you be?"

William didn't like the sound of that. Were things so black and white? "Just keep the engagement secret for a few more days. You've been very helpful keeping Deborah away while Miss Telfair visited."

"Yes, but I thought I was helping with something naughty, not downright respectable courtship. See you later." He kicked, and started his horse to trotting.

Chortling, William took a deep breath of the fragrant mint

and pine scent filling the air and walked from the stables. Stupid Stelford. Watching his fiancée play with Mary strengthened his confidence in his engagement. Gaia had a way with children. She'd make a wonderful mother to her. This marriage was the right thing to do for his child and his own comfort. Gaia was beautiful, and very desirable.

He marched to the entry of the great house and took the opportunity to scan the blooming landscape. Maybe he'd take Gaia for a picnic in the garden. Would that be good, or would being so close to flowers remind her of the botanist?

His jealous gut stirred. She was very pensive the other day, not even allowing a goodbye kiss. What thoughts were running wild in that pretty head? She said she had something to tell him. A new outlandish prayer? What could be the big announcement? It didn't feel as if she were going to beg off their engagement, but what?

There was something caught in between them, keeping them apart. And it wasn't her purity or layers of clothing. Thankfully, his military discipline kept most of his thoughts from seduction. No, the something was intangible, and it stole her joy when she didn't think he was looking.

Was it his lack of fully disclosing the horrid nature of his first marriage? Yes, he hadn't told Gaia everything of that brokenness or of the blackmail. Could that be it? Did she feel he didn't trust her?

He tapped his boot along the edge of the first the step and searched for truth. He did trust her, mostly. She wasn't marrying him for his wealth. The influence of his name and position settled it for her.

That wasn't such a bad thing. The honor of his title and all he could do for her three sisters and Timothy should definitely keep her scandal-free. Pity Elizabeth was an only child.

Whatever the cause of Gaia's shyness, a couple of kisses

and a joke or two usually set her at ease. The sooner they married, and she lived at Ontredale, the easier their relationship, and the less concern he'd have about Whimple coming to his senses and snatching her up. Could William persuade Gaia to elope? Had her affection for him grown enough to entrust her hopes with him now, not waiting for the summer to end?

Perhaps her announcement was to tell him she loved him. He stilled and breathed in the cool perfume of the morn, letting his heart expand with wishful pride. If only that were so. If only.

If she loved him first, then he would unlock that broken part of his heart to her. Yes, it was selfish to need her to go first, but what other way was there? He needed guarantees this time before he could stand to be that vulnerable.

Steady, old man. Patience. He'd keep courting Gaia until no memory of any other fellow existed. Yes, that was the plan. Whistling, he climbed the last step and entered Ontredale.

A servant grabbed his gloves, greatcoat, and top hat before he could trudge any further than the threshold. A few more happy footfalls, he planted at the show table, adjusting the porcelain rhinoceros. A strange notion to pray for Gaia filled him.

The first time he did, God had given him an agreeable result, an engagement. Perhaps it wouldn't hurt now.

Steam pushed out his nose as he shook himself of the notion of using God for coercion. The odd desire to pray must be arising from his anxiety of heading to church again. Yes, God mustn't turn him to salt this time either. Who then would raise Mary?

His cousin? A shiver traversed his spine. The temptation to toss the Dresden elephant vibrated in his fingers. With a slap to his forehead, he released the agitating idea.

William pushed open the doors to drawing room.

Deborah slammed the writing desk shut and marched to him. Her outfit of cream muslin seemed too light for the chill in the room. "I've been waiting for you."

He took her outstretched hand and patted it, then stepped toward the tray of fresh scones. He hadn't eaten this morning. Should he tempt a pastry? "This is your last morn here. It's been several weeks since the Masked Ball."

She crept up behind him and put a palm to his shoulder. "How can I leave when you are in danger?"

Was that her snide way of commenting about Gaia? Had she found out? He spun around and folded his arms. "What do you mean?"

"This came this morning." She waved an ivory letter with red writing.

His temper flared, and he snatched it from her. The blackmailer had started up again.

Deborah grabbed his tight palm and massaged his tensing muscles. "How long has this been occurring?"

"I don't want to discuss this. Mention it to no one."

"Come, have some tea." She shoved him toward the sofa then poured him a steaming cup. "It's a special blend to soothe your restless spirit. Then we'll discuss what to do."

His cousin seemed to possess a serene spirit today. She was very helpful the month Elizabeth died, until she started pressing him for marriage. He took the offered cup and downed it. "Thank you."

Her eyes widened. "You should drink more slowly."

He opened the letter and scanned the foul threats. Wiping his warm brow, his temper seethed. When would this be over?

Maybe Deborah would have an idea of what to do, or who was behind this. He searched her countenance, his anger blurring her image. "Where's the envelope?"

She blinked rapidly then nodded. "I opened it. Someone's

threatening to expose the late duchess's adultery. What will this mean for Mary's future?"

He leaned back on the sofa and filled his heavy lungs with air. "How the perpetrator found me, I don't know. If I knew who he was, he'd be jailed."

A gasp left Deborah. "But wouldn't that bring the whole sordid affair to life? You can't do that."

She sat near him. "They made a request. Let's pay it."

Steadying himself against the cushions, he squinted at her. "They want a thousand pounds, but, if I give it over to them, they'll just ask for more."

Why couldn't he make a new life for him and Mary without troubles from the past? Another horrid note had arrived. The heat of his frustration made sweat bead on his upper lip. He pulled at his cravat.

"Are you alright, cousin?" Deborah placed her cold palm on his forehead.

"I'm fine."

She crept closer and whispered in his ear, "You can't let anyone know. Mary will be plagued with rumors that her mother was nothing more than a prostitute." Deborah grabbed his face, as if to focus his moving eyes. "You can't let anyone think Mary's not a St. Landon. How will she bear the shame?"

"What...." He wiped his brow again as the room spun. "What do you suggest I do?"

She gripped his shoulder. "Marry me, Cousin. I'll protect Mary. I'll make sure society loves her."

"No..." Everything seemed foggy around him. He lifted, but didn't leave the couch.

Deborah tugged his jaw. "Ask me to marry you!"

The shrill notes made his head pound. He broke free of her and launched onto his feet, but his stomach lurched.

Deborah stood close. She tore her sleeve, took his hand and

put it to her naked shoulder. "Just say the words. Ask me to be your wife."

"Can't. Engaged to Gaia." He sank to the ground. His skull smashed into the carpet.

CHAPTER SIXTEEN

Losing William

Gaia and Seren walked from Southborne's gates toward Ontredale. The wind had died down and no longer moved the overcast clouds. It should shower and bring the fresh smell of dripping water to the woods, and remove the stench of wilting spring flowers. Summer blooms couldn't come fast enough.

A chill crept up Gaia's spine, even as a few rays of sun slunk past the edges of the gloomy fluff. Why weren't William and his daughter at church? Was his promise just another joke?

"Gaia? Are you listening?"

Seren tugged on Gaia's roomy sapphire gown. The pleating and puff of her cap sleeve flattened then fluffed back into place. Aunt's maid must be a master seamstress, far better than Gaia's meager talents, and the old mantua-maker seemed to enjoy rummaging through the fine fabrics William sent. The sound of the woman's giggles—

"Gaia?"

Seren now stood in her path. "What is consuming your thoughts? It's not like you to be this quiet or not mention Mr. Whimple or the duke once. Must be your *new* engagement.

You know Elliott is doing an exploration close to Ontredale. Maybe he and the duke will fight over you."

"What?"

Seren shook her head. "Wanted to see if you were listening."

Gaia trudged toward Ontredale, which stood beyond the bend. "I'm sorry; just so much on my mind. I am going to tell William today. He needs to know I am black. He needs to decide if he still wants someone like me."

Seren waved her arms and cocked a brow above concerned green eyes. She looked like a brown moth in her chocolate walking gown. "No. That will ruin everything. You are so close to being happy."

Blinking, Gaia swiveled and refocused on the pinkish brick of Ontredale claiming the horizon. "We can't begin with lies. I'm tired of living like this. Any moment, this could all go away. He could hate me."

Seren adjusted her straw bonnet as she lifted her tan kid glove to her giggling mouth. "You want this marriage, beyond just escaping Mr. Telfair's dictates, don't you?"

"What?" With a quick swat at her skull, Gaia stopped, her short heels stabbing the edges of a gnarled root. She stormed off the dirt path to lean against the mossy trunk of a grand oak. "Why are you questioning my mashed-up thinking?"

"That's what friends do." She cozied up and grabbed Gaia's elbows. "You seem different, happy. It must be the duke."

"It's the clothes and new shoes." She fanned her arms and showed off William's scarf. The silky tassels spun in the renewed breeze.

"No, Gaia, it's you. Maybe having someone special, noticing you, makes you glow. I want to glow someday."

Glow. Tanned skin and all. William thought her pretty. Today, as she sat in front of her mirror, sculpting her hair, braiding her hair tight, she felt pretty. Gaia shrugged and walked forward. "I don't know about me, but you will, Seren. You are beautiful, inside and out. We should hurry. Aunt Tabby might already be there, talking Cheshire to death."

Walking next to Serendip, she cast her gaze to Ontredale, with its round turrets and endless charcoal and chocolate roof tiles. She numbered twenty-six grand windows just on this side. How much did it cost to keep the glazing in good repair? Probably more than Mr. Telfair's income.

A tremble started in her toes and worked its way to her bouncing upswept chignon. Mistress of this place? Even if her race mattered not to William, how could she manage this?

Seren's arms surrounded her. "Don't be uneasy."

Her friend, her best friend, steadied her shaking limbs.

Throat thickening, Gaia held onto Seren, as if the ground had turned to quicksand. "He's so rich. I don't want to be someone whose association will bring him shame. I can't hurt him."

"You are worthy. Oh, Gaia. You are worthy, much more than your shallow friend or your tal—"

"Careful, Seren."

"I was going for tall, not talentless Julia." She lifted Gaia's chin. I think the duke sees what everyone but you or Mr. Telfair sees. You are filled with kindness and virtue. You didn't set down your vile cousin when she took Elliot. You congratulated her. When my mother lay sick with consumption, you visited her and read to her so I could get a few hours of sleep."

Was she worthy, God, despite her upbringing? "I've a strong constitution, so I wasn't frightened by the illness."

Seren tugged a four-leaf clover from her reticule and pinned it inside Gaia's stays. "No harm with a little extra luck. But you needn't be troubled. As you've told me when I fret about my brother's gambling, or my father's fury over an investment gone wrong, God is watching over us and guiding our footfalls. He might want yours to lead to this grand place."

Gaia dabbed her wet lashes. Maybe it was time to let God truly guide her, not her fears. Goodness knows she'd need strength to tell William the truth. *Help me, Lord. Don't let him hate me.*

"Come on, Gaia." Arm in arm, she and Seren marched up to the massive stone entry. Aunt's carriage wasn't about. Well, the woman was hardly ever on time.

With a grin as bright as the sunrise, Seren lifted the doorknocker. "Come, let's wait with *your* duke."

The door opened, and Albert, wearing a silver and blue uniform, took their bonnets and gloves.

Seren ran her fingers along the rhinoceros's nose, the porcelain statue sitting on the show table. "Cheshire has great taste. His duchess should be pleased."

"Where do you suppose the duke is?" William always made himself available whenever she visited.

Albert drew near. "He's in the drawing room, but Miss Smythen warned me. His Grace is not to be disturbed."

The man grimaced, as if he feared for his position. "The duke isn't easy on servants who do not follow his directions. Should I announce you, ma'am?"

The noise of horses and carriage wheels filtered through the open door, along with Aunt's screechy guffawing about the mason work. Albert should attend the newest visitor. Aunt Tabby loved pomp and circumstance.

"The drawing room is where he entertains. We'll go to him." Gaia towed Seren to the drawing room doors.

The room was vacant. Why did Albert say William was in here? She rounded the couch. "Where—"

The world stopped.

William lay face-down on the floor.

She ran to him and gripped his wrist. Her heart started

beating again when she found a pulse.

"Seren, go get help! Have Albert run for a doctor. Take Aunt's carriage if you must."

Eyes shiny with tears, her friend darted out the room.

With all her might, Gaia pushed William's shoulder. He was very large, very heavy. Bracing her feet against the sofa, she shoved him onto his back.

Underneath him was a cream-colored note. The sight of the red ink prickled her skin. A quick scan of the contents left her mouth open, gaping. *Adultery? The late duchess?*

William wouldn't want it discovered. She shoved it into her pocket.

She crawled close to his face and smoothed his curly hair from his forehead. "Please be all right."

Loosening his cravat, she stroked his neck, the base of his lean face. "Oh, wake up."

She pounded on his chest, as if that would make his inhalation less ragged.

His eyes opened. Bright circles framed his pupils. A shaky palm reached for her cheek. Then it dropped. His breathing slowed to non-existent.

Throwing herself onto his chest, water leaked from her eyes. "No, don't leave me. Never leave me."

"Gaia?"

"William, I've got to get you help. Mr. Whimple is near. Maybe he'll know some herb."

He jerked within her arms. "No Whimple."

Mr. Stelford pounded into the room. "What happened?"

Aunt Tabby sailed in behind him. The woman fell onto the couch like a wheat sack that flopped open. "Goodness, His Grace!"

Gaia rose up and wiped her face on her shawl. "Seren and I found him here."

His friend jerked William's wrist into the air, counting

aloud with his timepiece. Then he pried one of William's eyes open. "Belladonna? Come; help me get him to walk. I think someone's poisoned him with belladonna."

Gaia pulled on one of William's arms as Mr. Stelford grabbed the other. "Belladonna?"

"A wicked brew." Aunt fanned herself, and her voice strengthened. "Some ladies use it to make their eyes bright. Don't you ever go near it."

Stelford propped William up then pulled him to stand, and began walking him back and forth. "In large doses, it can be coercive or deadly. I think you found him in time. Get some milk and mustard. Let's see if he can throw off the toxin."

Gaia scrambled past Aunt's kicked out legs, almost tripping. Recovering, she bounced out of the drawing room and sent a servant off to the kitchen. Standing at the door, she held in her tears and pulled the shawl tighter about her.

The servant returned with a tart, smelly mixture, and she dashed back inside the drawing room. "Here, Mr. Stelford."

Holding William against the yellow wall, he poured the contents down his throat. "That should take hold in a second."

A gasp left her lips before she could stop it. "Someone has tried to kill him?"

William lunged forward onto all fours, and buried his head in a basket. Surely, the contents of the Thames flowed out of him. "No one's tried anything. I... mixed up the tinctures in my drink."

"Oh." Gaia moved close to him and smoothed his back as his face went into the basket again.

His friend's countenance squished up, as if he'd been stung. "But you don't—"

"Stelford, help me up!" his voice sounded like a command, not a plea. Even sick, William had a daunting presence.

A wailing sound, a child's cries, came from an upper level.

"Gaia, Mrs. Monlin, could you go see about Lady Mary? Stelford, walk me 'til my wits return."

Torn between wanting to stay and helping the girl, she remained paralyzed.

William waved at her to leave. "Please go to Mary; I need you to see after her."

She nodded and left the room. Aunt Tabby lumbered behind, adjusting her cream-colored turban. Lying against the other side of the door, Gaia let her eyes be leaky, and released the horrible feeling of loss from her weak shoulders. It was terrible to discover how much William meant to her when she thought he'd died. "God, thank You for preserving him."

Gripping Aunt's hand, Gaia headed for the stairs. She wouldn't be comforted until she felt his arms about her.

William filled his lungs. Heaving so much fluid from his guts hurt his pride. How could he have trusted Deborah?

Stelford walked him at least a hundred circles on the paisley rug, stopping only to locate the nearest container.

Ripping a handkerchief out of his jacket pocket, William wiped his mouth. "You'd think that nothing else could flow out of me."

"Tinctures? Say what really happened. You're not the liar in our friendship." Stelford eased him into a chair.

Laying his cheek on the cold top of the writing desk, William closed his eyes. "That horrible chit of a cousin. Deborah tried to drug me then make it look as if I forced myself upon her. What would make her so desperate?"

"How crude of Deborah. She could've killed you. Obviously, she's no expert with belladonna. Lizzy knew how much to use. But why not tell your fiancée about your cousin's scheme?

Opening his lids, he sat up straight and checked to see if the world still spun. It did. He sank back against the stiles of the chair. "I'd have to tell her the whole sordid story. Another blackmailer's letter came."

Stelford started to pace, his boots scuffing the rug. "But it had stopped again."

"Nosy Deborah thought she could use the hideous threats and concern over Mary's future to convince me to marry her."

Stelford's head whipped back in William's direction. "And, as added measure, to use the coercive belladonna to make you think you proposed. What a horrible thing to do to a single man!"

"Lucky for me, I was already engaged." Gaia, sweet lovely Gaia saved him.

What was it she whispered over him when he came to his senses before she mentioned his rival? Something about not leaving him, before she mentioned Whimple.

He let the cold, green haze of jealousy fade, and allowed a warm feeling to heat his soul. It wasn't nausea, though he had plenty to spare. He was blessed. Gaia truly cared for him. Maybe God did remember him. He rubbed his temples. "I think Deborah realized that no one would believe her, or that she'd killed me, and ran off."

Heading for the sideboard, Stelford picked up the nearly-empty decanter and put it near his mouth. "So what are you going to do? Should I get a constable?"

With a shake of his head, William tried to indicate no, but his brainbox seemed to bang against the sides of his skull. "This was the act of a desperate woman, her last grand play. She'll be too ashamed to show her face. If we get the law involved, the constable will uncover everything, not just Deborah's foolishness. Elizabeth and her lover will be made public. A bad prank is not enough to have my family run through the mud."

"Your eyes. They looked like Elizabeth's the night she fell."

"You're not suggesting Deborah had anything to do with

that?" He wanted to tighten his fingers into a fist, but it hurt too bad to tense his muscles.

Stelford's gaze floated to the right, as if he remembered something. "No, she wasn't near the place the night of the accident."

"Stelford, how do you know?" William's brow rose. Could Deborah be murderous? The woman had never liked Elizabeth. "She could have slipped in and out before you got there."

"I'm one hundred percent positive, but Elizabeth might have used too much, and lost her footing because of it."

His friend sighed, as if a weight lifted from his chest.

"You and Elizabeth were dear friends. I guess it's good to have a potential explanation, but it doesn't quite make up for the loss."

Stelford mumbled something under his breath, but a wail from above smothered it. Then all went silent.

The women must've gotten Mary to settle, but once the child had a fright, she'd be up the rest of the night. His stomach rolled again, but a few deep breaths kept inside what little remained of yesterday's dinner. Today's meals had surely exited him. Wretched cousin.

If the scandal of Elizabeth's infidelity broke, Gaia's lack of connections wouldn't help. Society wouldn't be thrilled with his marriage to begin with, so Gaia couldn't help Mary navigate the Ton. Probably make things worse. No, things must remain quiet.

The doors burst open, and Miss Hallow and an older man with a black case marched inside.

"Stelford, help me to my chamber so the doctor can give me a stamp of good health." Before they left the room, he pivoted and glanced at Miss Hallow. "Tell Miss Telfair I'm well. Thank her for caring for the baby."

* * *

The little girl finally settled down. Gaia placed the thin pink blanket on the child.

Mary closed her watery green-blue eyes, even as she rolled her head to the door.

"Looking for your papa?" Maybe she sensed he was in trouble.

One thing was certain… Mary had a voice. No one with that much lung capacity would ever be silent. The cries were so bad Aunt had to be settled into a room. She claimed her turbaned head would surely explode.

What had stunted Mary's development so she couldn't form words?

Sighing, Gaia moved to the rocking chair and forced her back against the column-cut stiles. She needed the rigid support. Her hands still held a small tremble. Thinking William had died hurt her more than she thought possible. How dull and invisible her life would be if God hadn't sent him to her special spot in the woods.

Perhaps the answer to why he mixed up tincture lay in the creased letter in her pocket. Maybe the shock of the duchess's unfaithfulness made him careless with his drink.

As if her fingers would burn if she held it directly, she lowered it by the corners onto the trunk under the window.

Using her pinkie, she unfolded the creased paper.

"What are you doing?" Seren walked into the room.

Gaia's heart stopped, as if she'd been caught doing something naughty. She put a hand to her chest. "I found this letter under the duke. I think it will tell me what the true problem is."

Stepping closer, Seren stood by the rocking chair. "Then you should open it."

Her best friend always knew what to say to get her into more trouble. One day Gaia would learn to do the opposite, but not today. She lifted the cream-colored letter and flattened it onto her lap.

Her quick read in the parlor had caught the word *adultery*. Hopefully, Gaia had misread something.

With her instigator looking over her shoulder, she scanned the expensive paper.

Seren plopped onto the floor. Her blush-stained cheeks matched the puce-colored rug.

Gaia blinked a few times as the words *adultery* and *expose* illuminated in the blood-red ink, as if the candlelight had set it aflame. A hundred different thoughts flooded her brain. Those passionate letters she'd found the other day… after such heartfelt words between man and wife, why would someone fall out of love and break their vows? Was it the same thing that caused her mother to be vulnerable? William and Gaia had a lot more in common when it came to scandals.

And why would someone want a thousand pounds to remain silent?

Poor William. No wonder he mixed his tinctures. This news chilled the marrow in her bones.

Seren flopped onto the trunk in a very unladylike heap. "Does that mean Lady Mary is not..."

At the Masked Ball, didn't he ask *how she knew* when she commented about how he took care of the girl even though she wasn't his? Gaia had meant Elliot taking care of his niece, not William and Mary. Could the little girl the duke loved so much not be his blood?

She reached for her friend's hand. "She's his daughter. I've never seen a father love a child more. Don't let those words ever leave your lips. Promise me."

"Yes; I'm not one for gossip."

Gaia lifted a skeptical brow at her friend, the blabbermouth. "I mean it, Seren. Don't hurt people I care about."

"I won't." Seren slumped, her perfect posture curving against the trunk. "This puts Cheshire in such a sympathetic light."

Oh, William; bearing such horrible news, and no one to share the burden. He had problems, too. How could she be such a bacon-brain?

Maybe he talked with Stelford. Still, her soul ached for William. Is that why he was trying so hard to please Gaia; to keep her from straying? From what, their friendship?

The gifts, the unending attention... maybe he wanted her love. That sent a fright in her bones. Again, she realized how much she'd miss William if they did not marry.

The pound of boot treads broke the silence. William stood at the threshold. His gaze seemed locked on the paper in her hand.

Gaia's heart broke at the hurt etched on his face. Could he forgive this breach of privacy? And could he now, finally, talk to her about his first marriage, as true friends, true mates would?

CHAPTER SEVENTEEN

The Nursery

Fury ignited in William's heart. No one was to know his shame, and now the young ladies did. He wobbled closer as his stomach rumbled and warned of another violent exodus. His attention stayed fixed on the blackmailer's note.

The paper fell from Gaia's hands. The scowls on their faces spoke volumes. They knew, and now pitied him. A wave of heat fled his nostrils. "Miss Hallow, can you please excuse us?"

The young lady looked toward his fiancée. Popping out of the rocker, Gaia came to him. "Serendip, go retrieve a cut of foolscap, or stationery, and check on my aunt; we'll need to stay the night to make sure all is well here."

Miss Hallow curtsied then sprinted from the room.

Gaia stood in front of him, silent, her lips threading to a line, everything he feared expressed on her face. She had to think less of him, a man letting his wife humiliate him. What did Gaia think of Mary? His stomach turned.

His hand fisted. Good, no breakables were near. He'd left Cheshire to avoid shame, and now it was all around him in his beloved Devonshire, enveloping Gaia.

She tugged on his lapels and pulled him near, then nudged

him into the rocker. Her hand went to his cheek, mothering him, extinguishing the flame in his chest. "You're warm. You should go to bed. Seren and I will make sure Mary sleeps."

He bent over and scooped up the letter. "So you know."

"Yes," her voice sounded nonchalant, as if being blackmailed over your wife's infidelity was a normal happenstance. She plucked at his cravat. "William, you shouldn't force yourself to stay up. You need to rest."

Clasping her hand, he pried her from his rumpled neck cloth. "Stop."

His voice must've sounded louder than he'd intended.

She stilled but didn't shrink away. Her hazel eyes widened behind her spectacles. With a turn of her countenance, she looked at Mary. "She's still asleep. We'll need to keep our voices low."

"I'm sorry. I've conquered most of my temper. The last time I talked to God about it, I asked him to remove it. As with most of my prayers, I received only a partial answer. Some foulness remains."

Gaia's countenance seemed serene as her bright eyes scanned him. The blue fabric pleating at her bodice hung well on her curvy frame. Her hands were again at his neck, loosening his cravat. His mind turned from shame to the feel of her fingers against his skin.

Her tone fell to a whisper. "I'm listening."

He closed his eyes and gave into the kneading of her thumbs, the needing of Gaia's calm strength. "I prayed for Elizabeth's heart to be filled with love. Must've forgotten the part of it being for me." A few bitter chuckles left his mouth.

"You hide in jokes. You don't need to with me." Her digits found their way to his temples, stroking and cajoling him.

He swept his gaze over her, but her smooth countenance gave away nothing. What was her opinion of him, of this sorry situation? "Tell me your thoughts, my forthright Gaia."

Her voice was soft. "When did the marriage sour?"

He caught one of her palms and looked to the ceiling, mentally tracing the plaster arches framing Mary's bedchamber. How to admit the blackest time in his life, with Gaia leaning on him, making him hope their future would be different? "When I met her, I thought Elizabeth was the prettiest woman I'd ever seen."

He slammed his head back on the chair and started it rocking. Memories of his late wife's smiles, their fast courtship, rushed over him, as did a chill to his soul. "Her beauty was only on the surface. She hated me. After Mary's birth, she wanted nothing of me."

"William, I know how it hurts to have your feelings rebuffed. My innards ached in ways I never knew they could when Elliot became engaged to my cousin. I'm so sorry." She knelt at his side. Her arms drew about his neck.

He dropped the foul paper and leaned his forehead against hers. His palms glided about her waist. This close to Gaia, he could tell her anything. "Elizabeth resented Mary. I think she wanted a boy, so her marital duties would be fulfilled. The woman wouldn't pick her up. Let wet-nurses care for her all the time. That's why I think she's mine." Another galling chortle left his lips. "But, then, she could be some lover's Elizabeth broke with."

Her hold tightened about him. "Mary is yours, all yours. She's a gift God gave you. Don't ever forget that. I'm a gift too. I have to remember that."

Any anger William felt over Gaia reading the note dissipated. There was something good about confiding in her. This simple gesture of embracing him, caring for him, outweighed his embarrassment. "You are a gift to me."

She leaned back and caught his gaze. "Do you have any idea who would write such notes?"

"Elizabeth and I released so many thoughtless maids and

servants. Anyone could've seen something and wanted to take revenge for their firing. I let some go here. I can't tolerate any person treating Mary indifferently."

She kissed his cheek. "Now go lie down. The doctor, if he's worth his salt, will want you to sleep."

"Rest, huh?" Gaia was so beautiful, tending to Mary and now him.

Her cheeks flushed. He must've gazed upon her too long. Righting his waistcoat, he slogged to his feet and saluted. "I will follow your orders, ma'am."

Taking her hand, he held it against his chest. "I do like where you lead."

"Then go and wash behind your ears. And don't forget to say your prayers."

Maybe he would pray. Who but God would give him such a friend? This time he'd be specific. Peace and faithfulness in this marriage to Gaia. Chin up, he left the room.

Gaia sampled an easier breath. She'd never seen William angry. He'd been understanding, funny with a ready joke leaving his lips, maybe caught wanting to kiss her, but not seething.

The wringing of his hands frightened her for a moment; until she remembered this was her friend, and he'd never hurt her. Was that the icy temper that Albert feared? She settled back into her rocker and released another sigh.

He had a right to be upset. She and Seren shouldn't have snooped. But at least Gaia knew and could now understand the depth of his pain.

Ten minutes later, Serendip poked her head in the room and shook two sheets of stationery like a flag. The blue tint of the paper reeked of expense... and familiarity. "All is well in here?"

Gaia waved her inside. "Yes, silly, come on in, but do be

quiet. Lady Mary is sleeping. Remember how hard it was to get her to settle."

The little one turned over. A foot kicked out of the thin bedclothes.

Fanning herself with luminous blue paper in one hand, Seren carried a writing set in the other. She swept into the room. "Mr. Stelford has a groom waiting to take the messages to our abodes. He's quite an interesting man."

Gaia took the ink and the blotter and placed them on the floor near the trunk. "Aunt might rouse and catch you flirting. You'll be in for a lecture." But one on how to do it better.

Seren cocked an eye and made a flourish with the paper, as if she were a senorita ready for a dance. "Until the banns have been read, there is always a reason to be a flirt. And Mr. Stelford is quite engaging."

Blue paper. The candlelight bounced down its weave. "Seren, did you get this from the duke's writing desk?"

"No, it's Mr. Stelford's."

Gaia's heart sank. "Mr. Stelford's?" She took the paper from Seren. Arranging the ink and quill atop the trunk, she scrawled notes informing the Hallows and the Telfairs their intentions to stay the night at Ontredale. Gaia was amazed she could spell her name, given the racing of her pulse. Folding the paper, she tore the excess off her note to her stepmother and put it in her pocket. "Can you give these to the groom, and come right back?"

Seren shrugged her shoulders, but took the letters. "If Mr. Stelford is not too attentive."

As soon as her friend turned for the stairs, Gaia closed the door and headed for the trunk. She smoothed her hand on the old roughed wood and unlocked the black iron hasp.

The hinge went easily. She rummaged past the linens and toys to the opening in the seam along the lining. Not breathing, she yanked out one of the letters. Holding it to the light, she examined the page, the weave, weight and coloring. An exact match to the piece of stationery she pulled from her pocket.

Air gushed out of her mouth like liquid in a toppled flask. The words of love scribbled on the love letter weren't from William.

Could it be a coincidence? The man who stole Elizabeth's affections and Mr. Stelford possessed the same stationery. She pried open another letter. This one had a mark at the closing. *S.*

She rubbed her forehead. Mr. Stelford, William's dear friend, was Elizabeth's lover. The realization stung Gaia's insides almost as badly as when her cousin Millicent sashayed into Chevron Manor, announcing her engagement to Elliot.

No. This hurt more. Poor William would be devastated by his friend's treachery.

A knock at the door made her jump in the air, almost tripping over the trunk.

"I can't open the door. It's stuck." Seren was on the other side.

"I'll open it," Gaia hoped her voice sounded steady. She stuffed the love letters and the cut of stationery into her pocket then closed up the trunk, before some other skeleton flew out.

Blowing out a long, frustrated breath, she slunk to the door, yanked, and spun the knob until it opened.

Seren floated inside. "The grooms have been sent. Is everything well?"

"I'm just a little nervous, given all that's happened."

With a fold of her arms, Seren came closer. "Are you sure?"

She wasn't. William was her every thought. How would he react if he learned of his friend's betrayal from the blackmailer? Gaia had to do something. "Is Mr. Stelford still in the drawing room?"

Seren's cheeks glowed as her sunny smile bloomed. "Yes, with Mrs. Wingate. She was quizzing him over the events. Poor man."

Gaia went over the threshold, but paused with her palms on the frame. "Wait here 'til I return."

"Oh, no. You can't have them all." Seren's laughter followed Gaia down the twisting stairs.

Gaia didn't want them all. She just wanted to protect William. She pushed open the drawing room's doors.

Mr. Stelford stood near the mantle. His dark tailcoat contrasted with the whitish marble of the mantle. "Miss Gaia, is the mad house enough for you?"

He poured himself another drink.

Mrs. Wingate shook her head as she walked past to the threshold. "Thank you for being here, ma'am. Keep bringing calm to Ontredale." A short smile blossomed on her face as she closed the doors.

"Well, the future duchess is already at work," Mr. Stelford's words slurred.

The old housekeeper looked aghast. "You are engaged to the duke?"

Every doubt in her head about herself shook her fingers, but she stuffed her hands behind her back. "Yes; it is very recent."

"The Telfair girl and St. Landon's son." She shook her head and marched from the room. The door seemed almost to slam shut.

Gaia marched to the couch, almost to the very part of the yellow rug where she'd found William. Her pulse raced. God must give her the freedom to speak her mind almost as much as He needed to erase the pain of nearly losing William.

She swallowed. "I hope you don't mix up your tinctures. One sick man in the house is enough."

"To be sure." He downed his glass.

Shoving her hand into her pocket, she fingered the paper and strengthened her resolve to aid William. "I noticed you drink a lot."

His dark green eyes narrowed. He put the glass on the sideboard's edge. "It's quite impolitic to discuss a man's habits. Besides, the man you should be assessing is the one called Cheshire."

"I know people are given to drink when they are mired in guilt."

"Well, I'm very ashamed of these people, wasting good liquor." He pivoted, placing his back to her. His onyx coat sagged on his rounding shoulders.

"I'm sorry for you." She came to his side, pulled the notes from her pocket, and waved them like a sword cutting the tense air. "It seems the Duchess of Cheshire's death hurt more than the duke and Lady Mary."

He put a hand to his face and wiped his brow, ruffling his deep brown hair. "Well, you are a shrewd one. Shan't mistake your youth for stupidity."

With a grunt, he folded his arms. "So what is it that you want me to do to keep this secret from the light of day?"

She handed him the notes. "I want nothing. You can burn these now, but someone else knows the truth. I think it would be better if Cheshire hears it from you."

He took them from her. As he murmured words from the page, something washed over him, weighing down his voice, wetting his green eyes. "You want me to tell him of my deceit?"

"Yes, sir, I do."

As if he were as thirsty as a camel, he dumped an ocean of amber liquid into his glass. He guzzled his beverage, as if his tongue burned. "Oh, you are too kind."

Unafraid, she took the glass from him and set it down on

the sideboard. "You'll never forgive yourself if you can't admit the truth."

Gaia knew in that moment that she too had to tell the truth. William would know her secret before the week's end, and if he chose to end their relationship, she would release him. She may not have been born in dignity, but she had it. And it would not allow her to keep another lie.

Mr. Stelford rubbed his neck, as if he could wrench it from his shoulders. "She was my childhood love. Our hearts were meant to be, before her father arranged their marriage."

Gaia couldn't understand. The feelings she had for Elliot were nothing compared to this man's anguish, or the duke's. "The news must come from you."

The glow of the hearth illuminated shadows on Mr. Stelford's cheeks. "There is nothing worthy in these bones to warrant forgiveness. He won't forgive me. He doesn't have it in him."

"It doesn't matter if the duke does or doesn't; I know you won't forgive yourself until you confess. Drink won't absolve you."

Stelford balled his fists, and then collapsed against the side of the mantle. "How can I? I lost the woman I loved and stabbed my best friend in the back to get another moment with Lizzy."

Strangling to get the words out, Gaia forced her voice to be steady. "There is something worthy in everyone, or God wouldn't have sacrificed His son for us. Tell the duke and start the path to heal."

"Maybe it's best that you tell him. That should gain you a few more points. Not that you need any, Miss Telfair. He already worships your footfalls."

She wiped at her eyes. "I care deeply for him, and I just don't want him hurt anymore. For the love I know you have for him, tell him the truth."

Mary started to cry again.

She walked to the door. No pleasure rested within her. Mr. Stelford might be as stubborn as William. "Just consider my words."

Sleep had barely taken a hold of William when Mary's scream pierced the darkness of his chamber. Between his stomach and the unsettled nature of his current affairs—a daft cousin, Elizabeth's scandals, a tenuous engagement to Gaia—he hadn't rested much.

Sliding out of his bed, he fumbled for a match on his bed table. A few blind stabs produced a sulphur-dipped stick. He lit a candle then threw on his robe. What happened to his reinforcements? Perhaps Gaia went to sleep. Poor girl; she wasn't used to Mary's night terrors.

He walked down the long hall even as the cries lessened. That was odd. The child usually didn't stop until he picked her up. Maybe Gaia was awake. His lips curled up, picturing Gaia holding his Mary, mothering his girl.

Dawn's early light filtered through the great window, guiding his feet down the long hall to his daughter's chamber. Anyone who could make it through this night at Ontredale was made of resilient stock. Gaia must belong here. She had to be the missing piece of his life.

He cared for her; so much more when he thought his last sight on this earth was her sweet face. Maybe they'd moved to a space where he could just say all that he felt, and not fear rejection. She already saw through his jokes. Except for Deborah's treachery, she knew the worst. Couldn't both admit to growing feelings?

Arriving at Mary's threshold, he twisted the knob, but the door wouldn't open. His pulse pounded as he thought of his little girl trapped and alone in the room.

Placing the candle on the show table nearest her door, he

took a deep breath, lowered his shoulder, and rammed the door. It shook in the frame but didn't open. The fouled belladonna must've tamped his strength.

"All is fine." The voice sounded muffled, like a hand covering someone's mouth.

His heart raced, and he rammed the door again. The paneled wood tore from its hinges, but did not fall. He pushed and propped it to the side. "I'm coming."

He stalked in. Mary's head pointed in the rocker's direction. A humming Gaia sat there, waving at him to leave.

"What is going on?"

Almost leaping, Gaia sprang from the chair and she charged him. She clapped a hand to his mouth and shoved at him, as if to make him leave the room. The woman would have better luck forcing a wall to move than to keep him from his daughter.

She reached up to his ear and whispered, "Mary is learning to soothe herself. You must leave now."

Torn between the visceral response of his heart when Gaia touched him and his anger, William eased her wrist away then bent over the crib.

His little teary-eyed child reached for him, and his ire heated again. "I would never expect you to be heartless and let a baby cry."

"Mary's not a baby. She has to learn to use words, not sobs."

He spun the child and held her tight. "She's my baby."

"She's a little girl." Gaia reached for his arm, but every muscle tightened, and he wrenched away.

Gaia moved in front of him. "The child needs to be given the instruction to develop. You must trust me."

Mary cooed at him as her chubby arms gripped his neck.

"Elizabeth! Your instruction made her eyes red. Is this how you treat your stepdaughter?"

Her face paled. "What?"

"All will be well, Mary. Papa's here."

Gaia backed away. "I am not your late wife. I would never hurt any child. Mary needs to soothe herself, or she will grow up nervous. William, you should know I wouldn't do anything to wrong this sweet girl."

He didn't answer, and plopped down in the rocking chair.

Gaia's breathing hitched as her bosom shuddered. She seemed to be full warrior, without the prayerful part. "I would never be cruel to Mary. Why would I, when we are the same, born under a cloud of adultery?"

What was she talking about? He squinted at Gaia even as the coldness of her statements about Mr. Telfair flooded into remembrance. "We'll talk when I get Mary settled."

"At least this child was born of love, not the opposite." Gaia pivoted to the threshold. She lifted her head and trudged out of the chamber.

Gaia was born under a cloud, too? If she wasn't Mr. Telfair's, whose daughter was she? And how did Mr. Telfair forgive the adultery?

Or did he?

William's heart dropped. The pain his Gaia must bear, and he'd just accused her of harming Mary.

He wanted to go after Gaia, but Mary hadn't settled. Yes, that would be the excuse he would use, not the guilt weighing down his feet.

CHAPTER EIGHTEEN

A Father's Love

Aunt's carriage rumbled away from Ontredale. Seren had left before dark, so it was just Gaia, Mrs. Monlin, and the lies.

The older woman shook. Her face pinched almost like Mr. Telfair's when he was really annoyed. "Tell me what happened. I heard shouting and wood breaking."

Refusing to answer, she turned from the woman's ashy countenance to the greenery of the woods.

Aunt pounded the seat. "Gaia, are you still engaged? Did you fowl things up?"

"I am to blame, Aunt?" Heated anger coursed through her. "No, all the lies I've ever been told. Those are to blame."

Aunt's mouth opened then closed. She wrung her hands.

"Keep your lies. Bury them again with my mother. Or with the mysterious black who stole her virtue. I don't care anymore."

Gaia spied the path to her favorite spot on the earth. She leapt up, pressed on the door, and jumped out of the moving vehicle.

Tumble, tumble, bump. She rolled to a stop. Her new gown had dirt caked on the pleats from the fall, but what did it matter? The frock was William's. Gaia had nothing, not even the illusion of hope.

She peered up and saw the carriage stop. Aunt would never traipse through the mud to follow, so Gaia marched through the bushes and didn't quit until she was hugging her oak.

Her chest still stung at William's accusations. The coldness in his sea-blue eyes; they might as well have been the pond that stayed frozen at the Hallows' three years ago, the year with no summer.

At least she saw William's true nature: irritable, judgmental. Surely he was just like his father, the harsh vicar, not the affable man William pretended to be.

"Arrgh!" she cried out her frustration, releasing it and all her breath. How could she be mad at a man protecting his daughter? Maybe it was envy making water gush from her eyes. No one would ever fight for her like that. No one.

She tried to swipe at her tears, and mud painted her cheek. She looked at the cold blackness of the raw earth, but saw herself, stained by birth, never to be washed clean.

"God, why was I born? If I am to hurt this much, what was Your point?"

"The point was to heal my dearest friend's heart."

"Aunt Tabby?"

"Your mother had lost twin babies before you. That is why there is a gap between you and Julia. She was sad for so long. My brother told her it was her fault, but men know nothing when it comes to these things."

The stillborn twins? How could Mother be blamed, when death in childbirth was so common? Gaia spun to look her aunt in the eye.

The woman fidgeted with her gloves, but her voice remained low and steady. "A man, a student from Africa, came to our village, Mr. Tialnago. He was here studying England to gain a way to help his people. He was the nephew of the king of the Xhosa tribe."

Aunt swiveled and looked around, as if there were a place to sit. There was nothing there but God's floor. "I've never seen a stronger attraction, and they were so different."

"Nephew of a king? But your brother said he forced her."

Shaking her head from side to side, Aunt strengthened her voice. "She loved Tialnago, and he her. It was wrong. She knew it was wrong, but couldn't let him be. I tried to dissuade her. Delilah and I were like you and Miss Hallow, always getting or keeping the other from straying, but not this time. She withdrew into herself. Only Tialnago could reach her."

"Did they want to run away together? What were their intentions?"

With a shrug, Aunt backed up and put her weight against the trunk. "I don't know. She became so secretive. Then, they were discovered by my brother. I've never seen Henry so angry. He wanted both to pay, but he didn't want the family slighted. Then Tialnago did the bravest thing."

The drop in Aunt's tone was like ice, and pelleted them. Gaia turned and grasped the lady's elbow. "What did he do? Don't stop. Let the truth reign."

Eyes wide, as if the event were reoccurring, Aunt Tabby continued, "Tialnago said he had coerced and confused her with his pipe music. He took the blame for the affair to protect your mother and you."

Gaia pulled away, hugging herself to prepare for the worst. "What happened to him? Did Mr. Telfair kill him?"

"It was his right to avenge Delilah's honor, but he didn't want the blood on his hands. He did worse. He shipped Tialnago into slavery."

With a heart pounding hard, she dropped to her knees. "How could that be? Tialnago was a free man. And don't slaves have rights in England?"

"Laws and wronged men's motives don't mesh. Henry wanted him gone and to pay most cruelly."

"How? Does he even know slavers?"

"Someone helped, but I don't know who. The scandal never came to light."

Aunt trudged in front of her and plucked leaves from Gaia's matted hair. "Know this. It was wrong what your mother and Tialnago did, but you are not a child of rape." She fingered and lifted Gaia's chin. "There is royalty in your blood."

An image of a woman brushing these frizzy locks flashed. Her mother was beautiful, but her lips formed a permanent frown. Now Gaia understood, and her heart shattered again.

"More love created you than any of your siblings. Tialnago loved you and your mother enough to take the full blame. He let his name be tarred. He sacrificed himself so that you might live."

Face in hands, Gaia wept. Her salted tears baptized her face with the truth. Her true father sacrificed his freedom to protect her. He wasn't evil, as Mr. Telfair had implied. Gaia wasn't evil either.

"Forgive my brother. He was very dark, shamed, more than anything, but he wouldn't take you from your mother, knowing how she grieved the loss of her twin boys. And when you came out so light, not looking black at all, I convinced him of the scheme to circulate Spanish roots. And when you became instrumental in saving Timothy, even he saw you had a purpose, a reason for you being a Telfair."

"My father became a slave for me. God, am I worthy of this sacrifice?" She dipped and picked up a stick to write her true father's name in the ground. Her fingers shook. Instead, she drew a cross. Her blood father sacrificed for her, but her Lord had already done so on Calvary. That, alone, made her worthy.

For the first time in forever, she felt whole. She even felt treasured. Standing tall, she looked at her tree. This place had always meant worship to her; now it meant truth.

"Come back with me, Gaia. Let's get you cleaned up. You can still be a duchess."

She took Aunt's hand and prepared to return to Chevron, the place owned by the man who had enslaved her father.

It took an hour for Mary to settle down. The child kept looking at the door, as if she looked for someone to enter. Could she be waiting for Gaia?

Trudging down the hall, he slunk into his bedchamber. Quiet and dull, his quarters stood, burnished with chestnut paneling. He flopped down onto the edge of bed, brushing back the burgundy and gold panel curtains flanking the sides to make room for his legs. Looking around, he had to agree. Gaia's wish of sunny blue paint might make the gloom of this place dissipate.

His valet snuck in, laid out an outfit, a turquoise vest and dark pantaloons, then crept back out without a sound. Was his staff expecting an explosion of his temper? Why would he take out his frustration on them? He wasn't the Reverend St. Landon.

Flinching, William scanned to see if a ghost were in the room; nothing but an empty bed and the breezy smell of salt blowing through an open window, fluttering the billowy, rust-colored curtains.

Ontredale sat three miles from his father's old vicarage. Closing his eyes, William could see the spire on the church, and the fire and brimstone man behind the pulpit.

After pulling on and lacing a shirt, William scratched the back of his neck and adjusted his cravat. His father taught him how to knot his tie. The pleasure of making it just so was a great accomplishment for a lad of seven. Even the old man had smiled. Then his mother broke a vase and the whole house was in uproar. A chill went up his spine at the memory of his father's shrieking at Mama or a slow maid. The man believed in propriety, but lived with so little grace.

With a tap to his head, William had to admit his temper was the match of his father's; awful, with an edge of bitterness, and lacking in forgiveness. And he'd just shown it to Gaia. "I must do better."

Although he was right about not letting his Mary cry, guilt gnawed at William's insides. It must be a lingering effect of the belladonna, not the hurt in Gaia's light eyes.

He yanked on his freshly-glossed boots. This would be a normal day; no mooning or dwelling in the land of second thoughts. He'd go to Chevron and apologize, and things would continue as normal.

As he bounced up, he caught himself pacing. Random thoughts of Gaia being lost to him started appearing, crowding out his convictions of being in the right.

In his mirror, he studied his posture. Where was the man with the beautiful child and the lovely intended to dote upon? Had he destroyed all his work to make Gaia comfortable in this marriage?

With the blackmailer still at large, maybe this was a chance to end the engagement. Exposure would come, and a divided couple couldn't help Mary.

With a final knot in his necktie, he left his chambers.

Mrs. Wingate dusted the massive canvases covering the cream wall.

She gazed at him with a frown, and then pivoted back to wiping the frame of a 17th-century landscape. The peace captured in the floral pastels wasn't on this landing, if Mrs. Wingate's stiff posture was any indication.

Tired of the false deference, he held his ground. "Fine, Mrs. Wingate; say what is on your mind."

Still dusting, the woman didn't turn. "The young lady, your future duchess."

His shoulders leveled. What was his housekeeper going to say that he didn't know? Gaia is too young. Too headstrong. All notions that had crossed his mind since their argument. "Yes?"

Mrs. Wingate turned, crossed her arms. The grey dusting cloth matched her neat uniform. "She's very clever, and devoted to your child's care."

Shocked, he rocked back on his boot heels.

"I earn my keep in silence. Your lineage has leased these grounds, done good or evil here, but I stay in the background. Miss Telfair, she attended Lady Mary all night."

The portly woman's soft brown eyes narrowed as she focused on him. "The young lady wouldn't let me relieve her. I watched her coax the child back to sleep, without picking her up and coddling her. You could learn a lot from her, sir."

"So, letting my babe scream is proper parenting?"

"No, but spoiling the child every time she is upset doesn't make her secure. What if you can't get to her? How will she go on?" His housekeeper folded up her cloth and picked up her bucket of pine-smelling polish. "Miss Telfair's in the right. In spite of how she came to us, things might be made right if she stays. There, I've said it. I'll go ready your breakfast."

William stood still, watching Mrs. Wingate's solemn form disappear upon the staircase. In spite of what things? How many knew of Gaia's illicit conception?

With the edge in her voice, it was as if someone in his family were the culprit. Oh, that couldn't be it. Could he and Gaia be related by an affair?

Oh, Lord, he felt ill and kept repeating, *cousins do marry, cousins do marry.*

In frustration, he stretched out his arms and knocked over a Dresden elephant. The silver and grey porcelain shattered as it hit the floor. He bent and picked up the largest shards.

Get a hold of yourself. Gaia looks nothing like a St. Landon. The old woman just knew of the affair.

He filled his lungs as his boot hit a chunk of the elephant's ear. Something broken. How many arguments did he have with Elizabeth that didn't end without one of them destroying an heirloom? Obviously, his ways of dealing with his anger in his early years of marriage weren't correct. Could his ways of raising Mary also be wrong?

He sighed deeply then returned to his room for a basket. He threw the pieces away, at least lightening the work for the maids.

Taking the stairs, he listened to the solitary thumping of his heels against the treads. God had helped to reform him of his temper, but it came too late. Elizabeth neither noticed nor cared.

Would God help him now make amends to Gaia? Had he ruined things so badly she wouldn't care either? There was no time like the present to find out.

Gaia sat back against the leather seats of Aunt's carriage. Her arm stung from the fall, her dress had stains that Aunt Tabby tried to brush out, but a little piece of her soul had been returned. Someone valued her enough to sacrifice their life for hers. Her father was loved by her mother.

"Now, Gaia, tell me; are you still engaged to Cheshire? Did you release him?"

"No, I did not say those words, but I think I should. He doesn't trust me."

Aunt's face was a mixture of relief and eyes shooting daggers. "You will do nothing of the sort."

Gaia folded her arms. She wanted a name; now that Aunt had provided one, wasn't that enough?

"You see, you are my brother's daughter, too; headstrong as

the day is long."

Aunt's hand became frenzied, pushing and tugging at Gaia's chignon. "There's a carriage at Chevron. The duke must've beaten us here. Oh, and you look as though you tumbled down a hill."

Until today, she believed everyone, that she was less than. She tugged Aunt's fingers to her heart. "Aunt, I'm not perfect. I am so far from it, but I refuse to make myself uneasy any more, even for the duke."

The words sounded confident leaving her tongue, until Gaia realized it wasn't the duke's carriage, but Elliot's.

"Now, Gaia. That one's for your sister. Maybe we could have a double wedding."

Her aunt should have no worries. Her head could no longer be turned by any man at this point. They marched out of the carriage toward Chevron, and, as if Elliot had been waiting at the window, out he came to greet them.

He held out his hand to her. "What happened?"

Aunt jumped ahead of her. "A little accident. She's fine."

"Miss Telfair, I came to speak with you."

Gaia's nose wriggled as she smelled raw earth and grass clippings. "What are you doing here?"

He tugged on the dusty lapels of his short hunting jacket. "I've just finished doing some research. I had some time to spare, and I thought I'd use it bringing you to your senses. Why are you engaged?"

As she looked into his piercing blue eyes, eyes she'd always wanted to be cast upon her, a wave of indignation hit her. Time to spare? That's what she was to him, leftover minutes. "Mr. Whimple, you've missed calling hours. I'm tired. Why not find my sister? She'll surely take this appointment. She might have spare time."

She brushed past Elliot and headed for the door.

He caught up to her and held it open. "What if I come

tomorrow? Will you give me a chance then?"

She turned her countenance to him. "If you come on time and not smelling of bogs, I will be very glad to speak with you. I'm busy today. I've already missed story time with Timothy today."

Head held high, she walked inside Chevron, visible and emboldened. She wouldn't let any man but her beloved brother, Timothy, dictate her days. The lad knew who she was, and had always honored her sense of worth.

Elliot caught her arm and pulled her into the parlor. "I insist, Miss Telfair."

Julia lifted from the sofa. Tears lined her face as she looked their way. Why had she been crying? It wasn't from joy of an engagement. "Julia, what's the matter?"

She shook her head, straightened her melon-green bodice, and slipped from the room, closing the door with a thud.

Her heart sobbed for Julia. The girl looked like broken china. "What has happened here?"

Elliot paced. "Why are you marrying the duke, Gaia?"

She pivoted from him and moved to the low flames of the hearth. A week ago, she had a prepared answer about marrying someone who knew her worth, but that was wrongheaded, with William thinking she'd hurt Mary. She rubbed her hands back and forth. "Well, uh, he asked me?"

Elliot tapped her shoulder, and she turned to face him.

His brow creased, as if he were disturbed. "I always thought your emotions went another way."

Her heart thumped as she looked into his deep blue eyes. "Whatever do you mean?"

He bit his lip for a second. "I always thought you liked me."

Elliot knew. Her stomach soured. "If you knew this, why would you propose to my cousin? Or make eyes at my sister?"

He rubbed the scruff of his neck. "You have always been like a little sibling. It wasn't until the Hallows' Ball that I saw you as a desirable young woman."

The gall of him. She leveled her gaze to his. "You mean it wasn't until I had the duke's attention."

Shrugging, he took to pacing again. "Perhaps. Maybe seeing another man hovering about you broke my fog."

"Well, I'm glad you can see things more clearly. That's not enough to change my mind."

He came closer and pried her hand from the folds of her jacket. "I think you should break with the duke and marry the man you've always loved. Marry me, Gaia."

The smooth sound of his voice wrapped around her, making her heart race with surprise. "What? Marry you? Are you sure you have the right Telfair? Wait a few years and Helena will be of age."

Stepping backwards, he held a sheepish grin, as if he dangled between full confession and a lie. "Well, you know your cousin is very fun, and pretty, and she had a dowry. Julia is also very pretty, perhaps prettier than Miss Rance, which made up for her small dowry. Everyone knows that very little or none exist for you or your younger sisters."

Her breathing became shallow as he lined out Gaia's prospects. "None of that has changed."

"It has. My father says the duke has offered to give Mr. Telfair four thousand pounds for your dowry if the engagement is broken. Now you're the equivalent of Miss Rance and Miss Julia. Our match would not be reprehensible."

What? This was about money. Lightning hadn't struck him. No grief over losing Gaia.

Yet William protected her again. He thought of her interests. She closed her eyes for a moment. William's arms were about her, rocking her near the cliffs. Lifting her lids, she stared at Elliot, the man she'd wanted forever, and felt numb. "So this new money is enough to make up for my looks and lack of charisma? Why, Elliot, you are setting the bar very low for a bride."

"I'm not saying this well. If you and Julia had the same dowry, I'd choose you. Your conversation is brilliant, and you'd understand the importance of my research more than Julia ever could. I'm not sure she'd know a lampiate from a nightshade."

Folding her arms, Gaia stamped her foot. "I don't either."

"But you have the capacity to learn. You are so caring, and a bit of sun would never hurt you. My father now says it is fine to wed you."

"Why?"

His brow pinched. "I'm older than you, and we have been Telfair neighbors forever. My father is aware of your mother's almost straying, but no one has seen that weakness in you or Julia."

Almost? So he didn't know the bigger scandal, and Julia didn't tell. Love for her sister battled the sour taste in her mouth. Elliot knew a tiny piece of Telfair baggage, but money, the duke's money, made a difference. "Mr. Whimple, you need to leave."

"Please, I'm clumsy at this. I know you love me. It doesn't matter how we got here. All that matters is I'm here now. My head is clear. It's you I want."

How many years had she wanted to hear these words? Something inside wanted to respond to the smoothness of his face, the strong jaw that she could draw in her sleep. However, it wasn't a kiss on her mind but a hard slap to his cheek that was what she wished to offer. "I asked you to leave."

"Please, give me one chance." He pried her hand free and kissed her fingers. His motion slowed, deliberate in nature.

She pulled away, as if his action were indecent. Maybe she was indecent, entertaining an offer when she was promised to another.

The door opened and Gaia chilled to the bone as William marched inside. "I think my lady asked for you to leave."

The duke looked furious, as if he would harm Elliot.

"Yes, Mr. Whimple, please leave. I am tired."

Elliot's head swiveled from her to the duke. "Just remember what I said. I'll be back tomorrow."

He brushed past William, their shoulders almost touching.

"Gaia, I'd like to speak with you, but what happened to you? Are you hurt?"

Though she wanted to turn from him, the pleading in his strong voice made her sigh. "I'm fine; a little tumble at my oak."

"If you were looking for me, you should've just come back to Ontredale."

"Why? To fight some more? Was there some damaged china you thought I broke?"

"No, I broke that after you left."

She squinted at him. "Shouldn't you be resting or accusing others of misdeeds?"

She covered her mouth. That wasn't generous, but she didn't feel generous.

"I deserve your censure. I shouldn't have suspected you, but you have to respect my wishes." He looked to the carpet. "Lovely Gaia, our friendship is new, and I shouldn't expect you would know how I want my household run any more than you should expect I have the good sense to know how to handle my temper."

"But to suspect me of—"

"I'm sorry, Gaia. I know you aren't Elizabeth. This is new for me, too. I don't seem any better at this marriage business than last time." He walked to the window and pulled back the curtains. Elliot's gig whipped by in the same instance. "Why was Whimple here?"

"He just learned of our engagement. He thinks I've lost my mind." She'd leave off the part about him proposing. Elliot didn't need the duke to be an enemy.

"With the blackmailer at large, maybe we should elope. Yes, you, me, and Mary, we should leave."

She folded her arms and moved closer to him. "So you still want to marry someone as dangerous as me?"

He leaned forward, his forehead tapping against the pane. "I was wrong."

The color of his face drained, making his golden skin ashen, as if he'd seen a ghost. He pulled the drapes closed, then towed her from the window. "You are dangerous, Gaia. I didn't realize you had the power to hurt me, to humble me in unimaginable ways; that a turn of countenance in anger slices through me. I don't want you angry or hurt, or worse, away from me."

He said words that stole the air from her lungs. Weakness settled into her as his gaze bore into her heart, stripping her anger away. It was as if she stood naked before him, cold and naked. "But you said a long engagement, so we could be sure."

His arms draped about her like a fine cloak. The heat of him made her warm and secure, but could this last? When he knew the whole of things, would he still want her?

She slipped from his arms and put a hand to her racing heart. "You don't trust me. Maybe we are a mistake."

A tremor pressed his lip. "The only mistake is to wait and lose you. Promise me that you'll stay away from the windows. Don't ask why; I'll explain later."

He reached out and gripped a lock of her frizzy hair, curling it about his thumb. With care, he traced her chin, down to the throbbing vein along her throat. "Don't be contrary this once, and I'll spend a lifetime making it up to you."

Her bones began to melt just from the scent of him, rich tarragon. "Why must you always smell so good?"

It wasn't clear if she moved or if he did, but his lips were on hers, her mouth opening more and more to accept his desperate kiss. His tone deadened, planting fire along her ear, the line of her jaw. "I am not losing you, and I'll do better at keeping you from my temper. I'll return tomorrow. Be packed."

He pounded out of the house. Breathless and confused, she peeked through the curtains and watched William ride away. Nothing should be hidden from a couple in love, nothing. He might be sure of their marrying, but she wasn't.

The cold glass chilled her nose. She stepped back and bunched up the collar of her pelisse. He had a power over her body that frightened her. Was this how her mother felt, swept away in passion that blotted out right and wrong?

It was dangerous to be this out of control, and now that she had a name, a true name, Gaia feared abandoning it for any other, even St. Landon.

CHAPTER NINETEEN

The Painful Truth

William stalked into the drawing room. Deborah rode away before he could catch her. Was it the barrel of a gun or the sparkle of a pocket lens she'd pointed Gaia's direction?

A fresh wave of anger washed over him as he glanced at the tea tray and the yellow carpet on which his head had bounced. His fingers folded into fists. Would she try to hurt Gaia?

The woman could've killed him with her poison, or worse, made him think he'd attacked her. Had her desperation turned against Gaia? He rubbed his skull. Deborah wasn't capable of murder. He'd find his cousin and set the chit straight. St. Landon baggage was tolling higher; scandal, evil cousin, too much for a peaceful marriage to Gaia here. No, they had to get away as soon as possible.

Stelford stood warming his hands by the fireplace. The man was unkempt, still wearing his waistcoat and breeches from the night before.

"I'm sorry, my friend. I guess this was not an easy time for anyone." William walked near and patted the man on the back. "But I must thank you again for saving my life."

Pivoting, Stelford caught his gaze. "You would have done

the same."

Clear, untainted eyes looked back at William. His friend must be so undone, he'd skipped his drink.

William outstretched his hand. "I owe you."

"You don't." Stelford backed away, and then paced from the mantle to the piano then to the bay window. "I'm the debtor."

Something in his manner made the hair on William's neck rise. He moved to the sofa and sank into the cushions. "I'm listening."

Stelford made an audible gulp. "Lizzy's favorite flowers were yellow roses." He pounded on his chest. "I gathered them near and far for her. Her face shimmered when she laughed and a tiny crinkle set in her forehead whenever she angered. And when we kissed, the world stilled."

Looking at the flintlock mounted on the wall over the sideboard, and back to his alleged friend, William held his breath.

"Yes, I was Elizabeth's lover."

It would take twenty seconds to grab the gun, but at least one minute to retrieve the shots from his trunk in his bedchamber. Hot air fell from William's nose. "How could you?"

"Elizabeth and I were always in love. We were going to be married until her father and the late duke decided you two should wed."

"That can't be. You would've—or she would've told—"

"How could I tell you when you fell in love with her at first sight? She knew I was your friend, but said nothing." Stelford balled his fist and pounded his forehead. "I think she thought it was the best way to keep us both close: I, her slave, and you, her respectable husband."

Stelford started moving. "We were together the night before your wedding. She said she'd call off the ceremony, but went through with it anyway."

Elizabeth was so withdrawn that day. William thought she was shy, and needed to become used to marriage. He dropped his head into his hands.

"I tried very hard not to succumb to her draw. I stayed away until you wrote me to check on her near her time of confinement. She was your wife, but she was so vulnerable with her lay-in, then depressed after Mary's birth. Her tears, her need to be loved. She broke me."

Blood rushing to his ears, William tried to slow his rushing pulse. "Is Mary mine?"

"She's not mine. We never technically broke her vows, but we loved in our hearts and in the letters we drafted to each other." He pulled from his pocket an off-white stack of notes, Elizabeth's stationery, and folds of Stelford's private, blue-tinted paper and put them on the mantle.

Bile filling his throat, William lifted from the sofa. "You were there the night she died, before she fell."

"I was. We were going to run away to Scotland, but I told her I changed my mind. We argued in Mary's room. The baby started to cry, and she backhanded her into the rail."

With slow, labored steps, William approached the traitor. "She hurt Mary?"

"Yes. I suggested we get a doctor to look at her. Elizabeth became enraged and struck me, then grabbed the baby. I didn't know what she was going to do. I gave chase and took Mary from her arms. She lashed out wildly, lost her balance, and fell down the stairs. By the time I situated Mary and got to Elizabeth..." Stelford's voice broke. "Lizzy died in my arms."

William came within three feet of the man who'd had an affair with his duchess. "Why are you telling me this now? Why not when I returned to Cheshire with a loaded gun?"

"The guilt has been eating me alive. Miss Telfair thinks that I'm trying to drink it away. She's right."

Gaia knew? She betrayed him, too. Unable to restrain himself anymore, he lunged at Stelford. In a blink, his hands were about the man's throat. "How does Miss Telfair know? Did you share this sordid business with everyone but me, or were you trying to strike again and steal the woman I'm to marry?"

Prying free, Stelford gasped, "Last night, Miss Telfair found letters in Mary's trunk. The woman suggested I had the good sense to come clean."

William pinned him against the wall and stretched for the spear on the suit of armor. Out of his reach by six inches. Instead, he reared back his fist.

"Go ahead. I deserve it. The guilt of breaking our friendship, of thinking Lizzy'd still be alive if I'd run off with her....I can't take it anymore."

Something held William back from pummeling the broken backstabber. His arm became heavier than lead, and he couldn't make a fist to darken Stelford's daylights. He released him and threw him to the floor.

While his flesh wanted nothing more than to snuff the life out of Stelford, a small part of William's heart knew the weight of the guilt the man carried. Perhaps, God now gave William the power to curb his anger. Wretched timing for that miracle. "Oh, get out of my sight."

Stelford crawled then sprang to his feet. "Someday I'll make this right."

"There's nothing you or anyone on this earth can do to correct this. Go! Be out before I change my mind."

"I will make amends." The door shuddered as the fiend departed.

William stormed to the mantle, picked up the pile of notes, and burned them in the fire.

Alone, physically and mentally, he sank upon his knees. His best friend stole Elizabeth, and now Whimple sniffed at

Gaia. A chill swept over him as he imagined his father pounding his altar, his voice echoing condemnation for Miss Oliver, Elizabeth, William, Stelford, and even poor Gaia. "God, I don't want to live in condemnation. I can't fix me or Mary, or anything without You. I surrender."

He covered his eyes from the glow of the flames. His misery-prayer warrior would be proud, but no peace ushered into his veins. Could he outrun the demons of the past with no good friend and no Gaia?

CHAPTER TWENTY

To Elope

William dropped onto the sofa. His note of apology for rushing Gaia to elope had surely arrived at Chevron hours ago. Two in the afternoon, according to his pocket watch, and no fiancée. The sun shot golden rays through the bay window. She should be here so that they could rationally plan what to do. He wasn't opposed to eloping, but he had to make sure it was what she wanted.

Where was she? Could she still be mad?

Women… well, men, too, were contrary. The house seemed frozen since Stelford's departure. He took the life from Ontredale.

Playing with the brass buttons on his waistcoat, he counted the flickers of the wall candles. Other than reading to Mary, he hadn't had a very productive day.

Right now, he wouldn't mind entertaining neighbors, but, as word spread of his engagement, the visitors thinned. No need for the matchmakers to darken his door. Well, that would be the case if he hadn't ruined things with Gaia.

He sighed out of frustration. This must be the low point his father preached from the pulpit, but where was the *way out of no way?* It couldn't be for him. There was too much guilt and shame piled on his plate even for the Lord to reach him.

He closed his eyes. Gaia's olive face floated near. Then, he heard her sweet voice talking to God.

A laugh started from his mouth, but it turned to sorrow. He swiped at a wet droplet on his cheek. Maybe he wasn't desperate enough last night. He surely felt helpless now. "God, are you there? Have you forgotten me?"

He sat up. "Lord, don't forget me or my Mary. Please accept my repentance."

Opening his eyes, he didn't feel foolish. Saying it aloud allowed cool air to fill his chest.

The doors to the drawing room flew open.

William jumped up and stared face to face with Stelford. "What are you doing here, Judas?"

Stelford yanked off his dark beaver cap. "I have some news. You must listen to me."

Turning to the flintlock on the wall, William chided himself. Still not enough time to go get those bullets. "I think you've told me enough."

His betrayer stalked around the sofa, and clasped William's shoulder. "My spy, the cook, said the Telfair girl is eloping. If we leave now, we can intercept them."

William staggered backwards, bumping into the piano. He gripped the edge of the curved music box for balance. That's why she wasn't here. How could this happen?

Stelford walked closer. "If we hurry, we can catch her at the post. That's where they'd buy passage for the post chaise. We can go get your intended back."

Looking to his boots, William scuffed the points. Not his Gaia. Why didn't he tell her he loved her last night? His pride stopped him. Maybe it was best this happened now, before she could scorn his love, just like Elizabeth.

Knowing Gaia was in Whimple's arms, laughing at William's heart, would kill him. His battered vanity couldn't take another disappointment.

He lifted his chin and caught Stelford's gaze. "Why have you come; to rub this in my face?"

Stelford ripped his gloves off and stashed them in his pocket, his gaze dipping the entire time. "No. I want to right my wrong. I need to prove my worth to you. You are my oldest friend."

Folding his arms to keep from strangling the bearer of bad news, William walked to the window. "If Miss Telfair has chosen to love another, what kind of fool would it make me to give chase?"

Stelford's voice boomed. "One in love! If I had been bold enough to confront you before your wedding, or if I had attended the ceremony instead of waiting for Elizabeth to come to me, none of us would be in this sorry shape."

Turning, he stormed a few inches from Stelford and glared. "Leave Ontredale. I haven't shot you yet. You know I'm not a patient man, but I am a brilliant shot."

The anguished fool twisting the brim of his hat took a step backward. "You are a good shot. Wellington couldn't have had a better man in the field, but the war is over. This is a new battle. Does the lady know she's broken through your armor? Did you tell her you love her?"

"Stelford, I'm done loving another man's woman."

"Fine, I'll go find her and convince her to return. I will earn your forgiveness by saving you from this mistake." The man stomped from the room.

William pushed at his hair, and then rubbed his temples. At least Gaia attained what she'd always wanted. He should be happy for that, but his insides churned.

Mrs. Wingate came in with a tray of tea. "Sir, anything the matter?"

"I am no longer engaged. Miss Telfair has flown away."

The woman's lips pressed into a frown. "I am sorry, sir. It is probably for the best, given the St. Landon-Telfair history."

"What are you talking about?"

She shook her head. "You don't know?"

"No riddles, Mrs. Wingate."

"Your father. He arranged for a free man to be sold into slavery for forcing himself on a white woman, but the man wasn't guilty. You could tell by the way the woman looked at him."

William's hands fisted as his impatience took control of him. "What are you saying?"

"Your father arranged for a black, an African from Port Elizabeth, to be sold into slavery, Gaia Telfair's natural father. He claimed to be of a royal line, here in England to help his tribe."

"Where did my father sell him?"

"To Jamaica; he sought help from here for the money to make it all happen."

Horror thundered in his heart. "Jamaica is a death sentence. They don't have the same laws. There are no rights for slaves outside of England."

The old woman put her hand to her mouth as her head swiveled to the door.

He turned and froze, too, for Gaia and little Timothy stood at the entry.

Her face dulled, as if she might faint, and William leapt up to go to her, but stopped with arms outstretched. How could he touch her? How could she want anything from the son of a slaver, the son of the man who surely caused her father to die?

Gaia shook her head, but the shock remained. William's father had done it. Money from Ontredale, the place she wanted to call home, had financed it.

She blinked hard and pushed the feeling of

lightheadedness away. St. Landon blood had made Gaia's birth father disappear. William said death sentence. Tears leaked from her eyes.

"Gaia?" William scrambled closer. His face appeared blank with no smirk, frown, or smile on his face. "Is this true?"

Her heart beat hard, and she could only stare. "What part?"

"Gaia, is it true?"

Edging to within three paces, he crossed the rug. His fingers fidgeted. One hand ran through his hair, the other tugging and straightening his dark colored waistcoat. "It can't be true. My father couldn't have been so cruel, and you don't look..."

His gaze went to his boots. "Say something."

What did he want from her? The shame of being the product of an affair had disappeared, but she was still of mixed race and almost illegitimate. "I know part of it is true. I am black. My father let everyone believe a lie to protect my mother."

Thinking of her blood father's sacrifice, she lifted her head high. "My brother and I will leave. Mr. Whimple may still be outside. He brought us to you.

William leapt over the sofa and pulled her stiff form into his arms. "Run to me, Gaia, not away."

Her breath caught, being held so firmly against his chest. She didn't think she'd ever be in his arms again once the truth was exposed.

His solid voice held cracks, almost stuttering. "Mrs. Mrs. Wingate, make the boy, Master Timothy comfortable. Sweets and milk. We… his sister and I need to go."

She pried out of his desperate embrace, with heart still racing from his touch. "I'm not eloping with you today. We need to talk. I'm here to talk."

He spun her toward the door. "Yes, but your sister has eloped and if it's not the botanist, it could be someone less worthy." Clasping her palm, he swiveled to Albert. "Bring my hat and coat. Send for horses."

Before Gaia could order her thoughts or voice a complaint, William had placed her on a mount and had come alongside her.

"What if Julia has found love, but it's not to someone who Devonshire would think deserving? What if he's of a different class or race? Why should I stop her?"

His hand went toward her chin but he fingered her bonnet. "Had she spoken of anyone?"

"No."

"Then how could the intentions be honorable? You have to try going through the front door before you find a window."

She nodded and gripped the reins. "I suppose sneaking about isn't best."

"This isn't like our meeting in the woods. Gaia, we have much to discuss about us, but we must save your sister first. Her ruin will make this even more complicated, hurting you and your other sisters even more."

"I was th..." The heat or hurt in his eyes made her speech falter. "I wasn't thinking of me, just of her happiness. She's tired of being overlooked."

Snatching up Magnus's straps, he made the horse lunge. "Keep up prayer warrior. We have some riding to do."

Either William was a great actor, or the news that he was engaged to a mulatto hadn't sunk in. Could he have known? Had he sought her out, made her dream of him just to assuage guilt? Was she nothing more than a pawn to spite his late father?

CHAPTER TWENTY-ONE

Riding to Salvation

The onyx mare beneath her moved at a steady pace. Riding had been a rare treat, but one Gaia relished. William's stiff posture bounced at least six paces ahead. When he looked back, only a frown filled his face.

She slowed him down. He must regret his decision for her to accompany him, but the more she thought it, she couldn't have sat idly by, waiting for a man to save the day. Men.

Tightening her fingers about the reins, she pushed and caught up to within a few strides. If she hadn't been so tired and confused by William's insistence they elope, she would've thought more of her sister. The girl had the opportunity to tell Elliot the truth about Gaia's paternity, but didn't. Sisterly affection won after all.

A wave of guilt slapped her stomach, churning it. Did Elliot use careless words in his break about her intelligence, as he had said to Gaia? Men. What words did Mr. Telfair use to blame her mother for the stillborn twins? Did guilt and loss of her father make her succumb to consumption a few years later?

William's strong figure bounded ahead. His eyes must be

focused on the road, not his mulatto fiancée.

What if he hadn't known and just found out? Would he remember every time his lips were on hers? Was he thanking his good fortune he found out now before they married?

Gaia remembered each time. This fantasy life of being happy with William needed to end. Wasn't it obvious how things had changed, with no jokes, no touches?

Anger rolled in her stomach, torching everything. His father, the fire and brimstone pariah of the parish, he was the guilty person. The awful man pounding his pulpit, divining God's words, twisted things for his parishioners. The Oliver dressing- down was nothing compared to sending a man into slavery to endure hard labor and death.

Her birth father was dead. She'd only had him for less than a day, but his sacrifice, his love for her mother and Gaia in the womb, filled her. And now ugliness stole him again.

Eyes watering with sorrow, she glanced again at William's straight posture. He looked as if he were going to war. If he didn't know, this news—her race, the actions of his father—must torture him. How could William and Gaia go on together?

With a tug, she secured her bonnet and tapped her spectacles to a higher spot on her nose. Leaning into her mount, she forced the horse to catch up to William. Now they walked side by side.

His head pivoted in her direction. The handsome planes of his taut cheeks looked as if he chewed nails. He was angry at her, surely at her blood. There was no future for them.

Before their engagement, she and William were friends. Was that gone too? Gaia patted her brown saddle. "You don't need to be concerned. I'm not going to fall from my seat."

He opened his mouth, but then snapped it shut.

"William?" Panic laced through her. She'd lost all of him. She clutched the straps with a stronger grip. "You can tell me what you are thinking."

He looked away. "Just hang on to that horse. We'll be at the coaching inn within the hour."

William spied the inn at the top of the hill. The wind pushed at his back. Normally, it helped to make up time, as when he led his men across the fields of battle. He sighed and forced Magnus into a reduced pace.

Slowing his gait for Gaia, it would be a miracle if he got there before the post chaise left.

His insides raged, twisting his guts. This battle between what he'd learned of his father versus Gaia not telling him would surely kill him. If he'd barked out the questions in his head, she'd run from him as she did over his foolhardy assertions about Mary. His bloviating was a match to his father. How could she ever think William was any different?

He spied Gaia. A tense crinkle assaulted her forehead. Oh, how he'd love to reassure her, but there was nothing he could do to make up for Vicar St. Landon's cruelty. What could replace the love of a father for Gaia? His soul burned, for that was a question he couldn't answer, being St. Landon's son.

Gaia made her mount move closer to his. "Did you say something?"

The glint of her spectacles blinded him for a moment. He blinked a few times and thought of something safe, far from his vulnerable heart. "Why would your sister leave all her family and friends? Does she know what this will do to your family?"

Gaia hung her head, as if she examined the filly's hooves. "We have not been on the best of terms lately. She probably feels alone. Loneliness can lead one down the wrong path."

William tugged at his collar as memories of one of his father's sermons sparked. Reverend St. Landon would already condemn Miss Julia as naturally given to wantonness and evil. How many lives had he ruined? "We'll stop her."

"We need to talk about us, our fathers."

Magnus stumbled over a rock, snapping William's attention back to the trail. He didn't have the words to make things better, but one person did. *God, give me the words, the right ones to say.*

Did he whisper that aloud? Must be Gaia's influence.

Going around a fence and slogging across a dirt lane, he steadied Magnus then pulled to a stop. They'd arrived at the coaching inn. With a quick breath, he leapt down and stormed into the livery, towing both the horses. "Let me help you."

Before he could get to her, she'd slid down. Wide hazel eyes settled on him. What was she thinking behind those spectacles?

Resisting the urge to hold her close, he turned to the door. "We'll find your sister."

She put her jittering palm in the crook of his arm. The touch felt as if she was scared to put her fingers on him.

As he handed Magnus and the mare to a groom, he saw Stelford's stallion. Maybe the man caught up with them and kept a vigil. In spite of everything, Stelford acted like the friend, the brother he once knew. A sigh left his chest as the years of confidences came to William's remembrance. "Gaia, we aren't too late. Stelford's here. I guess he wasn't lying about wanting to make amends."

Her hand tightened about his forearm. She seemed to mumble *Stelford*, and then looked up at William with the sweetest eyes, wondrous windows that had to understand the delicate balance he now bore. Stelford, friend and enemy. "I am glad he told you. What a disastrous two days, to discover such secrets. I'm sorry."

"We'll talk of *our* elopement, once we stop *this* elopement."

He ignored the way her face scrunched up, and walked her

toward the inn. Two days of chaos ended now. William pressed open the door and slunk inside. The scent of ale and cooked onions and mutton hit him. The crowded inn hosted many tables and travelers.

On the far side of the room, Miss Telfair sat alone, slumping at a rough-hewn bench and a dark-stained table, sipping from a cup. Clad in a chocolate walking gown, an innocent frilled collar, and a perfectly-pinned blonde chignon, she looked out of place, lost.

An arm tugged on his shoulder. He spun and spied Stelford.

"I followed the wrong sister." His former friend bowed to Gaia. "Good to see you, Miss Gaia Telfair. I bought off the driver to leave without all the passengers. The couple is stuck here until the next coach heading out tomorrow morning."

"Thank you so much." Gaia straightened her bonnet then marched toward her sister.

William grimaced at Stelford as his mind counted the lies shared between Elizabeth and this man. The scale didn't balance with this good. "Why didn't you leave?"

With a lift of his shoulders, Stelford shifted his stance. "I couldn't let your fiancée's sister come to disgrace."

Taking a slow breath, William focused on the Telfairs. He needed help to dissuade this elopement. If Gaia couldn't convince the sister, maybe the man would be a better route. "Where's the dance master?"

"Oh, that's what he is? I thought he looked the spinning type, all long and lanky. He took a room. Miss Julia Telfair hasn't moved from that seat."

"Good girl; already having second thoughts." He reached into his pocket and pulled out a small sack of coins. "Give this to the dancer, and tell him to forget about this entire incident."

As he started toward the sisters, Stelford clapped his

shoulder again. "I know we're not restored, but I hope we are on the path to reconcile."

William shook free. The Lord hadn't answered that prayer yet, and William didn't possess the grace to do it on his own. "Let's finish this, and we'll see."

Stelford dropped his head and walked away, rebuffed. Maybe now he felt a tenth of the spurn William had borne, trying to win Elizabeth's approval. Yet if there had been no Stelford, wouldn't Elizabeth have chosen another? William let the steam out of his nostrils. Elizabeth never loved him. And now, because of his father, Gaia wouldn't either.

Gaia stared at the girl who, next to Seren, had been her closest confidante. It was as if a stranger sat on the other side of the table, muffled in brown. Gaia gripped the edge of the wood separating them. "Why are you doing this?"

Her sister's eyes grew wide, and her tall posture sagged even more as William stepped near. "What is your fiancé doing here?"

"He came to help talk you out of this." Gaia gripped Julia's gloved palm. "The question is why you are here."

Julia pulled away, and lowered her gaze to the handkerchief she twisted around her thumb. "Eloping."

William sank next to Gaia and wove his fingers with her fidgeting ones, stilling them against the table. "For an eloping woman, you don't look happy."

Julia shrugged and started rolling the cloth tighter. Her brow raised as her chin lifted. "How am I supposed to look? Like Gaia? She's been proposed to twice."

"Twice?" William released Gaia's palm and rubbed his jaw. His shoulders dipped as he turned Gaia's direction. "Since your sister hasn't broken with me yet, we're still engaged. The botanist is free. Mr. Whimple is still available for you to go after."

"Oh, who cares about the leaf-searching man!" Water trickled from her eyes. "All my family's expectations have been on me. And my younger sister is the one to make two men come up to scratch." She patted her wrinkled handkerchief to her face. "What does that say of me?"

"Your fortunes are not tied to anyone." Gaia made her voice sound steady and strong, but fear for her sister set her spine trembling. "This isn't right. It's not like you to be this reckless."

With a roll of her eyes, Julia sat back against the bench. "What? To be married before my little sister is reckless?"

William rubbed his neck as a stream of air left his nose. "Never marrying might be better than wedding someone who can't or won't cherish you."

Julia bit her lip then sat up, eyes wide. "Being an old maid is to be preferred? I should aspire to be a governess or companion to your children?"

Gaia's cheeks warmed. The thought of having William's children, of building a full life with him, had teased her mind long into the night. But that hope was gone, wasn't it?

Emotionless, thinned lips graced his face, his gaze boring into hers. "So, Miss Telfair, you'll cast your lot to the first one to propose?"

"That's what Gaia did. She agreed to marry you, because you asked. Everyone knows she...." Julia looked William's direction then closed her mouth.

Tapping his fingers against the rough oak of the table, William closed his eyes for a moment. So much emotion seemed trapped behind his calm exterior. If only Gaia could know his heart.

"Things change. Hearts change too," his voice was low, and he folded his arms. "And if you've found happiness, we should celebrate it, but you are running off with no thought of your family. The dance master might be a wonderful and deserving young man, but you are a genteel woman. Some might not look well upon this match. You have to have enough love for the rough patches. Do you?"

"No gentleman has asked." Julia wiped her nose and held the cloth, as if she could hide her wet face. "I'm tired of waiting."

The pain in Julia's voice made Gaia tear up. "You're a good person. The prettiest spirit when you're not fretting. You deserve to be happy."

William reached into his pocket and drew out his handkerchief. The monogrammed fabric whipped in the stagnant air as he offered it to Gaia. "Did this young man, knowing the disappointment an elopement will bring upon your parents and your younger sisters, have enough respect for you to ask your father's permission?"

Her head bowed. "No, but he didn't care if my shyness robbed my conversation. He drew words out. I know he cares for me." Julia's gloved hand fisted. "None of the gentlemen did. They each abandoned me."

Something about her sister's tone alerted Gaia. Was it a streak of defiance or fear? "I don't think you wanted them, Julia. You've been sabotaging these matches."

"You two should go, forget I existed like the rest of our friends and family will."

"No, Julia. You've had opportunity after opportunity. Even Elliot. What are you doing, sister?"

She peered at Gaia, her eyes drifting to the right, as if a thought consumed her. "You don't remember, but our parents' marriage was not good. They argued, fought over things that shouldn't matter." Julia reared up and strengthened her voice. "No, I don't want to marry just anyone, but I fear being left alone. I hoped a gentleman would like me enough to lead me from my shyness, opportune me to converse. Then I'd know he truly cared about me, not my measly dowry, or looks that will fade."

"Only the dance master made you shed your facade?" A whip of air vented William's nostrils. His level shoulders hung lower and his gaze went high, maybe to the whitewashed ceiling. "I knew a woman, as beautiful as you. So lovely, it didn't matter that her conversation was small, as were her interests. She married, not for her heart, but to meet her father's expectations. The man possessed the right connections, but the things important to this groom did not interest her. She pretended it did, and the fool swallowed the act."

Julia rubbed her forehead. "Let me guess. They learned to love each other's differences and lived happily ever after."

"No. They both were miserable until one left the earth." He leaned in close. "She should not have pretended to be a certain way just to gain a husband. You can't be one way to attract someone, then change and expect a man to not care. Life is too short to make that kind of mistake."

No air of joke lay in his stiff demeanor. His torment over his marriage still sat on his chest. If Gaia could, she'd embrace him. William didn't deserve this yoke.

"You needn't marry." He took Gaia's hand in his, the first time since Mrs. Wingate's announcement, and kissed it. "With your sister marrying me... or her other beau, the Telfairs will be protected. Now you have time to make yourself happy."

"But what do I say? My fiancé's upstairs." Her cheeks flushed scarlet. "He's waiting for me."

Mr. Stelford marched into the front door and made hand motions, but nothing like what Gaia and Timothy practiced.

William nodded then leaned toward Julia. "Mr. Stelford has just returned from visiting the dancer. This honorable lad, who proclaimed to love you, has run off and left you for fifty pounds.

Julia fell onto the table, heaving with tears.

Gaia went to her sister's side of the table and scooped her up into her arms. "This is a blessing."

William glanced at Gaia. His gaze locked with hers. "When a man really loves you, he'll do what it takes to win you. He will try to earn your trust. He'll be patient and give you the world if you so desire. And he'll think of you and your family first. Running off would be a last resort, not the first. He'll even end a farce if he thinks it is for your good."

The intensity in his sea-blue eyes caught Gaia's breath. Her pulse raced as she hugged Julia tight. She lifted her sister's chin. "Rediscover what makes your conversation, your talents, sparkle. Show the world that you are not only beautiful, but also accomplished and witty. Let them love you like I do."

"But Gaia, Cheshire, I've ruined myself. The scandal will come out about this elopement." Julia wrenched from Gaia's embrace and banged her head on the table. "Now this scandal will impact all my sisters. I'm so sorry. I need to go away."

Gaia brushed her hair, stroked her cheek. "We'll be fine. William knows how to fix this. His family knows how to solve problems."

William looked at her as if she'd slapped him. He stood and adjusted the brim of his beaver hat. "I'm going to rent Julia a chaise to take you home. If we get this done quickly, no one will be the wiser."

After a final wipe of her eyes, her sister balled up her handkerchief and stuffed it in her reticule. "Please, send me home."

Thank goodness, Julia wouldn't toss her life away. Now if they could sneak her back to Chevron, life for the Telfairs could go on as normal.

But Gaia wasn't a Telfair by blood, so her life couldn't return to normal. It was time for it to be spectacular, but how could that ever happen without William being a part of her future?

CHAPTER TWENTY-TWO

Return to Ontredale

William adjusted his greatcoat. The wind had picked up, and the air held the scent of rain. The sun had set about an hour into the route home. Gaia rode at his side, silent.

"I should've insisted upon you going back with your sister. You must be tired."

Gaia glanced up at him. "My brother is waiting for me at Ontredale. And we haven't had a chance to discuss anything."

He craned his neck to look over the tree line. He could make out the roof in the moonlight. "Well, Ontredale's not much farther. We'll even pass the path to the old vicarage."

A yawn left her mouth. "You suppose Vicar St. Landon passed judgment over my father there or at Chevron?"

Turmoil stirred in his gut; part shame, mostly guilt of his bloodline. "It's late. You and Timothy will stay, and I'll send you home by carriage in the morning."

She shook her head. Her straw bonnet bounced with the effort. "We need to talk."

He nodded and motioned for Magnus to speed up. The last thing he wanted was to allow his muddled thoughts to rein. Something awful like the truth was bound to come out.

Gaia slumped in the saddle. "William, Ontredale's over the

bend. Pray, let's stop a moment."

Riding aside must've taken a toll on her. She needed to stop and rest. Tugging her mare's harness, he led them to a grassy knoll under a canopy of trees.

Gaia fell into his arms as he lifted her from her mount. "You are a very strong man, but what of your strength over the past?"

Patting away her arms, he stepped back. "Well, Stelford, the backstabber, wants me to forgive him. I'm grateful he made sure the coach left without Miss Julia and the dancer, and that he's following your sister's carriage back to Chevron, but he and Elizabeth were lovers."

Coming closer, Gaia's sweet whisper made his spine stiffen. "Maybe you should forgive him, and I will forgive your father."

He couldn't help eyeing her as if she'd lost her mind. "Well, if I'm dolling out these measures, I should forgive my father, too, for selling my fiancée's father to certain death. Slaves have no right outside of England. They are property again. I'm the son of slaver, perhaps murderer."

Gaia shook her fists in the air as frustration overwhelmed her. "Your father is dead and so is mine. What of us? Tell me what you are thinking on the matter. I can't take not knowing your heart."

His jaw tensed, but he forced out the words that had stuck in his head since Mrs. Wingate's pronouncement. "Can you honestly say you can forgive my father for selling yours into slavery, for lording over the adultery, being judge and juror, like there is no grace?"

Her shoulders hunched as she looked at the grass beneath them. "I didn't know your father. The only memories of him I have are his sermons."

Not a good enough answer, but she'd initiated the interrogation; he'd ask about everything that blocked their path. "Gaia, how long have you known of this business? Were you going to marry me without telling me?"

"I intended to tell you, but you promised a long engagement. There would be no need to expose this sordid affair if we decided not to wed. I was to tell you after church, but you had to mix up your tinctures and nearly die. How could you be so careless? Don't you know I need... Mary needs you?"

"What did you say?"

She covered her mouth for a second. "When you insisted we elope, I came today to tell you. I had no knowledge of your father's hand in my father's fate."

Gaia had doubts too, but more so about him, not his father's dealing. He wanted to raise her chin, but didn't know if he could without kissing her. And he could never again give into that draw without everything being clear, without knowing Gaia was his. "You didn't know."

"As you said, I look tanned from the sun, not an adulterous affair."

He rubbed at his skull, trying hard to keep ahead of his temper. He was so angry at his father he could punch a tree. "Don't put words in my mouth. How long have you known of these deeds?"

"The day you caught me crying in the woods; that's when I learned Mr. Telfair wasn't my blood father. But how long have you known of your father's role? Was your pursuit of me to spite Vicar St. Landon? Am I some black token to get even with your father?"

"No." He took her hands and lifted them to his chest. If he could, he'd push them inside so she could feel how his heart beating for her. "Your ability to teach a child to talk or to make signs with his fingers, that was my interest, but things changed."

She stilled and stared. The night sky reflected in her

spectacles. Behind the dark rims, her eyes beamed like the stars. The soft echo of her voice sounded like music, "How did it change?"

Against everything he knew to be safe for his soul, he held her close. Would he forever wrestle with Whimple to own these embraces? He'd come to love Gaia; not her race, or the baggage of their fathers, but sweet Gaia. "I don't when or how, but things changed for me. When they did, this marriage seemed right."

Her heart beat strong against his chest. "Things seemed right too, but then you thought I could hurt Mary. You believed me to be white. What do we do now?"

He dipped his head, almost touching her lips. "Do you love me, Gaia? If you do, we can survive anything."

Her hands locked on his neck. "I'm not sure what love is anymore, but what I feel for you is overpowering."

This close to her, all he wanted was to devour her in kisses and push away any thoughts of others, but he pulled away. "Gaia, release me."

She leaned into him, her arms skirting his waist. "I don't understand."

He stood tall, pushing out of her embrace. "I can't keep this up. Release me from this engagement."

Gaia stumbled backwards as she covered her mouth with her gloves. The fine cloth absorbed the moisture leaking from her eyes. "You're like Mr. Telfair. You want no part of a mulatto."

His pupils narrowed, as if she spoke gibberish. "That's not it. I was selfish in this engagement from the start, thinking of how this would help Mary, and then I let my attraction to you take over my reason. But you now have your offer from Whimple. It's what you've always wanted. I have to step out of the way for you to be happy."

Wide-eyed, she gaped at him. "What if I don't want you to

do that?"

He took off his hat and fanned his forehead. "Why didn't you tell me about his proposal? Still weighing your options?"

Gaia looked at the ground and the dust gathering on her ivory leather slippers, the ones William had sent. Perhaps she should have left them in tissue paper. "I didn't want you upset."

"Yes. You didn't want to see my temper. I have one, Gaia. It inflames over injustice. It explodes when I need to protect the ones I care for, but I won't let it boil over from the frustration of loving another man's woman. Not again."

She tugged on his elbow and came so close the tarragon scent of his skin filled her nostrils, more so than the tired horseflesh behind them. "Just because Elliot proposed doesn't mean I will accept."

"If Stelford had told me about Elizabeth, I would've stepped aside. If what Stelford felt for Elizabeth was one tenth of what I feel for you…" He rubbed his brow. "It is my duty to give you the desire of your heart."

"No, you're afraid; I never would have guessed it, but I see it now."

His head tilted above her, as if the sky would tell him what to say. Then he nodded. "I've done the vows of faithfulness, had the marriage breakfast. Can you promise our story has a happy ending?"

"Do you love me, William?"

"What I feel is irrelevant. The draw to your true love will be too deep." He tipped a rock and kicked it deep into the night. "I'm a widower with a special daughter. All the money in the world can't take away the fear that my unchecked temper will make you hate me. One day, you will regret the whim that has taken you from your precious Whimple."

She shook her head. "You're tired; you don't know what you're saying."

"Do I need to break something for you to listen? That got Elizabeth's attention."

"I'm not Elizabeth." She wanted to shake her fists at him again. Instead, she took a long breath. "If I knew you had enough room in your heart for me, that I could be safe in your love, then I would be yours forever. Can't you see that? I'm afraid that you will hate the mulatto you've married, that you will dread the dark skin our son may have or, worse, you think me unfaithful because of the past."

His gaze swept over her, but his mouth stayed a flat, grim line. He must not believe her.

"You want me to beg off our engagement? Fine, consider it done." She sprang back onto the mare's back. "I guess we'll never know what it would be like, but I was willing to try. I see you, William St. Landon, temper and all, with the questionable father, the baggage, and I still wanted to be in your life."

"Gaia?"

She turned her back to him. It was too late. His mulatto courtship was over. She sprang onto her mount, reached down at the dusty slippers that made her feel treasured, picked one off, and tossed it to him. "I'll pray for you to find happiness so you'll not become like Mr. Telfair, but at least I know why, when I reached for you, you can't reach back."

Gaia made her horse sprint to Ontredale. A few leaps away, she sank into the saddle. William shouldn't see her tears. He shouldn't change his mind out of pity.

With a leather slipper caught in his palm, William watched Gaia ride all the way to Ontredale's steps. The girl rode faster than he'd thought her capable. It was best she left him now. He couldn't live tentatively, waiting for the moment she decided their marriage was a mistake.

The rain started as he shifted his weight atop Magnus. The

initial drops obscuring his vision turned into a relentless pounding. He pulled his greatcoat tighter about him and waited until he saw the light of the entry brighten from the opening door. He might be soaked, but Gaia was safe inside; safe from his temper and his love.

He shook from the wetness seeping into his collar. The last thing he needed was to become so waterlogged he succumbed to an ailment. He'd never been so sickly. His blasted cousin's treachery gave illness a new meaning.

Frozen in place, he counted windows, and wondered what rooms Gaia visited.

Her heated words rang in his head. She admitted to wanting a life with him, and he'd rejected her. And now she wore the shoes he'd bought her. Now.

He fingered the slick leather of her shoe and wiped off droplets of cold rain. Blasted rain. The smooth ivory material hadn't stained in the water. Tough enough to endure long hikes, but stylish enough and dear enough to be treasured, just like Gaia. Tucking the slipper into his coat, he thought of the turn of her countenance as she fled on horseback. She didn't seem relieved by a break, but hurt. What was he doing, making decisions based on fear or hatred, or rain?

William slapped his skull. He needed to ride at full speed to clear his mind. He turned his gelding away from Ontredale, and took to the moors. The minute he broke free to the wide-open flat plains, his spirit soared. He could breathe.

The scent of freshness and splashing mud filled his nose. During Parliament, he longed for rain to cleanse the London air. When it did, for a few minutes, it smelled like this; clean and honest.

A high tor sat to his right. If it weren't so wet, he'd climb the slick point, as he'd done so many times growing up in Devonshire. A little older, a little wiser, he needn't risk life and limb. Mary would have a hard enough time. She needed one living parent.

His father would be proud of his caution.

Now William's stomach turned.

If he were truly honest with himself, he'd darken his own daylights for comparing Gaia with Elizabeth. The two were nothing alike.

His wife died more than a year and half ago, and his anger at her had not relented. Now, he judged Gaia by Elizabeth's failings. The leather strap of the harness slipped his glove and slapped his cheek. The sting made him refocus on the path. He pointed Magnus back toward Ontredale. With Gaia gone, he needed to be there if Mary had one of her terrible nights.

If he decided to forgive his child's mother, how would he do it? Cold in the ground, Elizabeth couldn't admit she needed forgiveness. Nor could his father.

Magnus slowed to the point in the road where he could journey to Ontredale or turn to his father's old chapel. If William were going to forgive the dead, he might as well start with the one toward whom he harbored the most offense, the man who sold Gaia's father into slavery. He nudged Magnus forward to his father's old vicarage.

Gaia eased out of the rocking chair and took a closer peek at Lady Mary. The child closed her eyes. One arm wound tighter around her doll, the other clutched her blanket. She did it… soothed herself, and went back to sleep.

Gaia leapt up but landed on quiet scrunched toes. Too much noise and she'd wake the poor girl. What a shock to enter Ontredale and hear the child shrieking! No matter how mad she was with William, she'd never leave Mary so upset.

With a little more work, maybe crying could be replaced by other gestures, then words. A joy raced in Gaia's heart. If she continued to help Mary, love her, the child might start speaking again. The thought of loving William might be gone, but she could still aid Mary. Rescuing Julia tonight would have to be enough for Mr. Telfair to agree.

Reaching into the crib, she tucked the pink blanket about the child. Mary smiled in her sleep. Maybe butterflies met her in this dream.

Gaia's heart beamed. She did love Mary, but children were her weakness. Pity William was such a dunderhead. How dare he want to end things, right when she thought she might love him!

She tiptoed out of the room and left the door cracked. Her fingers smoothed the fine mahogany grain, the fresh notches. William's steward must've been busy making repairs, but she wasn't ready to test the lock.

Gaia pivoted and backed into Mrs. Wingate. "I'm sorry."

"No harm done, ma'am." She smoothed her skirt and picked up her folded sheets. "I'm just glad you've returned. You're a good influence on his lordship."

Gaia influenced William? Influenced by a mulatto? Not possible. "Mary's sleeping. Make sure no one disturbs her."

"That I will." Mrs. Wingate's solemn expression lifted with the curl of her lips. "I couldn't get your brother to take a nap. I left him writing in the drawing room, but he might be getting a cookie from the kitchen." The housekeeper curtsied then walked down the long hall.

Gaia clutched the railing and took to the treads. With a glance at the window, she witnessed drops of rain growing on the amber glass.

Good and wet. Maybe the rain would wash away William's nonsense. Nevertheless, he'd been sick. The rain couldn't be good. He might be able to turn off his feelings, but she couldn't. "Lord, keep William in Your care."

God always heard her, even when she spoke nonsense, and He still loved her even when she turned away. Gaia's spirit lightened. She slipped past Albert and reached for the drawing room doors. What mischief could her brother have gotten into unattended? Entering, she didn't see him at the drawing desk. "Tim... Miss Smythen, when did you arrive?"

William's cousin stood up from the sofa.

The woman wrung her hands together. Her onyx cape was damp, and clung to her arms. "I've come to talk to William. I need... Why am I explaining myself to you?"

Any desire to make the lady more comfortable disappeared. With that horrible attitude, Miss Smythen could stay wet. "Cheshire is not here. I think you'll need to come back tomorrow."

Miss Smythen's countenance darkened. Her lips twitched then settled into a frown. "Not here? Then I'll go see Mary. I do miss the dear. Perhaps I'll take her on a walk."

Gaia squinted at her. What an absurd notion on a night like this. "It's the evening and it's raining. The child has just settled down."

With a huff leaving her lips, Miss Smythen moved near. "I am her nearest relation. If I want to go see her, I will."

Was that a threat? Something was terribly wrong. "You know the duke is very vigilant of Mary's routine. He wouldn't want his daughter awakened."

The woman pranced from the room and headed for the stairs. Gaia caught her. "Don't make a fuss. Why don't you go back into the drawing room? Let's have a civil cup of tea."

"If you insist." She walked back into the room.

Gaia approached Albert. "Please go to Mary's room. Let no one go into it without Cheshire's or my approval."

His deep brown eyes whipped over her. "I want to, Miss, but I can't leave my post."

"It's important."

He nodded his head and took to the stairs, just as Mrs. Wingate descended. "Albert, where are you going?"

His shoulders drew wide. "Miss Telfair says to guard Lady

Mary."

Mrs. Wingate dipped her chin. "She is to be the mistress of this house. It's fine to do the good things she says."

"Yes, ma'am." Albert pivoted, bowed toward Gaia, then continued up the stairs.

Her mind eased. Something about Miss Smythen's demands to take the child set the hairs of her neck on edge. She wouldn't let the agitated woman around helpless Mary, not without William to supervise.

Mrs. Wingate passed beside her. "Ma'am, where are your shoes?"

"One's caught in the storm, the other is in Lady Mary's room.

The old woman smiled and then headed toward the kitchen. "Seems as if you need to decide where you belong."

As she straightened her posture and put her finger to her sides, Gaia looked Mrs. Wingate in the eye and prepared for a dressing-down. Knowing her bloodline, she had to disapprove.

The housekeeper smiled. Her gaze set, as if she truly looked at Gaia. "I think you'd do more good here than outside Ontredale. Miss Oliver, the girl you befriended once, she was involved with my nephew, an under-gardener here. You did her a service, being kind to her. Your goodness outshines everything."

Gaia didn't know what to say, and she stood there, blinking at Mrs. Wingate traipsing down the hall. The goodness inside, manifesting Christ's love in her heart for others, made a difference in Mrs. Wingate's opinion… shouldn't it make a difference to Gaia?

Yes; yes, it should.

Smiling, she marched into the drawing room just as a maid left through the side entrance. Miss Smythen stirred the pot and poured two cups. Over tea, she'd get the woman to settle down and unburden herself. Maybe if she waited with his cousin long enough, she'd see William one more time. One last moment of privacy, she could tell him of her intentions to help Mary, even without their marrying. Hopefully, the rain cleared his fog long enough to listen.

"Let's toast to the new Duchess of Cheshire." The woman lifted the tiny china cup to Gaia.

Heat from the cup warmed Gaia's palms. The tea smelled like almonds and a hint of something else. Anxious over William still being out in such weather, she sipped the hot tea, hoping it would ease her stomach.

CHAPTER TWENTY-THREE

Forgiveness

Lightning silhouetted the outline of a cross atop the vicarage. The stars cast light over the small cemetery next to the main building. The last time William visited, the war had ended, and he came here to view his father's grave. Sadness filled him on that cold, grey day. His father never cared for his military successes, and William had stopped trying to earn his approval. They hadn't seen each other in years.

He should be alive today so he could be confronted over what he did to Gaia's father. How could he be so cruel? Who gave him the power to destroy lives?

Leaping down, he tugged his top hat a little tighter, so the wind wouldn't catch the brim. Miserable weather shouldn't stop William from having his say. He tied Magnus to the wrought- iron gate and stalked to the cemetery.

His boots sank into muck as he passed headstones and sculptures until he got to the grave at the base of the elm tree. The farthest from the rest seemed fitting for the aloof vicar. William bent down. A flash of light cast a rainbow on the stone. He turned to view the great stained-glass of the church. Another lightning strike illuminated the cross within the colors. His father had loved this living, the quaint church possessing the hardest pews in all of England.

With his gloves, William pushed dirt from the stone and gave the headstone a little polish. *Reverend Joseph St. Landon.*

As a lad, pride filled William's heart when his father preached from the pulpit. It wasn't until William read the entire Bible and discovered that the scriptures held more than correction for sin. It also possessed the word 'grace'. Reverend St. Landon never preached it or offered it to his household.

He definitely didn't offer it to Gaia's mother and blood father. He wouldn't offer it to Gaia. He'd shun her, and Mary too.

"Papa, how could you stand in that pulpit and offer nothing but condemnation?"

He let his voice get louder; maybe the old man could hear him. "Papa, why did you twist God's love, and show hate? Did you not know of His love?"

"Adultery is wrong. There is no right in it, but plenty of men and women commit it. Did Gaia's father have to be sent to death? If he'd looked like Stelford, would you have absolved him?"

"I love Gaia. Her race doesn't matter to me. If she will still have me, maybe her blood will cleanse our line."

Heat built in William's lungs, but he blew it out. His lips caught an extra portion of rain droplets. Thinking of all the bad things his deceased father accomplished would never heal his innards. He'd have to remember that, before he was Cheshire or St. Landon, or even William, he was called 'son'. With the man dead, did his crimes matter?

As Gaia would do, he called out to God this time. "Lord, how do I honor a father who is less than?"

All these years of believing he never measured up to the vicar's expectations. Well maybe that was good. He didn't want to be like him, a man who could hurt others; someone who could hurt Gaia. "Lord, let me not become him. Take away the guilt that has bound me all these years. Help me to forgive. Let me be slow to anger and fast to make amends."

He wiped rain from his face and didn't care if anyone saw him prostrate in a cemetery. Pride didn't matter; only true repentance.

"And God, please send word to wherever Rev. St. Landon and Elizabeth ended up, that I forgive them; that I'll raise Mary to know the best of them, even while acknowledging their wrongs."

Though the sky dumped water, soaking and weighing down his greatcoat, he never felt more liberated. Grace was freeing; offering it, even more so.

With a final look at the lone elm, the marble headstone, he stood and trudged back to the gate.

In an odd way, if Gaia's father had claimed her, William's love for her would never have grown. They'd never have danced at a ball or kissed in masks. If, by some miracle, they'd happened upon each other, their roles would have centered on employment. And he wasn't one to chase a servant into a closet, no matter how pretty.

Their worlds would have been so different. Could love have won, found a way, if she weren't viewed as legitimate, a proper Telfair? He shook his head as his soul overflowed with gratitude for knowing and loving Gaia. Maybe God *does* work good out of everything for those who love and trust Him.

From this day forward, he would fully trust God.

He leapt onto Magnus and headed to Ontredale. Would Gaia see this change? With his heart fully opened, would she have him?

Maybe Gaia should've had dinner by now. Food might give her the energy to keep awake.

Though Mrs. Wingate's tempting tray of cookies and

scones sat on the table, the smell of cinnamon and sugar turned Gaia's stomach. Her normally-straight posture slouched, and she leaned back on the couch.

A yawn escaped. Maybe she should go ply the housekeeper for a room.

Miss Smythen took her arm, "Let's go for a walk. The night air will be good for you."

Gaia squinted at the billowing window curtains. The musk of rain filtered inside, splashing against the glass. "It's pouring. Not good."

Responsibilities. She should get up and check on Mary and Timothy. Where was Timothy? With all her might, she pushed from the sofa. Swaying, Gaia headed to the writing desk.

Timothy's work sat on the marble top. In addition to Ms, he did red Ws and black Os. Red? Timothy must've rummaged through the desk and found the ink. Hopefully, it wasn't too expensive. The neat lines were smeared by her sweaty fingers. The squiggles ran together. "Oh, I ruined it."

Fanning the letter to push cool air on her neck, she turned to show Timothy's accomplishments. "See, it's ruined."

A gasp left Miss Smythen, and she fell back a step. "Clever; you found my paper and ink."

"Paper?" Gaia felt a little like Timothy as she mocked the woman's tones.

Storming over to her, arms swaying, lips twitching, Miss Smythen tried to yank the note from Gaia's fingers. "Yes; I thought that if I blackmailed William, he'd turn to me."

"Not a nice thing to do." In a low tone, mimicking the late scoundrel Vicar St. Landon, making sermons, she asked, "Have you thought about the consequences?"

She grabbed Miss Smythen's face and squished her cheeks. "No, I think not."

The woman pulled away. She folded her arms across her dark cape. Maybe Miss Smythen should save her outfit for the next Masked Ball.

Miss Smythen rubbed her jaw. "You unworthy thing. You're poor, from a family of nobodies; how could he think of marrying you?"

"I *am* somebody. My Father in Heaven made me somebody. My true father is royalty in Africa. I deserve." Gaia plucked at her skin, raised her hands and twirled, as she'd done under her precious oak. Dizzy, she fell back against the cold marble top of the desk. "If you stopped doing mean things, you'd realize you're someone, too."

The lady's voice sounded harsh and screeching, like when Gaia accidentally slid her nails against a slate board, "Africa? Are you a mulatto… a heathen, a horrid brown thing; how could William love you?"

"Ah, William; he's too angry to love anyone," her own fury had melted with the relaxing tea. Still gripping Timothy's work, Gaia swirled around, as if William held her in a waltz. "But little black me caught his attention; must not be so bad after all."

Miss Smythen caught her arm. "I think we should take a walk and see whether we can find him."

"I must run to him again. He's always telling me to run to him." Her pulse raced even more than before. "Lead the way."

The arched roof of Ontredale showed in the lightning. William kicked Magnus to spur him forward. Maybe Gaia stayed because the weather had become so foul. Oh, let her be there, waiting for him and only him.

A carriage swung wide near his gelding. A hand, lovely and slim, opened the window and waved.

Young women, flirting with a stranger on a night like this. Yet the curve of the fingers, the ivory kid glove looked familiar, like the pair that matched the shoe in his pocket. Must be the love in his heart for Gaia. Everything sounded of her voice, and now his heart made him see her in odd places, too.

With a dip of his hat, he nodded but then motioned for Magnus to trot the final leg to Ontredale.

It was late, maybe close to nine. *Please, let Mrs. Wingate have made Gaia stay.* Gaia had to know how he felt and would forgive him.

No more joking and hiding his love. She needed to know he listened to her. Their engagement must be kept. In fact, they should elope tonight, as he'd originally planned.

Magnus sprinted the last mile. The gelding muscled down the path and dropped William near the front steps. A groom ran out and grabbed the reins as William patted the horse's hind legs. "Give him an apple. Mighty fine job tonight."

He nodded to his groom then pounded up the steps and through the open door. The house was quiet.

Was everyone already in bed? Dropping his greatcoat, hat, and gloves on the table where Albert should be, he pivoted and moved to the drawing room.

He threw open the doors. Nothing. The room was empty.

Was Gaia with Mary?

Taking the treads by twos, he reached the landing. Albert sat in a chair by Mary's room.

His heart beat a little faster. Something was wrong. Mary!

William pushed past him and charged into his daughter's bedchamber.

The little girl slept in her crib. Her chubby little arms curled about her doll. He took a deep breath, but no Gaia sat in the rocking chair. Could she be sleeping?

He tiptoed out of the room and approached the footman. "Why have you left your post?"

"Miss Telfair asked me to stay here and let no one in without your permission."

"Why would she do that?"

Albert puffed out his chest. "You don't argue too much with that kind of woman. It's better to do what she says. You'll learn that. Should I return to the door, sir?"

Too much wisdom was packed in Albert's small words. He would dwell on them later, when he kissed Gaia. "If Miss Telfair felt you should be here, stay. Where is she?"

"The drawing room, sir, with Miss Smythen."

A pain lanced William's skull at the mention of his evil cousin. He sprinted down the steps. When he got a hold of Deborah, he'd wring her neck. Then he'd show the wench grace.

He marched into the drawing room, this time all the way inside, but it was as empty as when he first entered Ontredale.

An ivory piece of paper lay on the floor by the sofa. His heart pounded.

He picked it up. Only curly letters. No blackmail note. A sigh left him. The thought that the blackmailer could have gotten back into his home burned his gut. Yet, the red Os did look the same color as the villainous letters. Something wasn't making sense.

Where was Gaia? Where was Deborah?

A picture of his cousin sitting at this writing desk the night she put belladonna in his tea entered his head. He pulled open the drawer and found a stack of the ivory paper and an open bottle of blood-red ink. Could Deborah be the blackmailer?

A tinkle sounded behind him. He looked, but saw nothing out of place.

His stomach twisted as lightning flashed in the distance.

The doors of the drawing room opened. He spun, hoping Gaia would enter.

Mr. Telfair, pale and coughing, slogged inside. "Where are my daughter and my son?"

"Well, Miss Julia is on a post chaise. It moves a little slower than horseback, but she'll be at Chevron within the hour."

The man took a deep breath. "Well, that solves one girl's whereabouts, but I'm talking about Gaia. She and Timothy are missing. You've not married yet. She must be kept respectable, and not blemish my name."

His *name*? Was that all the man could see, not the pain he'd given to Gaia? William swallowed gall. "Is that the sentiment that led you and my father to sell a man into slavery?"

Mr. Telfair's thin hands shook, but he pulled them beneath his grey coat. "That business is none of your concern."

"It is when it makes Gaia cry; when she speaks of reaching for a father's love and missing it. Have you no care for her, other than your precious *name*?"

"It was a long time ago," Telfair's voice lowered, "a long time."

William moved closer to him, the picture of how hurt Gaia was when she met him at her oak reverberating in his head. "When I find Gaia, and if she will still have me, we will elope; so you don't have to worry about her using your name ever again. Pity. She's an excellent girl, and would have made any loving father proud."

Telfair's frown became more pronounced, his tone almost guttural. "She's the seed of adultery."

William could never look at his Mary that way, or Gaia. "She's a gift."

"I understand the lust of propping her up in your bed, but mulatto blood for your heir? Have you thought it through? Now that you know, I'll withdraw my consent, if we can keep things quiet."

The thought of Gaia welcoming him to her bed, of her bearing their children, filled him, put fire in his bones. "You will do nothing of the sort. I will marry her if she'll have me. Our children could be white as sheet or as dark as my boots.

My children will be loved."

The old man squinted and shook his head. "You don't care she's half-white?"

He thanked God in his heart that bitterness and prejudice never overtook him, as it did Mr. Telfair. Yet resentment could have, if not for William's prayer-warrior. "She has all my heart. That's what matters."

Clang. The suit of armor tipped over. Spry young Timothy stood behind it, his blue eyes wide as guineas.

Mr. Telfair motioned to his son. "Timothy, come here."

The boy stayed frozen to the wall.

"Tim—"

William waved him to be silent. He moved closer to the boy. "My friend, where is your sister?"

"Tea. Made ill."

"Tea?" His horrid cousin. "Did a mean lady give it to her?"

The boy nodded.

Heart almost in his throat, he put his hands on the boy's shoulders. "Did she take Miss Gaia somewhere?"

Again, Timothy nodded.

Mr. Telfair coughed, and then came closer to them. "Where is Gaia?"

"Left," the little man made hand signs, pointing to the door. He whinnied like a stallion, and then moved his fingers like a horse's gait along his coat sleeve.

The carriage he'd passed… it had to be Gaia. Pulling the boy into his arms, he offered an embrace, but they both trembled. Timothy must know the danger his sister faced.

"Thank you." He popped up and took his great-uncle's flintlock from the wall and aimed it at the writing desk. "Mr. Telfair, my cousin has taken her and means to do her ill. What will that do to the Telfair name, if she's murdered?"

Mr. Telfair grimaced and took his son's hand. "I'll get the neighbors to look for her. Gaia must be found."

"I'll start my servants searching."

No one would hurt the women he loved anymore. He'd stop Deborah once and for all from threatening Mary and Gaia. William ran from the room to get his bullets.

"Wake up, Miss Telfair," Miss Smythen shoved at Gaia's arm. "You need to cut in line and dance by the rocks."

The black walls of the carriage cloaked Gaia in darkness, making her more tired, even as her stomach rumbled.

"You're too heavy for me to lift. Move!"

The screechy pitch hurt Gaia's ears.

Another push to her shoulder made her punch at the air, as when Lydia or Helena awoke her too early. Gaia flailed again, but this time she struck something.

"Ouch! You hit my nose, you blackamoor," Miss Smythen stood over Gaia, grasping and shaking her. "I need you to do it yourself, just like Elizabeth. Then I can offer William true comfort when we find you."

Wham!

Gaia's face stung. She opened her eyes to peer at Miss Smythen's scrunched up mouth, her stare penetrating. "Why did you do that?"

Miss Smythen grunted and wrung her hands. "Wake up, you… nobody. You dark, poor, nobody."

"I'm not—" Gaia sat up and heaved her innards onto the floor of the carriage.

"Yuck!" Miss Smythen shrieked again. She reached into her reticule for a handkerchief, and sponged at her shoes.

Stomach still rolling, Gaia put a palm to her chest. "Well, you shouldn't try to wake someone up so cruelly. And I am beautiful, wonderfully made, in spite of what you think. My actions show me to be good. What do yours show you to be?"

"Please get out of my sight," Miss Smythen peered out the window. "A lantern's glow! People are coming. I'm out of time. I won't be able to watch you tumble from the cliff."

Gaia leaned back on the dimpled leather seat. She sucked in a deep breath of air to soothe her stomach. "Time is so precious. You should do everything in your power to do good."

Heat swept over her. The contents of her stomach needed to leave. This time she cracked the door, and vomited in the rain. "I think I soiled your carriage."

Miss Smythen pulled on Gaia's arm. "The belladonna should make you more submissive. I got the measurement right this time."

With a brisk slap to the lady's fingers, Gaia freed herself. "Why are you so mean?"

"If William finds you with me, he'll be so angry. What will it take for you to get out of my carriage?" The woman's eyes darted, as if her little brain searched for an idea. "He could be outside, waiting for you."

Settling back on the seat, Gaia closed her eyes again. "Then shouldn't you go running to him? You love him, don't you?"

"Well, yes."

Crossing her arms, Gaia shouted, "Liar! If you loved William, you wouldn't send him mean notes or lie to him. That's not love."

Screeching like a wounded animal, Miss Smythen shook her fists. "Please leave! Look, there's William now," she pointed outside the compartment, "near the rocks. Save him from the strangers coming."

"In trouble?" Gaia stepped down from the chaise. "William?"

The carriage door shut with a bang. Miss Smythen's vehicle moved at a fast pace, leaving Gaia all alone to enjoy the view. That was fine. The woman wasn't good company.

The soft sea air filled Gaia's lungs. The wind swirled about her, prickling her skin. The scent of salt was as strong as the day Mr. Telfair implied she was a child of rape. She wasn't that, or any of the mean things people had ever said. She was whole, wonderfully made, both black and white. Beautiful, descended from earthly and heavenly royalty. Tugging her William's shawl closer, she let the sway of the fringe guide her to the rocks lining the cliff's edge.

CHAPTER TWENTY-FOUR

Sermon of Terror

It took longer than William thought to rouse his grooms and his steward and get a search party engaged, but no one complained, with a hundred pounds as the prize for the man who found Gaia. His pockets lined with shot, he slung the flintlock over his shoulder and headed to the entry. Hopefully, Magnus had recovered enough for the hunt.

As he flung open the door, there stood Deborah.

Dressed in a dark cloak befitting an evil priestess from a London play he'd seen, she pressed inside. "Cousin, I just heard about Miss Telfair. What can I do to help?"

What was her game? A murderous wave of heat flooded his gut, but he took a deep breath. The wench knew where Gaia was. "Come inside, Deborah," he gripped her arm, tugging her into the drawing room, and closed the doors.

She squinted at him, and then smoothed her countenance, lifting her long nose in the air. "I know you're angry at me for my naughty trick, but we should forget that. I am here to make amends, now that you need me. I'll wait here and take care of Mary until you return."

His pulse raced at the mention of his daughter. *The babe in Deborah's foul clutches*. No wonder Gaia put a guard at Mary's door. His heart swelled for Gaia, but then his blood ran cold. This fiend, who dared to have St. Landon blood, harmed his love, and now was back for his daughter.

He rubbed his skull. No more games or pretense. Precious time was wasting. "Where is Gaia?" He peppered the chamber of the flintlock without blinking. As he'd done so many times with faceless, nameless enemies, he raised the weapon.

She backed away, almost crawling to the writing desk.

Intending to scare her, he took the shot. It missed her hand by inches, sinking into the marble top, the heart of the furnishing.

Deborah's eyes grew wide. She must know now he wasn't joking.

The smell of gunpowder filled the room as smoke emanated from the hole in the desk; so familiar, this perfume from the Peninsula. He primed the gun again. "I know you took her, and you're behind the blackmail. How dare you torture me for months, washing my face in this garbage about my wife, never giving me the time to heal?"

Deborah leveled her shoulders as her finger slipped along the beaded edge of her cape. "Elizabeth was nothing more than a prostitute. I had to make sure you didn't make that kind of mistake again. And now you are engaged to a mulatto." Her green eyes softened, and she took a step to him. "Can't you see she's gone? It's for the best. I didn't mean to hurt you, William. I love you."

His finger twitched along the barrel. Should he risk another shot? "This is your last chance."

The doors behind him blasted open.

"I heard a gun. Is everything… okay?"

William pivoted for a second then locked his gaze back on the vile woman. "Welcome, Mr. Stelford. This is Deborah Smythen, our blackmailer."

The man came closer. He reached for the sight of the gun.

His palm tightened on the iron shaft. "You don't have to do this. We all know the truth. We've stopped her before the gossip spreads."

William shook the gun free, and renewed his aim at the candlestick behind her head.

The half-smile on Deborah's face faded. She raised her hands high above her tight bun. "Help me, Mr. Stelford. You know his temper."

"Deborah has drugged Gaia and taken her somewhere," William's voice cracked. "If I hadn't been ashamed of scandal, I would have warned Gaia of this snake. My Gaia wouldn't have been vulnerable."

His friend reached again for the gun. "Instead of taking revenge, let's go find Miss Telfair. We'll deal with Deborah another way, and figure out how to cover this up."

No more hiding! Indignation burned hot and sweet in William's gut, as if a fire had been lit. Words from one of his father's sermons scorched his mind. He shoved the gun butt at Stelford. God powered a new weapon within William, His truth. "There is nothing covered, that shall not be revealed; neither hid, that shall not be known."

Deborah trembled. Even her rouged cheeks paled and her palms possessed a violent shake.

"Where is she, Cousin?"

Her eyes widened. "It's a simple misunderstanding. She was alive when I left her."

"On the moors, the cliffs… where?" His fists tightened as they dropped to his side. "Deborah, whatsoever ye have spoken in darkness shall be heard in the light; and that which ye whispered in ears shall be proclaimed upon housetops."

He leaned over her and lifted her chin with his thumb. She needed to look at his face and see the white-hot anger pent up in his bones. "Be not afraid of them that kill the body. After that no more harm can they do."

Deborah fell to her knees. A flood of tears strangled her high-pitched voice, "she's near the cliffs; about a mile or so by the rocks. The stubborn thing was very much alive when I finally got her to leave my carriage."

He scooped Deborah up by the elbow. "Stelford, take her to the magistrate. Tell the whole sordid story, from the blackmail to the attempted murder of Gaia Telfair."

Stelford grabbed her arm. "All of it?"

"Yes; I'm not afraid of guilt or scandal. Then get back as fast as you can to help me find Gaia."

Stelford nodded. "God will keep her safe until you get to her."

That had to be true. William ran out the door. It had to be.

Just beyond the line of boulders lay a black-velvet sky. Gaia's breath caught at the beauty, the few diamond lights illuminating the night like translucent sarsenet. The fabric appeared seamless, with no separation from the noisy sea. The color was beautiful. Black and comely, just like her.

The lapping water beat an even rhythm against the rocks below, sounding very much like the day Mr. Telfair hinted at her being a by-blow of rape. She'd come here, with her spirit so low. Right now it was high. If only she could find William. He needed to know he made her happy, and Gaia now fully believed she *should* be happy. The illicit nature of origin didn't matter. He thought her beautiful and, now, she did too.

Her heavy tongue tasted the fresh salt in the air. The storm must've set the water churning.

"Brr." If only it weren't so cold. Wrapping her shawl about her, she took a few steps.

Her stocking feet sank in the damp soil. Bouncing free, she moved a little closer to the sky. What would it be like to reach out and touch the clouds?

The ground seemed to move beneath her, and she swayed

towards a group of large stones. She stumbled and gripped a sharp rock to stay upright. Her palm stung, as it did the night she tried to sew the rose silk Sarah gave her. The bolt was as lovely as the distant sarsenet. To touch the sky fabric would be wonderful.

A wiggle of her fingers revealed no cut. She lowered her head and laid a cheek against the chilled creviced surface. With heavy blinks, she took another minute to fill her lungs.

So cold. A tingle coursed her spine, like the first time she danced with William. The wind blew hard, and it sounded like someone calling her name.

"William?"

With aching muscles, she wobbled to her feet. "I'm here. Do you see me?"

Something gripped her shoulder and gave her a hard yank. She pushed away, but not before the beautiful darkness enveloped her.

William hit his hands together to warm them. The temperature had dropped at least another ten degrees this past hour. However, his discomfort didn't matter. He punched his palm again. No sign of Gaia.

A fog had set in, mixing the wild scent of the moors, mud, and herbs, with the salt of the sea. He'd searched the cliff line and found nothing.

Perhaps if he lowered and swung the lantern over the side, he could see whether she fell. His heart thundered. He had to be able to get to her.

Another twenty minutes of leaning and looking stiffened the muscles in his back. The cold air would make him regret his age. He wasn't a spring chicken or a young soldier. He was a man, a father. *God, where is the spry Miss Telfair*?

He straightened his carriage, and ran his hand along his aching neck. Nothing but darkness and rocks.

No Gaia or crumbled form lay on the rocks below. Thank goodness. He blew out a weary breath. The tide was too low to have dragged her out to sea. It was as if she'd disappeared from the face of the earth.

Could Deborah have lied, in order to throw him on the wrong trail?

Unlikely. The woman believed he'd kill her. Well, for a few moments, he might've if not for the restraint of the Spirit. "Thank You, Lord, for self-control."

He walked back and hung against Magnus. The poor horse lathered again. The sweaty horseflesh filled William's nostrils, wriggling his nose. "Don't distress boy; I'm not going to ride you any further tonight."

Magnus shook him off, pushing him with the saddle. It was as if the beast encouraged him to keep looking.

Where was Gaia?

Timothy said she was sick. If she hadn't fallen, where might a wobbly girl go? He put down the heavy brass lantern and hit his hands together again. A flash of Gaia praying under her oak slipped into his head. How many times had he caught her there? Maybe her subconscious would drive her there tonight. It wasn't too far from Ontredale.

Retrieving the lantern, he stalked in the direction of the oak. Towing his tired Magnus up the hill and over to the soggy plains of moors, he trudged to a mighty oak in the clearing; the first place he had spied Gaia. His boots sank into the boggy mud and tangled in sagging weeds. He walked the distance to one of the drooping boughs and fingered the creviced bark.

No Gaia.

He dropped to his knees near the trunk. "God, where is she? How could You let this happen? Why weren't You looking after the weak and helpless?"

He put a vibrating hand to his mouth to shut up his

questions, and then wiped his eyes from the mist in the air. Looking at the puddles near his feet, he remembered God rains on the just and unjust, but Gaia didn't deserve this storm, another torrent caused by the St. Landons.

If he hadn't been ashamed at admitting his cousin's treachery, and banned Deborah from Ontredale, Gaia would be safe. He'd failed his love in the worst way.

"God, this isn't Your fault. It's mine."

"No it's not," the voice boomed from above.

He lifted his face. "Lord, are You speaking?"

"No, you daft man; it's Stelford." His friend lent him an arm and tugged William to his feet. "Why are you kneeling in the mud?"

"Gaia is still missing. I fear she's—"

"She's not. She's been found. I've been looking for you for the past half-hour to tell you."

"Praise God! Where is she?"

"Mr. Whimple saved her from toppling over the cliffs, and took her home."

A wave of weakness struck William, and he clutched the oak. "Well, that's fitting." A tornado brewed in his gut, spurred from relief that Gaia had been rescued and the abject fear of her hero being Whimple. "Well, the scholar is good for something."

William took a breath. "Is my fowled cousin rotting in jail?"

"The magistrate has Miss Smythen. The woman broke as soon as she got in the carriage. It seems your fancy shooting and sermon of terror did the trick. She confessed to everything, even strengthening Elizabeth's potion."

Deborah was partially responsible for Elizabeth's death. Wiping his brow, William stood erect. "At least she'll not be able to harm anyone else. Well, I'm heading home."

Stelford clapped William's shoulder, making him stop, causing him to sink into the muddy path. "You didn't cause this; Miss Smythen did. There's nothing that you or I could've done to make Elizabeth more careful that night. We both harbor guilt. It's made me drink, and kept you stuck in mourning until Miss Telfair came along. Actually, she saved me too. So don't give up. She's what you need."

William shook free and stepped to a grassy patch and wiped his soles. "Thing are as they should be. Whimple saved her. She'll want him."

Didn't Gaia say she fell in love with Whimple when he saved her brother? Surely, she'd fall for the plant man again. He sighed his frustration. "They'll announce their engagement tomorrow."

Stelford took Magnus's reins. "Here, take my horse to Chevron Manor."

With a shake of his head, William grabbed Magnus and started slogging toward Ontredale.

"You'll give up that easily?"

Stelford's words stung. "Haven't we all learned you can't win someone who wasn't meant to be yours? She's always loved Whimple. I can't risk another bad marriage. I can't hopelessly love another man's woman. Not again."

Running in front of him, Stelford blocked his path. The man was wetter and more stinky than he. His poor checked greatcoat could have been a blackened cape. "How do you know she's not yours? I was too self-righteous, and thought Elizabeth should refuse your proposal. She couldn't buck her father's pressure, and I didn't fight for her when it counted."

"So I should go to Chevron Manor and watch Gaia Telfair sail into Whimple's arms?"

"You need to go show her you love her. She can't have any doubts. Then she'll make the right choice."

"Well, I can't show up like this, smelling of horse, soaked to the bone; she wouldn't like that."

"Then let's go get you ready to go courtin'. And you stay

there until she knows your heart." Stelford gripped his arm. "Are we back to being friends?"

"I'm on a bit of a forgiveness spree. So, you, and even I, are on that list. Just don't... Don't ever put me in a position where our happiness is at odds." He slapped Stelford's back, even as his tone lowered, tightened, "I would have backed away, if I'd known about you and Elizabeth. I'm sure you'd let me be a doting uncle to Mary."

"Well, let me be doting to what you and Miss Telfair will conjure."

"That is, if she'll still have me." Saving one's life can change sentiments. He hung his head, tamped his brim, and headed for a shave and fresh shirt.

CHAPTER TWENTY-FIVE

A Soul Must Choose

Gaia sat up in her bed. With great care, she tugged her spectacles from the close table, slipped them on her nose, and scanned the room. Light poured in through the window, bathing her beautiful sunny blue walls. She was safe at home. But what of William? She hadn't found him.

Julia sprang from a seat by her bed, and put a cold towel against Gaia's forehead. "You're awake."

"Yes," low squeals sounded where Gaia's voice should be. She coughed and cleared her throat. "I don't know if my stomach agrees. I think it wants to flop over or run crawling from my body."

"You sound horrible." Julia lifted a glass of water to Gaia's lips.

Her sister's pretty face held shadows almost the shade of the sand-colored bodice she wore. "What happened to you? Why were you walking on a terrible night like that?"

Seren popped up from by the footboard. "Cheshire's scandalous cousin tried to kill her. She drugged her and tried to make her leap off a cliff." She gripped the bedpost. Her dark emerald walking gown made her eyes bright like clover. "The whole village is talking about it."

Everyone was gossiping about her? Now Gaia's head spun for sure. William must be mortified. Struggling to sit up, she took Julia's offered arm and leaned against a pillow. "Did she hurt Mary, Lady Mary?"

"No, you must've thought something was amiss. You instructed the duke's household to keep everyone from the child."

A long sigh whizzed from Gaia's lungs. Hazy images of her evening filtered into her memory, as did thoughts of Julia. She laced her fingers with her sister's and smiled up at her. "I'm so glad you're home."

Tears left Julia's eyes, and she leaned in and gave Gaia a tight embrace. "I'm grateful to have a friend who cares." She whispered in Gaia's ear, "Thank you for coming after me with Cheshire."

Stroking her sobbing sister's back, Gaia squeezed her again. God restored them, their sisterly bond.

Seren came around and put her arms about the pair. "Well, at least Deborah Smythen will be no more trouble. The duke told us Mr. Stelford took her to the magistrate. Seems she even tried to blackmail Cheshire. Talk about evil relations."

Sniffling, Gaia released them both and fought her covers to reach for a handkerchief from her bed table. "We need to stop this before we are all a pile of wet muslin."

Timothy scooted from under the bed. "Awake?"

"Come here," Gaia waved at him.

He bounced up onto the mattress, snaked through the maze of arms, and threw himself about Gaia's neck. "All is fine, though my voice is pretty rough."

With equal vigor, the boy leapt down and ran out the door. Such a hurry. Her friend and sister released her, too.

Julia tapped the book she held in her lap. "So, are you going to get up? It's well past noon. Or do you want me to read more *Romance of the Forest.* You like nature and mystery."

"Noon? And you were reading? I..." Gaia covered her mouth.

Seren started poking around in the wardrobe, pulling out the pastel rainbow of gowns now filling it. "I heard her. It shocked me too."

With a small roll of her eyes, Julia nodded. "One could never have enough self-improvement. Then, when God sees fit, if He sees fit, I'll find my own duke; someone who loves me just for me and I won't have to pretend, one way or the other."

Boot heels, too heavy for Mr. Telfair's, pounded outside of the door.

"Sir, you can't go in!" Sarah's voice? The lady sounded alarmed.

"We'll watch him, Mama." Helena was in the fray. Trouble.

The door opened and in bounced her twin sisters. And William!

Gaia sunk beneath her bedclothes.

Lydia neared. Her dark brown chignon shined with pearl pins. Gaia's pearl pins. *Little sisters.*

Grinning, Lydia eased onto the mattress. "See, she's still alive. Now you don't have to pace so much. He didn't sleep a wink since he came at midnight."

Helena grabbed Gaia's hand and jumped onto the bed. Her thin arms encircled Gaia's neck. Her brown eyes were rimmed red. She must've been crying. "So glad you're safe. No thanks to him."

Hugging the stuffing out of her little sisters, Gaia peered up and her gaze locked on William.

He stood still, as if he saw her for the first time. Yet his countenance seemed different. A morsel of fear and a hint of shyness covered it. A tremble set on his lean cheek. Even with him six or eight paces away, hanging onto her bed frame, she'd never felt closer to him. So open were his eyes, the windows to his soul.

"Blue walls?" William shook his head, as if freeing from a daze. "It is my fault, but I needed to see for myself that Gaia's well." He took his hands from the post and glanced at the floor. With a final lift of his chin, he backed to the door. "I can leave for Ontredale now."

Seren caught his arm. "No, sir, you will go back down to your post and wait in the parlor for our dear girl. Lydia, Helena, accompany the duke. Make sure he doesn't escape."

Like chains, the twins latched onto him and dragged him away.

William's eyes went wide, but he complied in silence with their tugs and giggles.

A measure of sympathy hit Gaia. William wasn't used to Telfair madness.

As he and the twins left, Sarah popped her head inside. Her mobcap shadowed newly-formed lines on her forehead. "Gaia, if you aren't well enough, I'll send everyone away. You don't have to make any decisions until you are ready."

Gaia smiled at the loving woman. "Mama, I'll be fine; just a little sore throat."

With a wipe to her misting almond eyes, Sarah nodded and closed the door.

Picking up the pink gown Gaia had sown from the wardrobe, Julia tossed it on the mattress. "You just need to get dressed and stand out in Chevron with all your beauty. The duke's been downstairs almost since Mr. Whimple brought you home."

"Elliot?" Gaia's heart beat hard for a moment. Old habit. The organ used to pulse every time she heard his name. He saved her? "He went looking for me?"

Julia bit her lip. Then a radiant smile blended with her pert blue eyes. "Yes, he found you. The duke had men searching everywhere, but it is Mr. Whimple to whom we are grateful."

"I'll have to thank him." She smoothed her fingers on the edges of the sheets. Elliot had always been a help to her family. He might be clumsy in his speech, but he did do his utmost for the Telfairs. He could always be counted on in tough times.

Seren lifted her chin and moved from the billowy curtains. "You have two men, who claim to love you, waiting downstairs. You must toss one back into the sea for others. Gaia Telfair is not a greedy woman."

"Sarah said God would let me know which one was for me. Safe, reliable Elliot, or exciting Cheshire. What if the duke has another insane cousin?" Or he again decides they couldn't be together because of her blood.

Gaia wrung her hands.

Seren picked up the jeweled mask from the wardrobe and waved it in the air. "Well, what shall we dress you as so that you can go choose your prince?"

The jewels of the mask shimmered in the sunlight streaking through the window glass.

Climbing out of bed, Gaia put her bare feet on the cold floor. She took the mask from her friend's delicate fingers. Peeling off her glasses, she put it to her face. Maybe there was a way to know which one was the one for her. "Ladies, help me dress."

William paced the small rug in front of the fireplace in the parlor, while his rival slept on the sofa. Whimple snorted an indelicate noise as his head fell deeper into the cushions.

Mrs. Telfair stepped across the threshold, bearing a large tray of treats and a kettle. "Would you like some tea, sir?"

"Ah, no, ma'am." Tea was the last beverage he wanted to consume. It would go on his prohibited list, like ale.

The lady adorned in a peach colored mobcap and matching muslin morning gown folded her arms. "Please sit, your

Grace, before you wear a hole in the floor."

Resigned, he dropped into a chair, the one closest to the fire. After such a chilly night, he couldn't seem to get warm enough.

"Your Grace, her fever broke early this morning. You saw for yourself; Gaia will be fine."

Mr. Telfair got up from his chair. His thin legs wobbled. "I'm too old for all these shenanigans. Take care of the birds in the parlor. I'm going to my bed."

With a sweet smile, Mrs. Telfair nodded, "As always, dear."

"Cheshire, let Gaia know I am sorry, and that I am glad she is safe."

William nodded. It was probably the closest the old bird could come to apologizing. If William had his way, Gaia would be gone from here, and he'd make up for any love she'd missed.

Mrs. Monlin, Gaia's aunt from the city, breezed inside and headed for the silver tray. The yards of lace on her gown, starched as much as a good cravat, made the woman stand out in the modest setting. "Oh, Sarah, why is my brother leaving, when we have so much company?"

Pushing at an errant red curl dropping from her mobcap, Mrs. Telfair shook her head. "Gaia can handle this. She's dressing now."

William slumped in his chair. Gaia was safe. Shouldn't he bow out now? "Ma'am, maybe it's best we go. We should all allow her more time to recover."

"Yes, you leave," Whimple sat up and stretched his arms. "Treats." He pulled at a scone and lumped on more than enough cream.

Timothy trotted into the room. A smile came to his lips, and he came to William.

He pulled the boy to his knee. "Thanks for the intelligence on your sister's awakening."

A smile, maybe the biggest William had ever seen, filled Timothy's face. "She's coming."

He patted the boy's head.

Mrs. Telfair heaved a deep sigh. "Excuse me, gentlemen. Come, son, Tabitha. Let's see whether Gaia needs any help." She gripped the little boy's hand and took Mrs. Monlin's scone-filled saucer, and led the two from the room.

Whimple stood and smoothed crumbs from his striped waistcoat. "I think it only fair of me to tell you, Your Grace, that I intend to marry Miss Telfair."

"Intentions can only get one so far."

The botanist smiled wide. A sparkle gleamed from his teeth. "An oversight. I proposed to her here in this very room. I'm sure once she's better, she will break with you."

A confident one, this Mr. Whimple. A good thing he didn't know William had already forced the break. "Well, we'll see whom she'll have." Or forgive.

Whimple stepped close to William's chair. "Do you know she's loved me all her life?"

Though he wanted to be snide and ask for the gentleman's expertise on broken engagements, he refrained. Gaia would not want her bucks going a round of fist-a-cuffs in the parlor.

"Nothing to say, duke?"

Was he trying to pick a fight? Though Whimple might be ten years his junior, he'd snap the impertinent fellow like a twig. "The dear lady has mentioned something about you." He tapped his finger to his nose, trying to conjure the least offensive slight. "I believe it had to do with a cousin, or her older sister."

Whimple looked away and ran a hand along the back of his neck. "Mistakes. You know mistakes; like that jade of a cousin. Or...."

"Or what?" Patience fleeing, he gripped the arms of the chair and stared through the man.

The scholar took a few steps back. "Just the rumors that are buzzing about."

Lacing his fingers together, William eased back into the cushions. "There will always be gossip about someone doing something untoward or foolish. One can smirk, tremble in fear at their discovery, or cling to God's grace."

William leaned back in his seat. "His grace is sufficient, and offers tolerance to those who don't know pain. May God never give you such a lesson."

The door of the parlor opened. Miss Hallow entered, with Gaia on her arm.

Why was Gaia wearing her mask from the ball, shrouded in a long black domino? His love sat at the piano near the entrance of the room. She slumped on the bench.

Whimple started her direction. "Miss Telfair, should you be out of bed?"

Gaia held out her hand, as if to say stop.

Miss Hallow blocked his advance. "Stay where you are, Mr. Whimple. Miss Telfair is still feeling under the weather, but she felt she should come down and address this situation. Take a seat."

The scholar complied, sitting in the chair next to William.

Why the disguise? William dipped his head in his hands. "What is the meaning of this?"

Whimple thumped his chest. "I am curious, too."

"Gentlemen, her voice is very hoarse, and to choose between you will be difficult. Hurtful. She'd rather do it behind a mask." Miss Hallow came closer and leaned on the back of the sofa. "Why don't each of you have your say to win her?"

This wasn't right. Wasn't he beyond games? Here William was, ready to tell the truth of his feelings, without jokes or omissions, and Gaia comes in costume. Maybe the belladonna made her act silly. "Shouldn't this be done in private?"

Whimple leapt to his feet." A lady has the right to hold court in the manner she chooses. I am not ashamed of how I feel. When you finally know what you want, you need to shout it from the roof."

The scholar moved to the edges of the sofa and looked into the niche where Gaia sat. "I love you. We've grown up together. I've known you for so long. It had to be why I was blind to how well we get along. You have always thought we should be together. You have loved me for years. It's our time to be together."

Gaia's posture slumped at bit more. She must be swaying, agonizing over this declaration. He'd always seen her sitting erect with her shoulders back, so this was unlike her. William's gut wrenched for the lass.

Whimple put his hands to his sides. "I know I should pay for my misdirected attentions. It was wrong. I finally see the beautiful creature you've grown up to be. You're the woman who should be in my life."

With her fingers, short and slim, Gaia adjusted her mask. Again, she leaned against the piano, as if she tried to shrink out of sight.

Miss Hallow waved a fan. "That was very beautiful, Elliot. I, for one, didn't think you had such a romantic side. But what do you, Your Grace, have to say to win the fair Gaia?"

Shuffling his boots, William toyed with how he should respond. Stelford said to tell her of his love, but was it that simple?

Everything could be ruined or saved by whatever came out of his mouth. Pulse racing, heart thundering, he glanced at the confident Mr. Whimple, and then at Gaia and her tiny hands, her fashionable slippers.

A lightning bolt hit William. He lifted from the chair. "I would like tell Miss Telfair I love her. I love her deeply, but I can't."

Miss Hallow fell back, as if she'd faint. "What?"

"Miss Gaia Telfair should hear how my heart beats for her and only her, and of the life I want to give her, but she's not in this room."

Undoing the ribbons of the mask, Julia Telfair exposed her face. "You are right. My sister is not here.

The door opened and the real Gaia stepped inside. Her bosom trembled as she seemed to return his stare. Her face appeared unnaturally pale, no doubt a lingering effect of the harrowing night she'd survived, but the rose-colored gown wrapping her skin clung to her curves in all the right places. The slight crinkle in her auburn hair adorned her chignon like lace. "Yes, I've been listening from the hall."

Beautiful woman. The only thing amiss was the stained slippers on her feet. He should've brought the ones left at Ontredale, but that would've seemed too Cinderella-like. With everything in his power, he would restore them to their owner before midnight.

Gaia gaped at William. He knew her. Of course, her true love would. "Seren, you and Julia can wait outside."

The girls scrambled from the room, her sister dragging Serendip the last couple of inches then shutting the door.

"What's the meaning of this?" Elliot ran a hand through his perfect hair. His troubled gaze went from her to the duke. "Is this a joke?"

William smiled. "I think it was a test."

"He is correct. This has been a very confusing time. I needed to know the heart of the man I marry. He needs to see me because I've been invisible."

"You're not invisible," Elliot came near and took her hand. "I see you clearly."

She shook her head. "You see me now. If Cheshire hadn't come around and danced with me, I don't think you would have ever seen me."

Elliot lifted his chin. His crystal blue eyes seemed sad, wounded. "Should it matter how I found you? Just that I did. With me, you are comfortable. We belong to the same sphere."

Patting away his arm, she turned and moved close to the fireplace. "A year ago, even a few months ago, those words would've been enough to melt my heart. I'd have been so grateful for your attention. It isn't enough now. It's not love. I'll always admire you as the first man I ever thought I liked."

He shifted his stance, his boot heel missing the rug and pounding the solid floor. "What are you saying?"

"I once thought what I felt was love, but it couldn't be. It can't compare to the depth of emotion stirring inside for Cheshire. I was running to him when you found me. I think I've been waiting for someone to see me for me, as God made me. That man is William St. Landon. I'm sorry, Elliot."

He wiped his mouth, as if the rejection took him by surprise, and then turned to William. "Take care of her."

The duke nodded, but kept his face solemn. "I will, if she'll have me."

Plodding from the room, Elliot offered one last glance her way and then trudged out of the parlor.

A sigh left her mouth. He may think he had feelings for her, but Gaia knew better than any that a one-sided love was not enough.

"Are you going to send me away, too?" William moved a few feet, but was still distant. "My cousin could've killed you."

She lifted a smile to him. "Miss Smythen did not. I'm so sorry that the whole sordid affair has come to light."

He marched near, with his arms locked behind his back, as though he didn't trust himself. The pearl buttons on his cranberry-colored waistcoat tugged from the pressure. "It needed to. If I hadn't been too ashamed to tell you about

Deborah, she'd never have had the opportunity to harm you. I thought I lost you. I nearly went out of mind."

She rubbed his forearm to coax him into relaxing. He needed to know he was blameless. "William, no lasting harm has been done. I have a hardy constitution. I'm well, though my voice is abysmal."

Pushing at his brow, he shrugged. "I don't know. You sound sultry. Maybe have a go at my given name again?"

With a stomp of her foot, she moved from his reach. "Be serious. You're always joking. Maybe I sent the wrong gentleman away."

William claimed her hand, and towed her to his wide chest. "I will be serious. I love you, Gaia Telfair. From the moment I caught you praying for misery in the woods, you captivated me. At our first ball, I felt my heart beat like never before. And when we kissed at the Masked Ball, I knew you had to be mine, but I was too afraid to admit my feelings. Nothing will suppress the strength of them now."

"Not even the truth?"

"None of it matters. Gaia, you are God's gift to me."

With weak fingertips, she touched his tanned cheek. "And my bloodline matters not? I am black. I am a mulatto as much as white. Knowing the sacrifices that made me, I am not sorry or ashamed. My husband must feel the same."

His gaze swept over her, his gaze so intense her neck warmed. "You are black and comely. Tell me. O thou whom my soul loveth, will thou have the son of the man who destroyed your father?"

She bobbed her chin, and a smile set in the calmed seas of his blue eyes. The turbulence of yesterday had disappeared. "Are you sure about us? This isn't some manifestation of guilt over your father's dealings?"

He stretched his hand to her neck and strummed the coral beads at the arch along her throat. With his thumb, he tugged a curly lock of her hair, warming her face with the heat of his breaths. "Quite sure."

Leaning, he kissed her brow. "You are the dream I didn't know I wanted until I found you at that oak. I need you. I want you. I can't wake up another day and not know you're all mine. Tell me, can you can love me, no other man but me?"

Slipping into his arms with an ease and a confidence that could only come from knowing she'd found her prince, she laid her head against his shoulder. "You are the one for me. I don't know why it took so long for me to realize."

He kissed her temples. "Well, you've been busy. It's a tough fight, falling in love with one person when you're dead set to marry another."

Tears sprang to her eyes as his lips brushed against hers, soft as a whisper. His hands wandered and warmed every aching muscle in their path. "Gaia, marry me, today. Let my name be yours."

A name she could claim with all its rights. Toes curling within her slippers, she brushed a droplet from her fogged spectacles. "Shouldn't you be on your knee?"

With a yank to his walnut-colored pantaloons, he knelt on the floor. Taking each of her palms within his, he kissed her wrists.

Her pulse raced at the feel of his mouth against her skin.

"My life will not be whole without you. If you can accept my Mary and these old bones, consent to be my wife. Make me the happiest man in England or South Africa."

She tugged him to his feet. "I just wanted to see you do it. Of course, silly man; I love Mary and you with all my—"

His lips were to hers, as was the dizzy lightness his arms stirred. Enveloped, safe, and warm, he tightened his embrace about her.

He relented his kiss just enough to allow her a breath. "Today, marry me today."

He could've said pray for war, and she would've agreed. "Yes, William."

"I know Mary will love you, too. You kept her safe. I cannot wait to see how you guide her. I'll never doubt your intentions, even when they differ from mine."

She wove her hand beneath his tailcoat and savored the tarragon scent of his skin. "It's just the beginning. I believe we can teach Mary her speech again. And they *will* differ, except in one instance."

His brow rose, as if she'd planned something sinister. "And that would be?"

Her lips curled up. "The color blue for our chambers."

"Like your room here?" Nuzzling her neck, he kissed her ear. "I'll get my steward to do it before night fall. In the interim, you, Mary, and I will head to Scotland. I want you as my wife as soon as possible. I'm not taking another chance on living without you. Then a wedding trip to Port Elizabeth; your father may be lost, but maybe his people still live."

She looked into his eyes and melted. William loved all of her. He wasn't ashamed. She wasn't either.

As if Gaia were a light parcel, he lifted her into his arms and headed for the door, her heart pounding with expectation. She was to be married, to know more of her father, to bear a man's name who wanted her to have it, and to possess all of William's love. A quick toss of his hat and draped in his cloak, they spun and bumped into Mr. Telfair.

His mouth twitched, as if he wanted to say something, but, instead, he moved out of the way and held the door. Little Timothy peered from behind his pant leg. "Sister going?"

Mr. Telfair clenched his son's hand. "Gaia's marrying today. You wish her well."

Timothy's cherub face held a grin. "Bye, Gaia. Happy Gaia."

She half-waved, her fingers suddenly becoming lead,

partially trapped beneath William's warm greatcoat. Staring at Mr. Telfair, the man who'd created her Devonshire world, who gave her the identity of an unloved dark daughter, an alleged child of rape, her throat constricted. In his eyes, she wasn't worthy of a goodbye or an apology.

She tucked her head beneath William's chin, her soon-to-be husband who saw her as God's daughter.

His arms tightened about her, but his low tone held the force of a command. "No sadness on your wedding day, Gaia St. Landon. No sadness at all."

There was some in her heart, probably always would be some, but, this time, joy overcame all.

Want More?

If you like this story and want more, please offer a review on Amazon or Goodreads.

Also, sign up for my newsletter and get the latest news on this series or even a free book.

Author's Note

Dear Friend,

I enjoyed writing Unmasked Heart because Gaia's story of finding the courage to know her worth and allow herself to be loved needed to be told. This is a forerunner to the Port Elizabeth tales. Visit the Duke and Duchess of Cheshire again in Unveiling Love. I added a sneak peek to Unveiling Love for you to enjoy after my notes.

I also added a peek at my exciting bride series, Advertisements for Love. If you loved Unmasked, you will love,Theodosia and Ewan in The Bittersweet Bride.

Enjoy these bonuses.

Stay in touch. Sign up at www.vanessariley.com for my newsletter. You'll be the first to know about upcoming releases, and maybe even win a sneak peek.

Thank so much for giving this book a read.

If you like this story and want more, please offer a review on Amazon or Goodreads.

* * *

Also, sign up for my newsletter and get the latest news on this series or even a free book.

Vanessa Riley

Here are my notes:

Slavery in England

The emancipation of slaves in England preceded America by thirty years and freedom was won by legal court cases not bullets.

Somerset v Stewart (1772) is a famous case which established the precedence for the rights of slaves in England. The English Court of King's Bench, led by Lord Mansfield, decided that slavery was unsupported by the common law of England and Wales. His ruling:

"The state of slavery is of such a nature that it is incapable of being introduced on any reasons, moral or political, but only by positive law, which preserves its force long after the reasons, occasions, and time itself from whence it was created, is erased from memory. It is so odious, that nothing can be suffered to support it, but positive law. Whatever inconveniences, therefore, may follow from the decision, I cannot say this case is allowed or approved by the law of England; and therefore the black must be discharged."

E. Neville William, The Eighteenth-Century Constitution:

1688-1815, pp: 387-388.

The Slavery Abolition Act 1833 was an act of Parliament which abolished slavery throughout the British Empire. A fund of $20 Million Pound Sterling was set up to compensate slave owners. Many of the highest society families were compensated for losing their slaves.

This act did exempt the territories in the possession of the East India Company, the Island of Ceylon, and the Island of Saint Helena. In 1843, the exceptions were eliminated.

Cheshire's Sermon of Terror

This was taken from Luke 12:2-4, King James Version.

Part One

Bonus - Next Book in the Series: Unveiling Love

* * *

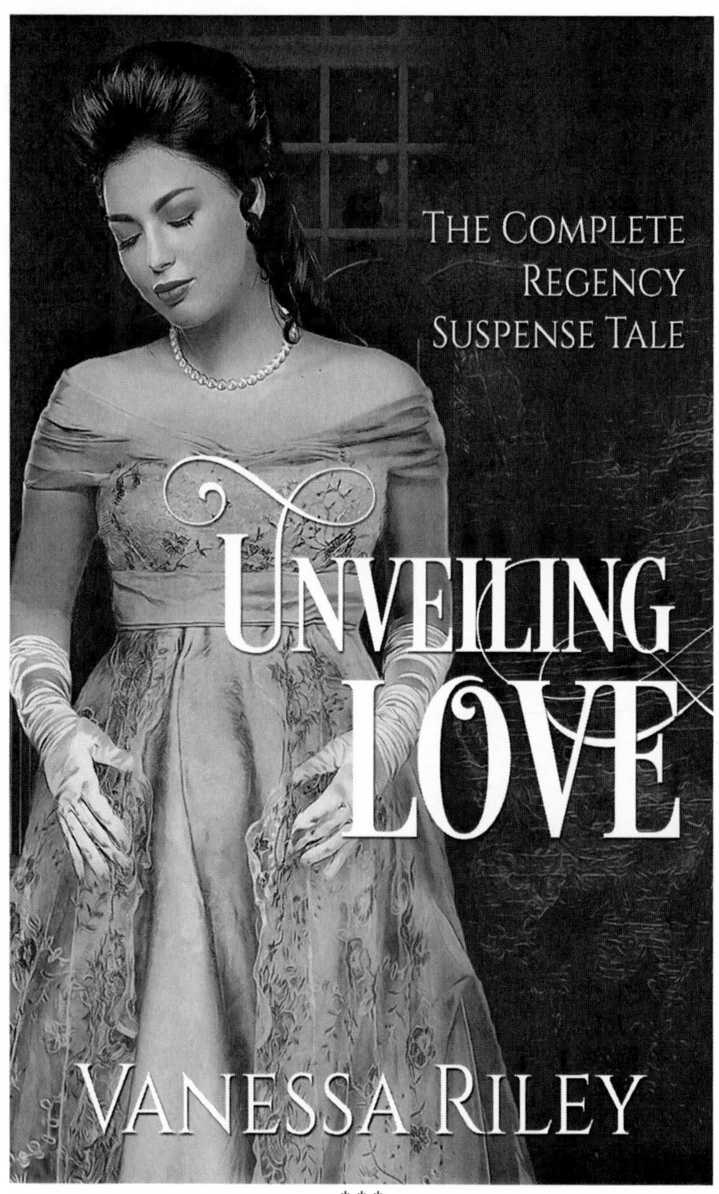
The Complete
Regency
Suspense Tale
Unveiling
Love
Vanessa Riley

* * *

Winning in the courts, vanquishing England's foes on the battlefield, Barrington Norton has used these winner-take-all rules to script his life, but is London's most distinguished mulatto barrister prepared to win the ultimate fight, restoring his wife's love?

Amora Norton is running out of time. The shadows in her Egyptian mind, which threaten her sanity and alienate Barrington's love, have returned. How many others will die if she can't piece together her shattered memories? Can she trust that Barrington's new found care is about saving their marriage rather than winning the trial of the century?

This is the complete novel with all four episodes. Enjoy this romantic suspense and meet old friends, William and Gaia, from Unmasked Heart. The love and drama continues.

Chapter One: London, England August 4, 1819

Barrington Norton loathed Newgate prison. The caustic smells, the cackles of the men driven mad awaiting release, the curses of the one's sentenced to die, many of whom he'd condemned — all churned his innards.

He popped off his top hat and fanned his face. Thinking and rethinking this visit twisted his resolve, tearing through his flesh like hot lead shots. Perhaps he should've headed home to his wife's fretful arms.

Hating indecision, he donned his hat again and climbed out of his carriage. He couldn't in good conscience forgo the opportunity to save an innocent life.

He shuttled toward the prison, away from his man-of-all-work. Good old James would slow him down offering wretched cockney wisdom. It was good to laugh. This just wasn't one of those days. Delay could antagonize Amora, shifting her into another of her strange moods, shooting a hole into all the good work he'd done these past months. He'd been on schedule, sent notes over the slightest changes. She seemed more at ease, more tolerant of his court work. That had to be good, even if he felt leashed.

The gaoler opened the massive door. "Barrister, what brings you here? Court finished hours ago. We're setting up the Debtor's Platform for tomorrow. Coming early for a good seat?"

"No. Spectators at an execution is reprehensible. Death is not a game for sport. I'm here to see Smith. Take me to him."

With a raised brow, the gaoler frowned then turned toward the long hall leading to the bowels of the prison. "This way, Mr. Norton. Smith's not on the list for tomorrow's ropes. Curious, ye wanting to see him."

Barrington followed. The sour scent of urine hit him, reminding him of years long past. Bad years. He pulled a cloth from his pocket and wiped his face, savoring the hint of lavender. Amora's fragrance. A symbol of their blooming love, of easier days.

Married for five years, engaged for three, things weren't the same as the day he spied her painting in the Tomàs Orchards. He wasn't the same either, changed by war and the positioning of London politics.

The gaoler stopped and unlocked an iron door. He stepped in front of Barrington. "Smith's in here. Mighty funny, ye trying to save the man ye convicted. Is that fickleness a custom for you people?"

Barrington glared at the man. He made his tone tight, a notch below menacing. "What do you mean my people? Did you mean mulattos or barristers?"

"Ah…I ugh, meant no disrespect. Barristers."

Barrington stepped around the gaoler. "Yes, that's what we barristers for the crown do. We fight for truth."

The fellow didn't retort with a more open slur. He shrugged and closed the cell behind Barrington as he went inside.

Smith lay on a small cot. He jerked up and raised his fists, storming towards Barrington. "Came to gloat?"

The words he'd struggled over still hadn't materialized. He coughed and stuffed the handkerchief back into his pocket.

"What do you want, barrister?" He lunged closer and

shook his knuckles near Barrington's face. "Get out of here, you half-breed, before I darken your daylights."

Barrington didn't move, staring, daring him to strike. Every muscle strained, pulling tight, tight, tighter, burning all the way to the missing bullet in his hip. "You let yourself be convicted for coining. You let the runners charge you with counterfeiting money. You let the sentence fall, started to dispute it, then stopped. I need to know why you chose to die."

Smith lowered his hand. His jowls dropped. His eyes drifted to the left.

Barrington knew that regret-filled look. It shoved his gut from hot indignation to sweet winning. He hovered over Smith using his height to crowd and corner him against the block wall. "They're building the hanging platform for the morning's executions. Hear the hammering. Pound. Pound. P-OU-ND."

He mimicked the sound again, exaggerating the echo, as if it were Justice Burn's gavel knocking against his desk. "Your name is not on the list this time, but it will be in a month. Tell me what you are hiding, and I'll get the sentence re-examined. I am your one chance to live."

Smith pushed past him and sank onto the mattress. "I have friends. They're going to help me, not the man who put me here."

"Unless these friends come forward and confess, you will die. Die with the truth. Whoever made you look guilty will die laughing."

"You and your smooth words. They will save me? You're dressed for a fancy party, barrister. Take your top hat and go."

Slam. A board or the platform's trap door must've fallen outside. It might as well have been the bailiff shutting up the doors to the Old Bailey. Barrington lost the argument. He turned and almost pressed upon the cell bars. Instead, he fished in his pocket and dropped onto a rickety table a couple of leaves of a Psalm, pages taken from the Bible he took to war. "If you don't trust my words, here's something that can save you. If you change your mind, send for me. I'll come."

Smith didn't move.

This visit was hopeless. A waste of precious time, time meant for Amora. He knocked on the bars to be let out. There wasn't a blasted thing Barrington could do. An innocent man was going to hang.

Amora Norton waited for the servants to clear her dinner setting as she sat next to her husband in the grand ballroom of Duke and Duchess of Cheshire. The soft strain of the violin's concerto caressed her ear as nineteen men with poufy powdered wigs and shiny blue liveries made the plates laced with garlicky fish remnants disappear.

Tonight, no shaking dread, no shivers of isolation seized her lungs, just a small swish of joy swirled at her middle. The pressure that pricked her high in the stomach eased when she shifted to the left against the dark stiles of her chair. Still not quite pain free, she pushed back in her dinner chair only to have its scrolled feet squeal and announce her restlessness.

Her husband continued his conversation with the gentleman on the other side of the crisp white tablecloth. Thank goodness he hadn't noticed the noise. Disappointing Barrington would ruin everything.

He'd been late to arrive at Mayfair, their London residence, but still wished to drag her to this ball. A deep frown marred his face. The stewing in his grey eyes whispered he needed care. She'd give him that, and more.

This proud man was her world, her anchor in shadow-filled London. So Amora didn't question him. She made him his favorite tea, wore his favorite bland dress. By the last course, the smelly fish, his mood had lifted.

The sultry tone of the songstress, Cynthia Miller, floated in the air, the lyrics haunting, soulful, man-snaring. She must be exhibiting to catch some new lover as she'd done for the beaus in their small Clanville village.

"Amora. Amora, dear."

Wanting to pinch herself for dwelling on the tart and not her husband's tall form, she blinked and looked up at Barrington. "Yes?"

Barrington's hands covered hers.

Her breath stopped, then curled in her throat. "Yes, Barrington."

"You are so beautiful, Mrs. Norton."

With a shy smile, she caught his gaze and counted the slow rises of his chest. Could he see how hard she'd worked to be pleasing? "I want to be here for you."

Like a slow, distant wave, the chairs were pushed away from the tables. A set formed. Would they dance? Usually he'd go politic or leave Amora for time with his patroness. "Do you think the floor is chalked? Can you see over the crowd?"

"My dear, what if we find out? Do you feel well enough to dance?"

"Yes."

Her pulse ticked to the timing of the violins. She came to his side savoring the crisp smell of his bergamot soap. The scent hung about his broad shoulders, wrapping him with appeal that stole everything — good-sense, decorum, and the desire to stay at this ball.

The lenses of his spectacles reflected the tall candelabras brightening the room. He tugged on his gloves. "Good, I wish to dance with the loveliest woman here."

Her cheeks heated. "After all this time, you still make me blush as if I wore pigtails."

She wished she'd stayed a hope-filled girl, not jaded, or

tormented, or fear-laden.

Barrington cleared his face of wanting, that caress until dawn heat in his gaze. He must have remembered they were in a public place and reigned in his passions.

She winced, put her hand to her stomach, then told herself it was nothing. A man had no time for a sick wife. He definitely wouldn't share a bed with one. And she needed him to be with her, distracting and holding her. The nightmares had returned.

"Your gloves, my dear?"

"Gloves?" Oh, the boring beige things. Twisting her naked fingers, she pivoted and searched her seat. They were missing. "They were here, Barrington."

The young servant who had attended her came from the edges holding the fallen mitts. "Here, ma'am."

The young man, blonde with pretty eyes of airy azure helped her tug on the satin, one after the other. With that hair, the servant could be a grown-up version of the little miracle, the orphan she'd read to this morning at the Foundling Hospital.

"Ma'am, is there anything else you need?"

"No, but thank you." Before she could pivot to her husband, the poor boy coughed and swallowed hard.

Amora's heart melted as she observed the creases under his young eyes. He looked so tired. Working at these long balls required so much, and an event for the Duke of Cheshire introducing his new duchess, must consume even more.

Called to that need, Amora put her hand to her half-filled water goblet and started to lift it to the servant, but Barrington claimed Amora's elbow. "Now, we are ready for a proper dance."

Proper. Barrington's need to be above reproach. The desire to help slipped away in a useless sigh. "Of course."

She was here for Barrington, not to make a spectacle of

herself acting out of station. What she wanted didn't matter anymore, never mattered, so she acquiesced to his gentle pull.

He led her to the center of the room and twirled her in the first motion of the reel.

Her husband looked handsome in his dark silken waistcoat with jingly silver buttons. The onyx jacket and pure white cravat covered his strong form. His gaze met hers, not looking over her head to find someone to ramble on about trials. But, this would end. It always ended, and she would be alone.

The set parted. His fingers stayed and lightly brushed her abdomen. His voice kissed her ear. He bent his tall frame closer. "Want some air?"

No, she wanted to leave and abandon the ball before something or someone stole his attention. Yet, a niggle of guilt swirled in her innards alongside his babe. *I should do more in public to benefit his career.* He so loved his career.

Borrowing some resiliency from the Egyptian kings within her bloodline, she reached for his cheek. "The Dowager Clanville is seated near the entrance. Go speak with your patroness. Her attention upon you will do more than mine. I've had you all evening."

His chin lifted then lowered as his nose wriggled beneath his silver frames. "I'll let her rakish son keep her company. Only you tonight."

Did he mean it? Her heart beat again, tapping faster and louder as his words penetrated her mind. "For me, it's always been you."

He dimpled. "Then to the balcony before Mr. Charleton presses this way and insists upon a dance."

Her husband was so fine looking with his jet colored hair lightly winged with gray and his swarthy brown skin. Built to be a warrior, he fought for justice with everything in his soul. Yet, that zeal seemed to blind him to other's faults and many times his own worth. "You needn't be concerned of any other."

"Well, I have a wide jealous streak and a boring road cut down my middle. And you've been so wonderful, Amora, never flirting or entertaining rakes, even whilst I was away three years at war."

"You're dependable and strong."

If tonight and every day forward, he used that strength to protect their marriage, to protect her and this baby, maybe her joy might be full again.

The smile forming on his lips could be no better than one of his kisses. His hand brushed the tiny swell of her abdomen as he steered her through the mob. Three months of carrying his babe had changed things between them, in so many good ways. Knowing where Barrington was, that he was safe, and that he'd always come home to her also did her much good.

He danced her onto the balcony. One step, two. He spun her under the bright stars then held her, sweeping her to the bricked corner along the stone railing.

Barrington ran a thumb under her chin. "You are very patient to attend these tedious things with me. The Duke of Cheshire hinted at needing my assistance. Perhaps that is no longer the case."

A sigh left his full lips, surely kissed with disappointment.

"You have nothing to prove to the ton, to anyone."

He pushed up his slipping lenses. "I like proving things. I like winning even more. But you must be rewarded. What bauble may I procure? Say a locket for the babe's first curl?"

"I want nothing but your love. To know you love all of me." She wedged her hands beneath his tailcoat and roamed the solid muscles of his back. This moment was not a dream, not a waking vision. Things had finally meshed. After his baby was born, their marriage would grow strong, strong enough to survive anything, even her secrets.

"Do you think it's a boy? I think so. I want to be a good father, a good man like my grandfather."

He would be a good one like her own, nothing like his. She peered up, catching Barrington's delighted gaze. "In a little more than a half year, we'll know. But if it is a son, may he grow as tall as you."

In the soft light, she made out his grin, heard the music of his chuckles. "I've never complained of your height, or lack thereof. You are the right size for me. I can pick you up in one arm and shelter you. And you've such wondrous raven hair. Is it a gift from your Spanish side or the Egyptian? A gift none the less."

They were both of mixed blood. That had to be why they belonged together. And yet it had to be why it was so hard to survive in London. They were different than this place, sunshine and shade. Back in Clanville, where his grandfather and her father ruled, no one dared question their marriage. If only home were an option.

Her pulse raced as Barrington's lips anointed her wrist. "What say you, my love?"

"Tomàs. Everything good is from Papa."

"I'm glad I can see that hue and your violet eyes, two colors to ever worship."

"You don't need to see the other colors." She stopped wearing them for him so he wouldn't struggle or get headaches from his blindness to them. "I want you to see me."

His mouth claimed hers, but she dared not shut her lids. To awaken away from this pleasure would surely crush what remained of her soul.

"Ahh humph." A masculine cough followed.

"Barrister Norton, I've found you. The Duke of Cheshire requests a private audience."

Barrington smiled broadly and spun letting the cold air

separate them. His joy at gaining the duke's notice was palatable, heart-crumbling.

"Where is he, young man?"

The servant adjusted the collar of his shiny livery. "In the study, sir."

Barrington took a step. Then, as if it dawned upon him that he'd be leaving her, he turned and extended his hand. "This will only take a few minutes."

She took his arm and allowed him to lead her back to her seat.

He kissed her forehead, then disappeared into the crowd.

She should be used to this by now, but every time he left, it felt fresh, cutting a little deeper. Someday he wouldn't return. Then the blade would run clean through.

The servant behind her coughed. He tried muffling the repeated cough by turning his face into his sleeve.

The poor dear thirsted. A dry throat scorched and sore was almost the worst. Amora lifted a finger, summoning him. When the boy popped near, she pushed her glass of water towards him.

Kneeling, the young servant choked and sputtered. His mouth trembled. "I…I couldn't, ma'am."

Flipping her fan, she covered him from the glare of onlookers, then slid the goblet into the servant's hands. "I insist. It's never good to be in want."

A smile bloomed beneath brightening blue eyes and blonde lashes. He downed the liquid. "Thank you, ma'am. Please don't tell."

Amora nodded. The one thing she'd learned well was keeping secrets.

Barrington walked behind the servant toward the duke's study. Could his heart hold both joy and sadness? Amora tried to appear supportive, but those eyes of hers said everything, more than he wanted to know. Did she have to think of this as an example of him choosing his work over her again? Did she not know what the duke's support would mean for his career? Imagine London's first mulatto judge.

"This will only take a few moments." He said the words under his breath and tried to make sense of the apprehension she'd cast onto him. Perhaps being with child made her more anxious. Five years of barrenness might do that, too.

"Excuse me, Mr. Norton. Did ye say something?"

Barrington shook his head and returned his focus to Cheshire and the dimly lit corridor. The sound of the music was squelched as if the walls had smothered it within a minute of this trek.

A rush of joy raced up his spine, tightening the knots of expectation in his neck. Battling every day to become the man known for finding and winning with truth had come to fruition. All the questions of his appointment to Lincoln's Inn had been trampled by a perfect court record. Now the Duke of Cheshire, one of the lead reformers in Parliament had need of him.

The servant pointed down a final hall. "The door at the end, sir."

The man bowed and returned to the party, leaving Barrington to take the final leg alone. What did the duke have to discuss and why do so in such privacy, away from all his guests, even his servants?

Getting close to the door, Barrington found it cracked. Voices stirred inside.

"Gaia, I know you are nervous about tonight. Don't be. You are beautiful. The ton will love you, my new duchess."

"William, I should be with Mary. Your daughter said her first words. Mute for so long. You don't know my joy."

"I've prayed for this." His tone sounded of a father's pride, loud and hopeful. "But *our* daughter will have her new mother tomorrow. Tonight at the ball, I need my duchess."

From the small slit between the double doors, the lady, the new Duchess of Cheshire, leaned into the duke. "I will try harder to do this public show for you, if that is what you desire."

The duke chuckled. His tall form enveloped her. "For now. But, later tonight in our chambers, I'll need my wife."

She backed away. Her gauzy gown billowed with each step of retreat. "William, you… I will…be so tired. Mary needs…"

The tall man folded his arms against his waistcoat. "You seem to be avoiding the subject of our chambers. I can be a jealous man, but I didn't think that tendency would be stirred from your devotion to Mary. Gaia, do I not make you happy?"

She pushed back into his arms. "More than anything. Yes. But I…I like just us three. A baby may come. It's so dangerous. My mother died—"

"Gaia, you are a strong woman. When it is time, all will be well." The duke dipped his head to his new bride.

Barrington removed his spectacles and knocked on the door. He didn't like eavesdropping, or interrupting this moment of privacy, but he needed to tend to his own wife.

The duke came to the door and opened it wide. "Duchess, I will see you in the main hall. Go mingle with our guests. Find your aunt and sister, but stay out of… I'll be along in a moment."

The lady was pretty with spectacles that glowed. Her face dimpled as she clasped the duke's hand. She was younger than he'd expected and more tan, more so than Amora's creamy cheeks. Neither had the milky-white complexion his fellow barrister's boasted of in their wives. Neither's tone was as indicting as his own.

When she swept by him, Barrington saw the crinkly pattern of her shiny bun, the slight flare to her nose. He knew why the duke wanted to talk privately. His stomach knotted from his deflated ego. Barrington marched inside and waited for the man to confess it.

Cheshire closed the door. "Mr. Norton, I am glad you've come tonight. I've a matter that only you can help with. I'm trying to find records on a relative of my wife's. You've been able to locate all types of documents and secrets."

Barrington looked over his lenses at the man who was almost his height. "I don't typically locate missing items unless it is a part of a crime." He pivoted and moved back to the door. "I can recommend my solicitor, Mr. Beakes."

"It has to be you. No one else will be as sensitive."

Barrington wasn't about games. The truth plain and simple was the best course. He rubbed his chin and turned. "Why would that be? I have a feeling this hasn't anything to do with my trial record."

Cheshire brushed the buttons of his waistcoat. "You are perceptive, and you are known to be a man who can find truth. That is what I need for my wife."

"Then say it plainly. For every moment I'm here, my wife is without me. All who I work for understand I need the complete truth or I cannot help. I despise lies and deception."

The duke squared his shoulders. "My wife is like you. She is a mulatto. I need to find out what happened to the man whose blood she shares. I want shipping records or even a bill of sale uncovered."

Bill of Sale? "The duchess's father was enslaved?"

"She only found out recently that she is of mixed race. Now, I need to give her as much information as possible. But this must be kept discreet. Not everyone is of an open mind. I thought surely you would be."

Barrington knew how narrow his world was. People sized up his race before anything else. That was why he pushed so hard for truth, for perfection. He'd long become the model for that one different friend, or the sole ideal the reformers proclaimed in fighting for the end of slavery or expanding education. Being the only was a heavy load; a gun cocked waiting to misfire.

Tugging on his tailcoat, Barrington hid his growing disappointment. "I'll think on it, your grace and send word."

Cheshire pounded closer. "It will be a great favor to me if you agree to take this upon yourself."

Barrington knew exactly what that meant. It was always better to have powerful allies than enemies. He nodded. "Yes, I will look into it. I cannot promise you anything."

"That's better than nothing. Thank you, Mr. Norton."

Barrington bowed and rotated. He walked down the corridor. It would have been nice to be singled out because of his abilities not his blood.

Yet, with ambition stirring in his veins, he'd use this assignment to prove his capabilities. The duke would see that Barrington was more than just in similar straits as the new Duchess of Cheshire.

When her husband reappeared at the entrance to the party, his face held a long frown; similar to the one he'd brought earlier to Mayfair. Amora's heart clenched. The meeting must not have gone well. What could she say to lift his spirits, to reassure him of his worth despite what the Duke of Cheshire said?

She rose from her seat to go to him. Forget this party. She'd tend to his spirits at home. They should leave now.

When she neared, he plastered his face with a short, tight smile. He surely meant it to keep her from fretting, but that never worked. She and anxiety were soul mates. "Are you ready to leave, dearest?"

His lips puckered as if to answer, but his gaze lifted. His eyes narrowed on someone. "Beakes?"

She turned and winced with frustration. His solicitor, Mr.

Beakes headed directly toward them. The man embodied work, more time for Barrington to be somewhere else where he could be injured or worse.

Beakes rent his chocolate greatcoat, putting large gloved hands to his lapels. "Mr. Norton, you have to come with me. Smith. He's asking for you."

A long blast of air left her husband's nostrils. "Smith? I just left him this afternoon. Tell him I will see him in the morning before court."

The man tapped his foot, then shook his head from side to side. "He won't be alive in the morning. Well, not for long. He's going to the gallows tomorrow."

Barrington wrenched the back of his neck. His shoulders slumped. "That wasn't supposed to be for a month."

Beakes shrugged. "Change happens. What do I tell him?"

"Y-e-s. I told him, I'd come if asked. I'll return to Newgate after I drop my beautiful family home." Barrington's voice sounded strained, weighted with obligation. But at which part, Newgate or family? "In an hour or so, I'll visit him."

The solicitor stepped forward pulling at his saggy cravat. He looked very grim with bushy furrowed brows and downturned lips. "He says he wants to tell you that truth. You're not going to risk him changing his mind over a delay?"

What did that mean, and why did Mr. Beakes seem to point his beady eyes at her?

"I'll take Mrs. Norton home, right away for you." The singsong voice of Cynthia Miller filtered near. The woman clad in a low clinging bodice of bright yellow traipsed near. Her ruby hair reflected the candlelight from the wall sconce. Not a tendril out of place on the vixen.

"How good of you." Barrington clasped Amora's hand. "Please understand. I'll be to Mayfair as soon as I can."

"It's no trouble for me to help, Mr. N-oor-ton." The breathless way Cynthia said his name made the flames in

Amora's middle more acute. Would the singer's two-faced tricks to lure Barrington start again?

Forgetting the vixen, Amora reached up and caressed his cheek. She so wanted to be understanding. "Is it that dire?"

Her husband's light eyes had faded even more. He tugged at his lapel and adjusted the brilliant gold pin, his grandfather's gift for acceptance into Lincoln's Inn. "Smith lied to protect someone. If I'd known the truth, I could've helped. An innocent man is going to die in the morning. I have to go to him."

How terrible! Breathless, hurting for him, Amora drew her hand to her mouth.

"If I'd had more time to organize my notes the morning of the trial, I am sure I would've seen the lies. I would've made him admit it. If I'd left..." Barrington's voice became muffled. His Adam's apple shook as he coughed.

The unspoken words stopped her heart. *If he'd left Mayfair on time.* If he hadn't attended his needy wife. This killing would be her fault. When would deaths stop being her fault?

He slid his fingers about her palm and drew the union to his chest. "Please be understanding. If he must die, he should have the opportunity to admit to everything, to go to glory with a clean heart."

No, some secrets should die, never to be said aloud. Amora thought this, felt this everyday with every nightmare. "Will you be very late?"

Mr. Beakes tugged his shoulder. "Time is of the essence. I have to catch up to the runners. There will be another good criminal catch tonight."

Barrington shrugged, then kissed her forehead. "I'll try not to be too late, but this may take a while."

Cynthia gripped Amora's arm. "Run along, Mr. Norton, and don't forget my debut performance week's end. Though you are the busiest barrister, you and Mrs. Norton must attend. It would be like having my brother there." Her tone pitched then lowered like a sorrow-filled harp. "Yes, having Gerald back would be so nice. You must come."

Barrington's lips turned up, then his countenance blanked again. "You're a dear, a credit to your great, late brother, Gerald Miller. Miller was such a good man, but Mrs. Norton can tell you of my work ethic."

On that, Amora could write pages. "No one is as dedicated. Be careful."

"Always." After a kiss to her fingers, he let go of Amora's hand and followed Mr. Beakes.

As she watched her husband, the dedicated barrister, wade through the crowd, sadness whipped through her, spinning her mind like a cyclone. Her palm dropped to her abdomen. Would their family be a priority to him, or another jot on his appointment list?

This son wouldn't be in second place for his doting father. Could she truly be happy if at least something of hers took first place in Barrington's heart?

She blinked away the anxiety building inside her mind, pricking her conscience. He was doing what he felt he must for his career, for their family. With a short breath, she placed a smile to her lips to avoid inciting Cynthia's questions. With this baby, Amora and Barrington would be happy. They just had to be.

Chapter Two: Confession And Omission

The guard fumbled with his heavy keys unlocking the iron door to Smith's cell. Barrington fumed. The gaoler was nowhere to be found, so no answers to why Smith's execution would be rushed. What had changed? And by whose orders?

Finally, the lock clicked. The guard flung the door open, allowing Barrington inside. Smith looked pale, white like the cuffs on Barrington's evening shirt. "You've come, Mr. Norton. I didn't think you would."

Barrington took off his hat and pitched it onto the table. "I am a man of my word. I'm here. Tell me the secrets that has sealed your fate."

The condemned fellow put down the Bible leaves. His fingers shook. "Does hanging hurt much?"

"Not for long. You'll hardly notice when you get the swing of it."

Smith's lips twitched in a half-smile as he nodded.

Trudging to the window, Barrington glanced at the finished platform. Smith's execution would begin at dawn. He fixed his gaze on the cart just outside the window bearing white hoods, the ones that would be draped on the prisoner before affixing the noose. As if a heavy weight sat upon his chest, he inhaled hard forcing air inside his lungs. "You asked for me. I said I would come. I left my wife to be here, so tell me now why you are dying? Maybe I could rouse the Lord Justice to stay this execution."

The rag thin man lifted red-rimmed eyes to him. "Barrister, I think it's unfair to die for coining. They should save the noose for true villains like the Dark Walk Abductor."

The man still wanted to talk foolishness. Barrington could be escorting his wife home, enjoying holding her until she slept. Amora had looked so beautiful in her lavender gown, the soft neck frill that fluttered when they danced. It was pure happiness slipping his fingers against the sweet texture of the fine pearls beading her bodice, sculpting the gentle rounding of her abdomen.

She was finally to bear him a child, a son to father. Barrington would be nothing like his own drunken one. No, he'd be a source of pride, not constant ridicule. A sigh sputtered out, releasing a portion of the disappointments filling his lungs.

With a grunt, he stopped his woolgathering and turned his attention back to Smith. "Coining is an offense against the Crown."

"And abducting and killing women, ain't?"

"All the laws must be obeyed, not just the ones we like. Believe me, if they find the fiend, and the magistrate's runners or the vigilantes don't tear him apart, he will see justice. But I believe it a fantasy like a ghost tale, made up to cover ghastly crimes or wanton runaways."

Smith's eyes widened. The man looked as if he'd choked on his tongue. "Ain't no fantasy. He's real. The crimes are real."

A tingle set in Barrington's ribs. His internal truth detector niggled. Smith wasn't dying for coining, but something worse. Folding his arms, Barrington decided to indulge him and softened his tone. "That's an old crime. No one's likely to pay almost two years out."

"He's been doing it for at least seven. Maybe more. Not

sure if he stopped."

Barrington's ears perked up. His blood heated to full boil. "What are you talking about?"

"I was paid to help him. That's why I die tonight. And if I'd said more, my only brother, he'll die too. My brother is all I have left. That's why I lied. I do deserve death for what I've done, for being in league with the devil. But my brother, he's got a young family. Mouths to feed."

Barrington paced over to Smith and grabbed him up by the shirt collars, shaking the miserable man's bones until they rattled. "What are you saying? You are the Dark Walk Abductor?"

Struggling in Barrington's grasp, the man's head bobbled. "Not me. I don't know his name, but I was in his service."

This was madness.

Ramblings.

Lies.

Evil lies.

"Smith, you have me here to spit falsehoods in my face."

"Not lies. When I die, the proof is gone. I contacted him again a couple of months ago 'cause I needed money. He said he'd help. The next thing I know, the coins he gave me were fakes. They found tools in my flat. He sent a note saying he'd help with the charges."

Barrington tossed the man on the bench. "Where is this note? I suppose it's gone."

Smith nodded. Barrington's innards burned brighter than the sun, hotter than hell's fire. "This fantasy won't save you."

"I've done some bad things, Mr. Norton. All for coins. So it is fitting I should die for coining."

A hundred and five thoughts pressed Barrington's skull but only three could be uttered aloud and maintain his Christianity. "Why tell me now and set me on this fleeting chase? You should've kept it to yourself. Is this a final revenge on me for your conviction?"

"No. But if there's anyone who can figure it out, it's you. You're smart. I don't know who he is, but he has means. I saw him once, tall, gentlemanly looking. I'm about to pay for my years of silence, but you can make him pay for all the bad he's done."

Recognition of his talents from a condemned man wasn't the acclaim he sought. Nor was being saddled with another man's burden. Barrington already bore enough. Wiping at his forehead, he pivoted toward the door. "Goodnight, Mr. Smith. Thank you for wasting my time."

"The abductor took a woman the night of June 10th. No, the 11th, 1813." Almost gagging on his lies, Smith raised his voice higher. "He killed her that night, dumped the body in a ditch. There's got to be a record of her murder. I'm telling you the truth."

A date? That could be checked.

"Find him. Before he gets to my brother, too. He won't be satisfied with just me hanging."

The pleading, the confession warbling Smith's voice could not be ignored. Barrington eased his fingers from the bars and rotated to the prisoner. "How can you be so certain of the date?"

"I was there. I drove the carriage. Check the records. You'll see. A woman's body was found on the next morning on the route from London."

"Where were you headed?"

"South. I don't know where. I know he didn't want to kill her there. He had other plans. He—"

Barrington sliced the damp air with his hand. The motion silenced Smith as if he'd struck his windpipe. The perversion never needed to be mentioned outside of the courts. All had heard the rumors of the shameless treatment of the Dark Walk's victims. Were the horrid tales true?

He rubbed at the back of his neck and addressed the witness, perhaps the only one to these crimes. "So your testimony is that you contacted the Dark Walk Abductor. How did you do it?"

"I left a message with the barkeep near the docks asking for help, a little money to get on my feet. That's how we always contacted each other. He knows I have a brother. My brother and his wife will be targets."

Could Smith be telling the truth? And if he was, did that mean the villain still lived and had the influence to get to Smith, to erect this conviction?

"Mr. Norton, you're married. My brother has a wife, one with a child on the way. I'll die for them tomorrow."

Barrington folded his arms and leaned against the bars, picturing his own wife and child on the way. She probably lit candles in every room she paced awaiting his return. A wave of protection, desire and caution encircled his chest pressing until a tired sigh sneaked out.

"Go after the real villain, Mr. Norton. My brother and his wife are happy, with a baby to come. They are innocent. You're married. Are you happy?"

Happy marriage? Scratching the light scruff of new growth on his jaw, Barrington narrowed his thoughts to his wedding trip and the last three months, the good times in his five-year marriage to Amora. "It's pleasant to find someone whom you can trust, someone who fusses over your eating, someone who ensures the bedchamber is warm enough so your hip doesn't ache." Or who calmed his spirit before a big trial. "You've given me much to think about."

He pivoted again and tapped the bar for the guard.

"Mr. Norton, would you mind waiting a little longer? The pages you left talked about repentance. I'd like to know a little more about that."

In for a pound. If he left now, by the time he made it to

Mayfair, Amora would be asleep. *Oh Lord, let her not have one of her nightmares, not without him being there to comfort her.*

Barrington swiped at his brow. Perhaps he could get Smith to admit to more details about the killer for whom he claimed to work. After tomorrow, there wouldn't be another chance to interrogate him.

Amora drummed her fingers against the tufted seat of Miss Miller's carriage. It was dark, stuffy, and reeked of chrysanthemums.

Cynthia had lied to Barrington, saying she'd get Amora straight to Mayfair. Once Barrington left, the tart spent her time thronged by gentlemen, tipsy in compliments on her singing. Trollop.

Tired and a little nauseous with pressure building below her bosom, she left the woman parked at the threshold of the grand portico. Cynthia stood there, flitting her fan at her audience of men. Maybe she enjoyed waylaying Amora. With all the bucks vying for the vixen, she'd never quit.

Since Barrington worked and Cynthia was being Cynthia, Amora might as well sit back and prepare for her lay-in, the birthing of her child here in chrysanthemum hades.

Another ten or fifteen minutes in the dark sent a wince to Amora's lips. Maybe she could wave at Cynthia to hurry her. Turning to the window, she spied Mr. Charleton. Heart thumping, then bumping to a stop, Amora ducked down, tucking her arms over her head. Did he see her? No no no. He couldn't see her.

She pushed foul air into her lungs, and forced her heart to beat again. A little faster than dead, but not quite a quiet rhythm. If that man knew she was alone, he'd want to converse about the past. Things that should be forgotten. He needed to march away and take the memories too.

Fidgeting, she peeked in time to see the gentleman retreat

into the party. Good. No confrontations, no fanning of gossip's flames. No infernos tonight.

The light disappeared as the moon dipped behind the clouds, making everything darker. Could she survive another hour in this small space?

Perhaps she could ask the footman for a lantern. Barrington always read, so riding with him, she never had to beg...beg for light. *Beg*.

A tremor rippled over her body. She gripped her arms about her to try to stop the shivers. Having an episode with Cynthia wouldn't bode well.

Filling her lungs, Amora wiped her brow. After counting twenty-three stars and forty-one nail heads, the carriage door finally opened.

"Sorry to keep you waiting, Mrs. Norton...Amora. My admirers can't get enough."

Cynthia slithered inside, taking the seat opposite her. She tucked her form fitting train against her long legs, and adjusted her red satin cape. "Hope you were comfortable. After all, what is a songstress to do?"

There were a number of things, Amora could list: stay away from Barrington, stop using her dead brother's memory to twist her husband into knots. Those pronouncements wouldn't be received well, so she made her tone pleasant. "I'm happy for you. You're the rage of London."

The carriage rocked and swayed forward. Hopefully, they'd take the short path back to Mayfair, about twenty minutes of finger counting. With the longer way, it would be difficult to think of more compliments for this *friend* of Barrington's.

"I have done well with the cards I've been dealt. But I'd give it all away for the love of a good man like…oh, I don't know. Someone like Mr. Norton."

One, two, three. She tried to ignore the viper's venom, but

it stung her chest to imagine Cynthia with Barrington. Amora smoothed her pinkie over the stitches of her shawl's hem. She must remain even-tempered, bland like the simple cloth shrouding her shoulders. "The weather is nice. Not too hot or cold."

"Is that all you have to say? We're alone. You could show off your wit. Well, you used to be witty."

No doubt, if Amora lost her temper, Cynthia would tell Barrington, ending the newly found peace of the Norton marriage. Nothing was worth that.

"Well, I can be civil too. The weather is delightful. See we can convey to Mr. Norton our nice conversation. That should please him. Don't you want to please him?"

This woman must possess something that made Barrington blind to Cynthia's faults. But what?

Truthfully, Amora would love for Barrington to miss her flaws, just like he missed the colors red and green.

Tired of careful speech, she grimaced. "You want something, Miss Miller, other than my husband, or you would be following him to the prison, offering to hold his hand as he walked the corridors."

Cynthia laughed. "You are a sly one. I need Barrington to represent someone dear to me, but I know he won't if he thinks it will upset you."

"My husband attends clients, with or without my approval." Amora bit her lip. She couldn't alert the singer to any marital difficulties.

"You can brag a little. You have more power over him than you think. No, it's going to take your urging to get Barrington to agree."

"Why would I help? You make veiled threats at taking my husband. Do you think I'm a fool?"

Cynthia slipped closer, planting her painted face directly in front of her. "I'm not the only one who'd love to borrow him, even for just a little while. His father was quite the man about town, and most men of Barrington's stature have mistresses. Usually a trinket or two keeps the wives happy."

A trinket? Or a bauble, like a pearl necklace. An ache stabbed her middle. She bit back the pain. The jade couldn't know her words cut deep.

With a lift of her chin, Amora leveled her shoulders. She hid her balled fists in the folds of her shawl. "Mr. Norton is not most men. He's quite honorable."

"He is a dear, but all males have limits. They can be driven into willing arms." She snatched a fan out of her reticule and whipped it about in the stale air. "Very willing arms."

There was no doubt, no misunderstanding of her words. Cynthia intended to seduce Barrington.

"Yet, I could consider leaving him alone."

Amora cut her gaze to the treacherous jade. "What?"

"I need you to let him take my case. It's life or death for my family. I wouldn't be here trying to seek this favor, humbling myself before you, if it weren't grim."

"If it's such, Mr. Norton will make the right decision."

"Not if working so closely with me, day and night, will upset you. Don't play the helpless wife. You are a force to be reckoned with, though Barrington says you don't paint any more or play the pianoforte. Afraid my talents will outshine yours, so you abandon the competition?"

Cynthia and Barrington discussed her? A lump formed in her throat. She forced herself to swallow.

"Will you support me?" The tart leaned forward. An errant curl flopped from her carefully coiffed bun.

A glimpse of streetlight exposed her narrowing emerald eyes and thinned lips. "You must agree."

"I can't tell him what to do."

"What if I promise never to tell of your little indiscretion?"

Amora pivoted to the window. She didn't want to think of

that time, but the memories returned almost every night. More so, when Barrington wasn't home. A shudder rippled through her. Would she ever be free of them?

Cynthia gripped Amora's arm. "Look at me."

The woman's silhouette seemed similar to her lost cellmate's, but that girl was kind. No cruelness in her, that precious soul.

"I know you didn't tell him of your *disappearance*? So, he married a liar." Cynthia giggled. The notes weren't merry, but harsh and threatening. She tightened her hold.

The pressure hurt, as did the pain in Amora's abdomen. She snatched her hand free. "Stop this now. You wouldn't want Mr. Norton to know of this unsightly nature."

Cynthia eased back onto her seat. Her fingers flicked at the bunches of fabric crowding her feet. "Barrington knows everything, everything about me. He was so caring about my child out of wedlock. If I'd been able to keep her, he'd treat the lass as if she were his."

Amora closed her eyes. Was that a hint? No, Barrington would have told her, if he and the singer... Her mind wouldn't complete the sentence. "Mr. Norton loves children. He'll never condemn a child for the mother's failings."

A hiss filled the dim cabin. "When he learns of your failing, we'll see if you're still so smug. We know how he hates liars, and you wed without disclosure. No man wants to be married in darkness."

The blood in Amora's veins froze. She chiseled free her gaze and peered through the glass. She spied the sign, Conduit Street. That was one block from the townhouse. She tapped on the roof of the carriage. With the gas street lamps burning, she could run and be on their Mayfair doorsteps within minutes. "Out! I want out!"

Her shriek did the trick. The carriage stopped. A footman appeared and opened the door. Amora stood and extended her hand to be let down.

"Oh, no, Mrs. Norton. I told Barrington I'd take you home. I'm not going to be accused of dropping you anywhere but your house."

"I'll take my chances. Besides, he'll forgive you." Amora leapt out of the carriage and wrapped her shawl tight about her trembling limbs.

"Suit yourself." The door slammed shut and the carriage moved away at a fast clip.

Even if she wanted to change her mind, it was too late. The carriage and horses disappeared at the end of the street. Amora filled her lungs with the chilly air. Staring at the lit street lamps, she paced toward the townhome.

The shuffle of her satin slippers echoed. The darkness of the night crowded her, squeezing her lungs, bringing heavy breath after heavy breath pouring out of her mouth.

Shaking, she gripped her tummy. "One, two, three." Counting aloud usually slowed her thoughts, but not tonight. Images of a darkened cellar with roots pushing through the floor crowded her head. The noise of falling brick clogged her ears. A sour taste rose from her stomach, drying her tongue.

If she blinked, she could be lost again, waiting in the dank prison, listening for the horrid footsteps of her abductor.

The shadows of trees swept across her path.

Her heart slammed against her chest.

Something was coming for her.

Even in London, she couldn't hide.

By the time she stumbled onto Mayfair's first step, the stabbing ache in her abdomen cut through her every few seconds. She couldn't stop shivering.

Pounding on the door, she sank to her knees.

It opened. Mrs. Gretling stood in the threshold bundled in a thick woolen robe holding a candle. "Mrs. Norton, are you alright?"

She fell against her housekeeper. The world grew darker, wrapping Amora in pure blackness.

With each weighted step, Barrington dragged into his carriage. His heart hung heavy, filled with hopeless burdens. The execution had lasted ten minutes. Ten whole minutes.

One to line up the men on the platform. A couple more to slip white hoods over Smith and the others. Another two to hear the building cheers of the wretched crowd. Then less than thirty seconds to feel the reverberation of the drop of the platform. Thud, Thud.

Ten minutes, the difference between life and death.

Barrington stretched out on the seat. The clip-clop of his horse team couldn't distract him from Smith's confession. Or the knowledge Barrington had been used to bring about Smith's death.

The fellow was innocent of coining, but not of this Dark Walk Abductor business? The clear-eyed confession. The palm-sweat Smith kept wiping on his breeches as he recounted of his vile participation in acquiring victims. A man facing death wouldn't lie about such evil transactions, would he?

Yet, one lie begat another. What words could be trusted from a liar's tongue.

Barrington rubbed at his skull. He had a date and a crime to give to his solicitor. Beakes was good at finding details. He'd put him on it later today once he made amends to Amora. How mad could she be?

The carriage stopped outside the jewelers. At well past ten in the morning, Bond Street typically hosted crowds of shoppers. Barrington didn't have the energy to face any of it and remained upon his seat with his eyes closed.

Hopefully, his man-of-all-work was the first in line at the merchant. The silversmith should be finished with the rattle.

A husband needed something to smooth any new thorns that might await him at home. One lesson he'd learned from watching his father drag in at all hours. A good distraction offered a chance at peace.

The dainty bauble, no bigger than his thumb, etched with his and Amora's initials should distract her. She'd think of their child and forget how late he was.

Maybe she'd realized that even if he weren't with her, she was very present in his thoughts. *Oh, Lord, let her understand.* A few months of happiness weren't enough.

The door to the carriage opened. A refreshing breeze blew inside. "Sir."

Barrington stretched and blinked at James.

His man, dressed in a dark coat steeped in braided trim, poked his ruddy face inside. "Here, sir."

"Thank you." Barrington took the velvet pouch. The smooth nape appeared gray, but it was probably emerald or red. How horrid not to experience all the shades of a rainbow. On the balcony, Amora had said she wanted him to see her. Clothing was one thing, but she shouldn't have given up painting, something that had once brought her joy. He'd speak to her about that.

Yet, his inability to detect certain hues didn't explain why she'd also abandoned the pianoforte. He adored music, and she was quite proficient before the war.

"Mr. Norton, I took a peek inside. Just lovely."

James's infectious grin filled his countenance. If not for the solemn night or the possibility of facing an angered wife, Barrington would smile too.

"The missus should love it. Might do the trick. You won't have to lounge in your study."

"Hope so. Get me home as quickly as possible."

"Yes, but be at ease. One night isn't long enough to change the locks." His man shut the door and soon the carriage raced towards Mayfair.

James was of a different race, different station in life, but no one understood Barrington's burdens better. Hopefully, his man was right about the locks, too.

Running a hand against his hair, Barrington shoved on his top hat and tried to relax. Nothing could ease his soul. Since the onset of her pregnancy, he'd been very careful to be in by at least ten each evening.

This should be a happy time for them both. His being absorbed in work always made her uneasy. Headaches, nightmares. He'd find her upset in her chambers, stewing as if she assumed something bad had happened.

With a last tweak to his wilted cravat, he bounded from the carriage.

"Good luck, sir." James tipped his tricorn hat and tugged the reins of the conveyance, hauling beasts and carriage toward the mews.

Partially blinded by the glare of the bright sunlight, Barrington walked up the path and onto the portico. All the lights of the house were a glow. Amora had a penchant for burning candles, but this was a bit much. Why?

He pressed on the door. It opened before he could settle his fob in the keyhole. Not locked?

Mrs. Gretling pounded down the steps with a bucket of balled up sheets. "Oh, Mr. Norton! You're home. No one knew where to find you."

Her tone sounded clipped. Their Scottish housekeeper was not shy with her opinions, but Amora knew where he was.

"My wife didn't say?"

The housekeeper shook her head. Her face pinched as she ran towards the kitchen. Were those tears in her light eyes?

Amora. He turned toward the stairs, but two men blocked his way. He recognized one as the physician who looked after Amora's odd headaches about eight months ago. But who was the other, the lanky man with walnut colored hair parted and converging upon a low brow?

And why were they coming from Amora's bedchamber?

The physician stopped in front of him and extended his hand. His countenance was ashen. "Mr. Norton…"

The other man also stuck his hand in Barrington's face. "I am Reverend Samuel Wilson. I wish we met under different circumstances."

Eyes widening until they hurt, a feeling of utter dread ripped Barrington's gut asunder. He pushed through them and pounded up the stairs to Amora's chamber.

This is the complete novel with all four episodes. Enjoy this romantic suspense and meet old friends, William and Gaia, from Unmasked Heart. The love and drama continues.

Part Two

Bonus - New Series - Advertisements for Love

* * *

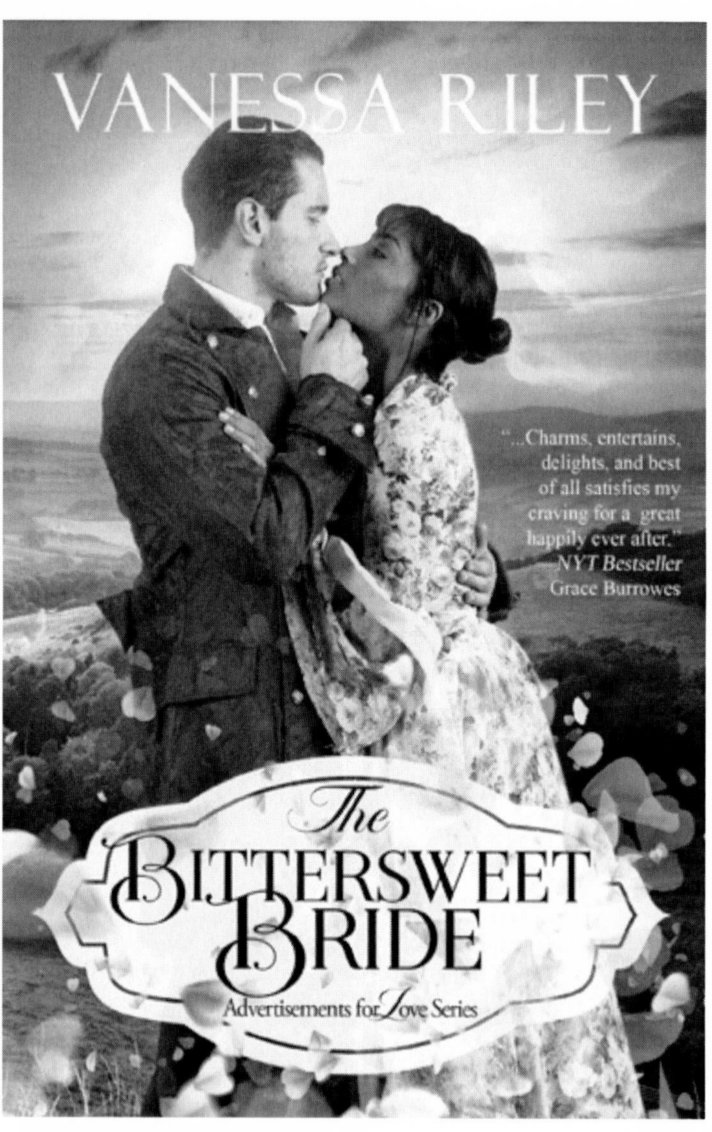

The Bittersweet Bride

* * *

Widow Theodosia Cecil needs a husband to help protect her son. The former flower seller turned estate owner posts an ad in the newspaper, and no one is more surprised than she when her first love, the man she thought dead, reappears.

Ewan Fitzwilliam has been at war for six years. Now, the second son of a powerful earl is back but his beloved Theo needs a husband and will not consider him. She believes Ewan left her—in desperate straits—so she denies the feelings she still harbors for the handsome, scarred soldier. Theo and playwright Ewan must overcome bitter lies and vengeful actions that ruined their youthful affair. Theo must reveal her deepest secret in order to reclaim the love that has long been denied.

Learn more: http://bit.ly/bsweetbride

Here's a sneek peak:

Chapter One

You Have Mail & Memories

London, England, September 7, 1819

Theodosia Cecil dipped her head, hoping her gray bonnet would hide her tall form amongst the crowd of Burlington Arcade shoppers. Her heart beat a rhythm of fear as her brow fevered with questions.

Could it be him?

Why was he haunting her now?

She spun, praying her wobbly legs would support her flight from the ghost. Spying a path between a chatty woman and her admirer, Theodosia claimed it and swayed toward the open door.

Safe in the shop, she put a hand to her thumping heart. Seeing the face of someone dead… It shook her, forced too many memories. The image of Ewan, her deceased first love, had to be a figment of Theodosia's conscience, nothing more. Why would this vision rear up now—questioning her resolve to be in town garnering letters offering matrimony from strangers?

Her hands trembled, puckering the stiff seams of her new kid gloves as she stuffed the sealed papers into her reticule. What if she'd dropped them in her mad dash? With all the people milling beneath the sparkling glass roof of the Arcade, the responses would've been lost, and with them, her dream of protecting her son. Hope in her plan slipped from her grasp, even with her onyx mitts. This time, there would be no kind Mathew Cecil to pick her up and wipe her clean.

She missed her late husband and his endless patience. He should be the only dead man in her head. Yet, there stood Ewan Fitzwilliam's ghost, vividly in her imagination. Perhaps it was her heart crying out at this unromantic way of finding a new husband.

"Ma'am, may I help you?"

Theodosia lifted her gaze from her gloves to a small cherry-red face.

"Our store has much to offer," the young girl said. "Did ye come for something special, Mrs. Cecil?"

Startling at the girl's use of her name, Theodosia raised her chin, then scanned from side to side at the pots. She took a breath and smelled sweet roses and lilacs. "What is this place? A perfumer?"

"Yes, Mrs. Cecil, and we use Cecil flowers to make the best fragrances."

The girl knew who she was, and the lilt in the young blonde's voice made Theodosia's lips lift. Respect always felt good.

A little less jittery, she nodded at the girl then turned to the walnut shelf and poked the lid of a greenish jar. The scent of lavender filled the air. Pride in her and her husband's accomplishment inflated her lungs. "Cecil flowers are the best."

The calm ushered in from the soft, sweet scents allowed her thoughts to right. Ghosts didn't exist. If they did, then it would be Mathew visiting her, guiding her, pushing her cold feet forward whenever she felt she couldn't do something, as he'd often done during their five short years of marriage. He had died almost a year ago.

The shop girl came beside her, dusting the shelves. "Would you like some of the lavender, Mrs. Cecil?"

That beautiful name, the only last name she'd ever possessed—the repetition of it inspired questions. "You know me from the flower fields? Have we met?"

"Everyone knew Mr. Cecil. God rest his soul. And all the flower girls know you. If a Blackamoor… Sorry, if a shop girl could be more, then we all can."

Theodosia, dark skin and all, an inspiration to others? If those shop girls knew the whole of things, they would be scandalized. Horrified at the things she'd done, Theodosia became teary-eyed. She'd received unmerited favor catching Mathew Cecil's eye and his mercy.

"Sorry, I didn't mean nothing."

Theodosia nodded and tugged at her sleeve, hitting her reticule against her buttons, which clinked like serving bells. Her fine clothes hid the past, the fatigue and hunger of living on the streets. She forced a smile. "Becoming more is the beginning."

"Yes, ma'am. Quite a good 'ne."

From the outside, it must look like that, but some secrets were best kept in the grave. She turned from the almost-hero worship look in the shop girl's eyes and counted the brightly colored decanters in hues of salmon and cobalt blue lining a near table. "This is a lovely place. Have you done well since the shop's opening?"

"Some days. Some mornings, we're good and busy. Others, slow and easy. So much different than selling on the streets."

That worn-out heart of Theodosia's started moving within her chest. She caught the girl's shy gaze and said, "Slow days mean no money, but they can give ease to the back." With her palm, she cupped her mouth. "I meant selling flowers…long days." There were worse things for the back than an honest day's work selling flowers. Her mother's work at a brothel—

that had been hard.

The younger woman nodded, but frowned as a shadow engulfed her.

A thick, portly fellow wearing a heavy burlap apron stepped from behind them. "Do ye belong here, m-m-miss?"

Theodosia blinked then stared at the man who stood with arms folded, disapproval flexing each meaty muscle. "Are you sure you're supposed to be here? Black servants don't come unattended. Blackamoor or whatever you are?"

"Sir, this is Mr. Cecil's widow," the shop girl said as her gaze dropped.

The man gawked as he glared at Theodosia. After an eternity of seconds, he said, "Oh…that Mrs. Cecil."

The pride she'd felt at hearing the Cecil name slipped away. It fell to the floor, ready to be trampled by her own short heels. With silk ribbons trailing her bonnet and an onyx walking dress stitched with heavy brass buttons, he still saw her as low. Was he thinking, as she often did: *mistress, half-breed, by-blow, whore*?

No matter what Theodosia felt about her past, she'd not let the sour shop clerk, or anyone else, stuff her into one of those names. She was a widow to a good man. "I'm not a servant, sir. In fact, you are one of the many vendors who use my family's wares for your livelihood." She took a step closer to the man. "I'm your business partner."

The man turned a lovely shade of purple, darker than fallen bee orchid buds. The veins on his neck pulsed.

As wonderful as it was to make him uncomfortable, it was never good to leave a bull enraged. Mathew had taught her that. She jangled her reticule, letting the *tink-tink* sound of clanging coins speak for her. "I'd like to be a patron."

The man harrumphed over his glasses. "We have many items." He pivoted to the shop girl. "Sally, go dust in the back. I'll take care of Mrs. Cecil."

The young woman nodded. "Good meeting you, ma'am." She offered another smile then pattered away.

Theodosia forced her shoulders to straighten and paced around the man. As a free woman and a proper widow with money, she could shop here. A glance to the left helped her settle on a practical item. "I'd like to purchase some soap."

The man nodded and pointed her to a table skirted in crimson silk. He dogged her footfalls, following close behind, as if she'd steal something.

She sighed. Hopefully, she wouldn't have to become used to this treatment again. The last year of grieving had protected her from outsiders, and the years of having her late Mathew's guidance had almost made her forget.

Almost.

She pressed her gloved fingertips against a jar colored lapis blue. "What type of soap is inside?"

The clerk pushed up his thick spectacles that had slid down his condescending nose. "A fine lavender. Very expensive, about four shillings a piece. Not so much for Cecil's widow."

Though she had the money to buy most things, years of thrift and haggling still pumped in her blood. She poked at the glass, tilting its heavy lid. The fragrance, honey-like, wafted from the pressed bars, stroking her nose. Surely, they had been made from Cecil spike lavandin—for nothing else could hold such strong perfume.

This had to be a sign from Mathew. He must approve of her actions to marry again in order to protect the son he'd so loved. She must buy the soap. She stroked the jar. "I'll take two pieces, and wrap it in paper. Make sure the scale is clear of fingers. I'd hate to pay more than what's necessary."

The man picked up the container. His head bobbed up and down as if it had taken this long to see past her face to her wealth. "I'll weigh this out…ma'am, without a finger on the scale."

Half watching the clerk, half watching the window glass, she decided the store front was more interesting than the man's balding head. She filled her vision with the sea of sleek top hats and crisp bonnets passing through the Arcade. None of them an apparition. She sighed again, the tight grip of apprehension further loosing from her spine. The vision had been her nerves.

Slowly, carefully, and in full view of the clerk, she dipped her fingers into her reticule pulling out the foolscap letters she'd retrieved from the stationer. She flipped to the first, a thin sheet of light gray paper, and mouthed the address. This was the second correspondence from a man with the rank of squire to her marriage advertisement. Though his crisp writing of her name, Mrs. Cecil, denoted elegance, their meeting last week had been far from elegant. It had been dull, lifeless, and made worse by his obvious discomfort in talking with her. He hadn't even had the courage to hold her gaze.

Surely, between the folds sat a polite *no*, and for that she'd be grateful. Theodosia was in want of a man's protection, but a new husband needed to be like Mathew, a Boaz protector. Yes, one of those gentlemanly fellows who cherished family above everything and who'd never be ashamed to be seen with her son.

What if it was a *yes*? She tapped the second letter to her bosom. If she had another offer she'd get her friend Ester to help pen a rejection to the squire. Ester's chaste brain had to be filled with clever ways of saying no.

Chuckling silently, she switched to the next response. This one addressed her advertisement number not her name. A first correspondence. New air filled her chest.

The primrose-colored paper felt thick beneath her fingers, and the thick glob of red wax sealing the note held an indentation of a crest. Could it be from a gentleman? Maybe someone titled? Maybe this could be the man who would stand up for her boy. The notion of such decency lifted her lips, even the bottom one she chewed when nervous or frightened.

"Mada…Mrs. Cecil." The shopkeeper's impatient voice sounded, cutting through her woolgathering. "I've more paper in the back. Another minute."

The heat from her kid glove made the wax melt a little. She should open it now and read the particulars, his age and situation, but having her dearest friends' dueling perspectives would help make sure she wasn't getting too excited. All the money in the world could not make a man want to father a sickly child and wouldn't help fight for the boy's interests.

Loud voices sounded from the backroom. The door opened and a shaking Sally came out. The blonde twisted her hands within her long apron. The stocky clerk passed in front of her and stood behind the counter. "That will be eight shillings."

Theodosia shoved her letters under the crook of her arm and fished out a half guinea.

The bright shine of the gold coin reflected in his widened eyes. They bulged like greedy hot air balloons. "Is there anything else you wish to buy?"

She shook her head and waited for two shillings and sixpence change. Everything her late husband had told her was true—money trumped questions. Pity all men weren't like her honest Mathew, or dreamers like her apparition. No, most were manipulative, lying as soon as they opened their mouths.

She picked up her package, shifting the treasure between her palms, and looked at the hurt painting the shop girl's face. She looked like Theodosia had used to look, contemplating the wrong choices. That couldn't happen. She flicked the edge of her parcel, making a hole. "Sir, might I have more paper? I don't want to lose these."

The man slapped the counter. "Aye. Picky. Seems money makes you the same as the rest."

Theodosia bit her tongue, then her lip, to keep a tart reply inside her mouth. She needed a moment alone with the girl.

As soon as the clerk headed into the back, Theodosia came alongside her. "Sally, was it? If you ever need an honest job, where you will be paid fairly for a good day's work, come visit Cecil Farms. Tell them Mrs. Cecil said to hire you. Whatever you decide, come to our Flora Festival in a few weeks." She dipped into her reticule and gave her three shillings to pay for transportation. The farm was a post ride out of London.

Amber eyes smiled at her. "Thank you, Mrs. Cecil."

The man returned, harrumphed, then settled the jar between them on the shelf. "Here's your paper, ma'am."

Theodosia took the blue material and carefully wrapped her soaps. Feeling good at being able to help another, she turned to the door. "Thank you, sir." Keeping another woman from making mistakes would honor Mathew's memory. Even Ewan's ghost would smile, if the shop girl could find a way to dream.

As she stepped back into the crowded throughway, her letters slipped and landed near a man's boot. She bent to retrieve them, but the fellow grabbed them first and held them out to her.

"Thank you." The words crawled out slowly as her gaze traveled up his bottle-green waistcoat and broad chest, past his lean cravat and thick neck, to a familiar scar on his chin. She didn't need to see his thick, wavy, raven hair. She stopped at his eyes, the bluest eyes, bluer than the sky stirred clean by a thunderstorm.

"It *is* you, Theo," said the man.

Her heart ceased beating. Theodosia looked down to see if

it had flopped outside of her stiff corset. Ewan Fitzwilliam stood in front of her. He wasn't dead. Didn't look the least bit distressed or deceased from the war. And he was no ghost, unless hell made apparitions look this good.

…

Six years had passed since Ewan Fitzwilliam had seen this beauty. The last time, the locks of her long, straight hair—a gift from her father, an Asian junk sailor, who'd been portside long enough to purchase companionship—had been free about her shoulders. Her deep bronzed skin, a blessing of the negress mother she'd barely known, had been exposed at her throat from a hastily put-on blouse. Her wide almond-shaped eyes, onyx pools of decadent wonder, had been afraid, like now. "Theo, the Flower Seller."

Chewing on her bottom lip, she nodded and blinked her lengthy, silky lashes, hiding the largest irises he'd ever seen. Before, those eyes had captivated him. He'd thought them passion-sated, but now, he knew them to be big with avarice, another of her deceptive guises. "It's been a long time, Theo."

She nodded and maybe took a breath, but still said nothing.

One look at her expensive frock, the tailored obsidian-colored walking dress that sculpted her hourglass form, and any doubt of her greed left his jaded heart. The sands of time had been good to her curvy form, and Theo had used her womanly wiles to attain wealth. Despite her humble background, she was no different than the ladies Ewan had met at the balls his mother forced him to attend. All were young women seeking advancement or larger purses, something a second son didn't possess. "Six years and you have nothing to say to me?"

"You died." Her alto voice dropped lower. "You are dead. An apparition."

"Very much alive. You look to be breathing, too. Barely."

She squinted and shifted the ribbons of her bonnet. "Whatever you are, can I have my letters? Then you may return to being dead."

Playfully, he waved the sealed papers fanning his chin. "Can you, or may you? A woman should know her capabilities. You know, like the ability to deceive."

He waited for her to respond. His Theo would offer a stinging retort, something with fire.

But this woman stood still, her fingers hovered inches from his as if she were afraid to take the letters. This wasn't his Theo.

Nonetheless, when she bit her lip again, he knew the folded notes held some importance for her. Out of habit, he swept them farther away, tucking them close to the revers of his tailcoat. Would this new Theo reach for something that was hers?

The woman glanced to the left and then to the right, but did not move. Part of him soured even more. Yes, she'd been shy when they'd first met, but never this cautious, not with him. This wasn't the girl he'd ruined himself over. Perhaps she had never existed, just a novel characterization his playwright mind had invented. "Are you sure these belong to you? Let me check for a name."

He read the markings on the folded papers and burned at the written name, Mrs. Cecil. "It doesn't say Theo the Flower Seller, but Mrs. Cecil. Is that you?"

She put a hand to her hip. "Yes. Give me those letters."

He waved at her again, fanning the pages near her cheek. "Then take them from your old friend. I don't bite. Well, not unless provoked or dared. Remember, Mrs. Cecil—my dearest Theo?"

She snatched the letters and stuffed them into her reticule. As she looked up at him again, her henna-colored cheeks darkened. "Too well, Mr. Fitzwilliam. How are you not dead?

They said you died in Spain."

He extended his arm to her. "Perhaps we should get a bit of refreshment and have a long chat. You seem rather faint. Let's go to your shop. I recall you *scheming* to get a flower shop."

"I…I have no shop."

She did look faint and the part of his heart that should know better made him take the tissue-wrapped package from her lean fingers and support her palm atop his forearm. "There's a coffeehouse, Theo. Let me buy you a sweet. That will give you time to recover."

"No. No, I must go. I can't be seen with you."

She pulled away, leaving him holding her parcel. With elbows flying, reticule swinging, the daft woman dashed into the hustling crowd. He stood there watching until her form disappeared beneath the triple arch at the south entrance on Piccadilly Street.

She'd gone from the Burlington Arcade. Where? Where did she lay her head at night? And, whose pillow now possessed her?

He wanted answers. But chasing after Theo shouldn't be done. His pride wouldn't let him. However, he was holding the schemer's bag.

Like breathing, his fingers automatically sought to fist, but her bulky pack sat in his hands. A few nosy pokes released the strong bittersweet scent of lavender. The flower had meant something to him once, not a sop for the soul, but of being caught in a thunderstorm. The scent came to him in his dreams. Isolated in one of his father's carriage houses close to the Tradenwood flower fields, trapped with the business-minded flower seller who hadn't talked about bouquets when he'd finally taken her lips.

Who was this Cecil who had them?

Did he know lies lived within each kiss?

Or had Theo lied only to Ewan?

Craning his neck toward the skylights above, he warmed his chilled blood with the sunshine. Yet more questions filled his breast.

Why did Theo think him dead? Was it another of her falsehoods?

Slinging her package under his arm, he spun in the opposite direction she'd fled and marched out the north side of the Arcade onto Burlington Gardens. Seeing the past twice in one day would be too much.

With each step, Ewan stewed a little more. His gut ached. The words of his father's letter, recounting how Theo had run away with another man, mocking Ewan's choice for love, burned as badly now as it had when he'd first read them, laying near death in Spain. *And this Blackamoor harlot you wished to make a Fitzwilliam.*

Blood started to hiss and boil in his veins. He walked down Bond Street, taking the long way back to where his brother's carriage awaited, all while repeating his father's slur.

Before a footman could jump down, Ewan gripped the pearl-black door and flung it open. Dragging himself into a seat, he prepared himself for questions and hoped his mind could swallow up the bitter dregs unearthed from seeing his past.

"Are you all right, Ewan?"

The concerned, low-pitch voice of his brother Jasper Fitzwilliam, the Viscount Hartwell, startled him.

Ewan gave himself a shake and dumped Theo's package onto the dark tufted seat. Theo. How could she still have a hold upon him? Hadn't he poured out all his anger at her lies into the lines of his latest play? He'd used his mad muse to re-create Theo as the perfect Circe, the goddess the playwright Homer had created to turn men into swine.

Risking everything for Theo had made him low, like his father's hogs. No, he wasn't a fool in love anymore.

"Hello, in there." Jasper leaned over and thumped Ewan's skull. "Not creating your next masterpiece, are you? Have you tried selling the first?"

"Not my first, but by far my best. My first would have been exhibited at Covent Garden six years ago, if not for Father's influence on the manager. He made Thomas Harris renege on his commitment to buy my play."

His brother poked his lips into a full grimace, so different from the man who loved to laugh. "Please, not that again. There are more things afoot than six-year-old misunderstandings."

The way Jasper said *afoot,* made the writer in Ewan sit up straight. He leaned forward to give the man his full attention. "I'm listening."

"I asked you to help me with these newspaper responses, but there's more I need to involve you with. You've been in London these past three months and haven't come out to Grandbole, yet. Why haven't you seen him?"

The *him,* their father, the Earl of Crisdon, hadn't yet summoned Ewan, and he hadn't had the energy to volunteer for another dressing down. *A Fitzwilliam doesn't write plays. The theater isn't a profession for a Fitzwilliam.* "Jasper, please. It's difficult enough to visit with Mother and listen to her constant complaints of how I was cheated of Tradenwood. But I was not cheated. Only bad luck."

"Well, the report of your demise did make your uncle designate a new heir, who was not your mother. Their feud never ended."

Ewan stared up at the ceiling. Counted to ten. Yet, in his head, he heard his mother's soft-voiced lament of his uncle changing his will to leave Tradenwood and all its fields to a distant cousin—all because of the incorrect report from the battlefield. He shook his head, banishing the loss. "Another subject. Your mystery woman had already picked up her mail. Our clever note is on its way to the intended victim. And since you corresponded as one of Father's lesser titles, Lord Tristian for his barony, your identity is safe."

Jasper rolled his beaver dome between sweaty palms. "Who else should borrow but his heir? Being the eldest has its privileges."

"And its headaches." Ewan shook his chin, wanting nothing to do with his father's grooming or any of the ways the man sought to control Jasper. "But you seem to manage."

His brother nodded as his smile shrank. "It's my humor. It comforts me. So, no peek at what the grand woman looked like?"

Beautiful as ever, but Theo wasn't the lady his brother was asking about. "Pardon?"

"The newspaper advertisement owner. The woman who placed the matrimony request in the paper."

"The new shop clerk hadn't seen her. I waited past the usual time you said the widow checked for correspondences. Sorry, old boy, your stationer has things wrong. Don't let Father know a Fitzwilliam failed to obtain secret information. That would bring the earl such misery."

Jasper dropped his hat and folded his arms about his jacket, a hunting garment with oversized sleeves. It was hard to make someone so big look even bigger, but the man achieved the impossible with dozens of tiny diamond shapes running north and south upon his copperplate printed waistcoat. "That's what I get for sending a writer to do a spy's work. Should've sent Father."

The unflappable Jasper seemed nervous, a side of his half brother Ewan had never seen. With his brow rising, he felt his quill finger cramp as if preparing to write dialogue for a new play. "I am surprised the earl's encouraging you to find a bride like this. Maybe he *has* changed after all these years."

Jasper shrugged his shoulders. "He doesn't know that I am. I'm taking a turn at being the rebellious one and doing something Father wouldn't approve of."

"How is that working?" Ewan chuckled.

"A few disappointments. Mostly, I've exchanged letters with women of the wrong temperament or situation." His brother shuffled his boots. "You don't know how I've missed your assistance. You visit with your mother in Town, but what of us?"

The *us* was Grandbole and all that came with the grand house. Ewan did miss it. He missed the land and walking it to clear his head. He missed all the Fitzwilliams under one roof. "There are many things to remember, many things to forget."

"If I hadn't spied you at the countess's party, would you have let me know of your return?"

"I missed your wit whilst I soldiered in the Peninsula, even the jokes at my expense. But I didn't miss the arguments with the earl. It is he that gives me pause, not you."

Jasper looked down again, as if a humbled posture could wipe away the vitriol of their father's famed rants.

Ewan had given up on the earl. The pressure of never measuring up would build inside, until his lungs exploded. He was glad the scars on his chest bound him together, kept the rage from showing.

He took a small breath. The pressure released. He wasn't that weak-minded person anymore. Hadn't the bad memories, the disappointments, become part of his sharpened sense of humor, the kindling wood for his farce comedies? Tweaking his cravat, Ewan sampled a little more air and sank into his beloved sarcasm. "Jasper, I would love to be the genesis of this rebellion, but take it from me, start small. Borrow the earl's hunting dogs without permission. Then work your way up to…oh, I don't know, petty larceny.

Then you'll be ready to take a bride without his approval."

Jasper sat back and drummed the black leather seat beneath his thick fingers. "I haven't picked the lady yet, for it is so important to do this well. Once a gentleman proposes, there's no taking it back. What if she doesn't like children, as she says? What if this one is like the others, not as young as she stated in her advertisement?"

"If you are fretting, go about finding a bride the old way. Pick a chit during the Season and propose. Lady Crisdon will help."

His brother's face grew more serious with his jaw firming, his eyes drifting to the right. "I can't bear to hear how none of them are like Maria. I *know* that."

The man quieted. If his eyes moved more to the right they'd fling from his skull. It must be hard losing a good wife. From the letters the brothers had exchanged over the years, Jasper had cared for her himself until the stomach cancer had taken its toll.

"I'm sorry, Ewan. It will be a year next month." Jasper tugged at his sleeves, readjusting his cuffs over his thick wrists. "Have you asked for your mother's matchmaking assistance? That might get her to come back to Grandbole. We should be unified now."

Unity? At what cost? Ewan pushed at his temples with fingers that now reeked of lavender, Theo's lavender. He put his palms onto the seat, gripping the edge, as if that would ground him from the memories of a fleeting romance with one of the Crisdon flower sellers. No luck. She'd be in his head tonight, tormenting him. "I've no time, or the finances, for a wife—not until one of my plays succeed."

Jasper rubbed at his chin. "What of that ginger-haired girl you danced with at your mother's dinner last week, the one with freckles? She didn't seem to mind the absence of a fortune."

That was unusual in London, to be sure. Mother must've whispered nonsense in the girl's ear. "She'll become enlightened by her own matchmaking mama. The second son from a second marriage can only do so much, particularly one recovering from banishment."

Jasper sat forward, folding his arms. "Father's irascible, but he only did what he thought was best. I will admit he is often misguided, but sometimes… Sometimes he's right."

Yes. The earl was right in the worst ways. He'd said Theo was after Crisdon money. He'd said she wouldn't remain faithful. Groaning, Ewan looked down again at his hands, his fisting hand. "The earl also does wrong. Lording his money over our heads, doling it out when we do as he wants. But then, he stops us from gaining the means to be independent. Not this time. My new play will succeed."

"How would Father put it?" Jasper held his nose up and made his voice strangled and low. "Fitzwilliams do military or religious service. We may go to the theater, but not perform in such. Ewan, use your writing talents for sermon making." He laughed and wriggled his nose. His voice returned to its normal energetic pitch. "That would've made Father very pleased."

Ewan's stomach churned, thinking of both the difficulty of doing as the old earl wanted and the image of himself being struck by lightning behind the pulpit. He spoke very slowly. "The black sheep can't wear white frocks, and I've already done my military service. Five and a half, almost six, years of service in Spain and the West Indies. My Fitzwilliam dance-card-with-bullets is jotted in full. I should be able to live as I want. I have stories to tell. They should be on the stage, no matter what the old man thinks."

Jasper dropped his hat as his shoulders slumped. "This new one is very good. It was a pleasure to read, but I hate being caught between you two. I'm not sure what has seeded the ill will, but this is a new day. We need family to pull together."

Not wanting to argue or mouth aloud Theo's name, Ewan sighed. "So, how do you intend to tell the old man of your plan for a new wife?"

"If advertisement number four lives up to the promise made in the newspaper, he won't mind adding another fortune to the family."

Ewan couldn't disagree with that logic, even if it felt wrong and unromantic. "Perhaps, but I still think you should give the traditional way a chance."

Jasper ran a hand through his curly, reddish-blond hair. His frowning lips turned up. "My rugged features do pale against yours, but I have three girls who will require dowries that my modest income will not profer. I don't want their fates to be under the earl's control. I need a young heiress who will be a good mother to my brood and add to my coffers. That can't be had at Almack's."

Maybe this finding-a-bride-by-newspaper-advertisement was a safe way for his brother to start living again. "A lovely brood, from what I can remember. Your wife gave you all she had. That is to be treasured."

Smoothing a wrinkle from his waistcoat, Jasper nodded. "I'm done with sentiment. You're only allowed one great love in a lifetime. The next will be a marriage of convenience."

That couldn't be true. His heart shuddered at the notion of only loving once. It would take a great deal of vanity for Ewan to convince himself that what he'd felt for Theo in those heady days before he'd left for war, was less than love. Oh, if only he were that vain.

What had started as an innocent, well, almost innocent, flirtation between the errand boy for the largest flower grower of greater London and a sassy street vendor had changed everything. Wanting Theo had cost Ewan dearly.

He'd been disowned, dispatched from the family, and had almost died in the war. He grimaced, allowing his gut to knot and twist with the horrid truth. Seeing how things had turned out: she'd apparently married a wealthy man, he'd written a farce of Theo's love that would draw all of London. Perhaps she had been worth the sacrifice. Yes, his humor had matured.

"Pay attention over there." Jasper smiled. It was his infectious weapon. "Do you remember your nieces? You should see them. My eldest is now a petulant ten."

He stuck a hand in his pocket and shrugged. Staying away had cost more than time. Deep down in his heart, he missed his family, that sense of belonging. "Perhaps you can bring them to town. My flat is small but clean." *And not under the old man's control.*

Jasper raised his brow. "You should come see them today."

Ewan shook his head. "No."

"But I will need your plotting abilities. I could pay you to help write my correspondences to number four of the *Morning Post*. If this woman is indeed young, with a fortune, and not so bad on the eyes, there could be competition." He shuffled his boots. "And if you are not courting, who's the package for? Smells like lavender. What secrets are you keeping from your elder brother?"

"No. I bumped into a woman in Burlington Arcade. She left it. I'll toss them away."

"Pretty expensive wrapping. A pity to disregard. When did you have time to make a new acquaintance? Did you miss my mystery woman when you were flirting?"

"I'd hardly call a pleasant exchange flirting." But what would he call running into his past? Though Theo wore expensive garb, she could be like him, all outside trappings. These perfumed soaps shouldn't be abandoned. Perhaps he should return them to their owner and have that final chat.

He whipped off his top hat. "Our mission is done today, Jasper. Drop me back to my residence."

"No, you must come with me for dinner with the girls… and Father."

Ewan slumped in his seat, wrinkling the vest he'd labored to pick out for an evening of cards at his mother's house in Town, not for seeing the earl. What type of mood would he be in after seeing Theo and his father in the same day? He shook his head. "I'm beginning to feel tired. Yes, very tired."

Jasper groaned, loud and long. "The chest wound?" His brother's voice raised an octave. "Does it still bother you?"

"Only on wet days…and during thunderstorms."

"Come to dinner, Ewan. So much has changed. The family needs to pull together. Don't be stubborn like Father."

Like the old man? His brother might as well have punched Ewan in the face to utter such horrid words. "I'm nothing like him. Stop the carriage. I'll walk."

Grabbing his arm like a madman, Jasper kept him from leaping out of the carriage. "I'm sorry, but it is true. I won't say it again. Have one meal. Get his complaints off my shoulders for a day. See my girls."

His brother had always tried to keep the old man at bay, even slipping Ewan a fiver upon occasion. "One quick meal, but as soon as he starts in, I'm gone. I'll steal a horse and return to London. In fact, give me money to stable a stallion now. For you know it won't take long for Father's harangues to start. It's about three jokes before he fumes."

"Fine, that will take care of one problem. For the second, you must also agree to help me with my potential newspaper bride, lady number four. I want to know more about her before I ask for a meeting. She'll respond to your quip. We'll need a clever note to follow. Help me write something to keep her attention. You're the clever one."

"You want to see her true character, then ask a question of

substance. Let me think on it."

"Well, come up with something to match your riddle, Ewan. Maybe it will be so good you'll use it in your next play."

Avoiding the temptation to roll his eyes, Ewan nodded. "All right…I'll help."

"You think you'll find the owner of the package, or do you think my girls might like it? Is it too personal?"

Anything regarding Theo was too personal. Yet, returning this package intrigued him. She had obviously purchased this in the Burlington Arcade. Perhaps, the perfumer knew where Mrs. Cecil resided. Ewan eased his head onto the seatback, preparing to sleep all the way to Grandbole Manor. Since she'd be in his brain, he piled up all the questions he wanted to know of Theo. Perhaps, he'd ask them the next time he saw the flower seller. "It should be returned to its rightful owner."

And there would be a next time. Fitzwilliams were good at finding things—weaknesses and secrets. Nothing else brought a smile to Ewan's jaded heart than the thought of improving his characterization of his play's villainess by visiting Theo, his personal Circe.

Chapter Two

Family, Friends & Enemies

Theodosia's carriage rumbled forward. With each passing second, her lungs constricted a little less. Her driver and horse team didn't know she'd fled a ghost. Surely, they assumed she needed to hurry back for her dinner guests. She wouldn't correct them.

By the time she'd passed Tottenham Road, the jarring and swaying of her ivory seat had jostled every bone in her body. The ache, however, didn't compare to the pain of seeing Ewan again. All these years, and the man was alive. *How could he not be dead?*

Six years of mourning him, of feeling ashamed for living and finding some happiness with Mathew, all while thinking a bullet had felled her poor dreamer.

How many times had she looked in those fancy glass mirrors at Mathew's Tradenwood, the home they'd shared, and had seen a traitor to the future she'd envisioned with Ewan? The man with the crooked smile that had set her heart pounding. Today, that crooked smile had crushed the useless muscle in her chest to dust.

Wait.

If Ewan didn't die in the war, where has he been?

Why did he stay away when I needed him?

Her stomach soured, thinking and rethinking their foolish dreams. His plays would be performed on London's grandest stages, and her flower shop would provide roses, the best ones—without a single thorn—to his actresses. And Theodosia's Ewan wouldn't be tricked by those ladies' beauty. He'd said he only had eyes for *Theo, his Theo.*

Lies.

Dreams were lies.

Ewan had gone to war and hadn't come back to her. The life they had whispered in secret was nothing but deceit, lines from a play he hadn't yet written. Her heart burst all over again.

Had he laughed with his brother at getting her to love him? Did he smile to his circle of friends about taking her virtue? Had he said pretty words about loving her to lower her guard, making Theodosia forsake her vow not to be like her mother? Theodosia had given Ewan all of her, and then he'd left.

She'd become Theo the Harlot because of him.

Her pulse raced and whirled so loudly, her ears hurt. Almost panting, she forced air into her hurting chest and gripped her reticule to her bosom. Her eyes were already weak from sitting at her son's bedside till well past midnight. Crying now about lies would only make them sting. Ewan Fitzwilliam wasn't worth another droplet.

Her hand clenched. Her nails dug into the fringe of her reticule. That ache should have died six years ago. Ewan and his lies were no more. He couldn't affect her future or destroy the life she'd built for her son.

Another two hours of ridiculous fretting occurred before her carriage passed the Fitzwilliam flower farm. Squinting from her window, she could see their house, Grandbole Manor. The cold gray stone looked small at this distance, but it overshadowed the lilac-colored flowers in the orderly fields. Hard to believe it neighbored Mathew's warm Tradenwood, with its pinkish stacked stones. Tradenwood wasn't as grand, but she believed it held more peace and much more understanding. Things Ewan had always complained were missing at Grandbole.

She slumped onto the seat. Ewan couldn't be staying at his father's estate. She would've seen him at least once these six years if he'd resided there.

The urge to know why he'd played her false might cause her to be rash, to do something crazed. No, Theodosia Cecil didn't look for trouble anymore. She glanced at her rows of flowers. She thought of walking in those fields, of finding answers and strength there. She'd found Mathew there, or he'd found her. If she were to go out there now, she might find peace, the peace he had so often talked about growing, like buds in those fields.

Her carriage began to slow. Peeking out the window, she saw the grooms and proud horse teams of vehicles lining the drive of Tradenwood. Her dinner guests awaited her inside the parlor. They couldn't see her so broken. The ladies were there for an early meal to discuss the Flora Festival, the grand picnic Mathew had started as a reward for his workers, one that had evolved to also include every one of his vendors and their workers. She chuckled, wondering if the perfumer she'd met today would come. She prayed the girl Sally would, and she wondered if she would seek employment with Cecil's Farms.

The carriage stopped and one of her attendants came to free her from her stewing. Marching through the doors of Tradenwood, she slowed her steps and stopped at the console. Her butler stood near.

Pickens, with his starched livery of dark crimson and gold braid, held out his hands. "Welcome back, Mrs. Cecil. I'll take your bonnet and bag. Your guests are waiting for you in the parlor."

She unpinned her hat and gave it to him, but held on to her reticule. She wasn't prepared to relinquish her letters.

Pickens's brow raised, but he didn't try again for her bag. Six years had given them a routine and, hopefully, a measure of mutual respect. If memories hid in the wizened creases of his forehead, he knew Theodosia held on tight to things that were hers, only relenting when she was good and ready. "Thank you, Pickens."

He pulled a folded paper from behind his back. "This came for you while you were out. The footman said it was important. It's from the Fitzwilliams family. The earl himself."

Swallowing her newfound reservation upon hearing the name Fitzwilliam, she slid off her gloves, stashing them on the console, then clutched the thick parchment. "Thank you."

Emotionless, always about his duty, Pickens bowed his graying head and pivoted toward the long hall leading to the parlor. "And Mr. Lester is visiting. He's in the nursery with Master Philip."

Lester. The name sent shivers of fear and hate up her spine. Who knew Mathew's faithful steward would turn into a vengeful frog the moment he understood the powers Mathew's will had given him.

The tapping of the butler's footsteps moving toward her dinner guests sounded like a muffled drumbeat, but the decision to go to the birds in the parlor or to the vulture near her boy, wasn't a question.

In as dignified of a manner as she could muster, Theodosia's short heels clicked hard against the polished marble with its shiny cranberry veining. The moment her foot dropped upon the first mahogany tread, her false calm shredded. Visions of Lester taking her sweet boy and shaking him for a response froze the blood in her veins. She lunged up the steps and sailed on fretful wings to the door of the second-floor nursery.

She didn't see the leech in the hall. He had to be inside with little Philip. How long would it be before he discovered the boy's illness?

Theodosia couldn't blow into pieces like a dandelion in strong wind. She steadied herself, clasping the molding. The stupid parchment crunched against the raised wood before relenting and curling about it. With a strangled breath, she pushed open the door.

Scanning to the left and then to the right revealed nothing out of the ordinary. Polished pine planks on the floor and a thick jute rug of blue yarn warmed up the pale beige walls. A huge closet hid enough space to house a small family.

In the middle of the wide room, swimming in a pinafore of cream and blue threads, sat little Philip alone with his governess, Miss Thomas. No Lester.

Fanning the paper, hoping to chase away the fear fevering her brow, Theodosia took a few steps inside. A hungry panic of losing Philip was stirring, growing, pressing at her temples.

Lovely, honest Mathew had protected Theodosia and Philip, writing his will to withstand the challenges his young family would face in his absence. But a dead man could only do so much from the grave. Her own wit and a new, trustworthy husband, someone as honorable as Mathew — that would have to be enough to keep vultures like Lester away. Where was the pushy brute?

Coughing from the growing knot in her throat, she moved closer to her son. She wanted to look in the closet or under the bed for Lester as she would hunt for a ghost. Lord knew she'd happened upon enough apparitions for one day.

Little Philip scooted forward, pressing his lean fingers against a carved block. His eyes were on the wooden toy, not looking at her.

That was good. He shouldn't see sadness on his mother's face.

She put a finger to her lips to keep the governess from announcing her. One heavy step after the other, clomping, stomping, she made her heels pound as loudly as she could as she approached his weak side.

The five-year-old didn't flinch. Never turned.

Her heart clenched.

The boy didn't hear her approach. The physicians, the old ones with gray on top, the young ones, trying to run experiments on the mulatto boy, even the ones who wouldn't see him until they heard his surname Cecil, all their words had been true. Philip was deaf on on his left side and losing his hearing on the right. This was the most painful consequence of her many sins.

Looking up to the ceiling, she counted her wrongs. Trusting Ewan—wrong. Holding on to pride too long—wrong. Not becoming a mistress to Mathew sooner, not trusting him sooner—wrong. Of keeping Ewan on a pedestal for so long, it had made it difficult for a good man to reach her heart—very wrong.

She lowered her gaze and looked at Philip. The boy jostled the toy between his small fingers. He still hadn't caught up to the size of other five year olds.

This punishment of barely hearing, of perhaps losing all of it, tore her up inside. Would he forget the sound of words? Would he remember an impatient giggle? It was too much for an innocent boy. Living as she had, speaking lies, listening to her dreaming heart, were the reasons her child suffered. She cleared her throat. "How's my Philip?"

The governess tapped the little boy on the shoulder and pointed. "We had a good day today. No more fever from last night."

Philip spun toward Theodosia and showed a toothy grin. Her worn-out heart stirred. His bright blue eyes opened wider. He rushed to her, stepping onto her feet, embracing her legs. A smile she no longer thought she possessed lifted her lips. "Love you, son."

She scooped him up. His pinafore bunched in the crook of her arm as he wiggled his way to her cheek, placing his face there. His pulse pushed against hers. She wove her fingers into his dark, straight hair. She'd do anything for Philip, the only person in this world who was truly hers. For the first time today, she breathed easier. Maybe her withered heart had a little more living to do.

"*M-mmm-m*," he said, before giving her a big, wet kiss.

The boy offered another hug about her neck. Theodosia needed to keep him safe, to keep his world secure and beautiful, even if that meant selling herself in a new marriage.

Footfalls sounded behind her.

She spun with her precious cargo, tucking him deeper within her stiffening arms. Anger rose inside seeing Wilhelm Lester, her late husband's steward, smirking at the threshold.

"Well, isn't this lovely? Mother and son. The usurper and her spawn."

Theodosia leaned down and gave Philip back to his governess. "Come with me, Mr. Lester."

She squared her shoulders, tightened her grip about the paper, and waltzed past the scourge who had dared to be Mathew's confidant. She kept moving until she stood yards from the nursery.

The beast followed too closely. Was it onions and mutton on his breath?

"Theodosia, what was it? How did you bewitch old Cecil and convince him to make his mistress his wife? Usually only fools do that and Cecil was no fool."

"Maybe the same reason you've been asking to marry me?

You didn't even wait for my dear Mathew to be cold in the grave."

The tall man laughed and flipped back a reddish-brown curl from his flat forehead. He would be handsome, if not for all the ugly evil spouting from his thin lips.

"No, can't be the same, my dear." His voice sounded like a fat cat's purr, one that had eaten its mouse. "You were penniless then. Now, you are a wealthy woman sharing the Cecil fortune. Yes, fifty-thousand pounds annually is more than enough reason to marry you, Theodosia."

"It's Mrs. Cecil to you. And I told you, you are not welcome in the nursery. Stay in the parlor."

"Can't. Your gaggle of hens is down there. Where did you find more educated dark ones?"

Ester and Frederica? Knowing her friends were near gave Theodosia more strength. "You heard what I said. Go downstairs."

"Then come with me." He held out his arm for her.

The thought of touching or being touched by Lester made her skin itch. It'd be like fiery ants who had stung her hands in the fields when she hadn't been careful cutting flower stems. Around him, she needed to be extra careful. She scooted past him and started down the treads, but he fell in step with her.

"The boy? Is he breeched yet?"

"No, he's five."

"Well, Cecil wasn't that tall of a man, but this one seems a might scrawny. As his guardian, I will need to make sure you're not coddling him too much. He might need to be sent away, if you're not taking good care of him. That's a guardian's job to make sure his ward is well protected."

She lifted her chin as she cut her gaze to the fool. "Philip is fine. Growing well. Don't threaten me."

Lester grabbed her and yanked her close.

Her reticule swung around her elbow swatting him in his midnight blue waistcoat. "Let me go, you bounder."

His grip didn't slacken. He leaned near her ear. "Things would be better for the boy if we worked together. You're not so bad with that mouth of yours closed or given to a common purpose."

She shook free and stared into his beady blue-gray eyes. "Don't touch me. Some of the coloring of my hand may slap onto your sallow flesh. It will leave you black and blue. You wouldn't like that."

He clamped her shoulder, shaking her. "The hellcat protests too much. And I'm an improvement over an old man. It's been too long for you, hasn't it, dear? It's almost been a year since his death."

She made herself stone, forcing away the disgust threatening to spew vomit from her mouth. "How dare you? I'm not even out of my mourning for Cecil, the man you claimed to love. What would he say to you if he saw this?"

Lester's sneer shifted into a frown as if for a moment a bit of humanity filled him. Mathew's endless kindness had made him a weak spot for many. Theodosia had noted Lester's affection for Mathew during her husband's illness. At the man's first threat, she'd invoked Mathew's memory, Lester's Achilles heel, but how much longer would it work?

The blackguard lowered his hand and yanked the parchment away from her fingers. "This looks important." He ripped it open and held it to the light. "Another offer to buy our flower fields. You're not considering this?"

Theodosia put a hand to her hip. "All the fields are mine and Philip's. Cecil left you an income to be an advocate." She softened her tone to keep the man's fragile ego intact. "It's hard to consider something I haven't had a chance to read, but you know I will consult you."

He ripped up the offer into bits, balled them up, then

stuffed the pieces into her palm. Lester stepped very close, his shadow falling upon her. "The Fitzwilliams ruined my father's business and took his lands. Land is everything. I won't let that happen here, and I've taken steps to ensure it." His brow rose. "The earl must think you stupid for such a low offer, though I think you know low."

He moved out of slapping range. "When you're done playing a lady and see that our interests align, mine for the Cecil business, yours for nurturing the heir, send for me. I'll come to you, Theodosia."

Lester grinned again, more evil than the first, and headed out to the hall. With a final smirk, he grabbed up his coat and cane. "See you soon, Mrs. Cecil, dearest woman. It will be good to see you out of your mourning garb. Maybe you and the lad shall come with me to Holland. Your head for numbers might come in handy."

No. Never would she go anywhere with him. Holding her breath, she made her response soft. "This is our first overture to those growers. You must go alone and represent us. I need you to do that."

"Yes, you are right. You do need me."

Even as he exited, his smirk stayed etched in her brainbox. Full of arrogance and condescension, it was a familiar response a Blackamoor woman faced in business. Exactly what she counted upon to be rid of him.

The footman closed the front door. The sound of the heavy thud made her hands tremble. If only Mathew had known Lester was vermin, worse than vine-rotting aphids. If he didn't go to the Dutch farms alone, her plan to outwit him would never work. How would she protect Philip then?

Pickens came near, squinting, creasing his brow even more. "Ma'am, do you need something?"

Yes, Mathew alive and here to keep me and Philip from harm. She shook her head and moved at the world's slowest pace down the treads. "How are my guests?"

"They are well. Enjoying your treats. I will go see if they are ready for more refreshments." The butler turned and left for the parlor.

Once she reached the console, Theodosia dumped the paper pieces onto the mahogany surface. Her reticule slid from her elbow down the length of her forearm, but that didn't stop her from arranging the torn pieces. She swirled the paper with her pinkie and made out the sum, ten thousand pounds. The devil was right. The offer was far too low for anything she and Mathew had worked so hard to build. The earl, Ewan's father, must think her daft. She put the paper into her reticule. Later, she would toss it in the hearth and watch the bits burn.

She started to reach inside the satin and peek at her newspaper responses but decided against it. With a room of guests to attend, she needed to complete the planning for Mathew's Flora Festival down to the tolling of the small parish bells. He had so loved this event.

She folded her arms, her fingers clanging the brass buttons of her dark sleeves. These mourning shrouds had become her friend, a comforting hug, like now, when she was weak. It was a show of respect for a good husband gone too soon. Was marrying again the only answer? "Madam?" The butler stood beside her. Woolgathering, she'd missed his solemn footfalls.

"Your guests are waiting. Mrs. Cecil never keeps her guests waiting."

It wasn't censure in his voice, but something thick and noble, almost like understanding.

She nodded. "Cecils do what they must."

Pickens nodded. "Yes, even when things are difficult." He bowed, back as straight as a new fence post. "I'll go see if Cook's pastries have run out."

The loyal man proceeded down the hall. She watched his

steady, easy gait until he disappeared around the corner.

Easy. Why did she think getting a husband by advertisement would be easy?

Go to the stationer's, pick up the latest response to her *Morning Post* advertisement, then return home safe and smiling with a suitable offer of marriage—all before dinner. Easy.

Easy, my eye. She took a breath, but it rattled within her chest until it found the right pipe to escape. She coughed, wiped her mouth, and tried to think of anything but fleeing. If Tradenwood wasn't safe, where would she and Philip find safety, find acceptance?

Still a little shaky, Theodosia commanded her wobbly legs to move toward the parlor. The meeting for the festival needed her attention. Tucking her reticule under her arms, she ordered her lips to form a smile. Once everyone left except Ester and Frederica—the Brain and the Flirt—she'd rely on her friends to keep her steady and follow through with their newspaper advertisement plan. Or… Theodosia would gather up all the coins she could muster and escape with Philip to the Continent.

…

Dining at Grandbole Manor after six long years wasn't as horrible as Ewan expected. His nieces grabbed ahold of him from the moment Jasper pushed him across the threshold.

Oh, how much time had slipped past? Three girls, three beautiful little girls. Only two had been here that last summer at Grandbole, before he'd joined his regiment. His heart burned, roasting with the memory of proud Jasper bundling two small girls in his arms as he escorted his pregnant wife to their carriage. Maria hadn't wanted her laying-in here, but at her mother's home in Devonshire. Dutiful, appeasing Jasper had defied everyone, even shouting down the earl to please Maria.

Ewan had never been more proud or more jealous of his brother. He hadn't yet experienced the burden of that type of love. Ewan hadn't yet met Theo.

Anne, a ten-year-old with blonde-like-her-father locks, put a palm under her chin. She appeared to be the head inquisitor of the three girls and chose to ask questions rather than peruse the long cedar table that held more food than a regiment of a thousand men could devour. "Uncle, so what temperature is the West Indies?" she asked.

"Very hot, my dear."

Lydia, nine years old and very much math inspired, drummed the table with her little fingers. "Is it hotter than Grandbole on a summer's day or an autumn day?"

"Very, very hot—hotter than both."

The little one whose name also started with an L, Laura, no Lucy, cast a big frown. "That's not very descriptive, Uncle."

Ewan looked at the cute upturned nose and the strawberry-blonde hair and released a smile. "You are right. I can do better. The heat of the day starts warm and inviting. By noon, it's enough to positively boil the tea. There. Will that do?"

Lucy closed her eyes and nodded. Ewan smiled again. He'd discovered the dreamer in the mix.

Jasper chuckled and finished dumping a piece of bread into his mouth. "Girls, save your questions for later or Uncle Ewan won't come back. We mustn't frighten him away, and no tricks, not yet."

It wouldn't be the three angelic moppets who'd make Ewan flee. No, it would be a curmudgeon whose chair at the far end sat empty. With a sip from his glass of cool water, he couldn't exactly measure the disappointment roiling in his gut alongside the succulent duck they'd had for dinner. Scanning the dark polished floors, the high walls strewn with family portraits of Fitzwilliams through the ages, a dormant sense of pride wet his tongue. Though he'd never mention it aloud, Ewan had missed Grandbole and his family, even the earl.

A servant came and whispered in Jasper's ear.

His brother nodded. "Father's finishing up business. He wants to meet with you in the library."

Ewan chugged more water and wished the wetness possessed the tang of liquor. He'd been formally summoned. With a slow motion, he stood, bowed to each of his fine nieces, then turned to make the long walk through the quiet corridors. He filled his lungs, savoring the scent of polish, noting the absence of flowers. It seemed that the family livelihood stayed outside.

After several turns guided by the swords strewn across every inch of the dark paint, he made it to the library. He pushed on the heavy door, folded his arms behind his back, and marched inside, entering a room of fine emerald-colored silk walls.

He was alone. Again, a sense of disappointment stirred. Turning to the exit, he decided against retreat and sank upon the inflexible straight-backed sofa centered upon the wide gold rug.

The grand walnut bookcases still towered as they had six years ago. Both were filled with books, among them Aristotle, Bacon, and Descartes, titles meant to sculpt the Fitzwilliam men's minds. But did not the shelves also hold the gilded pages of playwrights Hensley and Broome? How was Ewan to know those ideas were out of bounds?

Not able to help himself, he popped up and moved to a perennial favorite, Shakespeare, and poked at the torn spine. One he'd probably injured. No smile pressed his lips. Memories of dressing-downs filled his head.

The door opened like a lid to an ancient coffin, slow and moaning. His brother entered and behind him, their father.

Archibald Fitzwilliam, the Earl of Crisdon, had aged. A thousand more white hairs rimmed the balding spot he'd long tried to cover with powders. Now, that battle had been lost. However, the sneer over his glasses, the condescension that only his narrow dark blue eyes could bring, none of that had changed.

"Good of you to come for dinner, Fitzwilliam, finally," his father said. His head dipped up and down as if scanning a rose for an aphid bug. "About time for you to slink back here. At least you've seen your mother in Town. Haven't totally abandoned family."

Ewan released a low, tight breath, then straightened to his full height. He refused to look at his brother who, obviously, still served as a trickster. "I was told you wanted to see me. Surely, I've been mistaken." He turned to the heavy door. "I'll see you in another six years, sir. You, too, Jasper. Oh, don't mind me taking your carriage back to town."

Before he could touch the knob, his Judas brother leaped in front of him with hands outstretched. "Father, you know you wanted Ewan here. And Brother, if you were truly against visiting you'd have jumped from my carriage earlier. You're both too stubborn. I tire at being caught between you."

Ewan had no desire to feel his peacemaking pain. In fact, he wanted to be numb. He wandered over to the sideboard, moved the false panel book that hid their father's prized brandy, and poured a glass of the amber liquid. Perhaps, if he drank enough, quickly enough, the anger trapped in his skin would evaporate. "I'm here. Tell me what you want me to know, Father."

The earl came up beside him and filled another glass. "Your service to the Fourth West Indian Regiment ended three months ago when it disbanded. Why didn't you return to Grandbole?"

"Did you pay for it to disband? Of course, you did.

Something I was begrudgingly good at must have been horrid for you."

The tall man patted his thickening middle. "Son, you are being ridiculous."

Ewan took another slow swig, holding the honey on his tongue, missing the sweet rum of the Caribbean. "Well, you've done your best to stunt anything I've wanted to pursue."

"Your judgment has made me suspect."

Blinking, Ewan remembered how his actions had been judged in this room by the earl. *Your life will be a waste. She's a dalliance, nothing more.* With another slurp, his humor returned, for who couldn't laugh at the man being right? Theo's love hadn't lasted, but the memories of her, of shy, business-minded, insatiable Theo, had formed the play that would make Ewan a fortune, one independent of his father's. "You are right as usual, sir. I don't know why I came, either. That questionable logic thing is hard to outrun. The beefsteaks were good. Give my compliments to the cook."

Looking at the blank stare on his father's countenance reminded Ewan that his father had a poor sense of humor, another thing they didn't have in common. "Time to leave. Father. Brother."

The earl coughed, then said, "Sorry."

Ewan froze for a moment. Then put a finger in his ear to unplug it. "Did you say something, sir? My eardrums could be lying."

His father gritted his teeth. He partially opened his mouth, exposing the canine fangs that had sunk into Ewan's hide and that of any man standing in the way of accomplishing something the earl wanted. "I said sorry. I shouldn't have demanded you to go to war to prove your merit."

The old man apologizing. Something wasn't right. The repeated word, "sorry." What did that mean? Shouldn't there be thunder crashing, maybe a flurry of villainous violin notes, as would happen in the theater? "What is this?"

"Your mother hasn't told you?"

Only a Fitzwilliam fool offered information freely, and Ewan was done being a fool. He didn't blink or move.

"Your mother blames me for you not inheriting Tradenwood."

Oh. The nonsense about inheriting his uncle's lands. "My uncle read the same letter you did about my demise. Pity he passed on before he learned the truth."

The earl frowned and stood uncharacteristically quiet. There must be something more.

But Ewan didn't want to submit to any of the man's games. "I am quite resolved, Father. For what would a soldier or a playwright do with all that land, anyway?"

Pushing at his forehead and the deeply etched frown lines, the earl gulped down his brandy and poured himself another. "Not the theater nonsense again."

Jasper jumped between them. "This is not a time for family to be fighting. We need to come together. Crisdon lands are under threat. The competition for flowers is more than ever. And Tradenwood is withholding water. They're building dams on the springs. If that continues, we'll lose it all."

"We?" Ewan folded his arms and kept his gaze level, resisting the call back to the sideboard. "You need to pay the new owner more money. Who is the lucky fool to have the land you wanted?"

The earl wrinkled his nose beneath his brass wire frames. "That blasted uncle of yours left everything to a distant cousin. The new owner passed away, leaving his widow with control of everything. If she doesn't take my latest offer I may have to…"

Ewan spread his feet apart, slightly enjoying the concern rattling the earl's grumbly voice. "You may have to what?

Offer full value to my cousin-by-marriage, or is that once-removed?"

Jasper moved from blocking the doorway to perch on the large desk near the window. His face was strained, more serious than Ewan had ever seen.

"Father's done twice that on the last offer. I think she wants to ruin us. For a woman, she's a savvy one."

Back at the sideboard, the earl tapped the brandy stopper, but this time his hands shook. "Might have to resort to direct negotiations. It's been difficult, with her observing full and now half-mourning rituals."

There was something not being said by the old man. Something was in the air, heavier than the smell of dusty books or the warm cigar ash—the scents that stayed in his head embodying this library. "You've never had a problem being direct." Ewan lifted his gaze to the candles burning in the corner, counting flickers, counting direct slights.

No more playwriting nonsense. I didn't raise you to be a fool.

The regiment will make a man of you. Maybe even a good one.

If you serve with honor, then I'll turn my eye from your dalliances.

One dalliance was his first play. The second, Theo.

"Sir, I remember very well how you've made your opinion known. What's stopping you?"

His father nodded and downed his glass. "This situation is difficult, but Mrs. Cecil has a price. I have to figure out what it is."

Cecil? Ewan's pulse started to tick up.

His father stared at him as if hunting for something, but Ewan didn't know why, unless this Mrs. Cecil was the same Mrs. Cecil he'd met at the Burlington Arcade. Ewan's legs started him moving, even before he was ready to. He circled around the grand desk to the window. From the wide glass, in the tiptop corner, he could see the edge of Tradenwood.

Could that be where Theo lay her head? Had Theo gotten herself a rich husband, a cousin to his mother? And now she owned Tradenwood?

Ewan pulled the curtain closed, keeping him from looking for her again. When he turned and saw the guilt painting the earl's face with those cocky brows flying high above his quizzing eyes, Ewan knew Mrs. Cecil was Theo. Making sure the shock paining his chest had drained away, he cleared his throat and forced his tone to be even and steady. "I'm sure that a fair offer will get the response you deserve."

With a tug to his waistcoat, the earl sank onto the stiff sofa. "What do you intend to do now, Fitzwilliam?"

Was it too beneath the earl to ask his son to reason with an old lover? Perhaps. He scratched his nose and sniffed strong lavender. Theo's smelly paper package that he'd left in the carriage still stained his fingertips. Just like her to stay with him. "I…I'm working on a new play."

"Not much money in theater, Son."

Ewan jerked, tensing at the hint of a slight, then remembered his facade of not caring. "It's more than enough because it's earned by my hands, not yours. Except for the purchase of my commission, I haven't needed you—or your assistance."

Jasper chimed in. "This one is very good. He's created this villain. She's outrageous. London will adore this play."

"Ewan, you must stay at Grandbole and work on it. Become reacquainted with the land you once loved. The flower fields and its fragrances are in your blood, from your mother's family as well as my side. And you could be a help to Hartwell."

"My brother knows I welcome his help, but I can do more to manage Grandbole, if you let me, Father." His brother's voice sound unusually strained. "Your nieces would like to know more of Uncle Ewan, too. And they are getting started with their questions."

"Stay a while. Then, tell me of your desires. Maybe this time you can convince me of your passion for the theater."

Could the years have moved the earl from his harsh stance on the arts? Or maybe this war with Theo had changed him. Well, Theo had changed Ewan. "I turned down Mother's request to stay with her in London, I don't think—"

Jasper came alongside him and filled a glass with brandy. He drank one and then another in quick succession. "You're the perfect story crafter for the girls and for those whom *you* write."

Ewan sighed at the not-so-subtle hint at helping his brother with the newspaper bride stunt. With a shake of the head, he ignored the two faces waiting for his yes. It wasn't that easy. He set his glass down and again drew his hand along the bookshelf. These leathered spines written by playwrights had caught ahold of his imagination, never letting go, until he had spied a young woman gathering roses in the fields. Now, the thought of his Circe injuring his family wouldn't let go. Their common problem was less than a mile away. "I've missed a great deal. My nieces are fine girls. They make for a tempting offer."

Jasper clasped Ewan's elbow. "We need reinforcements. The girls outnumber us and with their pranks, we need you. Perhaps, we could have a chance at being a united family. Isn't that so, Father?"

The earl moved to the door. "Please stay, Son. You are welcome. Your room has been refreshed. Might even find a change of clothes to your liking."

He glanced at Ewan, dead in the eyes. It felt like an apology, but that was how it was between them, only going so far, never crossing the line. Respectable, distant, passionless. Yet, he'd never know if things could be different, if he turned away now. Ewan planted his boots apart and braced. "I'll stay for a few days. My flat and Mother's errands will keep."

The earl nodded. "Well, she's seen you enough these three months in London. If you stay, perhaps she will abandon her parties and return to Grandbole, too."

Being a pawn between his parents was an old game. One he'd hoped they'd stopped playing when he'd gone to war. Ewan shoved his hands into his pockets and shrugged. He'd let the earl fight that battle. Ewan would focus on his Circe and the package of smelly lavender that needed to be delivered.

Take a look at The Bittersweet Bride - http://bit.ly/bsweetbride

I hope you will enjoy this series.

VR!!!

Part Three

Glossary

Many of my readers are new to Regencies. I always include a glossary to help others learn more about this time. If you have favorite terms that you think should be included please email me. I'll acknowledge you in a newsletter or an upcoming book. Thank you. You are wonderful. VR

The Regency – The Regency is a period of history from 1811-1825 (sometimes expanded to 1795-1837) in England. It takes its name from the Prince Regent who ruled in his father's stead when the king suffered mental illness. The Regency is known for manners, architecture, and elegance. Jane Austen wrote her famous novel, *Pride and Prejudice* (1813), about characters living during the Regency.

England is a country in Europe. London is the capital city of

England.

Image of England from a copper engraved map created by William Darton in 1810.

Port Elizabeth was a town founded in 1820 at the tip of South Africa. The British settlement was an attempt to strengthen England's hold on the Cape Colony and to be buffer from the Xhosa.

Xhosa - A proud warrior people driven to defend their land and cattle-herding way of life from settlers expanding the boundaries of the Cape Colony.

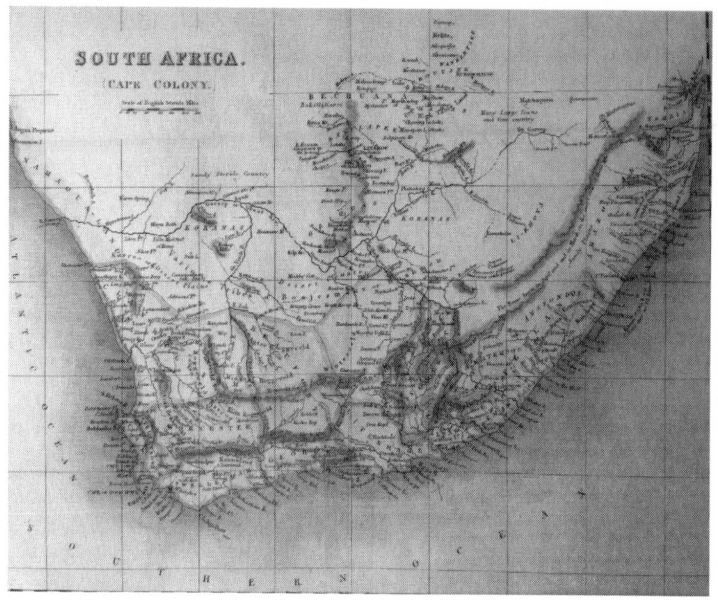

Image of South Africa from a copper engraved map created by John Dower in 1835.

Abigail – A lady's maid.

Soiree – An evening party.

Bacon-brained – A term meaning foolish or stupid.

Black – A description of a black person or an African.

Black Harriot – A famous prostitute stolen from Africa, then brought to England by a Jamaican planter who died, leaving her without means. She turned to harlotry to earn a living. Many members of the House of Lords became her clients. She is described as tall, genteel, and alluring, with a degree of politeness.

Blackamoor – A dark-skinned person.

Bombazine – Fabric of twilled or corded cloth made of silk and wool or cotton and wool. Usually the material was dyed black and used to create mourning clothes.

Breeched – The custom of a young boy no longer wearing pinafores and now donning breeches. This occurs about age six.

Breeches – Short, close-fitting pants for men, which fastened just below the knees and were worn with stockings.

Caning – A beating typically on the buttocks for naughty behavior.

Compromise – To compromise a reputation is to ruin or cast aspersions on someone's character by catching them with the wrong people, being alone with someone who wasn't a relative at night, or being caught doing something wrong. During the Regency, gentlemen were often forced to marry women they had compromised.

Dray – Wagon.

Footpads – Thieves or muggers in the streets of London.

Greatcoat – A big outdoor overcoat for men.

Mews – A row of stables in London for keeping horses.

* * *

Pelisse - An outdoor coat for women that is worn over a dress.

Quizzing Glass – An optical device, similar to a monocle, typically worn on a chain. The wearer might use the quizzing glass to look down upon people.

Reticule – A cloth purse made like a bag that had a drawstring closure.

Season – One of the largest social periods for high society in London. During this time, a lady attended a variety of balls and soirees to meet potential mates.

Sideboard – A low piece of furniture the height of a writing desk which housed spirits.

Ton – Pronounced *tone,* the *ton* was a high class in society during the Regency era.

Made in United States
North Haven, CT
18 February 2022

16212420R00252